SILVER BULLET

SILVER BULLET

STATE OF GRACE 2

COLETTE RHODES

CONTENT WARNING

Please note that this series contains sexual content,
violence, and drug references.

"Death doesn't discriminate between the sinners and the saints, it takes and it takes and it takes, and we keep living anyway..."

-Lin Manuel Miranda

THE STORY SO FAR

Our angelic agathos, Grace, met bad boy daimon, Riot, outside a club in Milton—a daimon town she'd moved to in a bid to escape her overbearing parents and community. At age 25, Grace had expected to feel a pull towards her four agathos soul bonds by now, but it never came. Instead, she felt pulled to Riot, even though a connection between agathos—worshippers of Anesidora and servants of humanity—and daimons, worshippers of La Nuit, and designed to lead humans astray, shouldn't be possible.

Grace's parents found out about Riot and had Grace taken from her job at a shelter and dragged to the basement temple in Auburn for a cleansing ritual to break the connection. Riot was given instructions by the mysterious Bullet on where to find Grace, and that is where our story picks up.

RIOT

CHAPTER 1

I pulled into the back parking lot of the Auburn Town Hall, Bullet's ominous countdown still ringing in my ears. The agathos had taken Grace, and this was my shot at getting her out safely. Maybe my only shot.

I didn't know much about what the agathos did to their own kind who didn't follow their ridiculous rules, but I doubted it was anything good.

She's fine. She's going to be fine. Bullet would have told you if she wasn't.

Right?

I shoved the modified bottle of vodka that I'd taken from Viper's bar inside my hoodie as I jumped out of the car and dashed around the building, sticking close to the brick walls. Bullet had given me a time limit, and I knew he'd probably be expecting an update, but he'd have to wait. I had a deadline.

Even if I was late, I wasn't going to give up. Bullet had told me there were different paths for Grace's future, including one she would walk alone, but I refused to accept that. So long as I lived, Grace would never be alone. I'd get her out of this creepy administrative tomb, then whisk her away somewhere safe.

Why had I let her go to work this morning? I should have fought her harder. Grace always wanted to do the right thing—the proper, respectful thing—and I'd followed her lead since I didn't have the first fucking clue how to function most of the time. I'd known today was a risk, but I'd let her take it anyway.

Was she hurting? Scared? I thought I was getting hints of fear through the connection between us, but it might have been mine. I was fucking terrified.

If we both got out of here alive, I was going to seriously consider handcuffing us together. And see where Grace stood on the whole completing the bond thing.

Do what scares you. That's what Bullet had said. I repeated the words like a mantra as I hovered in the shadows outside the front entrance to the town hall, back pressed to one of the enormous white columns that lined the front porch. The foyer looked to be mostly empty except for a bored receptionist, slumped over the desk with her head resting on her hand, idly clicking through something on her screen. All I had to do was get past her, then figure out where the entrance to the sub basement was.

And then... save my girl, somehow.

Did the Goddess of Night plan this? Or maybe Grace's scary goddess, Anesidora?

Who the fuck would ever ask me to be the hero?

1

"Goddess of Night," I muttered under my breath, my prayer skills rusty. If it gave me even a one percent advantage in getting Grace out, I'd do it. *"Please, please,* please, *help me get Grace out of here safe and unharmed. Whatever you need me to do, I'll do it. Just let me get her back."*

I exhaled, wondering if I was supposed to finish on an 'amen' or not. Fuck it, hopefully Bullet was throwing up some technically accurate prayers on our behalf.

The receptionist glanced over at something on the other side of the desk, and I watched impatiently as she fished a cell phone out of her bag, glancing around before answering a call. She turned away from the door, hunching over slightly to hide the phone, and I accepted that this was probably about as good as I was going to get.

Taking advantage of the receptionist's distraction, I slipped through the front doors as silently as possible, then darted across the open space to the wall, pressing my back to it. Conveniently, white columns also lined the foyer, keeping the walls and doors that led off in the shadows. How fortunate for me that the agathos were so ostentatious in their decor choices.

Now where the fuck do I go?

From the outside, I hadn't been able to see that the foyer *wasn't* empty. Hidden behind a column, pacing back and forth in front of a strange looking door, was a tall red-haired man with opal-colored agathos eyes.

I froze in place as he turned to look at me, my muscles tensed, ready to fight. I was prepared to fight as many agathos as needed to get to Grace, but I could have done with a few more weapons. Fuck.

He didn't look like he wanted to fight me as he took in my tattoos and dark red and purple eyes. Daimon eyes. If anything, he looked kind of *sad*.

The man gestured at me to come closer, before tipping his chin at an old-looking wooden door surrounded by a stone archway.

2

Should I go...? This really seemed like a trap. At the same time, Bullet had told me I needed blood to get through the door to the sub basement, and not *my* blood. I needed agathos blood.

Maybe I could smash his nose against the door or something. I still had the bottle of vodka tucked in my jacket if he tried to fight back.

I stopped a few feet away, and the man reached into his pocket, quickly slicing his finger on a knife before I had a chance to register the weapon. For fuck's sake. I needed a Keres daimon with me for this shit. I was not equipped for physical violence.

"Take care of my little girl," he whispered, holding my stare as he pressed his wound against the stone. The door opened with a light click, and the man moved back for me to pass.

"Always," I said awkwardly, tipping my chin at the man before shoving the door open and rushing down the dimly lit stairs. Was that one of Grace's fathers? He seemed a lot nicer than the dude with the pole shoved all the way up his ass who'd shown up at Grace's apartment yesterday.

The narrow passage was illuminated by fiery torches in wrought iron sconces, the steps and walls all made of dark stone that looked ancient and out of place compared to the foyer I'd just come from with its fluorescent lighting and ringing cell phones. This was the creepiest shit I had ever seen, hands down—like a scene straight out of *The Mummy*. The agathos were terrifying.

I followed the sounds coming from the bottom of the winding stairs, forcing myself to breathe in and out, to not panic for Grace as I went down, down, down into the earth. *What were they doing down there? Were they hurting her? Did agathos hurt each other?* The faint sound of chanting could be heard underneath some scrambling, panicked movements, and I forced my legs to move *faster, faster, faster.*

I could feel Grace's fear, but it was mixed with an unexpected hint of pride, and a heavy dose of disappointment. Of course she was disappointed. She'd trusted her parents, and they'd shown her very clearly how misguided that trust was. They'd twisted the faith she had in them into a weapon, then ran it right through her back.

At the bottom of the stairs was a single wooden arch-shaped door with a lit sconce next to it. There was no one standing guard, but I guessed if they thought only agathos could get through the creepy blood barrier, they didn't need anyone out here.

Convenient for me.

I pulled the bottle of vodka out of my jacket, checking that the soaked fabric was still in place, holding it at my side as I kicked the wooden door open with a bang, not giving a fuck about subtlety. This wasn't about stealth.

This was about perception.

Forgive me, Grace. I'm about to be every bit the reckless daimon they assume I am.

The room was pitch black, but the light trickling in from behind me illuminated the space, freezing all the scrambling people in place in the dark room. Why the fuck were there so many people here? Had they all come for a free show?

Shit, maybe I should just go full daimon and light this motherfucker up.

No, Grace wouldn't like that. Probably.

The small woman with dark hair wearing a bizarrely inappropriate power suit at the furthest end of the room spun to face me, her body obscuring a fucking *altar*. An actual real-life altar.

An old stone altar in the basement of an administrative building. What appeared to be a priestess, wearing a royal blue pencil skirt and matching blazer with 80s style shoulder pads. Chanting, burning herbs, the whole fucking nine yards.

I hadn't mentally prepared myself for the cult-like level of crazy I was going to face today.

Quickly, men materialized at the small woman's side, fully hiding the altar from view, but I'd already seen Grace's outstretched legs, bound at the ankles with rope.

They'd tied her to an altar. The realization made me nauseous.

Angling the bottle so it was visible in the light streaming in behind me, I pulled my trusty bronze dragon lighter out of my pocket, casually flicking it to life for maximum dramatic effect.

Fear crossed the faces of every agathos in the room, but I could feel Grace's relief, and her feelings were the only ones I cared about.

"I'm here for Grace," I drawled like I didn't much care either way, willing her to understand when I picked up traces of her confusion.

"Be gone, *daimon*," the woman in front of Grace snarled, the men next to her moving protectively closer to her sides. Did she seriously just "*be gone*" me? Like this was an 80s Catholic horror film or something?

"You don't belong in this sacred place," she continued. "How did you get in?"

My boots echoed with each slow step, but I didn't stray too far from the door. Just far enough inside to make them think I had no sense of self-preservation. Grace's fear spiked again, and I could feel that she was scared for me now rather than herself. *Feel how much I care for you,* I thought silently.

Feel how much I hate being this person.

"I'm here for Grace," I repeated in the same flat tone, like I was the soulless monster they assumed I was, flicking my lighter to life again.

I could almost feel Grace actively trying to settle her emotions, to keep calm for my benefit, and I wondered what she was thinking of. If she was remembering how it felt to wake up tangled up together in the morning and fall asleep in each other's arms, and if those memories soothed her the way they soothed me.

No matter how dire things got, we had those memories to sustain us. A connection ordained by a higher power that no jumped up agathos could sever.

The woman in charge—a Priestess perhaps?—began to object, but my patience had more than run out. A collection of amphora leaned against the wall next to where I was standing, and I clinked the glass vodka bottle against the top of the vase, a rush of satisfaction running through me at how ominous the noise sounded in the mostly silent room. The Priestess stopped protesting immediately, eyes wide with panic as she looked from the bottle in my hand to the door behind me.

"Is that straw on the ground?" I asked casually, as though the answer didn't bother me either way. I could see it spread out on the ground surrounding the altar beneath her feet.

It very much bothered me. If they'd put down straw to absorb Grace's blood, I was going to get her out of here and blow this fucking building up no matter how she felt about her parents. *Sorry, Gracie.*

"Don't do anything rash," the woman warned, a shake in her voice betraying the tough front she was trying to put on as she eyed up the lighter in my hand.

"Awful flammable, straw," I continued tonelessly. "Did you know that?"

"You'll hurt yourself," she pointed out, trembling where she stood. "Is it really worth it?"

Was she fucking serious? I thought these people were all about the soul bond thing. Of course Grace was worth it.

"Riot?" Grace whispered, another wave of fear rushing through her at the idea of me being hurt. My sweet Gracie, too fucking good for anybody in this room, including me. My heart skipped a beat at the sound of her voice, and I hoped she could feel how relieved I was to hear her speak.

"I'm not like you," I sighed impatiently, forcing the nonchalance into my voice. "You took something that belongs to me, and I want her back. But if you're going to be difficult... well if I can't have her, you certainly can't."

I flicked the lighter again, enjoying the way everyone in the room visibly flinched at the noise. In any other situation, I might be insulted at the low opinion these people obviously had of me. That they actually thought I would *hurt* Grace was laughable, but they obviously believed it.

Idiots. So far up on their high horse they'd lost sight of the world below them.

"Tell him to leave," Grace's mother hissed towards the altar, that traitorous fucking snake. "Tell him you wish to stay with your family."

"I can't tell a lie," Grace replied simply, the conviction in her voice strong despite the waver she tried to hide. My satisfied smile probably looked a little sinister to the agathos watching me warily. There was a strange coolness in the room that felt like it didn't belong, something *other*. It wrapped around me, not in a constrictive way, but like a cloak of icy shadows, making me look more intimidating than I was.

You're imagining things.

"You—" her Mother hissed.

"Let her go," the Priestess ordered, cutting her off.

"Basilinna—" Grace's father interjected, the one who'd been to the apartment yesterday. Snake number two.

"We know that daimons do not value life, not even their own. Anesidora would not want our ends to come this way. Not when we can still serve so many," the woman—the Basilinna—said, cutting him off. Goddess, she truly knew nothing about daimons if that's what she thought.

Even normal daimons like my dad cared about preserving their *own* lives. Besides, the *gall* of this woman to talk about my kind that way when they'd kidnapped my girl and tied her to an altar was fucking outrageous.

"Release her!" the Basilinna snapped at the men next to her who still hadn't moved. Her voice was shrill, and I picked up Grace's dark satisfaction at the woman's obvious fear. I was glad for it. I knew she tried to force herself to be sweet, to ignore any negative thoughts she had like they were something to be feared instead of a healthy defense mechanism.

Two men quickly moved to slice the ropes binding her wrists and ankles, and I watched carefully to make sure their knives didn't go anywhere they shouldn't.

The moment Grace's limbs were free, she shoved herself upright, half jumping, half falling off the altar. As much as I wanted to go to her and scoop her up in my arms, I wasn't willing to leave the doorway in case they decided to trap us both in here. No, I had to be tactical about this if I was going to get us both out of here alive.

The moment Grace's feet touched the floor, the light from behind me illuminated her face, and I didn't need to fake the rage I felt. What the fuck had they *done* to her? She didn't feel like she was in pain, but there was blood smeared all over her face, and her dress and hair were soaked and sticking to her skin.

Hold on a little longer, Gracie. I'll get you out of here. You'll never see any of these people again.

The Basilinna turned to face Grace as she stumbled away from the altar and my girl tipped her chin up, refusing to look away. Refusing to bow respectfully the way she had been conditioned to do her entire life. The pride I felt for her made my chest ache with its intensity.

"We will be praying for you, Grace," the Basilinna told her somberly. "We will come for you. We will *save* you. We will not give up on guiding you back to the right path, the path where you belong. "

"Keep telling yourself that," Grace snapped as she backed away from the woman, startling when she turned and saw the number of people in the room. They parted like she was the plague incarnate as she barreled towards me on weak legs, the relief she was feeling so palpable that it seemed to pulse through my veins.

She was here. She was fine. Mostly. I would get her out of here, and away from this fucked up town with its fucked up people and her fucked up family for good.

Before Grace could get to me, her mother stepped into her path, blocking her way, posture stiff with barely restrained fury, and I vaguely contemplated lighting the traitorous woman on fire.

"You are no longer part of this family. You are no daughter of mine. You are *Helen*," her mother spat, apparently not getting the Basilinna's message that this was just a temporary setback. Grace reeled back at the venom in her tone before regaining her footing and straightening her shoulders.

Do what scares you, Bullet had told her.

It was this. It wasn't going to work, or handing in her notice, or taking a step back from the agathos community while we tried to understand what this thing was between us.

It was this irreversible decision to leave behind everything she knew for good, because there was no coming back from this. Whatever happened, Grace would never be welcome among the agathos again. Among her own *family* again.

Of *course*, this was what scared her.

"I'd rather be Helen than Medea," Grace told her mother, holding her head high even as she blinked away the tears she was willing not to fall. Grace's father sucked in a horrified breath as the rest of the room grew somehow even stiller.

"Goodbye, Faith."

She'd actually done it. She'd basically said 'go fuck yourself' in agathos speak.

No time to reflect on that now, I had to get Grace out of here and find out why her face was bleeding.

Grace shouldered past her mother like a soldier marching to war, and the moment she was in reach, I draped an arm loosely over her shoulders like I didn't give a fuck either way, lighter dangling between my fingers next to her arm.

Grace's emotions were more tangible than they'd ever been. Her relief didn't so much brush over me as sink into my skin, settling some of the terror inside me.

"Pleasure doing business with you," I told the psycho priest lady, tipping my imaginary hat and dragging Grace backwards. The moment we were out of the main temple area, I threw the fake molotov cocktail into the room, smashing the vodka bottle and making the agathos scream in fright before slamming the door behind us.

I'd soaked the cloth stopper in some bottled water I'd found in the stolen car. I wasn't *actually* intending on burning them alive, but it was exactly the kind of thing they expected a daimon to do. "Come on, Gracie," I urged, helping her up the stairs as fast as we could go. "We need to get the fuck outta here."

"Agreed," she murmured, struggling to keep pace. Goddess, she was a wreck. Her long dark hair was drenched, as was the pale blue dress that was clinging to her like a second skin. Her golden brown skin was a bluish tinge from cold, with blood smeared over her like war paint.

"It's not mine," she assured me, seeing where my gaze had gone.

"That doesn't make me feel much better," I muttered, my chest ached with worry for her, and it was a weird and unfamiliar feeling.

We didn't speak again as we rushed up the two flights of dimly lit concrete stairs as fast as we could, both of us wheezing with the effort. The old wooden door apparently opened without blood from the inside, and I pulled Grace through, pulling it shut behind me as quickly as I could without making a sound.

The foyer had filled up with agathos, milling about with cups of coffee like this was their afternoon break spot, and I pulled Grace back against the door, still hidden in the shadows by the ugly columns, trying to think of a plan to get us out without being seen.

"Fuck," I whispered.

There was no way for a daimon and a blood-covered agathos to walk out of here hand-in-hand without causing a scene. They'd never let us leave. I should have kept the damn vodka bottle.

Grace shivered next to me and I quickly pulled off my black hoodie, angling my body in front of Grace's and wiping her face gently with the hood before yanking it over her thin dress. "You're going to freeze," I muttered, fixing the problem that was easier to address. I wasn't sure how to get us out of here, but I could keep her warm.

"I'll warm up later, we need to go," Grace urged, eyes wide with fear. She took the lead, pulling me along the wall, clearly more familiar with this building than I was, but we still couldn't access the front doors without crossing a few feet of well-lit floor. We were going to have to make a break for it.

Indecision warred in my head as I tried to figure out what to do. I *hated* being the decision maker. I had barely made a decision in my entire life, yet today had been full of them, and I'd been winging it the entire time. It was a miracle I hadn't gotten us both killed, honestly.

I got the impression Grace didn't like making big calls either. Maybe there was something to this multiple soul bonds business after all.

I glanced behind me, startled to see the tall, redheaded agathos man who'd helped me still hovering there. *Grace's dad.*

He examined her sadly for a moment before his expression blanked and his attention shifted to me. He didn't break eye contact with me for a moment as he pulled out a blue plastic lighter and flicked it to life before silently reaching for the fire alarm pull station and yanked down the lever.

Instantly, a horn started blaring, flashing strobes going off near the tops of the walls, drawing everyone's attention as they winced under the sudden barrage of noise.

Why the lighter? I wondered idly. That seemed unnecessary.

12

"Fire door!" Grace yelled over the noise, rushing towards a narrow door nowhere near the front doors I'd entered through. I broke eye contact with the despondent looking man as he slipped behind a column before Grace could spot him. We ran for the door together, Grace's freezing cold hand gripping mine like she would never let go.

That worked fine for me. After today, I never wanted to let her go again.

She fumbled against the fire door, trying to force down the bar, and I wrapped an arm around her waist, pulling her out of the way so I could force it open with my elbow and drag her outside. It took me a second to get my bearings, and I realized we had come out at the back of the building, closer to where I'd left the vehicle Dare had swiped for me.

Thank the fucking goddess for that.

"Nearly there, Gracie."

"Okay," Grace breathed, stumbling next to me. She'd been so fucking strong in there, and I knew she was trying to hold it together, but I could feel the cracks forming.

The alarm kept blaring behind us as I half dragged, half carried Grace to the black SUV I had commandeered. I lifted her into the passenger seat as gently as I could before jogging around to the driver's side, turning on the engine before I even had my door shut.

Grace slumped against the passenger side, buckling herself in with weak fingers before shutting her eyes and tipping her head back against the seat, totally trusting me to take the lead and get us away from this building, and all the people in it who'd so thoroughly let her down.

The tires skidded as I pulled out onto the main road and drove as fast as I could without attracting undue attention, fighting the urge to slam my foot on the accelerator and get the fuck out of this cursed Stepford Wives town.

I turned the heating up to full blast, hating the fact that Grace was only wearing a thin, soaking wet dress and my now damp hoodie.

"Thank you," she said gently, turning her head to the side to watch me.

"You don't have to thank me for that, Grace," I replied incredulously. It wasn't like I was going to just *leave* her there. The idea hadn't even occurred to me.

I glanced at her out of the corner of my eye and noticed the ghost of a smile flit across her face.

"I want to thank you, Riot. And I knew you'd come for me."

CHAPTER 2

There had never been any doubt in my mind that Riot would come to my rescue. Considering we'd only known each other for a week, my unerring confidence in that fact should have probably alarmed me, but it didn't. We were soul bonds—different pieces of the same puzzle—tethered by forces beyond our comprehension. Even if our bond wasn't sealed yet, we'd never let ourselves be torn apart.

The agathos who took me should have known that, but they weren't treating my connection with Riot like they would any other soul bond. They were treating it like an abomination that needed to be destroyed. That they *could* destroy, if they only prayed hard enough. I didn't think that was possible, but I wasn't willing to give them another opportunity to try.

I'd trusted them, trusted my parents, and learned a very hard lesson because of it.

"How did you find me?" I asked Riot, staring out my window. I knew he would never judge me for what he'd witnessed at the basement altar, but I couldn't help being embarrassed nonetheless. Embarrassed that I came from a community who'd treat *anyone* that way, let alone one of their own, and embarrassed that I'd been so trusting that I hadn't seen their actions coming.

"I could have probably found you just following the bond," Riot mused. "It feels like it's growing stronger. You don't have anything to feel embarrassed about, Gracie. *They* do. They should be ashamed, not you."

My hands were shaking with adrenaline and he absently reached across the console to grab one, interlacing our fingers. I wanted to use the growing connection we had to examine how Riot was feeling, but I was so overwhelmed by the fear, anger, relief, humiliation, and bone crushing disappointment that I was experiencing, I couldn't even *find* Riot's emotions. It was like I was lost in an ocean of my own feelings.

I was gripping his hand tightly, not quite convinced that he wouldn't suddenly disappear out of my reach. After a few calming breaths, I was able to recognize that the fear I was feeling wasn't entirely mine. Riot's hand tightened around mine, an edge of desperation in his touch that wasn't usually there.

"The bond does feel stronger," I agreed. *What would it feel like when it was complete?*

"Anyway, I used the tracker app I installed on the phone I gave you and realized you were in Auburn," Riot said unapologetically. "Then Bullet gave me your exact location."

"Oh," I replied lamely, trying to decide how I felt about that. The idea probably *should* bother me, but it didn't.

"I know it was an invasion of your privacy, but I can't apologize for it, Gracie. I didn't have the same faith in your parents that you did."

Riot grimaced as he made that admission, and I knew he was being careful not to rub my nose in the fact that I'd been so incredibly wrong about my family. So *naive*. I'd assumed that they'd give me the time that I asked for, and they'd run to the Basilinna at the very first opportunity.

Frankly, he had every right to say 'I told you so', but he wouldn't. Riot didn't think of himself as a good person, but he was one of the best people I'd ever met.

"I was stupid," I said quietly. "I didn't think they'd risk their reputation by telling anyone, but I guess they thought their reputation was more at risk by *not* saying anything. I didn't expect them to be happy—"

"You never asked them to be happy," Riot interjected sharply. "You asked them for time. They couldn't even give you a *day*," he spat, his knuckles turning white where he was gripping the steering wheel. "And you weren't stupid, Gracie. You trusted people you should've been able to trust."

"I don't trust them anymore," I said quietly.

It physically *hurt* to say the words out loud. They'd never been the perfect parents, and they'd certainly never seen me as the perfect child, but they were my family and were all I'd ever known. There were bad memories, but a lot of good as well—especially with Chance and Creed, the two dads I was closest to. Memories of beach days and holiday meals, birthday parties and winter vacations, movie nights and camping in the back yard.

Those good memories had been the reason I'd kept trying to please them, but I didn't even have those good memories now, not really. They'd been tainted by the past 24 hours. I'd never be able to see the *good* without the lens of the *bad* now.

No. I couldn't let Mercy and my two baby brothers, Leon and Tobin, be tainted by what had happened today. This had nothing to do with them.

"I'm sorry, Riot. I should have listened to you this morning," I managed to get out around the lump in my throat, blinking rapidly to hold the tears of sadness and frustration back. I should have *listened* to him, and we could have avoided all of this.

"Don't apologize," Riot said immediately, lifting our joined hands to press a kiss to my knuckles. "Bullet made it sound like this was inevitable anyway. The better option, even," he added with a grimace. He had made it sound that way, though I couldn't imagine going through anything worse.

We drove for a few miles in silence, both calming down after the intensity we'd just experienced. Riot's words had reminded me that we were en route to meet what was most likely my second soul bond, and I hadn't even had a moment to wrap my head around that.

I'd been scared to meet Bullet before today. It felt too real. A second daimonic soul bond couldn't be explained away as an aberration, and while I didn't even *want* agathos soul bonds—especially now—the idea that there were more daimons out there, destined to be mine, was a little overwhelming.

The dark monster who lived in the back of my mind didn't think so. The darkness reveled in the idea. I'd called on the Goddess of Night a second time, and received a response yet again. Being afraid of having a second daimon soul bond at this point seemed naive.

"I'd love to know more about whose blood is on your face," Riot said conversationally, clearly trying to distract me.

It worked.

"*Sugar*, it's still there?" I sighed, pulling down the sun visor to look at my reflection. "Gross. It's animal blood, probably sheep. Part of the cleansing ritual."

I looked frightening. This was not how I wanted to meet Bullet. The Basilinna had doused me in salt water as part of the katharmos, and my long black hair was hanging wet and stringy around my face. A face that was smeared in blood from the ritual over smudged black eye makeup that would have put any racoon to shame. I tugged the sleeve of Riot's hoodie down over my hand and attempted to minimize the damage as much as I could, horrified that Riot had seen me this way.

"I won't lie, I'm a little offended you believed that daimons drank the blood of virgins for sustenance, when you guys are bathing in sheep's blood at the temple," Riot told me drily, and a surprised laugh escaped me despite my heavy mood.

"That is completely fair," I replied, still shaking with silent laughter. "It doesn't happen a lot. It's an emergency measure for the heavily *infected*. They believe I'm polluted with miasma and that I need to be cleansed before I can ask Anesidora for her forgiveness."

"That is so fucked up," he muttered, some of the tension in his shoulders easing as we moved out of Auburn's city limits and got on the highway. We were heading towards the countryside, away from the coast, but this whole area was still heavily populated by agathos. They weren't as wealthy and elitist as the ones in Auburn, but they wouldn't hesitate to act if they noticed a daimon in their territory. I silently sent up a prayer to any and all goddesses that might be listening to give us safe passage.

No divinity owed us anything, but frankly, I felt like we deserved a break. I'd ask for forgiveness for my hubris later.

"We're switching vehicles up here," Riot warned me, and I nodded silently. I didn't want to ask any questions about where this SUV had come from, or about the car we were getting into next. Agathos couldn't lie, cheat, or steal, and I wasn't sure what my body would make me do if he told me the car was stolen. Stand stubbornly on the side of the road, probably.

Riot pulled over and cut the engine, leaving the key in the ignition, and ushering me towards the black classic muscle car parked a few feet away. He gave it an appreciative look as he climbed into the driver's seat, and I got the impression that this was exactly the kind of car Riot would choose to drive.

"How did this get here?" I asked in wonder, sliding into the passenger seat.

"Dare," Riot replied distractedly, the engine roaring to life as he turned the key. "Way to be discrete," he snorted, revving the loud engine and gunning it down the highway.

"Dare," I repeated slowly. Had Riot talked about him before?

Riot shot me a curious look. "The friend I told you about," he supplied. "Whose tattoo studio I've been working at."

There was something about the name that called to me. It wasn't quite a sense of familiarity, but it was something.

"Did he give you your tattoos?" I asked, my gaze trailing up from Riot's hand resting on the steering wheel up to his elbow, where the sleeve of his shirt was pushed up to.

"He did. Sometimes against his better judgment," Riot said drily. "They're not really Dare's style. You'll see his talent better represented on Bullet's skin."

Riot had tattoos everywhere, but his forearm was dominated by a Grim Reaper's head, covered by a gray hood, a scythe dripping red blood from the tip of the blade curled over its head.

The darkness and violence represented by each of Riot's tattoos should have frightened me, but they never had. If anything, it made me worry that this was how Riot saw himself. As a descendant of the Moros line of daimons, he ushered humans towards their doom, pushing them using his innate knowledge of their weaknesses towards their eventual end.

Perhaps he was thinking along the same lines as I felt his mood plummet, his self-loathing pricking uncomfortably at my skin.

"Your thoughts have taken a dark turn," I said quietly. I wanted to hold his hand again, but both of his were now gripping the steering wheel tightly. Which was probably a good thing, since I was sure we were breaking the speed limit.

"It's a dark thoughts kind of day," Riot replied with a shrug that didn't look as relaxed as he probably hoped it would.

"Does Bullet know we're coming?" I asked, taking a turn at changing the subject.

Riot shot me an amused look, the tension leaching out of his posture right away. "He's a psychic, Gracie."

"Right." I huffed a laugh, shaking my head at my own idiocy. Of course Bullet knew we were coming. What else did he know about me? I knew that his ability allowed him to visit people in their dreams, and Riot suspected Bullet had visited my dreams a *lot*.

But I couldn't remember any of those visits. It was unsettling to think that someone had been in my head so many times and I had no recollection of it.

"If I was feeling cooperative, I'd call Bullet," Riot continued. "But I'm still pissed at him for his non-answer about you going to work this morning, so fuck him. He can consult his stupid cards if he wants to know what's going on."

Sugar, this wasn't the best start to soul bond relations if Bullet really was mine. Hopefully, Riot wasn't the type to hold grudges. If he was... well, he might have a grudge to hold against me too. There was a secret that had been festering between us, and I couldn't let it go on any longer. I'd let it go on too long already.

"Riot, there's something I need to tell you before we get to Bullet's house," I sighed, chewing nervously on my lower lip.

"Did they do something to you?" he asked quietly, startling me. He'd responded so quickly, there was no way he hadn't been *waiting* to ask that question. "I should have set them on fire," he muttered under his breath.

"You'd have regretted it when law enforcement got involved," I replied, huffing a quiet laugh. "They sedated me at work to get me out of there, then did the cleansing ritual, but that's not what I wanted to talk about. It's about me. Something I did."

"Okay," Riot said slowly, eyes flitting to me before returning to the road.

"The night we met, outside Onslaught," I began, before pausing to take a deep breath. *Please don't hate me.* "Earlier that night, I'd prayed to Anesidora about finding my soul bonds."

"Alright," he murmured, letting me talk in my own time.

"And then, afterwards, when there was no response and I was feeling a little, er, *reckless*, I prayed to the Goddess of Night too."

I braced myself, shrinking back into my seat and waiting for Riot to erupt at me for not telling him this earlier.

22

"Did she answer or something?" he asked curiously. "I can't even remember the last time I prayed to the Goddess of Night. Daimons usually rely on Oneiroi like Bullet to connect with the goddess if we need to."

"It went really quiet. And the candle went out," I added, frowning to myself at how lame it sounded out loud. "It felt very profound at that moment. And then when they were doing the ritual, I did it again. I asked the Goddess of Night for help and all the torches went out and there was this *energy* in the room that sort of spooked them."

Riot hummed thoughtfully, and I wondered if he thought I was losing my mind, talking about strange energies and goddesses who answered back.

"It was smart thinking," Riot said approvingly, which only made me more confused. Why wasn't he mad? He looked over at me, lips twitching in amusement. "We've only known each other a week, Gracie. We're still learning things about each other, sharing our dark secrets, et cetera, et cetera."

He looked completely nonplussed, and I wondered if I should maybe share it again in case he hadn't understood me properly.

"So, you think that's what brought us together? A spur of the moment answer to your request from La Nuit?" Riot asked.

"You don't?" I asked, baffled. "Are you sure you're not angry??"

"You can feel that I'm not, Gracie. But I don't see La Nuit having that kind of power over your kind. I find it more interesting that you moved to Milton six months ago, which is when I finally refused to sell drugs for my dad anymore," he observed.

Apparently, Riot had been paying much more attention than I had because he was right, that was an interesting "coincidence".

"Besides, with everything Bullet said about him being able to visit you in your dreams, it seems pretty clear that whatever brought us together wasn't a spur of the moment decision," Riot surmised, reaching over to grab my hand again.

The obviousness of that statement hit me like a slap to the face. *Of course* I hadn't set things in motion with that prayer. They must have already been in motion if Bullet had been visiting my dreams. Maybe I'd accelerated things by reaching out to La Nuit, but I hadn't started them.

I'd been taught my whole life that soul bonds were determined before we were even born, but because Riot was a daimon, I'd sort of disregarded that knowledge.

"I feel kind of silly for being too scared to tell you now," I admitted sheepishly. I felt like a complete idiot, actually.

Riot glanced over, raising an eyebrow at me. "I hope I haven't given you any reason to ever be scared of telling me something. I'm not angry, but we do have enough mysteries to deal with without keeping secrets from each other."

"You're right," I agreed, tipping my head back against the headrest with a thud. "You're absolutely right."

"No more secrets?" Riot asked, giving my hand a squeeze.

"No more secrets," I vowed, tightening my grip on him in return. "So, um, do you have a plan right now? Aside from going to Bullet's house?"

I felt rude asking because Riot had been moving very decisively from the moment he'd burst into the temple, and he'd obviously coordinated with Dare to *acquire* us a vehicle, but I couldn't think when he'd had a chance to actually organize any of this.

"Sort of. You're clearly not safe from the agathos right now, and we need answers that I'm hoping Bullet can provide—especially since you've been communicating with La Nuit already. Besides, it's time you two met, since he's probably your second soul bond."

"Right," I agreed, looking out the window as my nerves rose again. *Knowing* I was probably going to meet my soul bond was a lot more intimidating than Riot and I's chance meeting outside a club.

"It's a good idea to get out of Milton. Agathos can't lie—when the Basilinna said she wasn't finished with me, she meant it. Maybe I could let my cousin know I'm okay..." I trailed off, chewing on my lip again before remembering the traces of animal blood on my face and stopping. "I don't know if I should burden Mercy with this. She'll be so worried about me, but if she knows where I am and my parents ask, she won't be able to lie."

Riot sighed heavily, and I got the feeling that wasn't the answer he wanted to hear.

"I don't think it's a good idea. I'm not going to risk losing you again, Gracie," he said eventually in a hoarse voice, shaking his head. "I've never been so fucking scared in my life. I know you might want to reach out to people or tie up loose ends, but it might be better to lay low for now. I have some *things* in motion to keep you safe—you'll probably think I'm overreacting."

"You have? When did you even have time to do this?" I asked, unable to hide my surprise.

Riot grimaced. "It was very last minute. I asked a daimon I know to cover your tracks, make you harder to follow. Honestly, I'd prefer to get you out of the country, but that'll take longer to organize. Whatever it takes to keep the psychotic people who tied you up on a fucking altar off our backs."

"But I can't lie," I replied instantly, seeing a massive hole in this plan. "Or cheat. Or steal."

I was already feeling a little tetchy about what he'd told me. Like I was approaching a lie and had to loudly announce my whereabouts to absolve myself. I took a deep breath and tried to exhale away the urge.

"I'll lie, cheat, and steal for you," Riot replied, like it was easy. "It's all sorted, Dare will grab the paperwork when it's ready. I just need you to be open minded about leaving your old life behind and leave the details to me for now. I know that's not a small ask."

"I *do* trust you, and I have to be open minded," I said sadly, looking out the window again as Riot turned off the main highway onto a winding tree-lined street, still filled with agathos mansions, though they were spread increasingly further apart. "I think that's what Bullet meant. Leaving it all behind is what scares me. Or *scared* me, past tense," I amended.

"I think Bullet's full of shit," Riot muttered under his breath. "What's the point of being psychic if you can't give us all the answers?"

"I don't know much about psychic abilities, but I doubt it's that simple. Are we close?" I asked, peering out of the window. Hopefully Riot warmed up a little to Bullet before we got there.

"Not far. I don't think so, anyway. It's been a while," he replied, scrunching up his face like he was trying to remember the last time he'd been here. Hopefully Bullet had other visitors, or I imagined it would be very lonely living out here.

"Why did your mother call you 'Helen'?" Riot asked quietly.

Sugar. Selfishly, I had hoped Riot wasn't listening to that part of the conversation.

"Helen left her true husband, her child, everything behind to run off to Troy with Paris. Helen was reckless and selfish, and started a war in which thousands died," I recounted in a monotone voice, staring unseeing at the trees outside. "She is the opposite of everything an agathos woman is supposed to be. It was intended to be the ultimate insult."

"It kind of sounded like you got her back though. What was it you called her?"

"Medea." My voice was impressively flat, considering the guilt that admission brought on. "Medea murdered her children."

Riot made a strangled noise of surprise in the back of his throat and my face heated. Much like my mother, Medea believed wholly that she was doing the right thing.

It was a cruel thing to say, and I should have been ashamed of myself.

"Daimons don't get the same extensive religious education that agathos seem to get," Riot began. "I don't know shit about Medea, but I sort of know the story of Paris and Helen. I'm a Wolfgang Petersen fan, I've seen the film."

I smiled in spite of myself, though catching sight of my bloody reflection in the window made it fall almost instantly.

"Helen and Paris were in love," Riot continued, giving me a pointed look. I kept my face impassive because I didn't *think* Riot was declaring his love for me, even if it could sort of be interpreted that way. We weren't at that level, that was for sure. I didn't know precisely how I felt about him, but I wasn't ready for *those* words.

"Love is selfish. That is why Anesidora chooses for us," I replied eventually, picking my words carefully as I thought back through years of classes and lectures from my mother. "She gives us our soul bonds and we can't feel desire for anyone else. There's no competition, no heartbreak."

"Your goddess is selfish," Riot replied, almost smiling at my horrified intake of breath. I wasn't even sure if I was horrified any longer, or if it was only a reflex. "Love can't be *assigned* like a chore list, and taking away your ability to choose isn't a gift."

"You're very wise," I said, finally turning to face him, feeling a little awed to be in his company, which he would probably hate. Riot set my mind at ease like no one else in my life ever had.

"Not even a little," Riot snorted. "Your mother may have a point though. If you're Helen, that makes me Paris, and I would happily risk a war to keep you."

"I think that ship has sailed," I replied with a tight smile. "The war may have already begun."

BULLET

CHAPTER 3

The best way for me to gain detailed insight into the future is to fall asleep. La Nuit delivered visions to me via dreams, and while they weren't always set in stone and I could always get insight from the Fates via my card readings, the dreams were by far my most powerful source of knowledge.

However, it was very fucking difficult to fall asleep when the love of my life was in danger, even though I'd given Riot explicit instructions for how to get her out, and I was ninety percent sure he was following them.

Fifty percent sure. Riot wasn't exactly great at taking directions.

How could I sleep anyway, when I was about to meet her for the first time in real life? My Amazing Grace, who had no idea who I was.

Semantics.

We'd meet, and she would realize she'd been in love with me her whole life because I was her LITERAL DREAM MAN. Visitor of her dreams, every night of her life. She couldn't remember any of them, which wasn't ideal, but she'd definitely fall in love with me. Right? How could Grace not love me? I was very lovable.

I'd check in with the cards, just to be sure.

The downstairs room which I called the 'parlor', even though it was a converted barn and fairly grim, felt almost suffocating today. This was the room I used for readings with paying customers because there wasn't anywhere else in this particular outbuilding, but I'd moved out of the big house when it was only me left here.

Originally, I'd lived in the 7000-square-foot main house in the center of the property with the other Oneiroi who had been here when I first arrived in my teen years, needing a reprieve from the sensory overload. They'd all died over the past decade and the enormous house was a bitch to clean, in addition to making me feel a touch lonely. These days, it was occupied by humans who leased most of the property, including the acreage for their horse breeding business, while I stayed in a converted barn on a quieter section of the property. The upstairs was my living quarters, and the downstairs was where I kept all the spooky mystic shit that humans liked, and occasionally did card readings for those who wanted them.

Sitting cross-legged in the nest of cushions I'd made in front of the low coffee table, I reshuffled my stack of black and gold tarot cards. They were hundreds of years old, passed on by generations of Oneiroi, but looked mint condition, preserved by the Fates' own magic.

With anticipation coursing through me, making me even more fidgety than usual, I picked through the Major Arcana cards until I found the one I was looking for. The Lovers. Two intertwined snakes wound their way from the bottom of the card to the top, the profile of a skull on either side of the snakes' heads, facing each other. One skull had a sun emblem, the other a moon. Life imitated art—Grace was the sun, except she had more than one moon man weaving into her life. Or she would soon, at least.

Riot better get used to sharing. He was going to be such a dick about it, I could tell. I didn't need psychic abilities to know that.

"What does Grace need to smooth her transition to this life?" I asked the Fates, closing my eyes and centering myself, opening my mind to their influence.

Ancient magic—the deep, heavy kind that predated the existence of mortals on this earth—rose up from within, moving like fine threads in my veins. Sending up a silent prayer of gratitude that they'd deigned to answer me, I let my hands reach forward for the cards with my eyes still shut, letting the Fates guide my movements. I didn't know what I'd done in life to deserve the Fates themselves almost always answering my call, but I was certain it had something to do with Grace. I was an anomaly in more ways than one.

The emblem of The Lovers appeared in my mind's eye, the snakes disentangling from each other, growing and changing until The Fool and Death stood facing one another. In the background was The Devil—Riot— standing stoically at The Fool's right shoulder, a constant support for Grace.

It was a clear sign from the Fates not to interfere in their burgeoning relationship, a reminder that Riot's place was as much at Grace's side as mine was. I knew that in theory, but I still wanted to keep her to myself.

Daimons weren't meant to share in general, and I'd spent my whole life meeting Grace over and over each night. It was a cruel joke that the Goddess hadn't allowed me to meet her first. To be her consort, as the agathos' first soul bond always was. Bitterness wasn't an emotion I indulged in—it would be a slippery slope—but I was fighting it off more than I was used to.

What did Riot even bring to the table? He was pretty, I supposed, in a brooding, petulant sort of way. Was that why Grace had found him first? Because he was more her physical type?

I could be brooding.

The threads of magic working through me pulled taut, like a snapping rubber band, the irritated Fates reminding me to pay attention. I exhaled heavily, forcing my concentration back to the cards playing out in my mind's eye. Vaguely, I was aware of my hands shuffling the deck, but I didn't "read" them the way humans did. I got a live action version in my head.

It was much more efficient. Too bad it didn't come with a soundtrack. A haunting rendition of *All I Ask Of You* would really set the mood right now.

Nine wands floated in the air around us, an almost constant presence in my card readings about Grace. The Nine of Wands represented courage, resilience, facing a battle and continuing on to the next one. Enduring just one more test, except it was always *just one more* test.

Do what scares you, I'd told Grace. It was an oversimplification, but I'd discovered in my years of psychic reading that most people preferred the cliff notes.

Death, representing me, kneeled at Grace's feet, skull head tilted upwards in supplication while The Fool looked fondly down. Death pulled a card from his robe and held it up for her to take. The Page of Swords. *Curiosity, new ideas, a thirst for knowledge.* I'd always known my role was to provide the answers to the questions that had always plagued Grace, the Fates were merely reminding me.

I'd been answering Grace's questions every night since she'd learned to talk, she just didn't remember the answers. I smiled to myself remembering what an inquisitive toddler she'd been. I'd been seven when she was three, and every night I'd suggested a game of hide and seek in the forest dreamscape we met in to get a break from her stream of questions of how anything and everything worked.

Riot, The Devil, pulled a card from his robe, black bat wings flapping noiselessly behind him. I watched as it passed to Grace, examining the image on the front. Six of Swords—overcoming hardship, calmer waters, relief, healing.

No time for bitterness, I reminded myself. Life was short and mine was shorter than most. I didn't have time for sadness, even though the realization that I may be Grace's teacher but Riot was her home pierced me right through the heart.

There was a reason I was kneeling at her feet, not standing at her side. The way ahead of her would be clear when I was out of it.

The Fates' magic in my veins dulled to a steady hum, waiting for my inevitable stream of follow up questions. I'd been tapped into their power for the past two days, obsessing over how this confrontation with the agathos would go, and the Fates had been patient with me. I'd already asked every variation of question I could think of to make sure Grace had safe passage, and give Riot the most specific instructions I could based on a combination of their answers to my questions and La Nuit's dream visions.

It was time to return to the real world. I had a soulmate to meet.

"Thank you for your guidance, sisters," I whispered, feeling the threads of magic pull away. It never stopped being uncomfortable, like strands of fiber pulling through my veins and out through my palms, dissipating into the air, but at least it was quick. I opened my eyes, blinking at my surroundings. It was a little destabilizing, coming out of my visions. The dancing, moving actions of the cards in my head happened in the dark—shining ochre figures moving against a pitch black backdrop. The real world was uncomfortably colorful in comparison.

It was probably what doing drugs was like. I wouldn't know, because Oneiroi didn't get to live like rockstars the way other daimons did, but I was going to assume that's what it felt like. Maybe I'd ask Riot.

I dialed his phone but it went straight to voicemail again, the sneaky devil. I was pretty confident based on the cards that he had gotten her out fine, and this was punishment for me not giving them more specific instructions and more notice—he was petty like that. It wasn't like I knew *everything*, there were always variables.

It was even trickier when the agathos were involved. The cards gave me some insight into the agathos—no one could escape Fate—but the detailed visions La Nuit herself granted me in the dreamscape never showed the agathos in the future because she couldn't "see" them. They weren't hers to guide, with the unexplained exception of Grace.

The Page of Swords card appeared at the forefront of my mind again, my heart pounding aggressively hard in my chest. My job was to answer Grace's questions, to guide her on her path. 'Unexplained exception' wasn't going to cut it anymore, I needed hard answers.

There used to be so many paths for Grace's future, but since she'd met Riot, the options had narrowed and all of them were hard. But Grace— The Fool—would have us by her side for as long as we could be there. The Devil. Death. The Chariot. The World.

Ugh, all these serious thoughts were giving me a headache. I was going to need a gallon of green tea and seven Disney movies to perk me up if this continued.

I meticulously reordered my cards and stored them in their black velvet bag that always lived in my pocket before lighting a small bundle of sage in a concrete bowl to cleanse the space. After a few moments, I realized my heartbeat hadn't slowed. It was still pounding incessantly against my ribcage at a borderline painful rate.

"Finally," I whispered to the empty room. Thank the fucking Goddess. I'd only been waiting my *entire life.* The past week since Riot first called me had been torture, and now it was time.

I was already scrambling over all the cushions and decorative throw blankets I'd collected from the big house to store here, hoping the almost burned out sage didn't set the barn on fire. It would probably be fine, that seemed like the kind of thing the Fates would have given me a heads up on.

Pushing my chin-length pale blonde hair out of my face, I made sure my navy shirt was neatly tucked into my cropped tweed slacks and my white sneakers were spotless. I didn't want to be making a bad impression on my girl right off the bat. I had *plenty* of time to scare her off with my weird personality. My sleeves were rolled up to below my elbows, showcasing the tarot cards Dare had tattooed on my forearms. If Grace looked closely, she'd see all of her soul bonds represented in the cards on my right arm.

Over my heart was The Lovers card surrounded by roses, also in her honor. Maybe Grace would demand I take my clothes off right away so she could inspect me? That wasn't what she was like in the dreamscape, but stranger things had happened.

Satisfied that I looked *fantastic*, I leaned against the door jamb at the entry to the downstairs shop like I was totally cool and not about to pee myself with excitement. Totally got this. No big deal.

This part of the property was accessed by a gravel driveway, but mostly surrounded by grass and trees that hid it from the main house. The sky was growing dark and the rain poured down incessantly, but I was so excited that I felt like the sun was shining and the birds were singing.

The front door where I waited was sheltered by the deck overhead which was also the external access to the apartment, but Riot had never been to this part of the property before and wouldn't know where to go. He and Dare had visited me out here about a month after I moved in twelve years ago, but I'd only seen them when I visited Milton since then.

And I was not offended about that at all, no siree. It was totally fine that the two closest friends I had abandoned me out here. Not. Offended. At. All.

Riot came up the winding driveway in the obnoxiously loud car Dare had procured for them—courtesy of my instructions—and I squinted to see the two faces in the front seat. Riot looked more stressed than I'd ever seen him, but I barely noticed him. Not when the beautiful, slightly traumatized woman sitting next to him was staring at me like she'd seen a ghost.

That's right, Amazing Grace. I'm your Ghost of Christmas Future.

Except not Christmas. Just Future. And not a ghost.

36

Okay, I needed a new metaphor, but it was hard to describe what I was to Grace.

Grace was the whole universe to me.

I knew everything about her. Everything. I recalled every conversation we'd ever had—from the fantastical tales of dragons and unicorns she'd told me as a kid, to the embarrassing school picture day she'd had in middle school, to the innocent flirting we'd shared in recent years.

Until this week, I'd never so much as hinted we were soul bonds— that was Grace's discovery to make when the time was right—but she'd always been more outgoing in her dreams than I suspected she was in real life. Still prim and proper, but a little more relaxed. A little more content to let the "darkness" she believed lived inside her rise to the surface. Only a little.

Would Grace be like that today? Would she be relaxed with me in person? Would I freak her out? Goddess, I hoped I didn't freak her out. Unrequited love was hard enough without her being scared of me.

Riot finally pulled up in front of the house, cutting the engine and shooting me an irritated look before exiting the vehicle. I gave him a beaming smile in return, knowing I was on his shit list, but it wouldn't last long. Riot wasn't a grudge holder by nature, he was too pessimistic to bother. What was the point in being mad at someone when everything was miserable and life was futile anyway?

What a way to live.

He quickly moved around the car to open Grace's door, helping her out of the vehicle.

My heart, still racing, flipped in my chest at seeing her like this—remnants of animal blood streaked across her face, clothes and hair wet, shaking from what the agathos had put her through. My feet were moving towards Grace before I realized I'd taken a step. I'd known it was going to be *unpleasant*, but what had happened today had been the best-case scenario. Better than them failing to sever the bond between her and Riot, and sending her on an outreach trip to the other side of the globe. It would have delayed me meeting her by *months*, and all the paths would have changed.

Riot wrapped his arms protectively around Grace's waist, and it was surprisingly un-weird to see him holding my girl like that.

Maybe because while his identity had only become clear to me in my visions recently, I'd always known Grace wouldn't be mine alone. I probably should have asked the Fates more questions on how Riot was going to handle the whole *sharing* aspect.

He didn't try to pull Grace back as I approached though. Just glowered at me, one arm around Grace, the other hand fishing his lighter out of his pocket to play with like a twitchy pyromaniac.

I'd win him over.

Grace stared up at me with eyes the color of opals—a fascinating mix of turquoise and lavender, flecked with gold. I'd looked into those eyes every night of my life, but nothing had prepared me for seeing them in person. She was... *breathtaking*. My heart was still working overtime, and I wasn't sure my lungs were even functioning. Maybe this was how I met my maker? Looking into Grace's eyes *in person* for the first time. Boom. Dead on arrival.

"Bullet," Grace breathed, her hand reaching hesitantly for me as I stepped into her space.

I'd imagined this moment a million times, and yet when Grace was right in front of me, panic froze my muscles in place before I could reach for her. Grace closed the distance between us, her hand coming up to cup my jaw, her cool palm as light as a feather on my skin. Tentative, like she was as nervous as I was.

A rush of memories swirled through my mind of every innocent touch we'd shared in the dreamscape—as sweet and chaste as this was—but this felt completely different. It felt so real. My hand came up to cover hers, holding her in place.

"Amazing Grace," I said, my smile taking over my whole face. "It's nice to meet you," I told her, the same as I did every night. This time the words felt like they were ripped up from the depths of my soul. Nice? Nice didn't even begin to cover it.

"It's so nice to finally meet you," she replied, her voice thick with emotion. For me? The idea seemed ludicrous.

"You're freezing," I said, blinking suddenly at the realization of how cold her hand was against my skin. She was wearing an oversized black hoodie that definitely belonged to Riot, but it was visibly damp, her long black hair was wet, and her full lips were looking a little more blue than I was comfortable with. "Come on, let's get you inside."

"Finally, he decides to be helpful," Riot grumbled, shoving his messy straight hair back, his hands covered in brightly colored tattoos. Between his all black clothes and the black hair, the tattoos and the red and purple eyes were the only splashes of color on him.

Luckily I'd bought him some clothes to wear while he was here that weren't hideously dull. He could thank me later.

"Oh hush, I have been very helpful," I chastised, reluctantly releasing Grace's hand and gesturing towards the building behind me. Instead of going through the downstairs shop, I led them up the staircase to the deck that made up the covered porch over the shop, and through the double doors into my humble home, jogging to get us out of the light rain as quickly as possible.

It wasn't the most comfortable home. The upstairs apartment had a central living area, with a small bathroom and one bedroom off to the side where Grace and Riot would stay. And maybe me, one day. The ceilings were low, and the exposed beams and sloping ceilings on either side of the building made it even worse. The kitchen was against a side wall and sometimes, when my back started hurting from hunching over, I'd kneel on the floor to work at the counter.

Luckily, Grace was a little shorter than me. Unluckily, Riot was not.

I made a beeline for the freestanding cast-iron fireplace to warm the place up. Fortunately, I'd already put the wood in earlier, so I got it going while Riot wrapped Grace in a quilt off the back of the couch. Everything in this place was sort of old-lady chic since this barn had been fitted out in the nineties. Or eighties. Or maybe the seventies. I wasn't really sure, but it was all still in pretty great condition since the barn hadn't been utilized until I'd decided to move into it.

"This place is so cozy," Grace said, looking around at all the varnished blond wood floors and furniture, with cream upholstery and quilts everywhere.

"It's missing something..." Riot drawled. "Crochet doilies, perhaps? A few dozen cats?"

I closed the squeaky fire door and twisted down the handle to secure it before standing and beaming at Riot. Look at us, bonding already. "You're right, we should get a cat. I'll name it though. You'd name it something depressingly pretentious like Poe or Morrissey."

Grace's mouth twitched as her gaze bounced between us, tugging the quilt tightly around her shivering frame. "Poe the cat sounds kind of cute, actually."

"Thank you, Gracie," Riot said, pulling her down onto the couch next to him. "I don't even want to know what kind of *Cats the Musical*-themed name you'd come up with."

"Mr. Mistoffelees," I replied instantly. It wasn't even a question. Mr. Mistoffelees was my fictional spirit animal.

"You're ridiculous," Riot huffed, shaking his head in bewilderment, though I saw the corner of his mouth twitch a teeny bit. "How did we get onto this topic? We're supposed to be discussing our clusterfuck of an afternoon."

"The agathos boss lady for the Northeast snatched Grace from work, you made some *arrangements*, Dare jacked a couple of cars, you rescued Grace with a little insider help, drove here, and now your new bestie is going to take care of the details," I listed, waving my hand absently, keeping the details about Riot's deal with Viper vague in case Grace's agathos aversion to lying flared up. "I'm guessing you haven't eaten," I added, making my way to the tiny kitchen.

Daimons were vegetarians, but agathos weren't. I probably should have stocked up on—*shudder*—meat.

"Insider help?" Grace asked, accepting the glass of water I got for her. Riot did the same, with a surly nod of thanks, before I returned to the kitchen for sustenance.

"I think it was one of your dads," Riot said sheepishly, keeping Grace tucked in close to his side. "Tall. Red hair. Freckled. Dressed like an accountant. He used his blood to open the sub basement door and told me to take care of you. And when we left, he started his lighter for some reason then pulled the fire alarm."

"They can't lie, remember?" I said, moving around the kitchen. "He couldn't pull the fire alarm unless there was an actual fire."

It was ridiculous, the way the agathos had to work around some arbitrary rules their goddess had imposed on them millennia ago and never bothered to change.

"My dad, Chance, works in the building. He's always been the most supportive of all my parents. If he'd known what they were planning, maybe he wanted to help? I wouldn't have expected that, though..." Grace said slowly.

I *felt* her sadness. It ghosted against my skin like the lightest breeze, and I froze for a moment, wondering if I'd imagined it. I'd found out as much as I could about soul bonds over the years, and I knew sensing emotions was part of it—after the first physical contact—but it was a whole different thing to experience it firsthand.

"I can't really *see* the agathos," I offered. "But I knew that help would be there for Riot if he made it in time. Chance wanted to help you."

"That's a nice thought," Grace said softly. "That not all of my parents were willing to throw me to the wolves. Just most of them."

Mm, only four out of five.

"Maybe you should shower while Bullet makes dinner?" Riot suggested, giving her a sympathetic look. "Wash the blood off, warm up a little."

Why hadn't I thought of that? Grace was going to think Riot was a better boyfriend than me. Damn it.

"That's a good idea," Grace agreed quickly. I knew from visiting her dreams that Grace didn't like to let people see her struggle, it was the agathos way. She probably wanted a minute to pull herself together without Riot and I hovering.

Grace stood, shooting me a sheepish look. "I don't suppose you have some clothes I can borrow?" she asked, gesturing at Riot's oversized hoodie and the pale blue dress she was wearing underneath that was clinging to her legs in a way that I probably shouldn't be appreciating, giving everything that was going on.

Grace looked up and gave me a startled look, probably because my excited grin was a little manic. "Clothes I can do. Follow me, Amazing Grace."

I'm about to blow your mind.

GRACE

CHAPTER 4

"What is this?" I asked, stopping in my tracks in the doorway, barely believing what I was seeing. The living area of the barn apartment looked like a perfectly preserved 90s sitcom set, but this room... this room was all the things I liked, distilled into one tiny space. Exposed wood floors, off-white walls, and a sloping ceiling. Textured throw cushions on top of cream linen bedding, and *plants*. There was a monstera in a terracotta pot by the door that was far more impressive than any I'd grown, and there was a spider fern on the window sill just like the one I had in the kitchen at my apartment.

My apartment. I wanted to weep. I was really going to miss my apartment.

"I don't know whether to be creeped out or impressed," Riot said with a low whistle, standing close enough at my back that I could feel the heat of his body.

"I vote impressed," Bullet replied cheerfully, though I could see the flicker of nervousness in his eyes that he was valiantly trying to cover up. "But if you're creeped out, don't look in the closet."

"Do look in the closet," Riot said instantly, like a devil on my shoulder.

I'd always been too curious for my own good. It's what had gotten me into trouble with Mother—*Faith*—my whole life. At least I didn't need to be ashamed of that curiosity anymore, I guess. I may be freefalling into nothing and hoping the universe would catch me, but at least the shackles had been cut loose. If I'd learned anything today, it was that I'd rather be uncertain about my future than unhappy with it.

Embracing my newfound boldness, I crossed the small room and pulled open the double doors of the whitewashed freestanding wardrobe that took up a decent portion of the room. There was a long rack across the top that was filled to the brim with hanging clothes, as well as built-in drawers that I assumed were equally as well-stocked, and a pull out shelf at the bottom with some of the prettiest shoes I'd ever seen.

Unlike the rest of the room, the inside of the closet was nothing like what I'd find in my apartment. There was so much *color*. Bright, bold colors I would have never dared to wear. And black! I was never allowed to wear black—it was strictly for funerals—but I'd always wanted to. It had always seemed so versatile and low maintenance, and now nothing was stopping me.

Silently, I perused the racks and shelves, pulling out fitted black jeans, a tank top and a buttery soft navy sweater. *Sugar, there was even an underwear drawer!*

It was better than having no underwear, but the idea of Bullet going out and buying it for me... My inner monster rose up in wanton excitement at that idea even as the logical part of my brain tried to muster up some embarrassment.

45

I didn't even *know* Bullet, though apparently he knew me. There was this *comfort* to the connection between us that made it feel older than it was, but at the same time my brain was rebelling, telling me he was a stranger. Even if he wasn't, I was sort of intimidated by Bullet.

The way he *knew* things was awe-inspiring, but beyond a little scary.

"How did you know my size?" I asked, verifying on the label that they were in fact exactly my fit.

"I asked you," Bullet replied as though the answer was obvious. "You always chose your own clothes in your dreams, I just followed your lead. Everything is always either bold colors or dark, and you wear jeans a lot."

"Well, I'm still leaning towards creepy," Riot volunteered, leaning against the door jamb. "But at least finding you some clothes is one item off the list. We'll leave you to get cleaned up, I'm sure you'd like to get the blood off your face."

I grimaced at the reminder that it was still there despite my attempts to wipe it off. What a day. I felt like I'd aged ten years since I woke up this morning.

"Bathroom is right next door," Bullet said. "I'll go start dinner. I insist," he added when I opened my mouth to object. We'd barged in on him and he'd done so much already, I wanted to be able to contribute.

"Don't feel guilty, Gracie," Riot called over his shoulder, already heading back into the living area. "He knew we were coming, remember?"

Logically I understood that, but I found it hard to believe. How could anyone be so relaxed if they'd seen this day coming? Maybe Bullet led a far more interesting life than I did, since he seemed completely unphased by our presence.

I needed to properly talk to him. I hadn't had a chance yet, and I felt awful about it. When Riot and I had met, we'd spent time alone together right away.

Soon, I promised myself.

It was only early evening based on the darkening sky I could see out the circular window, but the queen-sized bed with its pristine cream linen bedding looked *so* inviting. I would have been tempted to lie down for a minute if my gross clothes wouldn't ruin the bedspread. Instead, I gathered up my things and scurried to the bathroom, shooting the guys an apologetic smile on my way past.

The bathroom was also straight out of the 90s, but it was neat and clean, and I wasted no time cranking the above-tub shower and waiting for the water to heat up.

I could feel myself starting to fray slightly at the edges as the day caught up with me, but I forced myself to go through the motions, stripping off the soaked, stained dress I'd never liked anyway—definitely burning that—and climbing into the steaming hot shower. I barely registered that my usual brands of shampoo and body wash were already on the side of the tub waiting for me as I cleaned myself up, washing my hair once—then two more times—before scrubbing my face raw to get every trace of blood off it.

The agathos thought I was tainted, but I'd never *felt* dirty until they'd put me on that altar. It was their so-called cleansing that had made me feel polluted for the first time.

The water swirling into the drain ran clean. I knew I appeared to be normal on the outside, but that only made the weight of everything suddenly hit me harder, crashing over me as surely as the water did. My legs buckled underneath me and I fell to my knees, not even feeling the impact of hitting the porcelain tub when my emotional pain was so crippling.

47

I sat and drew my knees up to my chest, wrapping my arms around them and dropping my head. It was over. No matter what the Basilinna had said about it not being the end, it was. It was the end for me. I felt betrayed and violated, and I never wanted to step foot in an agathos temple again. Whatever they told themselves about bringing me back into the fold, I would refuse to go.

I was a permanent outcast. An exile.

Even though that realization came with a sliver of relief that I no longer had to try to force myself into a box I'd never fit, it also meant I was adrift in the world, and even with Riot and now Bullet at my side, that thought was terrifying.

And then there was Mercy, my younger cousin and bestest friend. My brothers were young and barely knew me as it was, and my parents would undoubtedly convince them that I was not to be trusted, that my name was forbidden. In time, perhaps they would forget about me. That realization stung, but knowing how hard it would be for Mercy hurt more. I didn't know if they would tell her the truth that I was soul-bonded to a daimon, or if my mother would cherry pick the worst things I'd said to her to pass on to Mercy without any explanation.

Forgive me, I asked her silently. *I would have never left you behind if I had a choice.*

I vaguely registered the bathroom door opening then closing with a quiet click, but I didn't have the energy to lift my head off my knees to check who it was.

Even if Mercy tried to contact me, my regular phone was back at the shelter in my bag from when the Basilinna's bonded had shown up at work to abduct me, and the burner phone Riot had given me was nowhere to be found. They must have gone through my pockets when they took me to the temple. Another violation atop a list of violations.

"Gracie," Riot murmured, already stripping down to his boxers to climb into the shower with me. He pulled me to my feet and wrapped his arms around my waist, holding me upright. I exhaled heavily as I pressed my forehead against his chest and let the tears fall, safe in Riot's arms.

I don't know how long we stood there—*while I was completely naked,* which I didn't even register at that moment—as one emotion after another ripped through me. I was afraid, and then relieved. Heartbroken at the way my family had turned on me, followed by a sense of hope and wonder that I'd met Bullet. Angry, exhausted, confused, *all of it.*

Slowly, I was able to find my way through my own emotional turmoil and find my way to Riot's calming presence. The connection between us had grown deeper, and I knew there was a lot more going on under the surface than he was letting on, but he was mostly calm. He was forcing himself to be calm for my benefit, and I couldn't have been more grateful for it.

"Come on," he said softly, rubbing my back. "You need to eat, then we'll get some rest, okay?"

Riot stepped away to turn off the now cold water and I knew my eyes were as wide as saucers when he turned to get out of the shower and get us towels. Rivulets of water ran down the strong muscles of his back down to his exceptionally great…

Grace! I scolded myself, crossing an arm over my breasts and using the other to shield my, er, *lady bits*. I forced my gaze up to the ceiling, so I wasn't perving on his butt, which his soaked boxers weren't doing a great job of hiding.

I was in no way *in the mood* with everything that had gone on, but I couldn't help being curious—this was the closest to naked I'd ever seen Riot. And I was *very* conscious of my own nakedness.

He wrapped a towel around his waist, turning back to me with a faint smirk on his lips as he draped a second towel over my shoulders, keeping his gaze firmly on my face.

"Who knew my ass was such a great distraction?" he teased, his amusement tickling my skin. I pulled the corners of the large towel up to hide my face. *Busted.*

"I bet *you* knew that," I mumbled, quickly patting my face dry, my cheeks stinging slightly from how hard I'd scrubbed them.

"I do have a great ass," he agreed seriously, pulling a fluffy cream robe off the back of the door and holding it up for me to slip my arms into. Was that a 'G' embroidered on it? For Grace? Surely not. "I'm going to see if Bullet has some non-pretentious clothes that I can borrow. I'll meet you in the kitchen, yeah?"

"Sounds good. Um, Riot?"

"Don't thank me," he said, dropping a kiss on my forehead. "There's no need."

"It's not just this," I protested, gesturing at the shower. "You came for me, and you sorted everything out—"

"It was my privilege," he said firmly. "I'm not... I'm not the hero. But I'll pretend for you, Gracie."

"You're always my hero," I replied, smiling at his rich chuckle.

"Cheesy," he chided, tapping the tip of my nose. "Get dressed. I have a lot of questions for our host."

I quickly dressed in the dark clothes I'd picked out, wishing I'd grabbed one of the designer lounge sets I'd seen in the drawer for comfort, instead of letting myself be tempted by the chic jeans.

The sweater was luxuriously soft—apparently Bullet had spared no expense when it came to my wardrobe. How could he even afford all of this stuff? Another question for my mysterious second soul bond, I suppose.

I plugged in the hair dryer and took care of the worst of my hair, examining the selection of makeup on the counter that definitely looked like it had been purchased by someone who'd never worn makeup before. It was a good distraction though. I picked through the items until I found a tinted moisturizer that would make my face feel a little less naked, then added some eyeliner and mascara. Even then, I still felt exposed.

A lifetime of expectations around how I should appear and my mother's rules around clothes and makeup. An extra addition to the ever mounting baggage I had to unpack.

Now that I was feeling calmer, I could feel Riot's strong concern as well as faint echoes of Bullet's, which was unexpected. Did the bond begin to form right away? Why weren't we taught more about that in our agathos classes?

Having procrastinated as long as I could, I joined them in the living room, which smelled strongly of cooked garlic and onion, as well as fresh basil.

"I'm making pasta," Bullet called from the opposite side of the living area, hunched over in the tiny kitchen with the sloping ceiling. "Won't be long."

"It smells amazing," I replied with a small smile, suddenly feeling shy. Riot grabbed my hand and tugged me over to the dining table, insisting I sit before I could awkwardly offer to help.

"You look nice," I told Riot, admiring the fitted jeans and charcoal cashmere sweater he was wearing.

He gave me an incredulous look while Bullet laughed. "Don't encourage him," Riot warned. "He's trying to dress me like his more muscular, dark-haired clone."

"You're welcome," Bullet sang, and despite everything, I couldn't help but smile at their antics. They definitely seemed like old friends, and I was a little sad at the idea they'd lost touch over the years.

"Bullet and I are going to head out for a bit after dinner," Riot told me with an apologetic grimace. "We need to, uh, *return* the car. Will you be okay on your own for a bit?"

"You'll be safe here," Bullet promised, moving confidently around the kitchen despite how cramped it was. "This place is kind of a haven for us, going forward."

"Oh, well that's good," I replied, not really sure how to respond to the certainty in his voice when speaking of the future.

"I'd say you get used to the vague statements, but I'm not sure you do," Riot said drily, his hand making its way under my mass of hair to rub my neck.

"You'll get used to them," Bullet laughed, setting an enormous bowl of pasta in the middle of the table, filled with bright cherry tomatoes, spinach and basil, before returning to the kitchen to grab bowls and utensils. "Sometimes I can say things with certainty, other times I can't. Destinations are set in stone, but the paths to get there are varied. Sometimes telling you things would change our course, so I'll keep that knowledge quiet. Great power, great responsibility, and all that."

He handed out the bowls and sat down across from Riot and I, shooting me a beaming smile. There was absolutely no question that Bullet was handsome, in an almost modelesque kind of way. He was leaner than Riot, and dressed in tailored clothes that wouldn't be out of place in a fashion magazine. His straight pale blonde hair was chin-length and shoved messily behind his ears, giving his gentlemanly clothes a rockstar edge, as did all the black ink that covered every inch of his arms that I could see. And the gold bullet that hung from a long thin silver chain around his neck.

And his *eyes*. All daimons had eyes that were a mixture of crimson and purple, like all agathos had opal-colored eyes, but I'd never seen daimonic eyes like Bullet's. They were almost pure amethyst, with the faintest hint of crimson around the edges.

That wasn't the only unusual thing about him. Bullet almost seemed to glow. Like there was an ethereal kind of moonlight inside him that shone from the inside out. It definitely made him a little less approachable—as if touching him would be like touching the stars.

There was no doubt about it—Bullet was incredibly handsome.

Riot snorted, pulling his hand away from my neck and brushing his thumb over the corner of my lip. "You got a little drool there, Gracie."

"What?!" I squeaked, immediately patting my chin with my fingers.

"You don't," Bullet assured me as my face heated up. "Though it would be understandable if you did. I am incredibly easy on the eyes."

"You sure you're feeling the soul bondy tingles for this guy?" Riot asked, side eyeing Bullet across the table.

"Definitely," I laughed, squeezing Riot's arm before serving myself some pasta.

"How come you're living here?" Riot asked Bullet. "We went to the big house first, the one I visited last time, but they said you'd moved to this barn."

"I moved about five years ago," Bullet retorted, raising an eyebrow at Riot though his lips were still upturned. He had an almost permanently amused look on his face, but I craved another one of his proper grins that showed off all his teeth and made the corners of his eyes crinkle. The way Bullet smiled with his whole face was addictive. "Once it was only me living there, the big house seemed a little drafty. I rented it out to humans and they run a horse breeding business on the grounds. Less work for me."

"No other Oneiroi have moved here in the last five years?" Riot asked with a frown before turning to me. "This property is passed down from Oneiroi to Oneiroi over the generations. It's not a family thing, just whichever Oneiroi wants to live here can. Right?"

"Right," Bullet agreed, filling his own bowl. "There are properties like this near all towns where daimons live. Oneiroi suffer from sensory overload, I guess you could call it. The more people we meet, the more futures we see. I managed to live a pretty regular life until 17, but that's a long time for an Oneiroi to stay in the real world."

His eyes flashed with some hidden emotion as he looked at me, and I got the distinct impression that he'd delayed moving out here because of me.

"And there were other Oneiroi here when you moved in?" I asked, clearing my throat as I twirled my spaghetti around my fork.

"Six," Bullet said thoughtfully. "All older than me. They've all passed now, they're buried in a cemetery at the back of the grounds. It's all very morbid. I assumed younger ones would come along after I moved in, but no one ever did."

I could feel Riot's confusion, but I didn't understand enough about the situation to know why he was confused. Maybe the younger Oneiroi weren't ready to move out here yet? Lots of young people tend to live more introverted lifestyles now anyway, hidden behind their computer screens, maybe they didn't *need* a country hideaway?

"So, any more vague, unhelpful advice about the future you'd like to give us?" Riot asked Bullet casually between mouthfuls, deftly changing the subject.

"I gave you instructions down to the *minute*," Bullet shot back, still smiling. "It was possibly the most helpful, least vague I've ever been in my life."

"I'm very grateful," I said quickly before Riot could reply. "Thank you for all your help."

"You don't need to thank me, Amazing Grace. That's what soul bonds do."

Bullet shrugged like he was the expert on the matter and Riot gave him a scathing look that almost made me giggle. It was a stark contrast from when I had to explain what a soul bond was to Riot, whilst also not entirely *believing* that's what we were, since it seemed impossible.

Now it seemed impossible that Riot *wouldn't* be my soul bond. Of course that's what we were to each other.

"How do you know anything about soul bonds?" Riot asked suspiciously.

"Grace and I have chatted about it before," Bullet replied easily, and guilt wormed its way through my chest that I couldn't remember any of those conversations. "Not about *us* being soul bonds, obviously, just the abstract idea. And I followed around a bunch of agathos over the years for observation purposes."

"You spied on them," Riot said blandly.

"I *observed* them. Like an anthropologist."

"Or a stalker," Riot shot back, struggling not to laugh before shooting me a concerned look, gauging my reaction.

I shrugged half-heartedly. "At least one of us will have some information, I haven't been much help on that front so far."

"You've been very helpful," Riot said automatically, giving me far more credit than I deserved.

I shook my head, giving him a small smile as I dug into my delicious bowl of pasta. Bullet could *cook*. How had he whipped this up while I was in the shower? I was pretty comfortable in the kitchen since I'd basically been raised to be a housewife, but coming up with a meal on the fly was a superpower I didn't possess. I needed lists and prep time and instructions.

"How did you two meet?" I asked, after demolishing most of my meal. The full stomach did wonders to make me feel better.

"School," Bullet said, eating at a much more leisurely pace than I had. "We all went to the same schools in Milton, and knew each other for years."

"Us and Dare," Riot added, giving Bullet an indecipherable look.

"Us and Dare," Bullet replied with a wide grin. "Anyway, I moved out here and those two stayed in Milton, so we haven't seen each other as much over the years. I still go into town sometimes. Dare does my tattoos."

"They're incredible," I told him honestly, looking at the ink on his forearms. They all seemed to be depictions of tarot cards, surrounded by vines and flowers that linked them together, with a breathtaking amount of detail on each card.

A good agathos girl would be terrified of tarot cards and all the black magic associated with them, but I'd never been a good agathos girl no matter how hard I'd pretended. Darkness called to me.

"I get visions that show me what I'll get," Bullet said, like that was entirely normal.

"Show off," Riot muttered. I nudged him gently with my elbow and he looked over at me with amused eyes, setting down his fork and reaching over the back of my chair to rub my shoulder. I didn't think he was actually that averse to Bullet, even if he found him frustrating sometimes. We'd all have to get used to one another.

"Grace, is there anything that happened today you'd like to talk about?" Bullet asked, unusually formal. Jokey and smiley seemed to be his default setting, and he definitely looked out of his element trying to be so serious.

"Um, I mean, you *saw* the gist of it right?" I stammered.

Bullet nodded and Riot gave my shoulder a supportive squeeze.

"How are you feeling about it all?" Bullet asked.

I opened my mouth then closed it again, trying to figure out a way to answer that question. "Betrayed," I eventually settled on. "I'm worried about the future, and nervous about leaving my old life behind even though there were parts of it I didn't like. But I mostly feel betrayed."

Riot made a distressed sound of agreement as Bullet shot me a sympathetic smile.

"The agathos are determined to... fix this, fix *me*, and the Basilinna, Harmony, said that they weren't about to give up," I added, because that really was the most important detail, and the thing they both needed to be aware of.

"I've seen that too," Bullet replied, nodding thoughtfully. "Don't worry, Amazing Grace. We'll keep you safe. We should probably return that car though, in case anyone follows the trail."

"I'll clean this up," I volunteered immediately, shaking my head when Bullet objected. "Really, it'll keep me busy, I want to."

Even knowing these two were my soul bonds, being openly honest and vulnerable was still something I wasn't entirely comfortable with. Agathos were meant to hide their emotions.

"Well, since you can't lie, then I have to take your word for it, don't I?" Bullet teased. "I'm going to find Riot the fancy jacket I bought him and grab the keys to my bike. Watch him act like he's not excited to snuggle up behind me on the ride back."

"Don't you have a car?!" he called as Bullet disappeared down the stairs to where I guessed his room must be.

"You're happy to see him really," I said softly, standing up and collecting the bowls to carry to the kitchen. Riot grabbed the rest, following behind me and hunching dramatically under the sloped ceiling, looking up like it personally offended him. "I can feel that you don't really hate him."

"He's annoying," Riot grumbled.

"Is he? Or is this whole situation just a little surreal?"

Riot leaned over, smacking a surprisingly affectionate kiss on my cheek. "Both. Are you sure you'll be okay here on your own? We'll be as fast as possible."

"I'll be fine," I assured him. As much as I enjoyed being in their company, an hour to myself might not be a bad thing. I'd been living alone for six months before I met Riot, and having time by myself to decompress each day had been quite nice.

After today, I had a lot of decompressing to do.

Riot moved to step out of the kitchen and I grabbed his arm at the last minute, tugging him back towards me. Before he could speak, I pulled his head down and pressed my lips against his, the taut, strained bond between us soothing almost instantly, easing an irritation I didn't even realize I'd had.

I hadn't planned to take it any further, but Riot's arms wrapped around my waist, pulling me tight against him and my lips parted as I forgot entirely that it was meant to be a chaste see-you-later kiss. My hands fisted Riot's absurdly soft sweater, and memories of how good Riot had made me feel when the bond was pushing us to consummate our relationship flashed through my mind.

I wanted to make him feel that good.

Now that I was free of the agathos community, I was running out of reasons not to.

A throat cleared from behind us and Riot growled in irritation as I pulled away quickly, looking back over my shoulder at an amused Bullet.

"Ready to go?" he asked.

"Obviously not," Riot gritted out.

"Go," I insisted, pushing him gently out of the kitchen and shooting Bullet a sheepish smile.

Apparently Riot wasn't the only one that would have to get used to our new living arrangements. I had plenty of learning to do myself.

CHAPTER 5

I looked around, suddenly finding myself standing in the abandoned grassy lot opposite Onslaught where I'd met Riot for the first time with no recollection of how I got here. I could hear the dull thud of bass from the dingy bar across the street, the low murmur of voices and occasional bursts of laughter, but they sounded far away. Like I was listening to it all with my ear pressed against a wall.

It was night, like when I'd first met Riot, but cooler. I shivered, pulling my parka closer around me before looking down at my outfit. A puffy black waterproof jacket, tight jeans, and knee-high boots. Did I choose this?

"Hm, you don't have a jacket like that in your closet," Bullet observed, seemingly materializing next to me and giving my outfit a critical onceover. "I'll order you one tomorrow."

"You've bought me more than enough clothes," I protested with a weak laugh, overwhelmed just thinking about the amount of stuff in the closet. "So we're still doing the dream thing then, huh?" I teased, bumping him with my shoulder.

Bullet blinked at me for a moment and I worried I'd overstepped, but then his face broke out in a wide smile. "It's weird not having to introduce myself. And we don't have to do this anymore, if you don't want to," he added, gesturing at the dream around us.

"I want to," I assured him instantly before sticking out my hand for him to shake. "Hello. I'm Grace."

Those mischievous eyes softened ever so slightly as he took my hand and shook it. "Nice to meet you, Amazing Grace. My name is Bullet."

I held his hand for a beat longer than I needed to, scanning his features. Did he look different in dreams compared to real life? I didn't think so. I kept hoping all of those years of dreams would come back to me, though I wasn't entirely sure how I'd feel if they actually did.

"You fell asleep on the couch while we were out," Bullet said, tucking his hands into his gray wool coat. "Riot carried you to bed."

Sugar, I must have been so out of it that I didn't even notice them coming back. I sort of wanted to ask Bullet where he was sleeping, but I didn't want to offend him.

"Sorry, I was exhausted. So, um, why are we here?" I asked, tucking my own hands into my pockets, feeling suddenly shy. "Recreating the first meeting between Riot and I?"

Bullet scoffed. "No. I wouldn't recreate anything at this shit hole. A less romantic location for a meet-cute could not exist, Amazing Grace. There are dirty needles on the ground."

I glanced down in alarm, though I guessed used needles couldn't hurt me in a dream. Right? Right.

"So then why this location?" I asked. I could hear vehicles in the distance, adding to the cacophony of sounds that was Milton by night.

Bullet's smile grew strained. "A little nudge from the divine. There's something she wants me to see, and bringing you with me while I was transported was instinct. Though I don't have the best feeling about whatever this vision is. Maybe I should send you back."

"Do you do that a lot? Send me away if your visions get bad?"

"You may not remember what happens, but you'll feel the aftereffects when you wake up. I would never intentionally frighten you," Bullet responded, a little sharply, like the very idea was upsetting to him.

Oh dear. I could very easily fall in love with these men, I could feel it.

It seemed strange to have any kind of physical affection with Bullet since we'd technically only met today, but the distance between us felt so wrong that I couldn't help moving closer and linking our arms together.

"I know you wouldn't," I told him softly, giving his arm a gentle squeeze as we both turned to face the street.

The sound of vehicles was growing closer, their engines revving intimidatingly. They were traveling fast, too fast for these narrow side streets. I didn't know that the sound of moving cars could be aggressive, but these vehicles definitely sounded threatening somehow. Like they didn't care if they plowed into whatever was in their path.

"What's happening?" I breathed, my heart rate picking up in my chest even though I could feel we were only observers to whatever was going on, not part of the action.

Bullet changed position, interlacing our fingers and gripping my hand securely as the first vehicles appeared. Not the kind of vehicles that were usually seen in Milton, but the kind that agathos like my parents drove—big, shiny, new SUVs.

The vehicles stopped in the middle of the road one after another and the doors opened, men spilling out of the SUVs with their faces partially hidden by scarves pulled high over their noses, baseball bats and cans of spray paint in their hands. One looked towards where we were standing, staring right through us like we weren't there with his pale, opal-colored agathos eyes.

"No," I whispered, horrified at what I was seeing. I attempted to move closer, but my feet were frozen to the ground like ice had formed all around them. Bullet gave my hand a supportive squeeze, and my grip on his fingers grew probably close to painful.

"We're just here to watch, Amazing Grace," he said with a sad smile.

"Why are they doing this?" I breathed as an agathos man took his baseball bat to the barber shop window, shattering it instantly.

"Where is Riot?!" one of them yelled, standing in the center of the street. His voice was familiar but I couldn't quite place it. "Bring us the kidnapper Riot and we'll leave! Grace! Come out!"

"That's a lie," I whispered. How were they lying? Agathos couldn't lie. "Riot didn't kidnap me. That's... absurd."

"They believe it's true though," Bullet replied. "That's enough, isn't it?"

He was right, it was enough. All the people at the temple would have to do was tell the agathos that Riot had burst in threatening to set the place on fire and kill us all if they didn't let me go. And conveniently leave out the part where I'd fought them and ran into Riot's arms the moment I could.

Daimons and humans alike spilled out onto the streets rearing for a fight, and I made a strangled noise at the back of my throat at the sight of all this carnage over me, even if the people fighting weren't aware of that.

Or maybe they were, since the agathos weren't being shy about yelling my name and demanding my presence. They avoided the humans, unable to cause them physical harm even if they wanted to, but the daimons were fair game. Our built-in nonviolence limitations didn't apply to daimons.

A clearly drunk daimon took a swing at an agathos, grazing the guy's jaw while shouting abuse. The agathos raised his bat and Bullet spun me into him, pressing my face against his jacket before I could see the bat connect, but there was no disguising the sickening crunch of bone and the howl of pain.

"We're leaving," Bullet said in a strained voice, his hands shaking slightly where they pressed me against him.

"No." I shook my head against his jacket before tipping my head back to look at him, struggling to put my reasons for needing to stay into words. My whole life had been a series of questions, and I wanted answers even if those answers were unpleasant. Worse than unpleasant.

"Even knowing you won't remember any of this?" Bullet sighed, seemingly reading my mind. Perhaps he knew me better than I realized?

"Will you remind me? When we wake up?"

"There's nothing I wouldn't do for you, Amazing Grace," Bullet replied easily, making my heart stutter in my chest.

Not entirely sure how to respond to that declaration, I grabbed Bullet's hand and began to run. My apartment wasn't far from here—though I'd never made this journey on foot—and I felt like I needed to see it, because that was definitely where this train of carnage was headed. I needed to see my own people break into my home, see the lack of care and respect firsthand. I don't know where this sudden masochistic streak had come from. The altar where they'd smeared blood on me, probably.

For so long, I'd diligently forced myself not to look, not to voice the questions that had kept me up at night, not to protest the unfairness that I tried so hard not to see.

I didn't have that luxury anymore. Not when the agathos were storming this daimon town with baseball bats and firecrackers were going off behind us. Not when my own parents had thrown me to the wolves at the first possible opportunity. The truth suddenly felt incredibly obvious in my mind— if I didn't pay attention, if I didn't make myself see the uncomfortable realities I'd been ignoring, I wouldn't survive this. I didn't know what this was, but that much was clear.

Bullet's hand squeezed my mind and I stumbled to a sudden stop in the center of my living room, gasping in surprise.

"Dream travel," Bullet supplied cheerfully. "It's handy. You can skip all the lines."

I barely heard him over the ringing in my ears as I looked around the remnants of my beautiful apartment, the sanctuary I'd created for myself. Though I guessed it wasn't as bad as it could have been—it hadn't been desecrated like I'd expected. There was just stuff everywhere. And no agathos in sight.

"What happened here?" I asked, not really expecting Bullet to answer.

He hummed quietly, picking through the books strewn across the floor. "Do you have a suitcase, Amazing Grace?"

"A suitcase?" I repeated dumbly. "Er, yes. In my closet."

Bullet smiled, gesturing towards my bedroom door and with one last confused look at him, I led the way. This room was even worse—the sliding door of my closet hung precariously on the track, every drawer had been pulled open, and there were random items of clothing strewn everywhere. The white hard-shell suitcase that usually sat in the corner of my closet was missing, and half my clothes were gone.

"Did someone pack my things?" I asked in confusion. Riot wouldn't have had time. I turned to look at Bullet who was lying on my rumpled bed, arms crossed behind his head. He was obviously well versed in the layout of my apartment, maybe he'd come in and packed my things? Not that he needed to—he'd provided a more than adequate wardrobe for me.

"Looks that way," Bullet replied, humming a tune to himself. I poked around my room, annoyed I wasn't solid enough to actually move things around. My jewelry was gone, as was my phone charger even though my phone was back at the shelter and probably in my parents' hands by now.

"What are you humming?" I asked absently as I left the room, heading to the bathroom.

"What'd I Miss," Bullet replied. "Another Hamilton classic."

I got the feeling it was also a pointed reference and smiled a little to myself, despite the circumstances. The medicine cabinet was empty—all of my makeup and beauty products were gone.

"Riot organized this," I said, thinking out loud as I made way back to the bedroom where Bullet was still humming to himself. "This was what he meant by covering my tracks."

"Not without great personal cost," Bullet sighed, staring up at the ceiling. "It was a necessary evil, but I hate to break it to you, Amazing Grace—if you thought the Fates were going to give you a break, you are sadly mistaken."

"Are you going to remind me of this conversation?" I asked, the helplessness I was feeling bleeding into my voice.

Bullet gave me a tight smile that didn't quite meet his eyes. "I'll tell you everything I can."

I suspected they hadn't told me about the lengths they'd gone to because they didn't want to put me in a position where I'd have to lie. Or rather, fail to lie. I didn't feel like I was being deceptive right now, though, looking at the lengths they'd gone to. Maybe because it was a dream, or maybe because I had been entirely upfront that I was leaving this life behind.

The front door opened with a bang and I jumped, impulsively moving to hide before remembering no one but Bullet could see me.

"Someone's been here," a masculine voice yelled as the sound of footsteps coming up the stairs followed him. Feeling a little lost just hovering, I made my way over to the bed, perching on the edge while Bullet lounged behind me. His body language was relaxed—bordering on comatose, actually—but I got the feeling he was paying more attention than he made it appear.

If it were Riot lying next to me, I wouldn't hesitate to snuggle up against him. Not that I'd known him particularly long, but he had taken the lead when it came to physical contact, and I was more than happy to follow. Bullet seemed to be waiting for me to make the first move, and I wasn't entirely sure how to.

Especially when we were here, and he was demonstrating the sheer magnitude of his gift like it was nothing. He'd popped into my head while I was sleeping and taken me on a field trip to the future. It was a mindblowing amount of power that made my ability to bestow luck on humans look like a party trick.

"She must have come back here," an angry voice complained from the living room. "Why did her parents even let her move here? Why'd they let him take her from the temple?"

"He would have set the whole building on fire if they hadn't. You know what they're like," someone else spat angrily. Their voices were vaguely familiar to me, and it hurt my heart to think of people who I had probably known my whole life speaking about me and Riot that way.

Don't let my fathers be here, I prayed silently, not entirely sure which goddess I was directing my pleas to. Any one who was listening, perhaps. I was sort of holding it together seeing agathos I barely knew behaving so shamefully, but I wouldn't cope if I saw my own family members stooping to this level.

A man barged into my room and I flinched instinctively. It was so bizarre being invisible, and I was frustrated that I would forget what this felt like when I woke up. The agathos was my age, searching my bedroom with wild eyes, dressed all in dark clothes with a bat in his hand that made me want to cry.

He'd pulled his scarf down at some point and I realized it was Pax, one of Verity Mae's bonded, a friend of mine back in Auburn. Or she had been a friend at least. I assumed I'd be meeting her first baby any day now, but that wouldn't be happening. Did she hate me the way my mother did? Or pity me as I felt the Basilinna did, thinking of me as a wayward daughter of Anesidora who needed to be guided back in line with a firm hand and cold animal blood on my face.

Prior nerves about touching him forgotten, I grabbed Bullet's hand on the bed and squeezed his fingers tight, exhaling slightly when he squeezed back.

"She's packed her clothes," Pax called to his acquaintances. "Her winter coats are still here. My guess is she's gone somewhere warm."

Bullet chuckled as my eyebrows shot up. Maybe there was more method to this madness than I'd initially realized.

"I've got Valor on the phone," a voice called back and my breath caught at the casual reference to one of my fathers. "He says her passport expired. He's looking at domestic flights out of Islip and White Plains she might have got on."

*A few idiotic tears slipped out and I ducked my head, not wanting
Bullet to see me in such an undignified state. To his credit, he only squeezed
my hand and said nothing, watching as more agathos I vaguely knew filed into
what had been my ultimate sanctuary with no regard for my space.*

"Enough," Bullet murmured quietly. "We've seen enough."

"Wake up, Amazing Grace," Bullet sang, perched on the edge of the
bed, beaming at me. I blinked awake slowly, rolling away from a groaning Riot.

"Fuck off," Riot grumbled, rolling onto his front.

"No can do, bestie," Bullet replied cheerfully. "You're going to want
to call Dare. Like ASAP. Emergency, and all."

"The fuck?" Riot asked, immediately sitting up and reaching for his
phone, concern rolling off him in waves. "What are you talking about?"

"Call him," Bullet reiterated, eyes still trained on me like he couldn't
quite believe I was real.

"You visited my dreams last night," I stated as Riot waited for the
call to connect.

"I did," Bullet confirmed, not a trace of embarrassment in his
answer. I guess it would have been weird if he hadn't visited me after doing
so for so long. Weird for both of us.

Bullet looked at me for a long moment and I fidgeted slightly
under his gaze. There was something... expectant in it. Or perhaps hopeful?
Like he wanted me to elaborate, but I had no recollection of the dream to
elaborate on, and I couldn't help but feel like I was letting him down.

"Dare?" Riot said sharply. "Are you okay?"

He was already pushing out of bed and moving towards the window like he was too agitated to sit still.

Bullet shot him a sympathetic look before turning his attention back to me. "The agathos came for you last night."

"What?" I gasped, digging my fingers into the blankets. There was another flicker of something in Bullet's gaze, almost like he was saddened by my shock.

"They came into Milton and said they were trying to find you and Riot, accusing him of kidnapping you. They also used it as an excuse to do as much damage to the daimons, their homes and their businesses as possible," Bullet explained with a grimace.

"What? How? He didn't kidnap me'—"

"Technically they were telling the truth, or the truth as they believed it based on whatever message the agathos in the temple passed along, but it was a very thin truth. And as you well know, all those do-good rules don't apply when it comes to daimons."

A mixture of fear and horror seemed to unfurl from the center of my body, spreading like ice through my veins. Some of it was definitely Riot's, perhaps even Bullet's, but most of it was mine.

I was horrified and appalled and ashamed.

For six months, I had lived among the daimons in Milton undisturbed. I had moved to the outskirts of their territory, and they had left me—a lone agathos woman—to my devices. As soon as the agathos had an excuse, they'd used it to attack a daimon town within hours.

"Where are you?" Riot asked Dare, rubbing a hand over his face. "You should've come out here."

71

Bullet shook his head silently, a serene look on his face. Did he already know where Dare was? I couldn't imagine knowing so much about other people's lives, before they even knew it. It would be a lot of responsibility.

"Fuck," Riot sighed. "But you're okay, right?"

"He told me daimons don't really have friends," I murmured, heart aching from the mixture of fear and panic Riot was feeling for the man who was obviously his friend, even if he didn't want to admit it.

"Most don't," Bullet acknowledged, looking at me while I looked at Riot. "We're not most daimons though, and you're not most agathos. You know that."

I did know that.

"The Goddess of Night answered me," I told him absently, twisting the blanket between my fingers. "Twice now. Anesidora has never answered me."

"I'm not sure she can, Amazing Grace," Bullet said amiably. He continued before I could question him on it. "There's this impression among both the agathos and the daimons of enmity between the goddesses, but it doesn't feel that way in my visions. When she talks about her sister, she seems sad. Regretful."

Riot hung up then, turning back to face us, his features tight.

"Dare's safe, he loaded up his truck with as much shit as he could from the studio and didn't stop driving until he got to his mom's place in Jersey."

Bullet nodded like this wasn't new information to him, and Riot gave him an assessing look, eyes narrowed.

"Did you know the agathos were going to attack Milton?" Riot asked Bullet, his voice dangerously low.

"Not really," Bullet replied with a shrug. "I just got a live show this time. Front row seat to the chaos."

"Then why didn't you *do* something?" Riot snapped, throwing up his hands in exasperation. While I understood Riot's frustration, the idea of Bullet running out into danger made me feel ill, and I was selfishly glad he hadn't.

"It was tempting, but this was necessary," Bullet replied with admirable calm, drumming his fingers to a silent beat on his thigh. "Daimons are loosely connected by a goddess most of them never interact with, bound to a moral—or perhaps *immoral*—code that is inherent rather than explicit, and follow that code on an individual rather than community basis."

Riot blinked at that, and Bullet gave him a smug grin.

"We need the daimons to rally. To rally, we need a cause. You'll see."

"Why would we need them to rally?" I asked nervously. This had all escalated incredibly quickly over the past two days, and I was nervous about it.

What the agathos had done was unquestionably wrong, but I couldn't bring myself to think of them *all* as bad people. Mercy was an Auburn agathos. So were my innocent little brothers. Sweet, if occasionally offensive Verity Mae who was due to give birth any day now, surrounded by her four bonded who worshipped the ground she walked on... they weren't bad people.

"They won't be launching some large scale counterstrike, don't worry," Bullet said with a bright smile. "Daimons aren't that organized. But they'll rally around you, and trust me, it'll come in handy."

Riot's mouth slammed shut, his objections apparently forgotten.

"Me? Surely they hate me. I brought all this trouble to their town, after they all left me alone when I moved to Milton."

Bullet snorted. "They don't hate you, not even a little. To them, you're a defector. You were from the moment you moved to Milton—a good girl that willingly crossed to the dark side," he continued cheerfully. "It's like you and Riot are Romeo and Juliet, and Juliet said 'fuck the Capulets, the Montagues have better parties and bigger dicks anyway.'"

"Weren't the Capulets her family? And I doubt, er, *that* had any bearing on her decision," I added, my eyes definitely dropping to Riot's crotch for half a second before I caught myself. *Sugar.* That desperate craving to cement the bond had been pushed down deep for the past day, but now it was rearing up again with a vengeance.

"Semantics," Bullet replied with a shrug. "The gist is, the agathos' actions made you a bunch of allies, and because whoever spoke to them about the temple debacle got them so thoroughly stirred up, they forgot to even try being subtle about it. There's no hiding what happened in Milton last night, the ripple effects will continue to move outwards. Nothing comes without a cost, Amazing Grace. You know that."

I definitely did. My own gift of Eutychia—good luck—could be bestowed on humans, but it always led to my own bad luck in return. I could ease their pain, but I would suffer myself. To be an agathos was to make sacrifices.

This hadn't been my sacrifice though. This was innocent people being caught up in whatever storm was always following me around.

Riot's phone vibrated in his hand, and his eyebrows rose in surprise at whoever was calling him. "Weird, it's my dad. He wasn't thrilled with me the last time I saw him," he added under his breath before exhaling and answering the call. I'd been naive to think that the incident on the altar was the *end* of something. The culmination of the agathos' efforts to destroy my bonds and somehow create new ones with the agathos men of their choosing. That failed attempt was only the beginning.

BULLET

CHAPTER 6

Grace frowned at whatever emotions she was picking up from Riot, whispers of her own concern brushing at my skin. I'd met Riot's old man, Kill, a few times over the years. He was like most daimons of his generation—an unfeeling robot programmed to go through life destroying humans, no matter the cost. No empathy, no paternal instincts, no 'off' switch. He was always enraged, all of the time. It was kind of sad.

For a couple of minutes, Riot just held the phone next to his ear while his dad ranted, the voice coming through the speaker too muffled for me to make out.

Bored of trying to read Riot's stoic facial expressions, I turned my attention back to my Amazing Grace, who was biting her lower lip nervously as she watched Riot.

Every morning since Grace had been born, I'd woken up knowing that she wouldn't remember anything that had happened while she was asleep. That was the reality of my relationship with her, and I didn't have time for negative emotions, so I didn't reflect on it.

It was bothering me a little this morning, with Grace within touching distance, in my home, looking at me like she barely knew me. *No time*, I reminded myself, humming *Seasons of Love* under my breath. *No time for bitterness.* Time was never on my side.

"Grace is mine."

Grace sucked in a surprised breath at Riot's words and I felt my eyebrows rise. That was unexpected. Riot had gone through life moping and bitching, but he'd rarely *fought* for anything. Grace had already had a positive effect on him, and they barely knew each other.

"I don't expect you to understand," Riot clipped as his father ranted on the other end of the phone. Sometimes it was so much easier having no parents. A little lonelier, but hey ho, such was life. "I'm not having this conversation with you. Grace is mine, and I'll fight any agathos that come for her. You're either on my side or you're not, I don't care either way."

Riot hung up with impressive calm, shoving his phone back into his pocket before letting the irritation show in the scowl on his face. I knew he wasn't an entirely changed man.

"What a fucking ball ache," Riot muttered, rubbing his temples. "I assume he's only going to complicate things?" he asked, directing his question at me.

I cocked my head to the side, trying to recall if I'd seen anything in my dreams relating to Riot's dad, and coming up short. Since I'd met him plenty of times, there was no reason for him not to feature in my visions.

"Nothing's coming to mind, but I'll ask the cards," I told him with a shrug.

"He sounded quite, um, passionate?" Grace hedged, looking between us. I guess as someone who'd never received vehement support from her parents, hearing Riot's dad so outraged might have seemed like a positive to her.

It shouldn't have.

Riot cleared his throat awkwardly. "I guess you could generously interpret his words as wanting to defend my honor..."

Grace waited patiently for him to continue, and I finally took pity on my soul-bond-once-removed and jumped in.

"Old school daimons like Kill—"

"Kill?" Grace squeaked.

"Please don't ask," Riot muttered.

"—they aren't like your boys here. You know—kind, benevolent, thoughtful—"

"We are none of those things," Riot deadpanned.

"Speak for yourself," I shot back. "I am all of those things. Probably great in bed too. Anyway, I'm distracted. Old school daimons tend to think of their offspring as extensions of themselves rather than as their own people. Kill will view the agathos attack on Riot as a personal affront against him."

"And that's... bad," Grace clarified, brow furrowed.

"Daimons can be very single-minded in their quests for revenge," Riot explained. "They go into this ragey, determined place that usually leads to the worst decisions and the maximum amount of damage."

He grimaced, and I wondered if he was remembering the time Kill had burned down a liquor store because he decided they'd shortchanged him.

He should really just tell Grace that story if he wanted her to understand what we were talking about. I'd have to take the lead with these conversations more often. Obviously, I was much better with women than he was.

"Can we circle back to the 'old-school daimons' bit?" Riot asked, frowning at me. "What do you mean by that?"

"Some of us are wired differently," I said, stating the obvious. *Hello, agathos soul bond, sitting right there.* "As has become apparent in recent years."

"Some?" Riot pressed. "Why?"

"Why do gods and goddesses do anything?" I shrugged. "It isn't our place to know unless they tell us."

"That's bullshit," Riot snarled. "We aren't puppets whose strings can be pulled at will."

I blinked at him. "That's exactly what we are."

Note to self: Riot needs in-depth history lessons.

"Well... fuck that," Riot sputtered eloquently.

The pressure! I'd have to be Grace's articulate soul bond as well as her wise and all knowing one. And the handsome one. Riot really needed to assess what he was bringing to the party.

Though I'd heard a rumor that Riot had gotten high and convinced Dare to give him a Prince Albert piercing one time, so I guess he had that going for him.

"Your brain must be a fascinating place," Grace said, looking at me with an entirely appropriate amount of awe. "Your emotions are so unexpected."

"Is he smug?" Riot groused. "I bet he's smug."

I grinned at him. I was definitely smug.

"Do you have a theory on *why* the goddesses changed things up?" Grace asked. "I'm guessing that's what happened to me, though I don't know of any other agathos quite like me. Do you know a lot of daimons like you?"

"Daimons mostly leave each other alone, even when we're weird. Take Riot for example." The man in question glowered at me. "His dad was mildly annoyed that Riot was such a failure of a Moros, but he didn't, you know..."

"Smear him in animal blood and try to chant the weird away?" Grace suggested.

"Charming," Riot scoffed, sulking that I'd called him a failure of a Moros. Accurately.

"Well, yeah," I replied with a sympathetic smile. "What I mean is, who's to say you were the first agathos oddity?"

Grace twisted the opal ring on her finger thoughtfully. "I haven't heard of any, but I guess it isn't a farfetched idea. When I was at the agathos library looking through the history books, I wondered if someone like me would even be written about or if they'd rather leave their records untarnished."

Riot's phone rang again, interrupting our conversation. Wasn't he Mr. Popularity today? Maybe that was what he brought to the party. People only called me when they wanted something.

"Shit," he muttered, answering the call and holding the phone to his ear without bothering to greet whoever was on the other end and striding out of the bedroom.

I pulled the black velvet pouch that housed my cards out of my pocket, tipping them into my hand and shuffling them with practiced ease while Grace stared after him in surprise. I couldn't hear Riot's voice, he'd probably let himself onto the deck for some privacy. My spidey senses were a-tingling.

Or maybe my *snakey* senses.

"Would it be terribly rude of me to abandon you for a moment?" I asked Grace. "The cards are calling to me."

"Oh no, of course not," Grace said hurriedly, looking curiously at the deck of cards in my hand. "Don't let me get in the way if there are things you would usually be doing."

"You could never be in the way," I assured her. Grace was The Way. Grace was everything. "Help yourself to anything in the kitchen," I added, leaving the bedroom and spotting Riot pacing on the porch before I headed back downstairs to the parlor.

I'd already stocked up on Grace's favorite brand of coffee and a few breakfast foods I'd spotted on my last inspection of her kitchen, so I was confident she'd find something she liked and be creeped out by me all over again at the same time.

The bedroom I'd set up for myself in the backroom at the bottom of the stairs was a neat and tidy reminder that I didn't belong in the cozy relationship Grace and Riot had already established, but I refused to dwell on that as I let myself into the parlor and dropped heavily onto a pile of cushions.

I took a moment to light the candles and center myself, breathing in the faint smoke from the candles and exhaling the negativity that was threatening to creep in on my sunshine-filled brain. Well, maybe not sunshine-filled, but definitely fluorescent light-filled, which was something.

Pulling my deck of cards, I shuffled them until The Devil appeared on top before closing my eyes and opening myself to the unfurling threads of the Fates' magic.

"Will Riot's arrangement to keep Grace safe cause him harm?" I asked the Fates, already suspecting I knew the answer.

The Goddess had been very clear in my vision that Riot needed to seek outside help to cover Grace's tracks—which made sense, neither of us had any expertise in that area—but I got the feeling the cost of that request was going to be steep.

The ancient magics pushed through my skin, winding their way through my veins until my hands began shuffling the deck in my hand unconsciously.

The Devil appeared in my head, Riot in all his winged glory. The bat wings extended behind him and he bent his knees as though he was going to leap into the air, but as soon as he jumped, a noose wound around his neck, yanking him back to the ground. The end of the leash materialized slowly, and a representation of Temperance appeared holding it, which was both expected and entirely unexpected.

That Viper needed to learn balance and moderation really shouldn't have surprised me.

The vision disappeared and magic hummed steadily in my veins, waiting considerately.

"How does Riot get out of it?" I asked, hoping the Fates would grant me a little more guidance today. I knew better than to ask *'when'*, they never answered those questions. Not spitefully, I didn't think. I imagined immortals just perceived time differently than we did.

There were no figures, only the appearance of three golden cups in the air, moving as if they were being clinked together by invisible hands. Three of Cups. Friendship. A sense of community and joyfulness.

It could mean the three of us—me, Grace and Riot—but I doubted it. They would have shown me our figures if that was the case, rather than the cups. No, my guess was that we needed Grace's third soul bond, and Riot's friendship with him would get him out of his deal with Viper.

"Thank you, sisters," I murmured, allowing the magic to dissipate and beginning my card cleansing ritual, sitting in silence for a moment as the sage burned to clear the energy in the room.

I supposed Viper *could* be Grace's third soul bond, but I didn't feel like he was. Daimons didn't really have friends, but I'd felt a kinship with Riot from the moment I'd met him, a sense of camaraderie. I'd gone to school with Viper, and after one too many bad encounters with him, I'd given him a nightmare so bad he'd pissed himself. There was definitely no camaraderie there.

No, I had my own theories about who Grace's third and fourth were, but Riot's relationship with them complicated those theories. Riot would be down on his knees thanking every god and goddess he could think of for making me his soul bond-in-law once he realized who the next in line was, if my hunch was right.

That was the kind of adoration I deserved, honestly. Oneiroi were once revered, but now there were so few of us left, I'd basically been forgotten about. I'd have to remind Riot later about the praise I was due.

By the time I rejoined my brand new family upstairs, Grace was setting bowls of oats and fruit out on the table for each of us and the apartment smelled of the fresh coffee I'd purchased specifically for them. Already it was *heavenly* having her here, even if I felt the faintest traces of bashfulness from my shy soulmate. That was okay, it'd take time to adjust to her new surroundings. Besides, we wouldn't be living in this tiny little apartment forever.

Or *they* wouldn't. My future was less certain.

"I need to borrow a car tonight," Riot announced, sitting at the table looking livid.

"You can take the Harley if you're willing to forfeit your life in return for any damages. When do you leave?" I asked casually, heading straight for the kitchen to make some chamomile tea.

Riot snorted. "Like you don't already know."

83

Grace gave him an exasperated look, but I didn't mind Riot's snarking. It was just a defense mechanism because he was a grumpy ol' daimon who'd never learned how to cope with uncomfortable emotions without getting as high as the moon.

"Believe it or not, I have more interesting things to do than ask the divine questions about the minutiae of your schedule," I deadpanned, earning a conceding nod from Riot.

"You're *leaving*?" Grace asked, looking at Riot with alarm. I focused hard to pick up her emotions, wanting to hurry this whole bonding process along, and found mostly fear.

Did she not want to be left alone with me?

It seemed crazy that Grace might be afraid of me when we'd spent every night of her entire life together, but I guess that was the downside of her not. Fucking. Remembering. Any. Of. It.

"I need to head out for a bit tonight when the daimons are all up and ready to work," Riot said, looking apologetic though I could hear the frustration in his voice. "There's a lot of property damage from the agathos, and I owe someone a debt so I have to help clean up."

Hm, that seemed rather innocuous. Perhaps the Fates had been overexaggerating. Or Viper was lulling us into a false sense of security, which was probably the more likely option. After all, Viper was descended from the Apate line, specializing in fraud and deceit. Even among his fellow daimons, Viper was wildly unpopular.

Not *just* because he was an Apate. Mostly because he was a raging asshole.

"That makes sense," Grace said guiltily. "If I thought it would help, I'd come with you, but it would probably do more harm than good."

"I'm confident that you're safe around daimons," I assured her, leaning on my elbows on the counter to watch them at the table. "You're basically one of us now, but you should avoid Milton for the time being."

I possibly had to work on my reassurance game, because Grace didn't look as comforted by that as I intended her to be. Damn it, it was so much easier talking to her in her dreams than in real life.

"Did you *see* something?" Grace asked, absently adding her favorite hazelnut creamer to her coffee. "In your cards?"

"Would you tell us if you did?" Riot added.

"Sometimes." I shrugged. "In my dream visions from the Goddess of Night, I often see the 'what' but not the 'how' or 'why'. Those are questions I can ask the Fates using my cards, but sometimes telling you the answers would render them moot, so I don't. Sometimes they don't answer at all, not if they don't want to. I don't have any control here."

Since we were but mere playthings of the gods, for the most part. Here and gone within a blink of their immortal eyes.

"Wow," Grace breathed, staring at me with wonder. "That's..."

"Amazing?" I supplied. "Awe-inspiring? Incredible?"

"*Terrifying*," Grace finished, shaking her head. "The Goddess of Night extinguished some candles when I spoke to her and I have been fretting over the implications ever since, I can't imagine what it must be like to receive visions from her. And the Fates... we learned about them, but they were always presented as goddesses just for humans."

"The Fates are goddesses for everyone—mortal and immortal. But don't worry, Amazing Grace. You're going to get a whole new religious education from me," I replied with a grin, finishing making my tea and joining them at the table.

That was my job after all, for as long as I had left. I guess if I had to spend my final days as an educator, being Grace's personal teacher was better than dealing with actual kids and their terrible parents for insulting pay.

Could be worse, I reminded myself cheerfully. I'd die young, but with maximum job satisfaction.

"If you could start those lessons today, that'd be great," Riot grunted, shoving his hand back through his black hair. "It'd be nice to start getting some answers rather than more questions."

There were dark shadows under his eyes, and I wondered how much sleep he'd gotten last night. Aside from the panic of Grace disappearing right under his nose, Riot wasn't accustomed to coping with this level of emotion in general. Daimons were masters of apathy.

"I'm sure we'll get a bit of both," I shrugged. "Some answers, a lot more questions. These things are rarely straightforward."

"So, you can make requests of the Goddess of Night or the Fates for knowledge, and they'll choose whether or not to give it to you?" Grace pressed.

"Correct," I replied, pleased that she was so interested in how my abilities worked. "If they want us to seek the answers ourselves, usually because that sets off a different set of dominos, then they'll play coy. I've been more *favored* than other Oneiroi, from what I understand. Hopefully that means they'll be forthcoming with me when it comes to questions about you. Us. This."

A flicker of relief passed over Grace's face at that, and I hoped on all the stars in the sky that I could deliver.

"Can you tell me anything about this *debt*?" Riot asked, looking miserable.

I did feel one percent bad for him—the Goddess had shown me that the deal with Viper was necessary, though she was working in mysterious ways because I couldn't for the life of me see why, unless Viper really was Grace's soul bond and my assumptions were way off. And while his assistance in keeping the agathos off her trail was helpful, surely I could have managed that alone with my visions? Things weren't adding up.

Viper was important somehow, but I couldn't see how.

"What's the debt?" Grace asked, staring at Riot.

Wow, it was frustrating that she couldn't remember our trip to her apartment last night.

"That daimon in Milton I mentioned who's helping out with the paperwork," Riot explained vaguely. "Dare was supposed to pick it all up actually, but at least now I can grab it myself when I help with the cleanup."

"Okay..." Grace said slowly. "You're going to help him clean up as payment?"

"Yes," Riot grunted, massively underselling the commitment he'd made. Viper's life was devoted to shady deals, mostly done with the kind of humans who struggled to uphold their ends of the bargain. He'd have plenty of use for an on-call bringer of doom.

Grace knew Riot was downplaying it too, the resigned acceptance was written all over her face. She was accepting we'd have to keep her mostly in the dark about the details so she didn't feel compelled to confess them, probably to her parents. The agathos sense of obligation was strong.

It was an extraordinary level of trust to place in relative strangers, but Grace had been raised with the concept of soul bonds. She'd expected to immediately merge lives with strangers one day, and that would be that.

"In the meantime, we're going to do some experiments," I told Grace cheerfully, trying to brighten the mood.

"What kind of experiments?" she asked.

"We're going to see if the Goddess of Night is willing to do more for you than blow out some candles."

I ushered Riot and Grace out of the kitchen after breakfast so I could clean up, insisting they have some downtime before Riot needed to head out. Considering Riot was going to be at Viper's beck and call for the interim, he'd probably need to switch back to nocturnal daimon hours. Especially since Viper's gym was out of commission, and that was his only semi-legitimate, daylight-appropriate business.

In my visions, I'd seen Viper and Riot strike a deal for hiding Grace's trail until she no longer needed it or for a year, whichever came first, and Riot would serve as Viper's errand boy for the duration. I knew a lot of what Viper wanted Riot to do would be things Riot wasn't comfortable doing—he hated being a Moros at the best of times and he definitely wouldn't want to be an on-call Moros for Viper—but that was something Riot would have to figure out. How to be a Moros without being a Moros. How to make decisions he could live with. Things he wouldn't have cared about before Grace.

Like a creep, I watched the two of them through the double doors that led out to the deck, looking out into the forest while I stood at the sink. Grace's arms were wrapped around Riot's waist while his were around her shoulders, his chin resting on her head.

Maybe I was feeling the teensiest bit jealous that she was out there giving him a cuddle. I wanted them to be happy and whatever, but I also wanted cuddles, and I wasn't quite sure how to get them.

Even in the dreamscape, there wasn't any physical touching. Not since puberty anyway. As a kid, Grace had always jumped all over me and demanded I carry her around on my back while she laughed hysterically because I got the feeling her family hadn't been much fun, and she'd made the most of having a willing playmate. As she got older and more stranger danger-y, we usually chatted about our days or I'd show her visions of the future, but there was never any physical affection involved.

Maybe I had to make the first move? What had Riot done? It had obviously worked.

No, fuck that. You know Grace better. You don't need tips from Riot.

My internal voice was right. I didn't need any tips. Maybe.

Grace came back inside, pasting a bright smile on her face that didn't quite meet her eyes. She'd picked out an outfit that was half-agathos, half-daimon—the black and bronze skirt fell below her knees, and the black top she'd tucked into it had a high neckline and drapey sleeves that fell below her elbows. It was agathos-style modesty combined with the dark colors she would have never been allowed to wear in her old life.

Riot followed behind her, yawning even though it was only mid-morning. "I'm going to nap for a bit since I'll probably be up late, is that cool?" he asked, narrowing his eyes at me like he knew this was the opportunity for quality time with Grace I'd been waiting for.

"Totally cool," I assured him, giving him my most charming smile and getting a borderline glare in return. Rude. I was going to return all the nice clothes I'd bought for him. "Ready to call on the *Goddess of Night*?" I asked Grace in my best spooky voice.

"Not even a little," Grace admitted with an uneasy laugh, tucking her long hair behind her ear. "I think... I think I should though. I never thanked her for helping me."

89

I nodded, making my way around the counter and gesturing for her to follow me down the stairs. "It's always a good idea to thank goddesses. They can be fickle if not shown appropriate gratitude."

Grace said a quick goodbye to a still sulking Riot before heading down the narrow staircase behind me. We had to go through the storage room that I'd converted into a makeshift bedroom for me while Grace and Riot had taken the upstairs bedroom. It wasn't much—a foldout couch and a makeshift clothes rail along one wall, but I didn't mind. Maybe Grace would invite me to share her bed one day. In her own time.

"Is this where you're sleeping?" Grace asked, sounding mildly horrified.

"Yup," I replied, ushering her into the almost pitch black parlor, hoping it would distract her from the storage den of bad sleep and borderline painful jerk off sessions.

"Oh wow," Grace breathed, stopping next to me, our arms brushing together. She didn't seem to notice the physical contact and I held myself as still as a statue, soaking it in as much as I could. From the sneaky investigative work-slash-spying I'd done over the years on the agathos, I knew physical contact was an important part of deepening the soul bond. Not that they generally waited long before having sex, which fulfilled the bond completely, but Grace clearly wasn't ready for that.

"Welcome to the sad barn parlor. It was set up to do card readings for clients," I explained, gesturing at the low round wooden table surrounded by black and purple cushions. The walls were lined with bookshelves that were filled with ancient texts, hidden in plain sight behind generic Halloween decorations. There was a selection of plain white soy candles on the table, a concrete bowl to burn sage, and a few crystals scattered around the space, mostly for the aesthetics.

"Most of my clients are intensely superstitious humans who travel out to the middle of nowhere to have their fortunes told, hence the over-the-top decor. It isn't ideal, but it works for now."

"Why isn't it ideal?" Grace asked, her arm breaking away from mine as she walked around the edges of the room, squinting in the darkness at the combination of books and knick knacks on the shelves.

"We prefer to read cards under the moonlight. Like the original daimons we're descended from, the Fates are children of La Nuit. Being under the night sky strengthens the connection," I explained as I flicked on the dim lamps in the corners.

"The Oneiroi who lived here converted this barn into an area for human clients to visit years ago, but I'll be honest, we mostly half-ass the readings. I can't be bothering the Fates with questions about whether someone is going to get a promotion, you know? I'm not a vision vending machine," I groused.

"Of course not," Grace agreed, sounding a little amused.

"Anyway, after I moved down here, I brought all the books and sacred items with me and disguised them amongst the plastic skulls and battery operated jack-o-lanterns on the shelves. The barn isn't so bad, but the storage space is definitely lacking."

"All of this is incredible. The more you talk, the more I realize I don't know," Grace murmured, elegantly perching on one of the floor cushions and folding her legs beneath her. She was so ladylike, I could watch the way she moved all day. "The card reading, and the moonlight, and the visions... It's all so amazing."

I sat down next to her, twisting to the side to face her and propping my elbow on the coffee table and grabbing the matches to light the candles closest to us. The light flickered on Grace's face, highlighting how pale her agathos eyes were.

"I'll give you an abridged history lesson to start, yeah? Let's keep it simple for now because it gets hella confusing. Basically, the Goddess of Night—also known as La Nuit, which she prefers because it's fancy, or Nyx if you want to be casual about it—was one of the two primordial goddesses who emerged from Chaos. Her children—some produced with her consort and some alone—are the daimons, pretty much all the dark and scary gods that aren't Olympians, and a few not dark and scary ones, like the Fates."

The Fates were also a little dark and scary to be honest, but theoretically neutral.

Grace nodded encouragingly, urging me to continue. There was so much absolute trust in her eyes in my words that I wouldn't have been able to stop myself from talking even if I wanted to. Maybe she didn't want me for cuddles and reassurance the way she wanted Riot, but I could give her knowledge. Even if she hadn't been my soul bond, I'd have told her everything I knew. My time was coming, and there were no new Oneiroi to pass on my knowledge to the way it had once been passed on to me.

"Basically everything else in existence is courtesy of your goddess," I said with a shrug.

"Anesidora," Grace said, though there was a hesitancy in her tone.

"Yes, but only the agathos call her that," I teased. "The meaning, 'sender of gifts' is apt, but the gods call her Gaia."

"It seems sacreligious to say that," she admitted, looking contemplative. "You know, I think that fits more. It sounds less..."

"Grandiose?" I suggested. "Gaia isn't a grandiose goddess, not really. She can be tempestuous, but she's life and earth and fertility. Gaia is the mother of the Titans, and the grandmother of the Olympians. Basically, every god not descended from La Nuit is of Gaia."

"And mortals?" Grace asked.

"Any that aren't daimons are courtesy of Gaia," I confirmed. "Though the lines are blurry now. The original immortal daimons, gods in their own right, were released on humanity and reproduced with humans as many gods did. The humans themselves come from Gaia's earth, they are chthonic births, formed in the dirt. Our daimonic side is like a parasite, I guess. It takes over the human part of us. It's more complicated than that, but that's the gist."

"Why don't we learn any of this?" Grace asked, more to herself than me, though I answered anyway.

"Most daimons don't either," I replied with a shrug. "The Oneiroi are the closest things daimons have to priests and priestesses. We learn this stuff, but other daimons don't bother. I guarantee you, Riot doesn't know what 'primordial' or 'chthonic' mean."

Grace's mouth tipped up as she tried to suppress a smile. "I can't judge, apparently I don't either."

"Fear not, Amazing Grace. I'm a great teacher." I winked at her. I mean, I'd never taught anyone before, but I'd probably be great at it. "There's nothing random about your soul bonds. We each serve a purpose in your journey, and mine is to teach."

"That sounds very predestined."

Damn it, I kept making her frown. I changed my mind. This job was the fucking worst.

"We all have a predestined journey to a degree," I said, though Grace's was way more complicated than most. Regular people didn't have the primordial Goddess of Night taking a personal interest in their journey. "Some people have more divine involvement than others."

"Right, I guess that makes sense," Grace agreed, nodding. "Do you think the Goddess of Night has any guidance for my journey?"

"Oh yes," I replied with a grim smile. "From the day of your birth, you've been on La Nuit's radar, Amazing Grace. You may only be becoming aware of your connection with her, but she's always been aware of her connection with you."

Grace grimaced, and I wished I had something more comforting to tell her. Or at least something she'd prefer to hear. I wasn't in the business of denying life's everyday unpleasantries though.

"Does she send you prophecies?" Grace asked. "Like the old oracles?"

I nodded approvingly at her line of questioning—she had more base knowledge than most daimons at least.

"Not quite. Or not *usually*, but I wouldn't be surprised if I got one soon. Or rather you did, if they wanted to communicate with you directly," I sighed, standing up and grabbing an enormous genealogy book off the shelf. I set it down in front of Grace, opening it to the family tree of the gods on the front page. "Oracles were mostly given their abilities by these gods," I said, circling the row of Olympians. "Mostly this one," I added, tapping on Apollo's name.

"But raw power comes from these gods," I continued, circling the top row of Primordials. "The kind of power that comes almost without limits. They are the originals, born of chaos or maybe even nothingness. Whatever was passed down through the Titans and then the Olympians is a watered down version of this true power. The Pythia was such a powerful oracle because Gaia herself spoke to her through the vapors that rose from the crack in the earth she sat next to."

Grace was listening to me with rapt attention, eyes wide as she absorbed every word. Ooh, this could be addictive. No one ever wanted to listen to me ramble about the gods.

"Anyway, my power comes from *here*," I said, running my finger under La Nuit's name. "The Fates and I are all children of the Goddess of Night, though obviously my bloodline is heavily diluted. My mind is capable of accepting visions directly, they don't need to come in through a filtered form as a vague prophecy to stop my head from exploding."

It would explode eventually anyway—no mortal was meant to have this kind of power for long—but I'd save that conversation for another day.

No time for bitterness, I reminded myself more aggressively than usual as I began humming *La Vie Boheme* rapidly under my breath, selecting a few more candles to light and arranging them around the table, putting a cleansing bowl of sage in the center.

Grace sat silently, watching me work as I hummed, lighting each of the candles and the sage. When I was done, I gestured to the arrangement on the table with a small smile, having successfully staved off my bad mood with the musical stylings of *Rent*.

"Ready to pray?"

"Ready to pray?"

GRACE

CHAPTER 7

"Okay. Let's pray," I murmured, staring at the flickering flames in front of me and wondering what to say. Where could I possibly begin? The Goddess of Night, La Nuit—*Nyx*, though I would never call her that—had come to my aid twice now, and I had yet to properly thank her for it.

I thought it had just been a random act of... well, not kindness, but compassion perhaps. A dark goddess taking pity on a lost servant of light, but Bullet had made it seem like it was so much more than that. Like I was already on a path towards a destination I had no idea I was traveling to.

"I don't know what to say," I admitted, twisting the opal ring on my finger. "I don't want to say the wrong thing and make her angry."

"Don't insult her," Bullet replied with a shrug. "Ask for guidance, thank her, say what's on your mind. As far as divinities go, La Nuit is one of the cooler ones, and you're one of her favorite mortals."

It was a little unsettling, the way he talked about the *Goddess of Night* as though he was on a first-name basis with her, but I tried to keep my expression neutral. Maybe the agathos were particularly out of touch with their spiritual sides? Then again, Riot was the least devoted follower of anything I'd ever met, so perhaps it was just a Bullet thing.

I closed my eyes, inhaling the strange scent of burning sage and remembering the gratitude I felt for the goddess as the sconces blew out and the agathos who'd trapped me panicked.

"Goddess of Night, thank you for helping me yesterday, for answering my call. For everything you have done for me so far, I am grateful, and I welcome whatever guidance you have for my future."

I hesitated, not knowing what else to say. Did I need to praise her more? Did she need some kind of sacrifice? As much as I recognized the agathos were wrong about so many things, I still had to unlearn their teachings. I'd been told terrible things about the Goddess of Night throughout the course of my life, and praying to her felt a little like I was sticking my hand into some flames and hoping they didn't burn me.

With a *whoosh*, the candles and dim lamplight disappeared and I opened my eyes with a gasp, realizing we were in complete darkness. The windows down here in the parlor were boarded shut, and there was no light source anywhere.

There was a chilling *presence* in the darkness. One that felt familiar, and I realized I'd felt something similar in the dungeon yesterday afternoon. A kind of ancient energy that I couldn't explain. Strangely, I didn't think this was the Goddess, or not how I imagined her anyway. There was no comfort or warmth to this presence, though it wasn't unpleasant either. It felt neutral, strong, and timeless.

Bullet began humming smoothly, another show tune, I imagined. It seemed absurdly out of context, but it gave me some comfort at the same time. If he wasn't worried, then surely I didn't need to be worried, right? He was more familiar with this kind of thing than I was. Nothing to worry about.

Until the scratching sound started, then I got a little worried.

Terrified, actually.

Bullet's soft humming became idle singing, not quite enough to drown out the sound of the monstrous scratching, carving noise, but I recognized the tune as a slowed down version of *The Bare Necessities* from The Jungle Book. He had a lovely soothing voice, and the combination of that and the intensity of the moment made my emotions rise, my throat growing tight and tears running unchecked down my cheeks.

I didn't even think about it, I just reached for Bullet in the darkness, my fingers brushing awkwardly against his surprisingly hard stomach before he linked ours together, giving them a gentle squeeze. It could have been seconds, minutes, even hours as we sat there in the dark, Bullet singing and the unseen *force* in the room chilling the space as it scratched away at something.

Bullet's fingers moved tentatively up my wrist, rubbing circles into my skin that were soothing, but also set off butterflies low in my stomach. His touch was impossibly gentle, even when he pressed his fingers into my wrist, undoubtedly noticing the way my pulse was thundering. The way he touched me made me ache in an unexpected kind of way. It made my *heart* hurt. Bullet touched me like I wasn't quite real.

I closed my eyes and let myself get lost in the moment with my soul bond by my side, in the presence of something ancient and primal. I doubted this was an experience many people had in their lives. Between the presence in the room, the scratching sound audible beneath Bullet's soft singing, and his agonizingly soft ministrations over my skin, the whole thing was the most moving, beautiful, terrifying experience of my life, and I knew I'd remember it for the rest of my days.

As quickly as it had come, the aura was gone. Bullet finished the song, patting the back of my hand before gently disentangling our fingers. Amazingly, he found the matches and lit the candles with no difficulty in the pitch black while I quickly wiped at my tears with the back of my sleeve before tucking my hands underneath me to hide the shaking.

My eyes adjusted slowly to the light, and it took me a moment to realize where the carving sounds had come from. The low wooden coffee table that once had a smooth surface was now engraved with letters that I definitely didn't recognize. The lines were so exquisite, it looked like they'd been stamped into the table rather than carved by hand.

Bullet snorted, remarkably unbothered by what had just taken place. "Couldn't have made it easy, could they?"

He stood, still humming to himself as he made his way over to the bookshelf, returning with an enormous Ancient Greek dictionary, a notepad and pen, while I continued to sit on my hands, possibly going into shock.

Why was he so relaxed? Was I overreacting, or was he underreacting?

"Was that," I began, dropping my voice to just above a whisper. "*The Goddess of Night?*"

"What? No," Bullet chuckled. "I mean, I can see why you might think that, but she only comes out to play at night and even then, she has a more maternal feel."

"Then who was that?"

"*That* was her consort. Erebus, God of Darkness. You have some big guns in your corner, Amazing Grace," Bullet added with a mischievous grin before meticulously copying out the message on the coffee table in his notepad, humming a different tune I didn't recognize as he opened the enormous dictionary.

Erebus. The God of Darkness.

I sat on the cushion like a statue, half worried that if I moved, I'd shatter the strange illusion I'd created. The illusion where dark gods and goddesses not only heard my prayers, but answered my calls. Visited me. *Left me a hand carved message on a table.*

When I imagined my life at 25, this is not at all what I had envisioned. I'd mostly assumed I was going to die alone, surrounded by houseplants and the potted roses on my deck, a disappointment to my parents in every possible way.

The last one turned out to be truer than I thought possible, but at least I wasn't all alone in the world.

"You can go watch TV or something if you want," Bullet offered, flicking through the dictionary. Occasionally he'd write something, before crossing it out and writing something else above it, still humming cheerily. "My Ancient Greek is rusty, and I don't want to render the wrong meaning by rushing this."

I was too nervous to read the words he was writing.

"Could I stay? If that's alright," I replied hesitantly, unsure if he was trying to tell me that he'd prefer to be alone while he worked.

"That's more than alright."

Bullet paused what he was doing for a moment, giving me a soft smile so filled with hidden meaning that it stole the air from my lungs. There was so much between us on his end, *years* of memories and conversations and emotions. It must frustrate him that it was so one-sided, but he hadn't mentioned it.

"Take a look at the books on the shelf if you want. There's a bunch of stuff that'll be helpful for you."

That was probably a better idea than sitting here, questioning my sanity.

I pushed myself up and moved around the room on shaky legs, turning the lamps back on again before making my way to the bookshelves. The shelves were deep, and the fronts were lined with an unusual assortment of decorations. I paused in front of a black plastic Jack-o-Lantern with bat wings protruding from either side that I was convinced had nothing to do with the Goddess of Night, gently pushing it aside.

Behind the odd decor were some of the oldest books I'd ever seen. The agathos had libraries in all the bigger communities, but they were hidden and accessed only by using agathos blood. The idea that these books with their faded leather spines were sitting here in Bullet's barn that doubled as a psychic reading parlor for humans, loosely hidden by Walmart Halloween decorations was hard to comprehend.

The writing on the spines—when it was in English—was often faded, and many of the books looked like they'd seen their fair share of fire or water damage over the years. Too nervous that I'd accidentally destroy a priceless book with my clumsy fingers, I settled on one of the newer-looking ones at the end of the shelf, with a slightly thicker layer of dust on it than the others. It had a black leather cover with a gold embossed image of a tarot card on the front.

The image was in the same style as the tattoos on Bullet's arm—a skull, surrounded by lines radiating from it like it was glowing, with different moon phases on the edges. This one had a tall hat like one a human priest would wear, and I traced the embossed leather with the tip of my finger, contemplating the image.

Bullet was still busy at the table, so I balanced the book in the crook of my arm and began looking through the pages, seeing detailed descriptions for each tarot card. The image on the front was The Hierophant. Spiritual wisdom, belief, initiating the next generation... It all reminded me strongly of Bullet.

I barely registered myself moving across the room and sinking down into the cushions again, totally absorbed in the pages. My mother would have me back on that altar in a heartbeat for *looking* at this book. I paused on a picture of a skull wearing a jester's hat that I'd seen once already, tattooed on Bullet's right arm, above his wrist. There were multiple cards inked there, all fanned out but in a group. His long sleeves were pulled down today, and I wanted to ask him to roll them up so I could see the design again, but I didn't want to interrupt him while he looked so focused.

This one was The Fool. *Innocence, beginnings, spontaneity.* The Fool is embarking on an adventure, there are challenges in the future, but The Fool has faith, still inexperienced and full of innocence. Sugar, it was me to a tee. Not that I liked to think of myself as a *fool*, but I had definitely embarked on some kind of adventure, though what kind was yet to be determined.

I was reading the description for The Chariot when Bullet shouted "Eureka!" giving me a delighted grin.

"I'm too scared to look," I murmured, glancing at the piece of paper he'd been working on out of the corner of my eye like it might burn me if I got too close.

"Don't be scared, Amazing Grace," Bullet said softly, gesturing me closer. "You've got a bright future ahead of you, I promise. I've seen it."

With that reassurance in mind, I shuffled over on my cushion so I was next to him, our shoulders brushing together, and pulled the piece of paper towards me, reading the words written in Bullet's impeccable, sloping handwriting.

Liberate the treasure held in the deep,

Where no sweet smelling smoke or prayer can reach,

Bring forth the Second Age of Heroes.

"What does that mean?" I breathed, staring at the words on the page. The English translation wasn't much more informative than the Ancient Greek.

Treasure? Sweet smelling smoke?

Heroes?

I glanced up at Bullet for a moment, just in time to see his frown before he smoothed the expression away. "The Second Age of Heroes is obvious enough in meaning, I guess. Heroes were mortals blessed by the gods—or sometimes sired by them—and tasked with great things."

I gave Bullet a wide-eyed blink. Did they want me to be a hero? I was the least equipped person in the history of humanity to be a hero. It had taken me 25 years of verbal abuse to stand up to my own mother.

"But that was when gods walked the earth," Bullet continued, frowning. "I don't know. Prophecies are vague and infuriating. It could refer to the immediate future, or it could refer to years down the track. But we'll work it out, Amazing Grace."

103

I nodded, having faith that if anyone could it was Bullet, but not feeling much better about it regardless. I sort of wanted to stick my head in the sand and pretend none of this was happening. Why couldn't I get the soul bonds without the scary destiny like other agathos?

Why *me*?

Of all the agathos I knew, I was one of the least confident, least articulate, and I definitely had the least helpful gift. I'd made my peace with all those things, but there was no universe where I was the most suitable person for any kind of prophecy.

"I'll do some card readings now," Bullet volunteered, probably sensing my rising panic. "Maybe the Fates will be willing to shed some light on this treasure in the deep."

"Okay," I agreed, selfishly glad he was volunteering for the task. "Maybe I'll go see if Riot is awake?"

I was craving Riot's comforting, unyielding presence as the world felt like it was disintegrating around me, but I got the feeling I'd said the wrong thing as soon as the words came out of my mouth.

The flash of disappointment on Bullet's face was gone as soon as it came. He was as much my soul bond as Riot, yet he'd gotten the short end of the stick when it came to my attention so far.

But I hadn't been given a prophecy by the Primordial gods immediately after meeting Riot, which had made it easier for us to get to know one another.

I hesitated, second guessing myself, but Bullet shot me a beaming smile that made all my troubles feel far away. For a daimon, he had an incredibly angelic face with his bright smile and sparkling eyes, and the candlelight made his pale blonde hair glow like a golden halo.

"You should go spend some time with him," Bullet said cheerfully. "The job he has to do tonight may take longer than expected," he added cryptically.

My heart sunk at that. The idea of spending a few hours away from Riot was awful, especially after everything that had happened yesterday.

"Thank you for warning me," I said softly, reaching out and giving Bullet's arm a grateful squeeze before making my way out of the dark parlor, through the soulless bedroom, and up the stairs, feeling like I'd left half my heart behind me.

While Bullet was charming and magnetic, there was also something almost daunting about him that I couldn't quite put my finger on. He was a similar height to Riot, but leaner, so it wasn't his overwhelming size. It wasn't how he presented himself either, with his trendy, almost playful outfits and loosely pushed back blonde hair. Maybe it was the bullet hanging around his neck? That was a bold fashion choice.

Or maybe it was his *aura*. There was something *otherworldly* about him, something supernatural. Bullet's energy felt like the way the room had felt the night I'd first prayed to the Goddess of Night. It was awe-inspiring, and a little overwhelming.

I kept my footsteps quiet as I crossed the upstairs floor in case Riot was still sleeping, opening the door to the bedroom silently and slipping inside.

If Bullet looked oddly angelic, Riot looked purely demonic, even in sleep. His messy dark hair fell over his forehead and long dark lashes rested on high tanned cheekbones. Sleep didn't make Riot look young and vulnerable—he always looked about a second away from opening those dark red and purple eyes, his mouth curling into a tempting smirk, inviting me to join him.

105

I didn't need the invitation today. My brain was too wired to sleep, but nothing could have been more appealing in that moment than curling up and stealing a bit of comfort from the man who'd been such an incredible support to me from the moment I met him.

As quietly as I could, I lifted up the blankets and slid in next to him, smiling to myself as he rolled towards me even in sleep and draped an arm over my waist. I buried my face against his chest, soaking in his warmth and comfort. I hoped Bullet was wrong about the job Riot was going to do taking longer than expected, but I got the feeling that wasn't how his abilities worked. If Bullet thought Riot was going to be delayed, he probably would.

I closed my eyes and vaguely attempted meditation for the first time in my life, trying to clear my overcrowded mind. I must have slept eventually, drifting in and out of wakefulness, Riot breathing evenly next to me. Eventually the quiet sound of Bullet moving around the kitchen filtered into the bubble of almost silence I'd been cocooned in.

It took a few more minutes for Riot to wake up and I suppressed a giggle at the rumbling groan he made as he stretched, rolling onto his back. I'd never spent much time around men growing up—I had four fathers, but quality time with them had been rare. It wasn't until I found myself living with Riot that I realized how *grunty* they were.

"Shit, did I sleep all day?" Riot muttered, squinting at the low light filtering through the circular window.

"I don't know what time it is, but I think so," I replied, wriggling up to sit leaning against the headboard. "I don't have a watch, and my phone is gone."

Riot grimaced. "You can always use mine or Bullet's."

"I don't have anyone to contact anyway," I pointed out, giving him a wry smile. "But make sure you use Bullet's to message me when you're in Milton. I hate the idea of us being apart right now."

"Same," Riot replied, sitting up next to me and tipping his head back against the headboard to stare at the ceiling. "I'm not looking forward to this at all. How was your day?" he asked.

My heart dropped into my stomach at the innocuous question, forcing me to confront the thought I'd been trying to avoid all day.

"Dinner's ready!" Bullet called from the other room and I took the out, jumping out of bed while Riot kicked the blankets off with a groan. I had to tell him what had happened downstairs, but it made more sense to discuss it with Bullet there too. Plus I was a bit scared, and wanted him to do the talking.

Riot tugged on a fitted maroon t-shirt that I was confident he would have never chosen for himself as he followed me out of the bedroom, removing the welcome distraction that had been his bare chest. I made a beeline for the kitchen to give Bullet a hand since I'd not only been a complete imposition on him since I arrived, I'd barely spent any time with my second soul bond.

It wasn't good enough, not by a long shot.

"Can I help with anything?"

Bullet shot me another one of his disarming smiles as he piled a platter high with every kind of vegetarian sandwich I could imagine, and a second with a generous helping of cut fruit. "Grab the juice from the fridge, everything else is done. I hope sandwiches are okay for dinner, I got a bit distracted with the cards and ran out of time."

"Sandwiches sound great," I said, shooting him a reassuring smile. It had been so long since breakfast, I would eat just about anything.

I squeezed around him into the tiny kitchen and headed straight for the fridge, noticing when I opened it how *healthy* the contents were. I'd always been a pretty health-conscious eater—mostly because my mother had given me a complex about calories—but my fridge definitely didn't have this amount of fresh fruit and vegetables in it.

Along the low wall, above a tiny counter, were rows of shelves stacked with dishes that also served as a pantry—surprisingly healthy as well. There were jars along the shelves filled with grains and lentils of every kind, all neatly labelled in a way that appealed to my aesthetically conscious self.

Riot groaned from next to the counter as I examined the shelf, bottle of juice in hand. "I forgot you hate good food," he said to Bullet.

"My mind and body are temples," Bullet replied cheerfully. "But fear not, I bought emergency processed snacks for your un-temple-like body to enjoy."

"You like to eat healthy?" I asked, grabbing a stack of glasses and bringing them to the table while Riot grabbed the platter of sandwiches.

"My mind is a weapon," Bullet replied with a grin as he brought over the fruit. "I have to keep it sharp with a nutritious diet, regular hydration, sleep, and meditation."

"I'm not complaining because this looks amazing," I told him, sitting down at the table while Riot loaded up my plate for me. "Every time I think I understand daimons, I learn something new and amazing."

"To give Bullet a small amount of credit, he's an *Oneiroi*. He's not like the rest of us. I'm just a Moros—it's like the mayonnaise of daimons," Riot scoffed.

I laughed a little in disbelief. "I think all daimons are some version of extra spicy chillies. The mayonnaise sandwich of abilities is the *Arete*. They're the agathos dispensers of knowledge."

I couldn't quite keep the bitterness out of my voice. The Arete were so holier than thou, going around dropping nuggets of wisdom on humans. They lost a little of their own knowledge in return, but they didn't *know* what they'd lost so it didn't necessarily bother them, and when they were bonded, that loss of knowledge was spread out over five people.

It was by far the easiest gift to manage and the most common type of agathos. I'd never allowed myself to resent Anesidora—*Gaia's*—gifts before because that was the height of sacrilege, but I gave myself a minute to feel bitter about it now. Whenever I used my gift to bestow luck on humans, I got stuck with bad luck in return, and I was *very* aware of the consequences. Why did some get such easy gifts to manage and others such hard gifts?

Then I remembered Bullet's gifts and instantly stopped feeling sorry for myself. I hadn't encountered any humans here, so my instincts hadn't demanded that I use my gifts. It was kind of a vacation. Bullet didn't have that luxury, he was always *on.*

"You really don't have any appreciation for what it is to be a Moros," Bullet observed, giving Riot an amused look. "The original Moros—God of Impending Doom—struck fear into the hearts of mortals and immortals alike."

"Really?" Riot asked, trying to look cool, but I *felt* his ego swell at that news.

"Oh yeah," Bullet said, nodding as he neatly arranged sliced apples on the side of his plate. "Driving mortals towards their deadly fate is a pretty big deal. Like the Fates, Moros' will was too strong to be subverted, even by other gods."

"How come I never learned all this shit?" Riot asked, looking genuinely disturbed at the amount of knowledge Bullet had.

"You didn't need to," Bullet replied with an easy shrug. "It was added to the burdens the Oneiroi had to bear, passing down this information to the new generation. That there are no new Oneiroi here to pass it on to is a little unsettling, but oh well. I've bestowed it upon you two now."

Riot gave him a strange look while Bullet grinned, and I noticed that wasn't the first time he'd finished speaking on a deliberately positive note. Like whenever he felt like he was being too negative about something, he'd deliberately push himself to be happy.

Was that a good thing? There was nothing wrong with looking on the bright side, but this seemed like more than that. Like he didn't let himself be anything other than positive.

"Did you discover anything during your prayerfest this morning?" Riot asked before taking a bite of his sandwich.

Bullet looked at me curiously, probably wondering why I hadn't mentioned it yet.

Because I'm a coward?

"Maybe you could explain it?" I hedged.

"Sure," Bullet agreed. "Grace asked the Goddess of Night for help, then Erebus, God of Darkness, showed up all dramatically and carved a prophecy into my perfectly good coffee table."

Riot choked on the mouthful of food he was eating and I hit his back, giving him a sheepish smile.

"What was the prophecy?" he managed to get out, reaching for his glass of juice.

"Liberate the treasure held in the deep,

Where no sweet smelling smoke or prayer can reach,

Bring forth the Second Age of Heroes," I recited quietly, the bite I'd taken of my cheesy pesto sandwich sitting like lead in my stomach.

It didn't feel any less terrifying after saying it out loud.

BULLET

CHAPTER 8

"The what? What treasure? The deep like the ocean?" Riot asked. He looked appropriately disturbed, which was good. Most daimons weren't the religious type, the gods were merely abstract figures that they came to me to understand on the odd occasion they needed to.

That wasn't going to fly anymore. Not for Riot, not for any daimon out there. They were going to need to brush up on their religious education real quick if my suspicions about this prophecy were accurate.

"I don't know," Grace replied hesitantly as both her and Riot looked at me.

"What's the Age of Heroes?" Riot asked, eyebrows drawing down even further.

"The cards hinted at an age where mortals and the *divine* interact again." That was what I'd spent the rest of the day obsessing over, holed up in the parlor. "Possibly the divine in that equation is us, since neither Gaia nor the Goddess of Night have ever shown any interest in living on the mortal plane. Maybe it's a world where humans know about us, or agathos and daimons aren't sworn enemies."

That made the most sense to me—why would the Fates connect us as soul bonds if not to herald an age where we weren't pitted against each other?

"I don't like it," Riot grumbled. "Whatever it is."

Riot didn't like anything, except Grace.

Maybe me on a good day.

"I don't feel great about it myself," Grace laughed uncomfortably. "But if Bullet's guess is right, the potential..."

Her hope was so strong that I felt the brushes of it against my skin like rays of sunshine, even though our connection was flimsy at best.

"Wouldn't it be amazing if the agathos and daimons didn't despise each other?" Grace asked wistfully. "Even better if we had some measure of control over our lives. Not subject to the needs and weaknesses of whatever humans we encounter?"

"I guess," Riot replied uneasily, his six lonely brain cells probably working really hard to imagine how that was possible when we were designed to exist in opposition to one another. "It's a nice dream, but what happens if, you know, you can't do what the gods are asking you to do? Or if you just chose not to? What then?"

Grace blinked at him before looking at me again.

I shrugged. "If you were given the chance to make a difference, if the Fates had that path laid out for you, could you really walk away from it? Say no and live a life of mediocrity in a world you knew could be better?"

"Yes," Riot replied immediately.

Grace frowned. "If I had the chance to change the way the agathos did things? To show them that daimons aren't necessarily the enemy? Ease the plight of humans who are caught in the middle of this invisible war?"

Her hesitation was obvious, and in that moment I understood entirely why Grace had been singled out for this task. She couldn't be wooed by the allure of fame and eternal glory, though that might be a byproduct. Grace cared about *people*, maybe too much, and she'd be prepared to do whatever she had to do if the wellbeing of others was on the line.

"Tempting, is it not?" I teased while Riot looked on in a state of mild panic.

"Very," Grace agreed with a frown.

"And *that* is why Fate is impossible to outrun," I shrugged. "It's not that you'll be herded onto the path they want you on, it's that you won't be able to resist it. It's designed specifically for you."

That being said, I got the impression this wasn't *always* Grace's path. There'd always been some uncertainty in my visions about Grace's future that wasn't there anymore. It was like she'd been hovering at a crossroads until she'd finally picked a direction, and now there was no turning back. Maybe it hadn't been as conscious as that, but Grace had set things in motion when she'd chosen Riot.

Grace sighed heavily and I wished I could offer her more reassurance, but I would never outright lie to her. It was basically psychic code—always tell the truth, just maybe not the whole truth.

It was a pretty quiet meal after that, which was a shame, because I'd gone all out on the pesto grilled cheese sandwiches, and now no one was enjoying them. *Such was life when you learned what your future held.*

Ignorance may be bliss, but knowledge was power. That might be the most painful lesson I had to teach Grace.

I insisted the two of them sit at the table and spend some time together while I cleaned up, humming *Don't Rain On My Parade* as I washed the plates and Riot teased Grace about the teen movies she was so fond of watching. He was trying valiantly to brighten her mood, and it was sort of working, though she couldn't hide the waves of distress underneath all that as Riot's departure grew closer. I didn't even have a strong read on her emotions yet and I was getting hints of it, so it must have been driving him crazy.

Eventually Riot stood, scrubbing a hand through his messier than usual hair, and Grace's entire demeanor changed instantly.

"It's time for you to go," she said softly, standing as well and wrapping her arms around his waist.

"I'll be back before you wake up," Riot assured her, his arms around her shoulders and his chin resting on top of her head. Their embrace spoke of comfort and a relaxed kind of warmth that Grace and I didn't have yet after one day of knowing each other in real life.

And a lifetime of knowing each other in our dreams.

Despite spending most of the day apart, I got the feeling I wasn't wanted here at that moment anyway. It stung a little more than I cared to admit.

No time for bitterness. Grace had been through a huge upheaval in the past couple of days, and that was without the whole prophecy revelation. I'd waited this long to spend time with her in person, what was one more night?

"I'll leave you to it," I announced, grabbing the bike keys and tossing them to Riot. "I'll be downstairs if you need anything, just shout," I told Grace before shooting Riot a sympathetic grin. I'd hate to spend my night—and probably longer—taking orders from Viper, that was for sure. "Good luck."

"I'll need it," Riot sighed, swinging the keys around his finger and looking resigned. The cards had been clear that he needed to do this, and I assumed that whatever obstacles this deal would bring would lead to other necessary things.

Knowing that it served a purpose didn't always help. Sometimes Fate was shitty, and doing things that *had* to be done felt shitty.

"Um, well, goodnight?" Grace said, still clinging on to Riot but giving me a hesitant look.

Did it feel like a stab in the heart that she didn't have the physical chemistry with me that she seemed to have with Riot? *Absolutely*, I decided. But I had to trust that these things would come in time, so I brushed it off and gave her my most charming smile as I made my way down the stairs to my dungeon of a bedroom.

I'd see her in her dreams anyway.

After hours upon hours of mundane visions about strangers, and a fairly harrowing vision about how Riot's week was going to unfold, I felt myself being pulled into the Goddess' arena. It was like a hook in my sternum, dragging me where I needed to go, my body disintegrating then rematerializing in the process when I landed on solid ground again.

The Goddess of Night was practically invisible whenever I met her. She was always covered by a veil as dark as pitch that covered her entire face and body, and it sparkled like the stars were sewn into it. The most visible thing about her was the silver crown she wore over the veil. The moon phases were depicted around the edge of the crown, held in place by thin rods in the shape of intricate constellations that glittered as she moved.

It was a privilege afforded to very few to see La Nuit even in this form. I immediately dropped to one knee and bowed my head, waiting for the Goddess to speak, staring at the almost black grass below me.

We always met here, in this colorless garden. There were flowers here from every corner of the world, but they were all in shades of gray, occasionally shining silver like moonlight if La Nuit touched them. There was no sky above or land on the horizon, just endless darkness beyond this ashen oasis.

I could feel her moving towards me, though her steps were silent. Her ice cold fingers brushed lightly over my hair, encouraging me to look up.

"Rise, the Spirit of Dreams."

Weird. Usually I was just 'Spirit of Dreams', no 'the'. The additional word made it sound so singular.

I stood, keeping my head respectfully bowed as the Goddess conjured an onyx throne out of the darkness for herself and a small bench for me to sit on, placing me appropriately below her.

She may be friendly as far as goddesses go, but she was still a goddess. The differentiation in hierarchy must be maintained.

"You are now the only living Oneiroi," the Goddess sighed, lowering herself elegantly onto her throne before slumping sideways like the effort of maintaining her dignified posture was too much effort. *"Charon is escorting another across the Styx as we speak. The world is changing once more."*

I took a seat on the bench, silently waiting for La Nuit to continue. I selfishly hoped she wasn't going to elaborate on how the other one died. I had no idea who they were, but I didn't want to hear about another 30-year-old Oneiroi's brain melting because they couldn't deal with their connection to the divine.

We sat in silence for a long moment. I watched the gray roses next to me bloom and die before my eyes, everything about this garden was constantly in motion. Life was a fleeting thing in this realm.

"I never cared for humans," the Goddess said idly. She conjured up the silhouette of a woman in front of her, the two dimensional figure glowing like it was made of moonlight. I watched as the woman fell to her knees, crouching over like she was digging in the ground with her hands. She reached forward and an amphora appeared in her hands before the image stopped.

I knew this story like the back of my hand, but I didn't wish to shorten my already short life any further by pointing that out, so I kept silent.

"The first humans were all men. Mindless little playthings for the bored, spoiled Olympians. Molded and made from my sister's earth. Irritating, but ultimately harmless. They were pure, unblemished souls, and the spirits of those untainted first mortals were eventually used to make the first generation of agathos, the beginnings of each line."

The image of the woman remained frozen in place while above her the figure of a man appeared, darting down a mountainside with a fennel stalk of fire. The fire that gave human beings true consciousness, a will outside of what the gods imposed upon them. The earliest beginnings of the Age of Man.

"That soft-hearted fool Prometheus could not stand to see the humans so weak, so subject to the will of the gods. He gave them divine fire, and their mindless, unquestioning obedience was lost forever."

The image of the man fizzled out and La Nuit sighed. "Zeus always feared me, but in this matter he asked for my assistance. He and the other arrogant little Olympians created the first woman, a gift and a punishment in his eyes. Pandora was the gift, my children were the punishment."

There was no hiding the pride in her voice. The figure of the woman, Pandora, opened the jar and out flew the daimons into the world in their monstrous original forms, the first of each of our lines. The woman opened her mouth in a silent scream, shoving the lid back on the jar and trapping Elpis inside, the elusive daimon of hope. She stays with mankind to this day, not as a physical representation on Earth like the other daimons and the agathos, but as an idea. A lifeline that mortals can hold onto in the darkest of times.

"Gaia loved the mortals she had created, at the time at least, but she was too ambitious. I loathed the mortals for spoiling the perfectness of Earth, but was too resentful of the divinities that created them, too vengeful. Now Gaia is self-destructing, the Earth I loved so well is in disrepair, and mortals have forgotten the gods altogether."

She fell silent as I mulled that over in my mind. It was as close to an admission of wrongdoing as a god or goddess would ever make, and I didn't quite know how to process it.

"Your love is troubled," La Nuit noted eventually, sounding rather bored as immortals tended to do despite the sudden change in topic.

It was my usual practice in these meetings to sit diligently and listen until the Goddess told me whatever she wanted to tell me and sent me on my way, usually into a vision of her choosing. As much as she favored me, it was never a good idea for a mortal to get over familiar with a god—we weren't friends, and I was in no rush to get cursed for impertinence.

But there was only one Oneiroi left, and my time was running out. I guess if I got cursed now, at least I'd met Grace first. I'd at least had one day with her in person, and she'd actually remember me. Maybe the time for silence had gone.

"Why her?" I asked quietly.

Why Grace? Why were the paths open to her suddenly closing? Why now?

I felt rather than saw the Goddess' amusement.

"It has taken much trial and error on the parts of my daughters to create agathos and daimons suitable for this task," she replied serenely, and I knew she was referring to the Fates. "There are others, and the prophecy could have fallen on any of their shoulders. Your Grace volunteered herself when she requested my guidance for her future."

Well, fuck.

Grace and I were going to have a chat about suitable prayers to make to shadowy goddesses who possessed the powers of life and death.

"Do not be sad, the Spirit of Dreams. A mortal life may be short, yours more than others, but there is always the afterlife. Heroes are well rewarded for their feats. If you needed further incentive to succeed, you now have it."

Abruptly, the vision disappeared from around me, the dark of La Nuit's lair sucked away into the night. She wasn't the type for drawn out goodbyes, but the sudden withdrawal of her presence never ceased to be disorienting. Especially since she usually dropped me somewhere else when she left, showing me another glimpse of the future that I might find useful.

The promise of an eternal happy afterlife with Grace wasn't one I could easily disregard. Most mortals went to Asphodel, and the worst of the worst went to Tartarus, but those who'd done something amazing in their mortal life got to the Elysian Fields.

The ground solidified beneath my feet and I took a moment to absorb my surroundings, setting aside my morbid thoughts of the Underworld for later. I didn't think I'd ever been to this place, though I'd seen so many futures by now I couldn't remember all of them. I was standing in a small loft apartment with exposed brick walls, next to a leather two-seater sofa. There was a comically large bed dominating the nook behind the couch, another armchair and coffee table next to where I was standing, and a cozy kitchen with a breakfast bar in lieu of a dining table.

The whole apartment was done in light shades of wood with dark furniture, and there wasn't a single personal touch anywhere. I made my way over to the bookcase that dominated the wall behind the armchair, trying to figure out whose place this was from their taste in books.

Fitness books and autobiographies. Thrilling stuff.

Where was the romance? The YA fantasy? The smut? Whoever this was, I was going to write them a book list when I woke up and slip it under their door.

I heard the lock click and the front door opened, and my eyebrows shot up in surprise as my Amazing Grace walked in, looking around the apartment like she'd never seen it before. Apparently I was only here as a spectator, since she didn't acknowledge my presence at all.

Cool, cool. Not upset at all by that. Everything is fine.

I had no idea when this future was supposed to unfold, and Grace's outfit made me even more confused about it. She was wearing one of her agathos-style green dresses—one I hadn't bought her—but she'd paired it with flat shoes with ankle straps that I knew were sitting in a box downstairs. There were a whole bunch of things in a cupboard down there that I couldn't fit in her main closet.

With her long dark hair pulled back in a simple ponytail and a determined look on her face, my girl always took my breath away with her beauty. I'd worked hard to keep my thoughts about her not creepy over the years, but now I let my gaze linger on the fullness of her lower lip, the swell of her breasts in her modest dress, the way her waist nipped in before her hips flared oh so temptingly.

Would my hands span her entire waist? Was she ticklish around her ribs? My mind spun out an elaborate fantasy of Grace unzipping her dress, looking shyly up at me as she pulled the sleeves down and crossing an arm over her breasts as she let the garment fall to the floor.

Damn it. Even in the dreamscape, my dick was hurting.

I attempted to calm myself down and think unsexy thoughts before jumping up onto the counter, my ghost legs silently hitting the cupboard beneath me as I settled in to see whatever it was the Goddess wanted me to see. A few minutes passed with Grace hovering awkwardly just inside the apartment door, twisting the opal ring on her finger nervously, very much not acting out my amateur porn fantasy. I wanted more than anything to reach out and touch her—if only to hold her hand—but I couldn't in this form, not when La Nuit was in the driver's seat.

I'd definitely be paying Grace's dreams a visit after this. We were due for some quality time. Maybe she'd give me a cuddle.

The sound of heavy footsteps coming up the stairs outside the apartment made Grace jump. She moved as quietly as possible behind the door like she was about to jump whoever came in, which was not very Grace-like. Maybe this was further in the future than I thought? I knew there would come a time when Grace grew more sure of herself, of her relationship with her soul bonds and her place in the world, but a lot had to happen before then.

The front door swung open and I groaned in frustration as The Chariot appeared. The figure was masculine, and outfitted with the traditional signs of The Chariot card—a tunic under an armor decorated with crescent moons, a laurel crown on the figure's head with a star in the middle—but everything else about them was hidden in a cloak of moving shadows.

Was it too much to hope for a solid confirmation of identity at this point in the game? Apparently so.

The moment the figure moved inside, Grace slammed the door shut behind him and slipped in front of the door, inches away from his body when he spun around to face her. I may not have been able to see his face, but there was no denying the mixture of nerves and quiet determination in hers.

"Why are you avoiding me?" Grace demanded, hands balled into fists at her side. It looked more like an anxious reaction than an angry one, like she'd been steeling herself for this confrontation.

The man said nothing, but I didn't think I was imagining the stiffness of his shoulders under the stupid tunic.

"Why go to the effort of helping us and bringing us back here if you want nothing to do with me?"

"Tell him, Grace! You got this!"

I whooped and clapped even though no one could hear me, and I had no idea where this was or who this man was who'd apparently brought "us" somewhere. Was I part of the us?

123

I wished I could get into Grace's head at that moment. She was staring at him with so much confusion and hurt and lust, it was like a tornado of emotion taking place behind those pale eyes, ready to burst out of her at any moment.

Dressed like the "old Grace", but acting like the Grace I knew she was growing into. The brave, confident young woman who bore the weight of the world on her shoulders with endless calm, even when she felt like there was a storm raging in her head.

There was an eerie silence from The Chariot. I couldn't tell if it was part of the vision or if it was La Nuit making absolutely certain I didn't guess his identity, but apparently that was all I was getting for tonight.

The vision disappeared into nothingness around me, blowing away like dust in the wind. I had no idea what time it was, but surely there was enough time to bring Grace into a dreamscape of my choosing for a little visit before she woke up? I hadn't missed a night yet, even if it was only for a few minutes before her alarm went off because I'd been pulled into a bunch of visions about people I didn't care about all night.

One of the many downsides of being an Oneiroi—aside from the short life expectancy—was being exposed to visions about everyone we'd ever met. Talk to the grocery clerk that day? See them break their leg at a family football game on Thanksgiving in ten years' time.

What a gift.

There were a few go-to dreamscapes I created for Grace, mostly designed to make her comfortable back before she knew who I was. Hmm, where to take us tonight?

I concentrated on building the scene in my mind before I reached out for my girl, searching for the glowing thread that connected our souls and tugging it towards me. Grace was the only one I could do this with. Anyone else, I had to visit them where they were in their head. Grace was part of me though, so she could mostly go where I went. Just not to see the Goddess.

Grace materialized next to me with a start, glancing around in surprise, though a lot less surprise than I was accustomed to since she at least knew who I was these days. "Are we... on a lake?"

"Lake Union to be exact," I replied. "You have to move your feet," I added, nodding at the paddleboat we were sitting on. "To get the full Kat and Patrick experience."

I wasn't as confident as I'd expected to be with Grace in person, but I did know almost everything about her. Including that she had a borderline unhealthy obsession with 10 Things I Hate About You.

"Bullet... this is the most romantic thing I've ever done," she murmured, same as she had the last time we'd done this. She'd subconsciously chosen workout gear and was wearing her thick dark hair up in a messy ponytail, the ends curling over one shoulder. "What's the occasion?" Grace asked.

"To take you on a romantic date you won't remember?" I laughed. "Do I need one? Maybe I just enjoy your dreamy company."

Grace hummed, tipping her head back to feel the fake sun on her face. "What about my real life company? You seem a lot more relaxed here than you were today."

Wasn't that the truth? This was my element. Real life was definitely not, even though I should theoretically be great at it. I'd done all the research! Everything from agathos soul bonds, to whether or not the G-spot was real, and if so, where it was located (Cosmo's changing stance on this had caused me a great deal of consternation).

My hesitation was ridiculous. Tomorrow, I'd be a total boss boy at life.

"This is where I spend most of my time," I answered evasively. "I am a Spirit of Dreams after all."

We paddled in silence for a moment and I focused on making sure the sound of the water lapping against the paddleboat was appropriately authentic. I didn't skimp on the details for these excursions Grace couldn't remember.

"How do you really feel about me not remembering any of this?" Grace asked, startling me as she landed on the exact topic I'd been thinking about. "You can be as brutally honest as you like, since once I wake up, this will all disappear," Grace added wryly.

Could I? My initial reflex was to belt out a jaunty rendition of Put On A Happy Face, but now that Grace knew who I was, I couldn't redirect the conversation as easily and pretend this was nothing but a dream.

Why not be honest for a moment? I could already feel the tendrils of wakefulness drawing me away from the dreamscape. In a few moments, this would all disappear, and Grace's recollection of the conversation with it.

"I hate this. I hate that we have a lifetime of conversations and moments like this that you don't remember. I hate that I know all the fears and hopes you've shared with me over the past 25 years, and you know none of mine. More than anything, I hate that I'm a stranger to you when you're everything to me."

"Bullet," Grace breathed, looking stricken. The dreamscape swirled aground us, blowing into nothingness like grains of sand in the wind. "Bullet!" Grace yelled, reaching for me as we were pulled apart.

That was one sound I hoped I wouldn't hear after we met in person. The anguished noises Grace made when we were forcibly parted. No time for bitterness. I'd indulged in the forbidden emotion, and now it was done. Now it really was time to Put On A Happy Face.

I woke up alone on the uncomfortable foldout couch downstairs, feeling annoyed and unrested, though I was determined to shake it off. Today was a new day, and I always felt a little off-balance when I'd seen the Goddess directly and been exposed to whatever she wanted me to see that night.

There was more to unpack than usual—whose apartment was that? The third soul bond or the fourth? Why was Grace stomping in looking all sexy and issuing ultimatums? Where were the rest of us while that encounter took place?

Was Grace going to wake up upset after my mini meltdown?

Why was I the last Oneiroi?

That one I *really* didn't want to think too hard about. It had become clear over the years that less and less Oneiroi were being born, but this was much worse than I anticipated.

How long did I have left?

Nope, no time to think like that. It was even more crucial than usual that I didn't think like that. I had to focus on concrete questions, not abstract ones. Like where was Riot? The bike was way too loud for him to sneak onto the property. Maybe Viper had found a few other jobs for him to do while he was there.

I grabbed some clean clothes and aggressively hummed *My Shot* under my breath while I jogged up the stairs and quietly let myself into the bathroom. I was pretty confident Grace was still sleeping, and hopefully I'd have time to shower, call Riot, and maybe make some pancakes before she woke up.

No time for bitterness. No time for anything. I was going to cram as much information as possible into my history lesson with Grace today, just in case. Everything I knew about the gods, about the agathos, about daimons, *all* of it. It would all be hers. There was no time to waste when any moment with Grace could be my last.

GRACE

CHAPTER 9

"Amazing Grace," Bullet called softly, crouching next to the bed. It had been a night of broken sleep, and I had woken up not much earlier feeling *distraught*, before falling back asleep again. I just wanted to burrow down under the blankets and rest for a few more hours. "Wake up. Riot's on the phone."

I jackknifed upright, narrowly avoiding a head-on collision with Bullet. "Sorry," I winced.

My breath caught in my throat at seeing Bullet first thing in the morning after missing him so much last night and feeling so far away from him. My face was so close to his, an inch further and our lips would've touched...

"Don't apologize for being excited," Bullet replied, an amused glint in his eye as he passed me the phone. "Though you should probably temper your expectations," he added with a grimace.

That poured cold water over any kissing thoughts I had

"Riot?" I asked, holding the phone to my ear and shooting Bullet a confused look. Sugar, I probably looked awful with my hair falling out of a braid and skin all blotchy from sleeping on one side. Though Bullet still looked at me like I was beautiful.

"*Gracie*," Riot sighed, sounding both relieved and exhausted. "*Probably best to put me on speakerphone, though I'm sure the psychic already knows what's going on.*"

"I don't know everything, you know," Bullet replied cheerfully, settling on the edge of the bed as I put it on speaker and held it between us.

"*Just most things,*" Riot scoffed, though there was no heat in it. "*The bad news is I won't be back today. I'm not sure when I'll get back.*"

"I'm not sure either," Bullet added, sounding genuinely apologetic. "I'm trying to get more insight, but the answers are elusive."

"What's going on?" I asked, panic making my throat feel tight. "What have they done?"

It had to be the agathos. Nothing else would keep Riot away from me.

"*The Governor's declared a state of emergency for the whole county,*" Riot sighed irritably. "*There was some, uh, retaliation last night. That, plus they made it sound like the Milton residents were responsible for a lot of the original property damage. It's a flimsy excuse to close down the town and try to flush us out, I think.*"

The Governor was an agathos—Felicity Wilkes. She ran in the same circles as my mother, even though she lived further away. Milton may be almost all daimons, but the rest of the state wasn't.

"What does a state of emergency mean?" I asked faintly. "You can't leave?"

"Well, they've brought in the National Guard," Riot replied, and if I weren't so worried I would have smiled at the eye roll in his voice. *"It's ridiculous. The city's on curfew, there are troops swarming the streets, and we can't congregate. That kind of thing. They're making life difficult, both in order to find you, and to annoy all the people here who have taken up your banner."*

I gave Bullet a helpless look, hoping he'd have something reassuring to add, but he only gave me an apologetic grimace.

"They're looking for both of you," Bullet replied. "They want to make an example out of you, and hand Riot to the authorities so they can pin him for abduction or whatever."

Riot snorted while my alarm spiked exponentially.

"But you're there!" I spluttered. "In the viper's nest!"

There was silence on the other end of the phone while Bullet's eyebrows shot up towards his hair.

"What've you been saying?" Riot growled.

"Nothing!" Bullet laughed. "That was just an excellent coincidence."

"What was?" I asked, feeling like I was only getting half the conversation.

"The name of the guy Riot's working for is Viper," Bullet replied, still chuckling. "He is quite literally in the viper's nest."

"Not literally," Riot groused. *"Not at the moment, anyway. I cleaned up the gym and headed straight to Dare's apartment when the troops started rolling in. The downstairs studio is trashed, but the upstairs living area is habitable."*

Nausea rolled in my gut at the idea of Riot racing through the streets of Milton on Bullet's motorbike to find somewhere safe to hunker down. Unlike daimons, the agathos worked in all areas of human society, including law enforcement. They could punish the entire town of Milton and make it look entirely legitimate. They already *were*.

"Maybe—"

"Don't get noble on me, Gracie," Riot said flatly, cutting me off before I could suggest turning myself in. *"If you're feeling like you need to confess, then Bullet better hide his phone and physically prevent you from doing it. I made a deal with Viper to keep you hidden—if anything, this just proves that he needs to up his efforts."*

"Agreed," Bullet said, twisting on the bed to lean back against the headboard, deceptively relaxed. "Are you feeling noble, Grace?"

"I don't feel like I *need* to confess or anything," I said slowly, trying to decide if my agathos instincts were going to force me to act or if it was just *me*. "I don't owe them knowledge of my location."

"You're damn right you don't," Riot agreed fiercely. So long as I didn't know about whatever it was Viper was supposed to be doing, I didn't feel the need to do anything about it.

"I don't want anyone to suffer because of me," I admitted quietly. "That isn't my nature talking, that's me."

"No one here is suffering," Riot said firmly. *"If anything, they're excited,"* he added with a snort. *"Inconvenienced, but excited. This is the most exciting thing that's happened in Milton in years."*

Bullet nodded enthusiastically. "Violence is in our blood, Amazing Grace. There's nothing more satisfying to our kind than a good fight."

I wasn't sure if that was strictly true—Riot and Bullet didn't seem like they particularly relished violence, but then they weren't quite like other daimons. From everything I'd been told about Riot's dad, he was probably quite keen on exacting some revenge on the agathos who had intruded on their town.

As much as that thought *should've* horrified me, it didn't. Not really. I didn't like the idea of anyone getting hurt, but the daimons in Milton had every right to defend their territory.

"Take me off speakerphone," Riot instructed. Bullet chuckled as I did as Riot asked before discreetly slipping out of the bedroom.

"Okay," I told Riot softly as Bullet shut the door behind him. "It's just us now."

He hummed softly, but there was a hint of sadness in it and I wished more than anything that he was here and I could wrap my arms around him.

"It'll never be just us again, Gracie."

"No matter who else comes into our lives, we're still Riot and Grace," I assured him, surprised at the fierceness in my voice. "What I have with anyone else doesn't take away from us, and if you ever feel like it does, then promise me you'll tell me so I can fix it."

"I didn't mean to make you feel like you had to fix anything," Riot replied with a heavy sigh. *"You don't, there's nothing broken between us. You grew up with this whole multiple lovers idea, but it's all new and weird for me. Give me some time, okay?"*

"However long you need," I promised. Bullet was handling the concept of sharing better than Riot was, but I guessed he'd had his visions to prepare him for it. Not that we'd actually discussed it, but he seemed more open to that side of things.

"You should, uh, sleep next to him tonight," Riot said, sounding tired. *"If you want to."*

"Really?" I asked in surprise.

"Yeah. I'm being a moody bastard about it, but Bullet isn't that bad, and I hate the thought of you being alone. Being so far from you is agony, I bet it's doubly bad for you now."

Having twice the number of unfulfilled bonds was definitely no picnic. The constant emotional turmoil was distracting me, but the physical side effects were definitely getting hard to ignore.

"I'll think about it," I replied softly. Sleeping next to Riot was still a strange concept, let alone a different man, but the bond was pushing for more physical intimacy with Bullet, and cuddling was the easiest way to appease it. "Are you going to sleep now? You sound exhausted."

"Yeah, I'm shattered," Riot replied around a yawn. *"Hopefully Viper will leave me alone for a couple of days. I'm going to spend some time cleaning up Dare's studio before he gets back."* Riot paused, sounding rather emotional for someone who claimed he didn't have friends. *"It'd kill Dare to see the place like this, he put so much work into it, you know?"*

"I wish I could help you. It feels very indulgent to be lazing around in the countryside while you're there doing all the work."

"You're not lazing around anywhere," Riot scoffed. *"I've never put much stock into Bullet's ramblings before, mostly because the future was an abstract thing I didn't really give a fuck about, but I can recognize now that there's more to it than I thought. The things you're learning from him are important, without a doubt. That's where your focus needs to be."*

He was definitely alluding to the prophecy. "It is. I'll focus," I promised.

"I know you will," Riot said confidently. *"Go get some breakfast. I'll call you when I wake up, okay?"*

"Be safe. I miss you."

The words slipped out of my mouth before I had a chance to stop them, and my face flamed immediately. Were we at that stage where we could say things like that yet? We hadn't known each other for very long, but it felt like forever.

"I miss you more than I can even comprehend," Riot replied with his low, quiet laugh that always gave me goosebumps. *"Talk to you soon."*

I hung up with a heavy sigh and climbed out of bed to get dressed, taking a moment to admire the selection of workout clothes Bullet had picked out for me. Mostly in sleek black, which my mother would have had a fit about and I was thoroughly enjoying.

Black was so *convenient*. Everything matched all the time, no thought process or laying out of clothes the night before required.

Once I was in my thin slouchy black pants and a gray long-sleeved top, partially tucked in, I ducked into the bathroom to freshen up, awkwardly waving at Bullet in the kitchen as I went past.

Today, I promised myself. I wouldn't stop worrying about Riot, but I would make an effort to connect more with Bullet. He deserved at least a little of my undivided attention, and I wanted to get to know him better.

Once I looked somewhat presentable, I joined Bullet in the kitchen where a stack of pancakes were sitting in the center of the table, surrounded by bowls of accompaniments—fresh berries, sliced banana, chocolate sprinkles, whipped cream, maple syrup, peanut butter, and more.

"This is amazing," I gasped, staring at the spread he'd whipped up in awe. Buttermilk pancakes with berries and syrup was my absolute favorite indulgent breakfast—my dad, Chance, had made them for me before my Saturday agathos lessons when I was growing up to perk me up because he knew how much I struggled with them.

Maybe it was a coincidence. Or maybe Bullet already knew that.

"Coffee's in the pot," he replied with one of those disarming grins, sipping his herbal tea.

"You're too sweet, thank you." I quickly mixed my coffee in the kitchen as Bullet chuckled, adding hazelnut creamer before rejoining him at the table. I had no idea why both he and Riot seemed to find the idea that they were sweet so ludicrous—both of them had been nothing but sweet to me.

"Are you worried about Riot?" Bullet asked conversationally as he covered his pancakes with peanut butter and sliced banana. Apparently no man was perfect after all.

Peanut butter was the worst food in the world.

"Yes," I replied, filling up my plate. "But I'm selfishly hoping you'd see if something was going to go wrong and let me know."

"That's not selfish at all. But sometimes I don't see things in time to change them, because that's the way Fate was meant to unfold. I didn't see the original agathos attack on Milton until it was in progress, for example." He gave me a searching look, like that was meant to mean something, and I couldn't help but feel like I disappointed him with my clueless face.

"Anyway," Bullet continued, pasting a smile back on his face. "I don't think Riot is going to get hurt or anything, but I'll keep an eye out. He's going to get *very* sick of Viper though."

"He never told me how long this arrangement with Viper lasts. It's obviously more than simply cleaning the gym," I pointed out wryly. Yes, they had to hide some things from me, but not *all* things.

"Until he can get out of it," Bullet replied, mouth downturned for half a moment before he cleared the expression again. "In the heat of the moment, Riot basically signed a blank check to keep you safe. If Viper keeps slacking off like he's been doing, Riot might be able to get out of it that way. I had hoped the agathos would be following a fake Grace to Hawaii or something by now."

I blinked at him. That seemed very elaborate.

"What's Viper like?" I asked, pouring a generous amount of syrup on my pancakes.

"Oh, he's the absolute worst," Bullet chuckled. "A money grubbing leech who deals in favors. He has a little fiefdom in Milton built on shady deals, but he's a little fish really. He just thinks he's a shark."

"This is not making me feel better," I said faintly, my knife scraping against the plate, my pancake long since cut through. "What kind of daimon is he?"

"An Apate—daimon of deceit and fraud. He's a dick, but I'm confident that he serves a purpose in this journey we're on. What that purpose is, I'm not entirely sure."

It was a difficult lesson to learn, that bad things would happen and I had to just accept them as part of the process. It seemed instinctively wrong not trying to stop unpleasant things from taking place.

"He and Riot struck a deal with La Nuit as witness," Bullet continued. "Those deals can't be broken unless both parties agree without incurring her wrath. La Nuit has a strict code of honor for her human-torturing daimons, you know."

Bullet held up his forkful of peanut butter covered pancake like he was saluting me before popping it into his mouth.

"So, do we have another lesson today?" I asked.

Bullet grimaced. "Not right away, though believe me, I wish we could. I forgot that there are a couple of human clients coming in this morning for their regularly scheduled psychic readings. I'm going to cancel all future bookings for the next little while, but I was hoping you'd be okay killing time with Netflix and some of the books from downstairs for today."

"Oh, that's fine," I assured him. "I shouldn't have assumed you'd be free, I'm sure you have to work—"

"Hardly," Bullet interrupted with a wry grin. "Between previous Oneiroi who made smart investments—definitely with help from psychic insider knowledge—and a few other money-making schemes related to the estate, no one who lived here had to "work" in the conventional sense for years. This is more about tradition, I guess. Upholding the legacy or whatever."

He shrugged like it wasn't a big deal, but I got the sense it was more important to him than he let on.

"That's really cool," I told him genuinely. "I know most daimons aren't big on religious tradition, but I grew up with a lot of ritual and I always enjoyed that aspect even if I didn't enjoy a lot of the other agathos trappings."

I felt Bullet's gratitude like warmth on my skin, but his face gave nothing away.

"I'll be as quick as I can," Bullet promised. "Fortune cookie style readings all day, no follow up questions. Enjoy your day off, Amazing Grace."

A few hours away from Bullet, and now a whole night since I'd seen Riot, and I was lying on the couch very seriously questioning if someone could die from unfulfilled sexual desire?

That really seemed like a question they should have covered in the How To Be An Agathos lessons, though I supposed people usually found their soul bonds, quickly consummated their relationship, and never had to deal with the agony I was experiencing.

Surely, Bullet would have seen my death by lack of intimacy in the cards.

He was still downstairs with a human, and I guessed he wasn't in as much pain as I was or he would have come up, right? Then again, I was getting a double whammy from the lack of bond and the physical distance between me and Riot.

Oh sugar, I might genuinely die from this.

Unless I handled it myself. Which was *extremely* frowned upon for an agathos, but also... better than dying.

In my teen years, when my curiosity had been more *volatile*, I'd tried touching myself. I knew it was strictly forbidden to entertain any sexual ideas that weren't about one's bonded, but I'd been so curious, and thought one time wouldn't hurt.

Agathos couldn't feel true desire until our first soul bond awakened it in us, but without anything to compare it to, I hadn't realized what I was missing out on when my fingers ventured south. After a dry, painful, borderline clinical examination of my lady bits, I'd run to the bathroom and promptly thrown up everything I'd eaten that day, wracked with guilt.

For years after, I'd watched my friends find their soul bonds and convinced myself it was Anesidora's punishment for that one indiscretion that I never found mine.

Except they'd been there all along, I just hadn't met them yet.

Sugar, I hoped I hadn't mentioned the failed touching experiment to Bullet when he'd visited my dreams. Apparently I'd been very chatty about other topics.

I could try again. It wouldn't be like last time. In fact, it would probably feel nice, now that the nerve endings in that part of my body had awakened. And I wouldn't have to rely on Bullet to ease this ache when we really didn't have that kind of connection yet.

And I just kind of *wanted* to. Crossing this forbidden line was another step away from my old life. One I was ready to take.

I set down the book I'd been pretending to read and made my way to the bathroom, feeling a little bit like I was sneaking around. This was fine, wasn't it? Bullet wouldn't want me to be in pain.

Who are you trying to kid, Grace? Pleasuring yourself in your host's shower is a flagrant abuse of his hospitality.

And yet I turned the water on and got undressed anyway, nervously setting my clothes into a pile and tying my hair up in a bun.

No goddess was going to emerge from the heavens and smite me for seeing to my own, er, *comfort*, surely. This was a perfectly natural practice that people indulged in every day, and I wasn't hurting anyone.

I was not going to throw up this time.

I climbed over the side of the tub, letting the warm water wash over my keyed up body, and knew I wouldn't be able to talk myself out of doing this, regardless of what my moral code tried to tell me.

I *needed* this.

Tentatively, I pumped some body wash into my hands, intending to wash myself while I worked up some courage, but the moment my palms ran over my skin it was like a fire had been lit, burning me from the inside out. My breasts, whose existence I barely registered most of the time, were heavy and aching, and the slightest brush of my fingers against my nipples sent a spike of awareness between my thighs. I kneaded at the sensitive skin, sighing heavily at how good it felt to have hands on me, even if they were only my own.

Sugar.

It was clearly not natural to have met two soul bonds and not have bonded with either of them. My body was letting me know that it was very much not natural.

There was a persistent throb between my legs that I couldn't resist any longer. One hand slid over my stomach, down to where I was aching the most, and the amount of wetness I found was frankly alarming. It most definitely had not felt like this the last time I'd attempted this.

This was much more pleasurable.

I closed my eyes and tipped my head back, remembering the way Riot had touched me, trying not to be embarrassed that he knew more about what made my body feel good than I did. I dragged wetness up to my *clit*, blushing furiously at just the thought of the word, and sucked in a startled breath at the impact. It jolted through me like electricity, and I swallowed the urge to groan at the sensation.

This was dangerous. I could get addicted to this.

Using my middle finger, I circled the sensitive nerves slowly, curling over myself and bracing one arm against the tile wall as the strength in my legs threatened to fail me.

I craved the feeling of Riot's confident hands on me, imagining his body wrapped around mine, his front pressed against my back, his hand guiding my movements. What would it feel like to have Bullet standing in front of me, holding me up, those long elegant fingers exploring my body as I struggled to keep quiet? Would his face still be bright with amusement when we were lost in each other this way?

I imagined Bullet's lips on mine while Riot's pressed against my shoulder, and tightness coiled low in my belly before exploding. I pressed my mouth against my forearm to muffle the sound as pleasure threatened to drown me.

Oh, there was no way this was frowned upon. This felt too good to be anything other than a gift from the gods.

I took a moment to recover before washing up and climbing out of the shower on weak legs. The immediate edge had been taken off, but it wasn't nearly as effective as my experiences with Riot had been. Even the gentle brush of fabric against my sensitive skin was too much.

It may not have cured the ache, but it had relaxed me at least. I headed back to the living room and curled up on the couch, tugging a throw blanket over my legs and grabbing the remote.

I passed a good couple of hours binge watching a reality show about attractive humans finding love, and reveled a little in the frivolousness of lounging around in the middle of the day, watching television. But even with all the distractions, I was hyper aware that Riot wasn't here, and that he may well be in danger in Milton, despite Bullet's words of comfort.

I hated being away from Riot at the best of times—just a few hours at work had felt like utter misery—but this was infinitely worse. Feeling more than a little sorry for myself, I switched off the television and headed for the bedroom, flopping down on the bed and pulling the pillow Riot had slept on towards me to try to pick up his scent.

This was not how it was meant to be among new soul bonds.

I didn't even have my own phone to contact Riot with, and he was all alone. As lonely as I felt without him, at least I had Bullet. I was only lonely because he wasn't with me right this second.

As much as I wanted to ask Bullet to consult his cards again, I got the feeling I'd drive us both crazy if I went down that path. He was confident Riot wouldn't get hurt, and I needed to trust that.

I *did*. I knew Bullet even less than I knew Riot, but I felt incredibly at ease around him. It helped that he talked to me like he knew me, which I guessed he sort of did.

"Don't be sad, Amazing Grace," Bullet called, the stairs creaking as he made his way up them. "We're going to watch *Mamma Mia* and eat fancy cheese. Your number one boyfriend will be home before you know it."

I smiled in spite of my worry, Bullet was the kind of person it was almost impossible to be sad around. Tugging on a lavender sweater and woolen socks, I slipped out of the bedroom to join him in the living room.

Bullet really did have phenomenal taste in clothes. He'd picked out gorgeous outfits for me, and he was dressed in a sharp tan waistcoat over his white shirt, with a navy tie. He may not think of his psychic readings as work, but he was definitely dressed for a day at a very trendy office.

"I'm not sure I like the 'number one boyfriend' title," I confessed, moving to the kitchen where Bullet was hunched over the counter to avoid banging his head on the ceiling.

"No?" Bullet glanced up, cocking an eyebrow at me before returning his attention to the platter he was arranging. He'd already assembled such an impressive array of cheese, crackers, sliced fruit, and hummus, with sliced pita bread grilling in the oven, I almost didn't notice the absence of meat. "Isn't he your *consort*?"

There was nothing in Bullet's tone or body language that implied it was anything more than a casual question, but I felt the hint of his deep curiosity against my skin.

"I've never been overly fond of that agathos tradition," I admitted, leaning against the end of the counter with my hip. "It seems so unfair."

He hummed in agreement, working efficiently to finish the platter.

"How was your day?" I asked. If he'd felt traces of my sadness when he came upstairs, had he felt my emotions while he was downstairs?

Surely not. Surely he would mention it if he felt what I'd been doing in the shower. My face heated up just thinking about it.

"Boring," Bullet replied with a cheeky grin. "Rich people only ever have questions about their money, which has always seemed weird to me. Like, you've already got money. Ask about your future soulmate, or whether your kids will grow up happy, something like that, you know?"

He rolled his eyes, adding the warm pita bread to the platter and carrying it to the couch. I trailed along behind him, feeling distinctly out of my comfort zone. I'd been out of my comfort zone with Riot too, but I'd still had my everyday life to ground me—my apartment, my job, my car, my *clothes*. I had none of that now, in Bullet's 90s time capsule above-barn apartment.

"Do you know why Gaia elevated the first soul bond above the other three?" Bullet asked, catching me off-guard. I sat at the other end of the couch from him, pondering the question.

"Because she had the most children with Ouranos?" I hedged. Agathos didn't like to discuss Anesidora—*Gaia's*—own consorts in great detail, given how incestuous the relationships were. The gods were very different from mortals in that regard, and it wasn't something the teachers enjoyed reflecting on in Saturday morning lessons.

"Guilt," Bullet replied easily, slicing himself a piece of brie and giving each cracker an assessing look before settling on one. "He locked some of their children away, and Gaia went to all the others in turn, asking them to depose Ouranos. Only Kronos agreed. He castrated his own father with the sickle Gaia made before taking his throne. Ouranos, who was a sky god, took his place permanently in the sky after predicting his children's downfall."

None of what Bullet was telling me was new information. I'd learned it all in agathos history lessons over the years, but I had never found those lessons as engaging as listening to Bullet was. I'd never heard of the gods being discussed with such *human* emotions.

"Gaia deemed that agathos women would have four soul bonds like she had four consorts, but the first would be elevated above all others like hers was, as penance for her crimes. But you're not designed quite like other agathos, it would make sense you're missing that urge to elevate Riot above me."

With that pronouncement, he grinned and shoved the cheese and cracker into his mouth, then hit play, the sound of Amanda Seyfried singing *I Have A Dream* filling the quiet. I contemplated asking some follow up questions, but I got the feeling Bullet needed to unwind after his day and this was how he did it.

He hadn't been in a bad mood before, but he noticeably perked up as soon as the song started, and I could feel the faintest sense of relief brushing over me. Perhaps Bullet's love of musicals went a little deeper than merely enjoying the songs. It was very lonely out here, maybe musicals kept Bullet company.

He had me now. Things may feel a little bit new and awkward at the moment, but I wasn't going to let Bullet feel lonely ever again, that much I was sure of.

For a while we watched the movie in almost silence, broken occasionally by Bullet humming along to the songs or me eating crackers which sounded obnoxiously loud when I was trying to be demure and ladylike about the whole process like I'd been trained. Riot was never far from my mind, but Bullet's presence soothed the agitated edges of my thoughts.

It was a different kind of reassurance to how I felt around Riot, but no less potent. Where Riot felt like a safety net who'd never let me fall, Bullet felt like a lifeline, tethered to me and feeding me a steady stream of everything I needed to know.

Did my mother experience this with her four soul bonds? Did they each give her something different that she wouldn't have otherwise had? I couldn't understand how she was such a bitter person if that was the case.

"Donna really should have had a harem," Bullet remarked, tilting his head to the side as he drummed his fingers against his thigh along to *Take A Chance On Me.* "Not sleeping with Sam, Harry and Bill all at once really seems like a wasted opportunity."

I coughed slightly on the mouthful of pita bread I'd been chewing, my face suddenly so hot I was sure I could fry eggs on it.

"You disagree?" Bullet asked with a mischievous grin. "Wait til we watch *Mamma Mia 2*. Young Bill looks eerily like me, but without the tattoos. You'll join Team Foursome as well. "

"I don't know about that," I laughed before taking a swig of my water. "I can't imagine being Team, um, *Foursome* ever." I whispered the word like *Gaia* was going to burst through the apartment door and smite me just for uttering it.

"With all the soul bonds you're collecting, *that* would be a travesty," Bullet shot back with an unrepentant grin that made me smile in spite of myself. For all his suggestive talk, Bullet was still sitting at the other end of the couch with enough space between us to fit two more people. I didn't know him well enough to say for sure, but it seemed like he was more shy than he was letting on.

"You think I'll meet more of them then?" I asked, choosing to gloss over the flirty banter. I *wanted* to reply, to say something funny and a little bit cheeky that would make Bullet blush as hard as I had, but I didn't know how. It was basically the total opposite of every conversational skill I'd been taught my whole life.

"Soul bonds?" Bullet asked, sounding surprised. "Definitely, Amazing Grace. You're going to meet all four of them. Sooner rather than later."

The idea of meeting two more of them was equal parts exciting and intimidating. *Where* would I meet them? We were holed up here for the foreseeable future, and it seemed like the only visitors Bullet had out here were his human clients.

"I don't know for sure who they are," Bullet continued, though he sounded like he had his suspicions. "They're both daimons though. If you were hoping for a couple of clean cut agathos gentlemen to balance out Riot and I, sorry to disappoint you, but you won't be getting them."

"I think I'm fine with that," I mused. "You're more likely to get along if you're all daimons, right?"

"Definitely not," Bullet snorted.

"Well, *more* likely to get along than you would be with an agathos guy. Especially one who may or may not have taken part in the destruction of your town," I added, wrinkling my nose. "When the Basilinna told me her grand plan was to break the connection between me and Riot to try to somehow bond me to a dead woman's bonded, there was absolutely no part of me that *wanted* that outcome. I was—I *am*—happier with my own soul bonds than I would be with any agathos ones."

Bullet's mild expression sharpened instantly. His amethyst eyes which had been twinkling with amusement since I'd met him narrowed, and his lips that were almost permanently upturned flattened into a thin line.

"That's what they had planned?" he asked in an icy voice. "They wanted to reset you like an old computer?"

"They thought it was a sign from A—, from Gaia, that the day I met Riot was the same day an agathos woman named Joy died," I explained. I struggled to keep my voice even when the darkness in my mind raged at the memory, then wondered why I was even bothering to be polite about it. I didn't have to pretend to be okay with the worst parts of the agathos world anymore.

Old habits die hard, I reminded myself, but I was determined to put them to rest.

Waterloo began playing on screen and I watched in fascination as Bullet hummed along for a few bars of the song and the tension bled out of him like he was forcing it out. The cold, enraged look was gone like it had never been there, leaving a smiley, bright-eyed Bullet in its place.

Suddenly, I *craved* a completed bond with Bullet. There was so much going on in his head that he refused to let show, and he obviously had incredible emotional control to keep those feelings locked down. I admired his control, but hated that he was hiding pieces of himself from me. Hated that he felt like he had to.

"Well, aside from the fact that their whole theory is *ridiculous*," Bullet said cheerfully, though there was a bite to his words I doubted he wanted me to hear. "Riot and I would never sit back and let them sever the connections you have with us anyway. If they somehow succeeded, we'd rebuild them. Fact."

"I believe you," I told him with a small smile. I'd believed with absolute certainty that Riot would come for me when I was on the altar, and I believed with absolute certainty that Bullet and Riot would fight for me again if push came to shove. I *felt* it.

I really hoped push never came to shove though.

BULLET

CHAPTER 10

I seemed to be getting a night off. Instead of being pulled around from vision to vision, I was languidly relaxing in blissfully dark nothingness, my magic waiting for me to choose the direction I explored tonight.

Maybe it was because I'd gone to bed with such a restless mind that I wasn't being yanked around the dreamscape like usual. Grace had excused herself to go to bed after the movie ended, nervously suggesting that I could sleep next to her if I wanted before running like there was a fire on her ass.

I wasn't about to say no to that offer. Aside from the fact that I was in abject misery from not touching her with the incomplete bond hanging like an anvil around my neck, I just wanted to hold her.

I'd waited until Grace was asleep before joining her in bed though. To save us both from the awkwardness.

"Show me Grace's future," I asked the darkness, hoping La Nuit was listening. I asked every night in the hopes I'd get some insight into the challenges *ahead of her, but it seemed the Goddess of Night wanted us to go into that blind since she usually gave me visions in the more distant future.*

Ones where I wasn't around. Still, I always asked. Just in case.

The darkness swirled around me, fracturing like a broken mirror before disintegrating into sand and forming into something new.

Sunlight hit me first, temporarily blinding me until my eyes adjusted. I hadn't brought Grace with me this time, the vision of her that appeared in front of me was only a vision, like watching a film reel in 3D. I could feel the sand under my feet, but it was too soft to be real. The sun beat down overhead, but it hit my skin like it was filtered by an invisible bubble.

I was here, but not. Because this future may not be mine.

I stood on the sand as Riot ran down the beach in a pair of black swimming shorts, Grace thrown over his shoulder, squealing and laughing as they approached the waves. Grace's hair was bundled up on her head, and her swimsuit was a pair of tiny coral hot pants with a matching crop top, surprisingly revealing compared to what she'd worn in beach visions before this, so maybe this happens much further in the future?

Despite how left out I felt, I couldn't help but smile as Riot crashed into the water and dropped Grace into the waves, keeping his arms around her waist so she wasn't fully submerged. She regained her footing, turning in his grip and laughing as he pulled her back to his chest and held her close when she tried to splash him.

I couldn't see them, but I knew they weren't alone here. Behind me, but somehow invisible were two more male voices and a child laughing as they played on the sand. Grace looked back to the shore, and I was struck by the maternal devotion in her eyes as she sought out the child. Satisfied there was nothing to worry about, Grace's attention returned to Riot, her eyes tracking straight over me without pause.

It was a blessing and a curse to see these visions. A blessing to know whatever happened to me, Grace had a beautiful future ahead of her, filled with love and laughter. Without me.

That was the curse.

Nothing in this vision gave me any indication as to what the immediate future held. The Riot in front of me had a few more tattoos than he had now, and I thought I glimpsed a hint of ink on Grace's inner wrist, but it was too hard to tell while she splashed in the water.

I didn't even know exactly where we were. Whatever Grace's long-term future held, it seemed to include a lot of travel since they were always in vastly different locations in each vision. I liked that for her. It was nice to think she would see the world outside the Eastern Seaboard when whatever her trials came to pass. That was another thought I could take comfort from to stave off the bitterness. The promise of a happily ever after, or so I hoped.

Whenever I had these visions, I usually visited Grace right away because spending time with her in the dreamscape made all the pain worth it. Every night of her life, I'd spent at least a little time with her before she woke up. She'd never remembered me, so no matter what mood I arrived in, she was politely curious and happy enough to talk to me.

But if I went to her like this now, Grace would know something was wrong. Grace knew me, and she wouldn't settle for a non explanation if she felt something was bothering me. Even knowing she wouldn't remember it, would never know the interaction had occurred, I couldn't stomach the idea of her seeing me like this.

This wasn't me. I didn't have the luxury of letting these emotions rule me. I definitely didn't have the luxury of wasting the precious amount of time I had with Grace—in this world or any other—feeling bitter about my lot in life.

I'd always known how this would end. I'd always known there was an early expiration date on my time, because that's what being an Oneiroi entailed.

So instead of creating an idyllic dreamscape to wow the love of my life and pulling her into it with me, or even showing her this happy vision of her future, for the first time in Grace's life I returned to the dark alone.

I woke up early, slipping out of bed where Grace was still sleeping and creeped out into the still dark living room. I brewed myself a cup of chamomile tea and took a few minutes to meditate away my bad mood. We had bigger things going on than my existential crisis, and those things deserved all of my attention.

Settling in on the couch, I turned on the news, sad but not surprised to see another giant earthquake had ravaged the globe overnight. I pulled out my phone and added it to the list I was keeping along with the date, making a note to check online to see what disasters I'd missed while I'd been singularly focused on Grace over the past couple of days.

Gaia was restless. She'd fought for this level of control, battled her way to the top of the divine food chain, only nominally kept in

check by La Nuit. But Gaia didn't really want to lead, she wanted power. Eons ago, gods and goddesses had all but micromanaged humans. Now they were left to their own devices.

Perhaps Gaia thought that without competition, mortals would only worship her. Instead, they'd ravaged the land she'd created and forgotten about her existence.

"Liberate the treasure held in the deep."

In the very depths of the earth, beneath the Underworld, laid Tartarus—both a deity and a place. Tartarus the god was one of Gaia's

153

consorts, and Tartarus the realm was his shadowy prison domain. Despite his connection to Gaia, he'd given the Goddess of Night a home there. Maybe that was where whatever treasure Grace was supposed to seek was lying.

Or maybe it was buried at the bottom of the ocean, and I was overthinking things? I wasn't accustomed to *not* having all the answers at my fingertips and I had to say, so far I was not a fan of all this thinking and guesswork.

This must be how normal people felt.

Grace emerged from the bedroom while I puzzled over the prophecy, looking adorably rumpled in her monogrammed fluffy robe with her hair coming loose from her braid.

"You woke up early," Grace said in a raspy voice, shooting me a soft smile as she made her way to the kitchen to make coffee. I could sense something bothering her, a discontented emotion brushing insistently against my skin, but one I couldn't identify.

"Couldn't sleep," I replied cheerfully, drumming the beat to *In The Heights* on my knee because it was an uptempo-or-I'd-breakdown kind of day.

"Oh." For a while, Grace made her coffee in silence while I messaged Riot to check in on him, humming a little aggressively under my breath because I wasn't doing a good job of resetting my mood, and Grace was obviously picking up on it.

This wasn't what I was here for. This wasn't why she had me. I was supposed to be her teacher, her guide, not the mopey dude who brought down the entire mood.

She already had Riot for that.

"There's a takeaway cup in the top cupboard," I said, injecting as much cheer into my voice as possible. "Do you want to get ready and we'll do our lesson outside today?"

The trees were all shades of gold and red, and the early morning sun was shining, making them look particularly soft and glowy if you were into that sort of thing. It seemed as good a location as any to talk about Mother Earth.

Grace's eyes lit up. "I love that idea. I've been missing going for my morning runs outside. Give me five minutes to get dressed."

She quickly finished making her coffee in the takeaway cup then disappeared into the bedroom with it, looking far more excited than she had been yesterday.

Idiot. Why didn't you show her where she could go running? You know she likes to run in the mornings.

I was letting Grace down in more ways than one.

While she got dressed, I quickly headed downstairs to grab my coat and boots, then dug out the box containing a brand new pair of dark green Hunter boots for Grace since the ground was a little muddy outside. Maybe I should have moved back into the big house. I had a whole second wardrobe's worth of things for Grace in storage down here, which I could have put in a walk-in closet in the main house.

It had just been so depressingly quiet up there after everyone had died off, one by one. Besides, I'd never had any visions of me living in the big house again, so I assumed the barn was where I died.

A comforting thought to start the day with.

Grace was emerging from the bedroom, wearing the fleece-lined black leggings and matching jacket I was glad I'd remembered to buy her, hair fixed in a neat ponytail and some subtle makeup on her face. Her eyes widened as I handed her the box with a flourish.

"Bullet," Grace squeaked. "You shouldn't have— oh my gosh, I love them," she sighed, pulling the lid off the box. "You still shouldn't have though."

"Agree to disagree, you can't be traipsing around the mud in sneakers," I replied confidently. I pulled on my own coat and shoes while Grace unpackaged the boots, giving them a borderline adoring smile as she pulled them on.

It hadn't escaped my notice how *tight* Grace's outfit was. She'd already lost some of the self-consciousness she usually had when she was wearing anything other than the kind of agathos-approved pastel clothes that would look at home in a nunnery. Grace leaned forward to admire the boots on her feet and I had all kinds of non-teachery feelings at seeing her ass in spandex.

Concentrate.

It was so distracting, noticing for the first time all the little things that I didn't see in the dreamscape. She never had to push her hair out of her face in her dreams—there was no wind unless I wanted there to be wind. The first time I saw her yawn, I could have

fainted from shock. She never yawned in the dreamscape. Her nose had scrunched up so adorably that I'd wanted to faint and make out at the same time.

I was feeling that same weird combination of emotions as I watched her wriggle her feet into the boots, getting them comfortable before tugging down the hem of her jacket. They were such mundane

movements that reminded me she was a real person and not a fantasy that existed solely in my head.

She wasn't *just a dream*, but she was still my dream.

"Right, let's go!" I announced, thinking happy thoughts before I dropped to my knees and begged her to be as obsessed with me as I was with her.

Grace snagged her coffee off the table as she followed me out, gripping the rail tightly as we made our way down the dewy outside stairs that led to the gravel driveway.

I should go outdoors more often, it was nice out here.

I wouldn't, but I always told myself that every time I dragged myself out the door. All the fresh air and birds singing, it was so... real. I spent so much time absorbed in visions that the real world was a little unsettling sometimes.

Grace inhaled deeply, clutching her coffee close to her chest and shooting me a beaming smile. "It's so beautiful here."

"You don't miss the city?" I asked, leading her down the gravel driveway towards a field at the furthest edge of the property. There was a pond there with a bench we could sit on, and damn it, why hadn't I packed a picnic? Ugh, I was letting myself down with my lack of forethought.

Grace hummed thoughtfully, taking a sip of her coffee. "A little. I *like* the hustle and bustle, but I also haven't seen much of the world, so spending time out here is nice."

"You've been to Saskatchewan a couple of times, right? Plus that trip to visit your grandparents in Montana. And that one trip to Florida when you were eight," I replied, remembering all the times over the years I'd visited Grace's dreams while she'd been away with her family, usually visiting *more* family.

Agathos had a borderline absurd number of relatives, but population wise, there weren't *that* many of them, at least in relation

157

to humans. I was pretty sure the soul bond thing was a way for the Fates to ensure they didn't all end up bonding with their own cousins.

"It'll never stop being weird when you do that," Grace laughed. "It's kind of nice, having this history together, but weird that I can't remember any of it."

I gave Grace a tight smile and resisted the urge to belt out *Singing In The Rain* at the top of my lungs. 'Weird' wasn't the word I'd use to describe it. More like 'tragic', but I was trying to stay positive.

"Super weird," I replied instead, leading Grace off the path onto the dewy grass, sticking close in case she slipped. "So, today's lesson."

"Teach me, master," Grace said teasingly, her smile soft.

"We need to spend some time talking about your goddess. That's why we're out here," I added, letting my fingers brush through the damp golden leaves hanging overhead. "This is all her creation. The *Earth*. When she's unhappy, the earth is unhappy. Her frustration comes in earthquakes, landslides, volcanic eruptions, flooding, that kind of thing. She's been unhappy a lot lately."

"Why?" Grace frowned as she sipped on her coffee, and I thought about how best to proceed.

"I mean, I sort of get why," Grace continued. "Not even the agathos honor the land, and that was her creation. I've always found that strange."

"I imagine a big part of Age of Heroes Part Two will be a renewed appreciation for the world the gods built for us," I agreed.

"I worry a lot that if we do what this prophecy tells us to do, that there will be consequences we couldn't predict," Grace said, twisting the opal ring on her finger. "My instincts push me to put humans above myself, and I can't help but question if an Age of Heroes would be bad for them."

"Things will be pretty bad if Gaia implodes the Earth," I pointed out, earning me a wry look.

The wind picked up around us, rustling the golden trees and bringing a chill. Was this a sign from Gaia? It was hard to tell with her. The wind gods were from her line, she could communicate through any of her children if she so chose. She just never chose to.

She grieved and fought and struggled.

"Why me?" Grace asked quietly, staring at the ground below her feet as though Gaia would split the earth open and rise out of it the way Hades did when he stole Persephone out of her mother's garden.

"I asked the Goddess that question myself," I replied, knowing she'd be waiting a long time if she expected answers from the earth.

"And?"

"Well... I guess you kind of asked her?" I said hesitantly. Why did I always end up being the bearer of bad news? Why couldn't I bring some light and joy to Grace's life for a change? "You reached out to La Nuit first, you asked for her guidance for your future."

Grace's eyes widened in recognition.

"I get the feeling that there are others like you. Like us. That there were other options, but you chose when you prayed to her for guidance. I think that's what she was saying," I continued. "Maybe not quite like us, but daimon-agathos combos of some kind."

"It was made very clear that there was never another agathos like me," Grace said instantly, shaking her head. "It was mentioned a lot as I got older and hadn't found any of my soul bonds. My parents even checked with the Elders."

She had known one of her soul bonds all along, she just didn't remember me, but semantics.

Not bitter.

Totally fine.

"Agathos society is very structured," I pointed out. "Something that happens in one part of the world might not make its way to the Elders in your region if they didn't want that news to spread. If they didn't want the news about you to spread, it wouldn't have. They obviously decided, for whatever reason, that the consequences were worth it."

Grace sighed heavily, hurting from yet another shitty revelation because that was all I seemed to give her. She twisted the coffee cup lid between her thumbs and resumed walking to the pond, striding straight past me. I knew from a lifetime of talking to Grace that she didn't like anyone to see her vulnerabilities, in her family that was an open invitation for criticism, and it didn't surprise me that she needed a minute to collect herself.

But if Riot was here, she would have walked straight into his arms. He'd gotten past Grace's defenses, and she felt comfortable reaching for him when she needed support.

I started humming Listen under my breath, not wanting to admit that her reaction had stung.

A lifetime of loving Grace and I still hadn't earned that right yet.

No time for bitterness.

Listen was too pensive, it wasn't helping my mood. I switched to *You Can't Stop The Beat* from *Hairspray* and joined Grace on the bench, drumming my fingers against my thighs and forcing myself to stay positive. The burgeoning bond between us wouldn't let me hide behind a smile and a catchy showtune. I had to *feel* it.

160

"What happened to the Olympians?" Grace asked eventually, breaking the borderline awkward silence between us. "They were the gods that intervened in mortal lives, right? Where did they go?"

I leaned back on the bench, tipping my head back and letting the sun warm my skin. "The Goddess of Night was never a fan of mortals, and they were reproducing at a rapid rate. The agathos were already there, the remnants of the original prototype humans I guess, and La Nuit released the daimons to counter them, with Zeus' approval. The more humans there were, the more arrogant they became—there were less sacrifices to the gods, less prayers, all of that stuff. The Olympians enjoyed watching mortals and interfering in their lives for sport, but they couldn't let their hubris slide."

I opened one eye, peeking at Grace to make sure she was paying attention. She was staring at the water, but I was pretty confident she was listening.

"The Olympians thought mortals needed them, but without worship and offerings, they're weak," I continued. "They'd gained strength from mortal worship, mortals gained life from the gods who could also take it away. It was a delicate balance."

"So, the Olympians just faded away without worship?" Grace asked, sounding unimpressed.

"They were weakened. And while they may have been descendents of Gaia and were respectful of her sphere, she never stopped wanting power. From the moment she had her son cut off her consort's balls to overthrow him, she'd craved that ultimate spot at the top of the divine food chain."

Grace's eyes were as wide as saucers, and I guessed it was a little different from the benevolent version of Anesidora that the agathos were fed from birth.

"The details are very sketchy here—my information comes from La Nuit, and even she doesn't seem to know what really happened. Gaia attacked Olympus with some of her children, the Olympians were already weak from human indifference, and then no one knows. Gaia's children died in the battle, and the Age of Man began—a world mostly devoid of gods and magic, where regular humans do whatever they want, might makes right, and so on."

"Gaia took power for herself?" Grace confirmed, frowning like that idea was foreign to her.

I chuckled at the disapproving look on her face. "The agathos were made in Gaia's image. Is a power grab really such an unexpected move?"

Grace shook her head slowly, slumping back against the bench, some of the defensiveness leaching out of her.

"There's no real heroes or villains in this story, Amazing Grace. I can see you looking to pick sides in your head, but gods and goddesses don't operate by the same moral code that we do. It's difficult to say if one is good or bad, they just *are*."

Grace twisted her agathos purity ring around her finger, chewing nervously on her lower lip. "Gaia may be indifferent, but she isn't cruel to mortals. Maybe it was a good thing she seized power…"

"Gaia might blow the Earth up out of sheer frustration if things go on as they are, which does limit options somewhat, unless you're fine with the apocalypse."

I'd be dead anyway, so it didn't particularly bother me. Grace was already shaking her head vigorously though, and I understood at that moment why the Fates had chosen an agathos for this particular task.

Even the very worst agathos were compelled to give a shit about humans. If Grace saw a human in need of help, she wouldn't be able to walk away without bestowing luck on them, knowing full well she'd suffer the consequences of it later. They were Gaia's sacrificial lambs, always willing to serve.

I could have done with Riot right about now. He had a more direct approach to pointing out the bullshit injustices of being an agathos.

"If it makes you feel any better and somehow restoring the old ways is what needs to happen, most of the gods won't be in a hurry to return to whatever state of weakness they've been subsisting in, wherever they are. I'm sure they'd interfere in mortal lives—sometimes for good, sometimes more questionably—but humanity has a weapon to use against them now."

Grace's relief tickled my skin and I exhaled slowly. Oh, maybe I didn't need Riot for this conversation after all.

As if I'd summoned him, my phone buzzed in my pocket and I fought the urge to screen the call, knowing Grace would want to speak to him.

"Hey," I said into the receiver, verifying it was in fact Riot before I handed him over to Grace. I had to make sure Viper hadn't somehow bargained for his phone as well as his soul.

"*Hey. Grace there?*" Hm, I needed to figure out what that Three of Cups message meant, because Riot sounded like shit. I handed the phone over to Grace, whose pale eyes lit up immediately.

"Riot?" she said, voice thick with relief.

Not even a little bit jealous.

I stood up, wandering around the edge of the pond to give them some privacy and ponder our next move. We needed to find the

163

"treasure" the prophecy referenced, whatever that was. In the past, the gods had given heroes weapons and items that would help them on their quest. Maybe that was what we were supposed to find?

Grace would look sexy as hell with sword and shield. I wondered how she'd feel about Amazonian-style leathers. Specifically the tiny skirt thing.

The pond water rippled as a gust of wind blew, evidence of Gaia's creations all around us. She didn't usually respond to mortals, too busy wallowing in her misery, but maybe for Grace she'd make an exception. Not for regular agathos prayers obviously, but if Grace went through the cleansing ritual that Oneiroi had to go through...

When I came of age, like all local Oneiroi, I fasted for two days and traveled to Enders Falls to submerge myself in the natural spring water Gaia provided. It was an ancient practice that the Goddess of Night herself had deemed necessary—her ire had always been saved for mortals, not for her sister who'd created them.

I paused my pacing to stare at my girl, sitting on the bench with the phone still held to her ear. The early morning light showed a few reddish strands in her dark hair, and made her already pale eyes look even more ethereal. She was hunched over, an arm wrapped around her middle, the absence of Riot like a physical ache in her body.

There was no way she'd be willing to make a two-hour trip to Enders Falls right now. Not when Riot was stuck in Milton and she was already struggling with the distance. No, I had to figure out why the Fates had wanted us to get involved with Viper in the first place, and what the Three Of Cups card had meant. We needed to get Riot back.

GRACE

CHAPTER 11

I ended the call with Riot, satisfied he was safe at least even though he sounded miserable, before rejoining Bullet who was waiting for me next to the tree.

"Do you mind if we head back?" Bullet asked. "I think I need to meditate."

"Oh, of course," I said quickly, handing the phone back to him. His pace back to the barn was quick, and I was almost jogging to keep up. Something was obviously on his mind, but I couldn't tell if he wanted to talk about it or if meditation was his own way of handling whatever was bothering him.

Bullet was clearly someone accustomed to always having all the answers, but the answers weren't forthcoming right now. That was a frustration I *could* understand. The connection he had with the Goddess of Night and the Fates—that was not something I could understand. I was more than a little scared of it, and it was affecting the way I connected with Bullet. I hated it. I hated that I was letting my fear of the unknown affect us so much.

Last night, we'd slept in the same bed, but it was nothing like when I shared a bed with Riot and we woke up tangled in each other's arms. Bullet slept like a statue—probably because he was lost in visions the entire time—and I'd felt awkward snuggling up to his still form. It had taken the most ragged edge off my need to connect with him, but it hadn't been satisfying either.

Get it together, Grace, I chastised. Bullet couldn't help the fact that he was an Oneiroi any more than I could help the fact that I was a Eutychia. Neither of us asked for these gifts.

Bullet led me up the stairs to the apartment, and we both ditched our coats and boots just inside the doorway.

"Will you be alright on your own for a bit?" Bullet asked, looking fidgety. His fingers, which were usually drumming a constant rhythm against his thighs, rubbed against each other like he could already imagine the feel of the tarot card between them.

"I'll be fine," I assured him. "I'm going to make some breakfast."

Bullet nodded, already moving towards the top of the stairs. He paused, fishing his phone out of his pants pocket and leaving it on the dining table before taking a few steps back and disappearing down into the lower level of the barn.

Strange.

I made a bowl of yogurt and granola which I ate standing over the kitchen counter, before washing up and tidying the kitchen. Bullet had really been pampering me since I'd been here, but I was missing my usual routines. Little things like my morning run, or deep cleaning the kitchen on a Thursday, or changing my sheets every Tuesday. I was someone who thrived on structure, with checklists and color coordinated reminders on my phone.

I felt a bit adrift out here, killing time until… *until, until, until.* Until we had more answers. Until Riot was back. Until the agathos stopped looking for me.

There were so many 'until' scenarios, I couldn't even keep them all straight in my head. It was making me twitchy.

The morning sun streamed in through the double doors that led to the deck, catching on Bullet's cellphone that he'd left sitting on the dining table, calling to me like a siren song.

Don't do it.

I wasn't entirely sure what Riot's agreement with Viper entailed, but I knew he was trapped in that deal to keep me safe. All I had to do was not tell anyone where I was.

The phone was practically calling out to me though. No, it wasn't the phone, it was a whisper in my ear. Something ancient and powerful that seemed to push me towards the device with promises of friendship and rebellion, alliances and change.

My feet were moving before my brain had caught up. There was no passcode on the phone, and I immediately opened the browser and searched for 'Lyon Construction', relieved that there was a cellphone number listed for the owner, Felix Lyon. I had no idea how I'd even attempt to explain my call to a receptionist, and not for the first time, I wished I could tell the occasional lie.

That sense of rightness was still in my ear, telling me I was doing the right thing as I hit 'call' and held the phone up to my ear, my heart thundering in my chest. I forced myself to take calming breaths on the off-chance Bullet could feel my emotions from where he was meditating downstairs. It was only a few rings, but they seemed louder and slower somehow, like the phone was making this as ominous as possible.

"*Felix Lyon,*" he answered gruffly.

Felix's voice was steadier than it had been the last time I'd heard it—at his bonded's memorial service—but I swore I could still hear the grief in it from those two words. Nausea churned in my gut and I very seriously questioned my sanity for making this call even as the ancient presence in my mind seemed to whisper that it was okay, that all would be well.

"*Hello?*" he asked impatiently. "*Anyone there?*"

"Um, hello," I rasped, voice shaky.

I should have written this down or rehearsed in front of the mirror or something.

"*Miss? Are you alright?*"

That was a very nice question. Goddess knew what was going through his head as I basically hyperventilated down the line.

I took a deep breath, willing my nerves to settle and forced the words out. "I shouldn't be calling you. I'm calling at great personal risk to myself and people that I care about, and I'm hoping you won't throw me to the wolves, but I had to warn you..."

Why did I have to warn him? I didn't owe him anything. At the same time, it felt wrong not to say something.

"*Grace Bellamy,*" he said softly. "*You're the talk of the town, you know.*"

"I'm sure," I replied with a shaky laugh. The agathos had always whispered about me behind my back, now it was happening on a bigger scale. There were probably prayer circles being held in my honor.

"Are you in trouble? They said a daimon snatched you away and threatened to kill them all. That he would have killed you if they hadn't let you go."

I opened my mouth to argue and realized that technically was the truth. Truth enough that they could run with that story, leaving out their own sordid involvement.

"Riot is a daimon and *my soul bond*," I said firmly, ignoring Felix's gasp of surprise. "He said what he needed to say to get me back when the Basilinna and the Elders took me from my workplace *"for my own good"* and dragged me down to the altar. They began the cleansing rituals with the intention of breaking the connection between Riot and I, and installing me as a replacement for your bonded, Joy."

There was *silence* on the other end of the phone and I cringed to myself, thinking I could have probably handled that more tactfully. Once I'd started talking, the words just seemed to explode out of me.

"I am very sorry for your loss," I added hastily. "It was obvious to everyone at her memorial how much you loved Joy."

"Yes," Felix rasped. *"Which is why I can't understand why anyone would think we'd be interested in replacing her. I mean no disrespect—"*

"I'm sure we both find the idea appalling," I reassured him, smiling a little to myself at the discomfort we both obviously felt at the concept. "I met Riot the day of... of Joy's accident. The Basilinna chose to interpret that as a sign from Anesidora."

This was a risky conversation. I wasn't pulling my punches with my criticism of the Basilinna, and frankly that was cause enough to get shipped off on an outreach trip, never to be seen again. But I wasn't going to play by the rules of a community I was no longer a part of.

Let them try to send me away. I was already gone.

"It is convenient that Anesidora's silence can be interpreted to fit the agenda of the Basilinna and the Elders so well."

Relief seemed to unfurl like a tight ball in my chest, flowing out through my veins.

"It does seem convenient," I agreed, not entirely sure what to say now I'd thrown all the information at him.

"Convenient also the way they described the confrontation with your soul bond. I don't know much about daimons, I haven't interacted with them much, but I do know what it feels like to find part of your soul in another person, and I wouldn't wish the breaking of that connection on anyone."

I wanted to break down in tears thinking about it. I couldn't even comprehend the pain he and Joy's other bonded were in.

"There was a meeting the night you left," Felix volunteered. *"All adults were required to attend. It was heavily implied that your daimon took you because he could. That all agathos women were at risk of being snatched off the street. I'm ashamed to admit, I bought into the paranoia myself. Most agathos women in Auburn are cooped up at home right now for their own safety."*

Oh no. I didn't want that. The daimons were already suffering because of me, I didn't want any agathos to suffer as well.

"But when three of your parents stood up to speak at the meeting," he continued, and I held my breath. *"There was a sense of discomfort in the room. No one was speaking openly about it, but the way Faith and Valor spoke about the situation... They didn't speak about you at all."*

"Well that's not entirely unexpected," I muttered. I could imagine it now—the two of them stoically standing side by side, making moralistic arguments about the evils of daimons.

Felix scoffed. *"I have a daughter. Liberty. If it were me up there and I thought she was in danger, I would have done nothing but speak of how much I loved her. I'd beg to get her back. I'd have told everyone in the room about how sweet and kind she is, and I'd offer them my worldly goods on a platter to ensure her safe return."*

Wow.

Was I so used to having indifferent, bordering on hostile, parents that I hadn't even realized how abnormal their response was? I didn't even have children, but I knew in my bones that I'd feel exactly the way Felix described if I thought my hypothetical kids were in trouble.

"Earnest cried," Felix added. *"And spoke of how much he missed you and just wanted you to be safe. Creed and Chance weren't there."*

The only ones who'd been in the basement were Valor and Faith, and by the sounds of it, Chance had been the one to help Riot come to my rescue. How much did the others know through the bond with my mother?

"I'm not sure Chance approves of their actions," I said carefully. "I doubt Creed would either, but he's busy with the two boys."

Felix hesitated for a moment. *"Can I pass on a message to Chance for you?"*

The idea was *so* tempting, but the risk…

"I want to, but I don't know how easy it is to keep secrets with a bond. I don't want to put him in a difficult position." I blushed, realizing I'd just admitted that I hadn't consummated the bond with Riot.

"You're right, it would be difficult for him. If you change your mind, tell me. There's always a way."

"Thank you," I breathed. "Will you stay in Auburn?"

Felix sighed heavily. *"My younger brother, Harbor, was sent away. Outreach trip, you know how it goes."* I nodded even though Felix couldn't see me, my throat tight. *"His messages are… cryptic."*

I stilled. "Cryptic?"

"My family have wondered for a long time what he's really doing. Where he really is. Joy wanted us to find him…"

"Where was he sent?"

"Russia, in theory."

"And in reality?"

"He sent us a postcard from Maine."

Maine was definitely not Russia. At the same time, agathos couldn't lie. My parents had been truthful when they were talking about the plan to send me to Indonesia.

"I don't want my kids here with everything that's going on," Felix said heavily. *"And I want to know what happened to Harbor. But you have my number. Don't be afraid to use it, Grace. You always have an ally among me and my family."*

"Thank you, Felix. Take care of yourselves."

I hung up, staring down at the phone and trying to keep my whirlwind of emotions under control so as not to alarm Bullet. I wanted to delete the record from his call history, but I physically couldn't make my finger move. My agathos instincts roared in my head, telling me it was dishonest. *Not allowed. Not acceptable.*

Growling in frustration, I set the phone down on the table, and paced back and forth. There had been such a strong sense of *rightness* when I'd made that call, like there was a goddess whispering in my ear to do it, but now that it was done, I wondered if it was more a temporary break in sanity than instructions from the divine.

I was hiding from the agathos and I'd *called* an agathos. That seemed like a monumentally idiotic decision in hindsight. It would be different if it was someone I knew, someone I trusted, but Felix was basically a stranger to me and I'd put a lot of faith in him not to sell me out.

Still, he'd put a lot of faith in me too by telling me about Harbor. I didn't know him—from memory, Felix wasn't originally from Auburn, he'd moved there when Joy had found him. I'd only seen Joy's bonded around at community events, I'd certainly never met their families.

I should have asked where he was from. If Elders everywhere were like the ones in Auburn who'd been so happy to send me away just for not fitting their prescribed mold.

The phone seemed to be staring at me as I thought about the one agathos that I *could* trust without question. The one I really *did* want to talk to.

It was a selfish desire. I had given up every part of my old life in the span of a few hours and just walked away. While I was glad to be gone, there were definitely things that I missed—my apartment, the humans I helped at the shelter, my routine, but mostly Mercy. I missed her like crazy, and I couldn't help but feel that by upping and leaving, I'd caused her to suffer.

If only I could send her a message to let her know I was okay...

I drummed my nails on the wooden table, staring at the phone.

Don't do it. Someone will ask if she's heard from me, and she'll be forced to say yes.

Mercy wasn't stupid, though. If I gave her enough plausible deniability...

Mercy's number was one of the few I had memorized, and I quickly tapped it in and opened a new message. When she'd first moved to Auburn, she'd been super intimidated by the enormous houses and ostentatious wealth of the agathos community compared to the small town in Saskatchewan where she'd grown up. For the first few months, we used to quietly come up with the worst dad jokes to whisper to each other at social events to put her at ease, though she hadn't needed the crutch in recent months.

Still, hopefully she'd remember our little game.

Me: *Did you hear the rumor about butter? Well, I'm not going to spread it.*

I watched as two little ticks appeared, nervously waiting to see if she'd respond. If I got a random joke from an unknown number, I'd probably assume they either sent it to the wrong person or they were a creep.

Three little dots popped up and I sucked in a hopeful breath.

Mercy: *Where do young trees go to learn? Elementree school.*

I giggled quietly, forcing myself to exit the messaging app and put the phone down. I still couldn't make myself delete the messages, but I rationalized in my head that with the evidence right there, I wasn't really lying to Bullet.

There wasn't even any guarantee that Mercy knew that message was from me, but I was choosing to believe she knew. I was choosing to believe that had given her some peace of mind, in the way her response had given me some peace of mind.

I was choosing to believe that in prioritizing my own safety, I hadn't cost myself my relationship with my best friend, and that maybe someday we could get that relationship back. That Mercy could stay safe and content while I dealt with gods and prophecies, and yet we could eventually find some kind of normalcy in whatever world emerged from this. Hopefully, a world where agathos and daimons were two sides of the same coin rather than mortal enemies.

My head ached, my brain physically rejecting the lie I was trying to tell myself. Maybe that world would exist, and maybe Mercy and I could have some kind of friendship again in the future.

But things would never be the same again.

RIOT

CHAPTER 12

I dragged my tired, aching body up the metal stairs to Viper's office, wondering if the Goddess of Night liked Grace and Bullet enough to give Viper a slow and painful death as a favor to me. I was on day four of servitude to the biggest dickhead in Milton, and was feeling relatively homicidal. Maybe I'd be coping better if I was at least going home to Grace each night. At this point the achy lethargy of being apart from her with an incomplete bond had morphed into something more vicious that seemed to be clawing me apart from the inside.

I'd sworn I'd always take things at Grace's pace and I meant that, but I was going to bring up the whole bond thing when I got back to her. If I ever got back to her. We at least needed to have that conversation. I needed to have hope we'd get to that level some day. That I wouldn't spend the rest of my life living with a steady hum of agony seeping through my bones and an itch on my skin.

Fuck, or be in pain.

What a benevolent goddess the agathos had.

With the state of emergency and Milton full of troops, Viper couldn't utilize me to the extent he wanted. I was one of the two people they were looking for, after all. I'd spent my downtime boarding up the window in Dare's studio and cleaning it as best I could, but today my reprieve was over and I'd been summoned.

As usual, the agathos' lack of knowledge about daimons was playing into our favor. The patrols were mostly active at night and practically non-existent during the day, since they clearly thought all daimons were vampires or something. Morons.

Aside from all that, Milton was our turf. It was daimon through and through. The agathos could huff and puff all they liked, but they weren't blowing our town down.

"How's my favorite servant today?" Viper asked with a smug grin that I desperately wanted to punch off his stupid face as I shut his office door behind me.

It was worth it, I reminded myself. Yesterday Viper had informed me that two of Grace's dads had flown to Florida, following the wild goose chase Viper had sent them on. He'd upped his game after the agathos had shown up here looking for Grace. There were now two human body doubles on his payroll, acting suspicious as they made appearances on security cameras around Orlando.

Viper was a prick, but he was a useful prick, so I had to accept the fact I'd sold my soul to him. I didn't have to act happy about it though.

"What do you need me for?" I asked flatly, crossing my arms across my chest, mostly to disguise what rough shape I was in from being apart from my Gracie. I wasn't about to show any signs of weakness in front of the snake. Not that I could do much about my face.

Viper tutted ominously. "Maybe I should make you bow so you learn a little respect."

"You're a seedy dealmaker that lives in your office above a shitty gym, not fucking Littlefinger. I've already given you more respect than you deserve," I drawled.

"Careful," Viper warned, eyes flashing dangerously. "Would be a terrible shame if your girlfriend's parents suddenly discovered her whereabouts."

I tamped down the rage that rose in response to any threat against Grace before Viper had the satisfaction of seeing it. "By all means, break the deal. I'd love to see how the Goddess punishes her least favorite daimon. Maybe we can find you a new nickname while we're at it. Oathbreaker, perhaps, like in the old days. Liar. Shell of a person filled with self-loathing and daddy issues—"

"The Goddess won't consider the deal void if I slit your fucking throat," Viper snarled, slamming his hands down on the desk and rising to his feet. "Your life was not part of the arrangement."

"Ah, but then you'd lose your favorite servant. So, what'll it be, oh wise reptilian one?"

I was being a little more cavalier than I usually would in the face of someone threatening to slit my throat, but maybe some of Bullet's confidence was rubbing off on me. I doubted he would have sent me here if my life was in danger, and I was choosing to trust him.

I mean, I was already trusting Bullet with the most precious thing in my life. My life was nothing compared to that.

"There's a human by the name of Gary Moss who owes me money. I told him I'd make his life hell if he didn't pay up, and I intend to keep my word. You'll find him at the casino on Stratford, probably at the slot machines. Go on, *Moros*. Make his life hell."

Viper sat back down, pulling his laptop towards him in a clear sign of dismissal.

"Of course, your most slithery one," I replied, inclining my head sarcastically before leaving Viper's office, fishing my lighter out of my pocket and flicking it to life, only a little tempted to burn this whole fucking place to the ground. Thanks to my hard work, the gym was now in decent condition after the agathos attack. In some respects, this place had gotten off lightly because it didn't have any windows to smash on the ground floor. The agathos had still thrown a firecracker through the door though.

If I hadn't been the one stuck cleaning it up, I would have celebrated. Dare and I worked out here for lack of any better options, but Viper deserved a serving of humble pie. He thought he was such a gangster, but he wasn't even the biggest powerbroker in Milton.

I stomped down the stairs, wanting to check in with Grace again, but I never chanced calling her anywhere Viper might overhear our conversation. As far as anyone knew, Grace was only my girl—the connection between her and Bullet was still under wraps, which was exactly how I wanted to keep it. Even though a weird part of me felt guilty that he wasn't being acknowledged. Like I was taking something from him or whatever.

I was going soft in my old age.

I put the lighter away and shoved on the bike helmet before I walked out the door, grateful that it disguised my identity as I made a beeline for the Harley. Also grateful for the Harley in general. It roared to life underneath me and I wondered how nice I'd have to be to Bullet to convince him to let me keep it. It was really more my style than his, it seemed only fair.

I sped towards the casino, no clue what I was going to do when I got there. I had to do *something* though, to honor my end of the deal. But I didn't want to use my Moros abilities on some human just because he'd been dumb enough to make a deal with Viper. It's not like I had room to judge on that front.

Fuck, I might *have* to use them, unless I could think of a way to make his life hell that didn't involve shoving him roughly in the direction of his mortal downfall. Being around humans was a constant battle with my Moros instincts anyway, and I was irritable as fuck from being away from Grace and stuck under Viper's scaly thumb.

At least I'd be able to get into this place. The casino was owned by a daimon named Creep who didn't entirely dislike me, unlike most of the other club owners in Milton, which was a positive.

I parked the bike in the underground garage and made my way through the dilapidated foyer, forcing my mind to concentrate on Grace and her soft smiles and eyes like jewels to give me a sense of peace. Subconsciously, my hand found my lighter again, the noise of flicking it on and off grounding me.

It didn't quite drown out the whispers—the Moros in me telling me what exactly would push these humans over the edge, set them on their path to self-destruction. Often it was drugs, but for others it was violence or greed, too much confidence and not enough caution. My head pounded at the effort of rejecting each one, forcing the instinct to act on them away.

Grace. I need to speak to Grace.

I stumbled out to the front of the building to find somewhere quiet to talk, constantly looking out for any agathos in uniform that might be hanging around. They tended to stay close to her old apartment, assuming I guess that she would return there at some point.

She probably would, if she had the chance. Grace loved that place, and she'd made it into the perfect little sanctuary for herself. I hated that she had to leave it behind.

Fuck, I missed her more than I could comprehend. Grace's sweetness was a better cure for my bad mood than any drug on the planet. It wasn't only that the urge to seal the bond with her that was riding me hard, it was also that I knew Grace and cared for her—bond or not.

Maybe *more* than just cared for her, but I wasn't entirely sure I knew what that emotion looked like.

There was an alleyway along the side of the brick building which I turned down, intending to find some privacy to call Grace, but the sound of voices gave me pause. I couldn't see past the giant dumpster in the way, so I leaned back against the wall, listening to the agitated man on the other side.

I'd know my dad's voice anywhere.

"Listen here, you little shit."

Wow, it was like being transported back to my childhood. I was almost offended that 'little shit' wasn't a term of endearment saved exclusively for me.

"You have one day to pay me what you owe me. Did I not give you the best experience of your life? Did I not tailor a concoction specifically to your liking?"

I almost snorted at that. He'd tailored a concoction based on what would create the most effective addiction.

The human stuttered and mumbled some apologies, and that gnawing guilt I got whenever I used my abilities reared its head. There was no way I could use my abilities on the human Viper had sicced me on. I didn't want to look in the mirror and see my dad's soulless eyes staring back at me because I didn't have the courage to find a different solution.

Grace deserved a better man than the one I'd been. She deserved better than me, period, but it was too late for that. I'd sunk my claws into Gracie and I wasn't going to let her go.

I pulled out my phone and searched for cop siren sound effects on YouTube, setting the volume to the lowest setting so it would sound further away, then letting it play.

"*Fuck*," Dad hissed. There was a thud that I assumed was the sound of the poor human being dropped on the ground. "I'll be back for my money."

I pressed my back against the wall, letting the shadow of the dumpster hide me as my dad legged it out of the alleyway, moving faster than I'd ever seen him move in his life. An out-of-it looking human stumbled after him, and I rolled my eyes as I watched him follow my dad's exact footsteps.

You could lead a horse to water, but you couldn't make it not follow the fucking drug dealer who'd just been threatening him.

I let the sound loop for a few minutes, turning it up occasionally so it sounded like the sirens were getting closer, before closing the video. But before I could call Grace, my phone started buzzing.

"Dare?" I asked in surprise, holding the phone to my ear. "Everything okay?"

He laughed. *"You're asking me that? You're the wanted man, I'm fucking bored out of my skull. Let's gossip. Talk about your girlfriend. Anything."*

"Is your mom not stimulating enough company for you?" I teased. Dare's mom was pretty great, as far as daimon parents went. Philotes daimons weren't as psychotic as the rest of us though, since their thing was sex. In the 21st century, wanton sex with whoever wasn't quite the taboo it had been way back in the day anyway.

Dare blew out a long breath. *"My mom is cool, but the stress is driving us both crazy right now."*

"The stress over what happened here?"

"It's not just Milton, man. News about you and your girl has spread all over the place. Tensions are high as fuck out here in Jersey. Someone followed me back to my mom's place the other night and slashed my tires. People are fighting in the street, not as discreet as they should be. That kind of thing."

Oh shit. This whole situation had spiraled way beyond what I'd expected. Grace would be devastated if she knew there was more violence unfolding because of our relationship.

Then again, there was that whole prophecy thing. Regardless of what was happening in other cities, our relationship was obviously already bigger than us.

"It's not your fault," Dare said, reading my mind. *"Sometimes I think they were waiting for an opportunity, you know? This was the excuse they needed to drop the thin veneer of civility. How are you holding up? And the girl? Grace, right?"*

It was weird that I didn't get that same protective instinct over Grace when Dare asked about her as I did when Viper so much as hinted at her existence. I'd never got that weird protective instinct when Bullet talked about Grace either, even when he occasionally irritated me.

I may not be the smartest guy, and I doubted I'd be the brains of Grace's harem, but I wasn't a total moron, and that gut feeling I had about both Bullet and Dare wasn't a coincidence.

That wasn't a conversation to have over the phone though.

"She's safe," I replied, unwilling to elaborate on the off-chance this phone call was being listened to somehow. "And I'm stuck with the snake, trying to uphold my end of the bargain."

"Which was?"

"I mean, it was pretty much a blank check," I admitted. "Apparently I don't make good decisions under pressure."

Dare snorted. *"I could have told you that. Fuck's sake, Riot, what were you thinking?"*

"Yeah, yeah. Help me out of my dilemma. I'm supposed to give some guy hell at Creep's casino because he owes Viper money. You know how I feel about using my gifts," I snorted.

"So don't?" Dare replied, like it was obvious. *"Sounds like a vague enough order. If I was a guy who loved the casino, I guess my hell would be not going to the casino anymore. Tell Creep I'll fix that abomination of a skull tattoo on his chest free of charge if he bans the guy."*

That... that was a very smart idea. Maybe Dare would be the brains of the harem, if my hunch was correct.

"I guess you're not just a pretty face after all," I teased, relief coursing through me that I had a plan that didn't involve me following in my father's footsteps.

"I also have a huge dick," Dare agreed. *"I'll leave you to your plotting, there are some shifty looking fuckers across the street in their pressed khaki pants and white polos who need reminding about which part of town they belong in."*

I grimaced at the thought. Dare could hold his own, but he was a lover not a fighter. His line wasn't violent. They were mostly horny.

"Good luck. Don't get arrested."

Dare laughed. *"This face is too pretty for prison. I'll be good."*

The line went dead and I forced myself not to worry. He was a big boy. He could handle himself.

Maybe I'd ask Bullet to check in on him, just in case.

I quickly scanned the alleyway to make sure I was alone before returning to my sad spot by the dumpster and dialing Bullet, tapping my foot impatiently as I wanted for him to pick up. If he didn't, I'd plow through the agathos barricade and head out to his place myself, consequences be damned.

"Quiet Riot. How's the snake den?"

"About as unpleasant as you'd expect it to be," I replied curtly. "Can you check in on Dare for me?"

There was a beat of silence on the other end, probably surprised that I'd asked him for help. It wasn't that I didn't *believe* in Bullet's gift, I just didn't like it. I didn't want to believe that the future was all laid out for us, that we had no control over our fate.

"Of course," Bullet said, unusually serious. It was rare that Bullet's cheerful mask slipped, usually he was so careful about keeping it up. These days, at least. When Bullet was younger, he hadn't tried so hard to conceal his bitterness about his fate.

"And you? How are you doing?"

"Worried about me, Riot?" he teased, deflecting as always. As much as I wanted to complete the bond with Grace, assuming it would give me a better read on her emotions than I got now, I suspected Bullet needed it more. He was better at making sure people only saw what he wanted them to see.

"Don't be a dick for a minute," I sighed. "How long until your birthday?"

The big 3-0. No Oneiroi had ever lived past that day. Bullet would though. I had to believe that. He was Grace's soul bond, he already wasn't like other Oneiroi.

"Still three months to go," Bullet replied, his bright tone sounding significantly more forced.

"Does Grace know about the, er, possibility?"

"She has enough on her plate," Bullet said dismissively. *"I'll get her for you."*

I heard a shuffle of movement in the background and my stupid heart skipped a beat knowing that I was about to talk to Grace again, even though I'd spoken to her at least once every day I'd been stuck here. Once I got back to the farm and he couldn't run away, I was going to make sure Bullet and I finished that conversation.

"Riot?" There was so much worry packed into that one word that I wanted nothing more than to go straight back to the countryside and pull Grace into my arms.

"Hey, Gracie. How's everything going?" I asked, forcing myself to not sound like I was so tightly strung I was about to snap, because that probably wouldn't make things easier on her end.

"I'm extremely worried, and your everything-is-fine voice is not persuading me that I shouldn't be," Grace replied. The bite in her voice was weirdly soothing. I liked when Grace's impeccably polite facade slipped a little.

Making emotional confessions didn't come naturally to me—it would have earned me a beating from my dad back in the day—but that was a hangup I was determined to overcome for Grace's sake. She deserved to hear how I was feeling, and I got the impression from meeting her psychotic family that she hadn't been told nearly enough that she was wonderful and beautiful and special.

"I miss you like fucking crazy," I said matter of factly. "I feel like my skin is on fire and I am exhausted, but I can't sleep. Whatever shit I'm dealing with here is *nothing* compared to being away from you."

"Riot," Grace breathed, her agitation replaced by that soft tenderness she possessed in spades and I had none of. *"I'm losing my mind without you."*

This better fucking improve after we were bonded, because this crawl-out-of-my-skin sensation was no way for anyone to live. At first, I'd thought the incessant itchy discomfort was an improvement over the genuine *pain* we'd both been in with the unfulfilled bond. Now, I wasn't so convinced. Either way, Grace's goddess was a psycho for punishing us just because we hadn't had sex yet.

"Can you tell me what you're doing?" Grace asked, sounding like she already knew the answer. I couldn't, knowing it might challenge her instincts not to lie, cheat or steal, but I didn't want to anyway. I didn't want this shit to touch her.

"Running errands for Viper. How are you holding up? Are you getting comfortable with your new roommate?"

"He's been nothing but kind and hospitable," Grace replied immediately. *"A perfect gentleman."*

Hmm, a perfect gentleman, huh? Was Grace into that? I had been mostly gentlemanly, as much as I could with the bonding urges driving me out of my fucking mind. But they also drove her out of her fucking mind, and the gentlemanly thing to do in those situations was to give her a hand.

Literally.

"Are you not getting what you need, Gracie?" I asked, my voice instinctively dropping a little lower.

There was a heartbeat of hesitation, enough to tell me that she wanted to say she was, but she couldn't lie about it.

Apparently Bullet needed to up his game.

The voice of noisy chatter as people exited the casino pulled me out of the moment, reminding me where I was and that I still had a job to do.

"Fuck. I need to go, Gracie, but I'll call you later, okay?" I hesitated, hating to help him out because while I didn't *hate* the idea of Bullet around Grace, the idea of *sharing* her with him was still foreign and sort of horrific. Fuck it, this could be my kind deed after all the psychic help he'd given me. "Bullet never dated when we were teenagers and all went to school together. He never so much as *looked* at anyone that way. You've always been his endgame, but maybe you're a little more intimidating in the flesh."

"I'm the intimidating one?" Grace repeated in disbelief. *"He's so... mystical. The gift he has is incredibly intimidating. I see what you're saying though. Maybe I should be more, um, forward?"* If I closed my eyes, I could imagine her face as she said it, nose scrunched up. *"Don't forget to call me, Riot. The only time I'm not panicking about you is when I can hear your voice."*

I rubbed at the sudden ache in my chest, wondering what the hell was happening to me.

"I won't forget," I managed to get out hoarsely, hanging up before I did something stupid like blurting out that I loved her when I didn't even know what that felt like.

Get your shit together, Riot. I pushed off the wall, shoving my phone into my pocket as I stalked towards the entrance to the casino. *This is for Grace.* I'd do whatever I had to do to keep her safe, to uphold my deal with the devil, because there was no question in my mind that she was worth it.

DARE

CHAPTER 13

Well, this had proven to be an anticlimactic afternoon.

The moment I emerged with a switchblade and violence in my eyes, the two agathos in front of me had turned tail and fled. I'd been stalking them now for two blocks, herding them towards a daimon neighborhood so I could give them a proper warning to fuck off back to whatever gated community they'd emerged from.

Sure, the switchblade alone was intimidating when I looked this feral, but a well-worded threat to cut their dicks off if they ever hung around my mom's house again would probably be more effective, and I was nothing if not a perfectionist.

In general, I was a pretty peaceful dude. Philotes were the least violent daimons in existence, and it took a lot to piss us off. But the agathos had been a thorn in my side for days now—first in Milton when they trashed my studio, and now here in my mom's town. News spread fast, apparently. Riot was *famous*.

The two agathos in front of me were walking at a rapid clip, heads ducked, which is why they didn't spot the daimon who stepped out of the bar in front of them, a feral grin lighting up his face when he saw who was headed his way.

"Boo," he whispered, advancing on the two agathos.

They stopped with a gasp, and I closed the distance between us, giving the daimon a nod over their heads before grabbing them by the scruff of their collars and dragging them into an alleyway, surprised at how easily they came. I worked out and I had decent upper body strength, but I was like some kind of giant, stacked Keres daimon who could easily pick up two dudes and throw them across the room.

Their lack of struggle cooled the rage in my blood, and I shoved them back against the brick wall with more exasperation than anger. If they were smart, they'd recognize I was a safer bet than the grizzly old dude who looked like he'd been gunning for blood.

They spun to face me, backs pressed against the wall, and I half expected them to piss themselves, they looked that afraid. On closer inspection, I doubted they were older than 14. They were tall, but gangly, like they hadn't quite grown into their limbs yet, and their faces were still youthfully round with a few stray whiskers in place of a beard.

Huh. One of them was of Asian descent like me, and one had olive skin with dark hair. They reminded me of myself and Riot at that age, except we'd worn skinny jeans and Green Day hoodies, not khakis and polo shirts.

Maybe the resemblance was why I couldn't find it in me to teach them a proper lesson. That, and they were kids. I wasn't a total monster.

I groaned, running a hand through my hair. "Why the fuck am I spending my day chasing after *teenagers*? Don't you have homework to do? Dance challenge videos to make? Whatever the fuck teenagers do these days."

You're 29, not 89, I reminded myself. I just felt old on the inside.

"You, you people have been taking our women," my little agathos clone said in a shaky voice, glancing nervously at his friend, aka Baby Riot, who nodded in encouragement.

I pinned him with my best *'you can't be serious'* face. "*One* agathos woman in Milton has a connection with a daimon. Like one of your supernatural, Goddess-y connections. Whatever bullshit you've been fed is just that—bullshit. I literally know the guy, he didn't *take* anyone."

"We can't be soul bonds with your kind," Mini Dare replied, shaking his head. "He must have taken her against her will because he realized our women are better than yours. And it will keep happening if we don't stop it. We have to show you that we won't stand aside and let you take our women. That we don't want daimon women in return either."

I laughed before I could stop myself. "A daimon woman would eat you alive and you'd thank her for the privilege. I know your kind can't lie, but it sounds like you've been fed some half truths designed to freak you out."

I crossed my arms, waiting patiently for them to process that. I didn't know much about the agathos, and Riot had been hella secretive about his girl, but one thing I knew for sure was Grace's people snatched her out from under him and dragged her back to Auburn against her will.

"You're young and stupid for coming here, but I also think you're being fucked with by the powers that be. Ask some more questions, be a little more observant, and for the love of all the goddesses, do not come back here if you want to leave with your faces intact. Got it?"

Baby Riot nodded, elbowing Mini Dare to get him to move while I lounged against the opposite wall, watching them flee. This whole situation was fucked up. Hopefully those *kids* had chosen to come here and start shit because they thought they were tough and not because the agathos leaders were sending boys whose voices were still breaking out to do their dirty work.

Nothing would surprise me—I didn't know what was going on anymore. It felt like the world as I knew it was falling apart around me, but everyone was too deep in their rage to see it.

I pushed off the wall, making sure the switchblade was safely stowed in my pocket before striding out of the alleyway. I was intending to head straight back home, but I ducked into a convenience store for a giant energy drink to tide me over for the walk back.

Fuck, I was tired. One time, Riot and I had skimmed some pills from his dad's stash and stayed up for 48 hours straight at a music festival, and I thought I was tired *then*. That was nothing compared to the bone-deep exhaustion I felt now. I generally didn't sleep much anyway, but even when I laid down to rest on the shitty foldout in Mom's study, I never felt like I could actually switch off.

Not when a war was low-key breaking out around us. It wasn't even that low-key anymore—humans had started noting the increase in violence on the news. What had started in Milton had spread up and down the East Coast, and I got the feeling it wasn't going to stop.

Especially not if the agathos were convinced that daimons were out to steal *all* their women. Fucking drama llamas. I'd already had to convince a few local daimons that I actually knew Riot, that no, he hadn't abducted his girl, and that there seemed to be bigger forces at play here. We weren't the most religious bunch, but most daimons respected the Goddess of Night enough to mind their business if they suspected she had a hand in something.

If anything the daimons were *excited*, which didn't necessarily help the situation. The older ones in particular were practically foaming at the mouth at the idea of kicking some agathos ass. I didn't have to worry too much about my mom getting involved with her Philotes blood, but I dreaded to think about what Riot's dad was up to back in Milton. He'd probably made a decorative wreath out of agathos bones and intestines to hang on his front door.

I dragged my feet along the sidewalk back towards my mom's place, not particularly rushing to get back in case Mom had a "guest" over again. An affinity for sex and physical touch was a pretty good trait to have as far as daimons went, but it was a little traumatizing when it was my mom. Worse still, she'd been on my case about the *lack* of action I was getting, which was not doing great things for my ego. No one wanted their mom pointing out that they hadn't got laid in a while.

I wasn't just a piece of meat with a great dick attached. I had feelings. I wanted sex with *feelings*. Was that too much to ask? It was a constant struggle with the constant urge to fuck everything that moved, but the idea of going out and hooking up with someone to satisfy cravings imposed on me by a higher power was so demeaning.

Usually, I was able to get by flirting with humans and encouraging them to get frisky, as well as getting my own fill of physical touch from tattooing. Well, not really, but it was enough to take the edge off. I didn't even have that at the moment.

Too bad Riot wasn't here. Back in high school, he used to let me cuddle him sometimes when I was feeling particularly needy, because he was a bro like that even though he was all "daimons don't have friends". I was missing my bestie, for sure.

I wound around the obnoxiously large pool in the center of the complex where my mom lived and pulled out the key she'd given me to let myself in the door.

"Hey, Ma," I called, stopping in the doorway to remove my shoes and put them neatly on the shelf in the entryway so she didn't disown me.

"That didn't take long," she replied from the kitchen where she was making nikujaga for dinner. If I was going to be stuck here for the foreseeable future, I was going to bully her into making all my favorite meals.

She had taught me how to make them all myself before she moved away from Milton a few years ago, but food just tastes better when other people make it.

"Yeah, they were literal children," I said, veering left towards the small dining nook and galley kitchen. This place was the antithesis of my style. It was a serviced apartment type place—a bunch of connected units built around a communal pool area, with an on-site gym and cafe. Mom had always dreamed of resort-style living on a tropical island somewhere, but she hadn't quite achieved that goal.

I was 90% sure she was banging the human owner of this place, but I tried not to think too much about that. We all had to get our touch fixes somewhere. Whenever gentlemen callers showed up, I disappeared into the small study with the foldout couch that I was sleeping on and blasted the volume on my headphones so loud I was surprised I hadn't popped an eardrum yet.

Mom pottered around the kitchen, her long black hair clipped messily out of the way, and her chic black clothes looking at odds with the beige-on-gray-on-beige color scheme that was this entire house.

She glared at the empty energy drink can in my hand, swiping it for the recycling while muttering under her breath about how I needed to respect my body more. She'd lose her shit if she knew how many things I'd sampled while Riot was dealing.

"They're sending children now?" Mom scoffed. "Disgusting."

"I don't know if they're *sending* them or not. At first I thought the agathos men were all riled up and acting of their own accord, but these two were kids who'd been fed some half truths and were confused as fuck. They didn't seem that bad, honestly," I said, ducking behind her to grab a beer from the fridge before sitting at the dining table, out of the way.

"You're too soft," Mom scolded, stabbing her wooden spoon in the air at me. "You can't even go home right now because of what those people have done to your city."

I hummed absently, not agreeing or disagreeing. Maybe she was right, but those kids weren't like the psychos who'd shown up in Milton in the early hours of the morning with baseball bats and firecrackers. They were just... kids. If it weren't for the freaky eyes, I might have mistaken them for regular human teenagers.

We all did dumb stuff when we were young, right? Not *hang around outside people's homes and harass them* level of dumb, but regular dumb. My willingness to take on any dare anyone ever gave me was how I'd earned my nickname.

"I personally have had enough of living in the shadows," Mom continued, aggressively adding potatoes to the pan with the sizzling beef and onions.

"We can't *not* live in the shadows," I pointed out. Our existence was so thoroughly hidden from humans, even our human *parent* had no idea their offspring was a little baby psycho, programmed to destroy humanity.

"Pah, you know what I mean," Mom groused. "We will always live in the shadow of humans—they were always the gods' favorite mortals. Only the Goddess of Night favors us. But I am sick of living in the shadow of the agathos. No matter what other daimons claim, we don't have the freedom the agathos have. They're organized, *militarized*, and efficient. They shut down a whole city in less than 24 hours! Ridiculous."

"Are you suggesting that daimons also get organized?" I asked, unable to keep the doubt out of my voice. "Daimons would never answer to anyone the way the agathos do."

Mom sighed irritably. "You're probably right. In the olden days, the agathos weren't so structured. But in the absence of their goddess, they made idols out of each other. If their *Anesidora* ever wakes up, they will be in for an unpleasant surprise."

"You think so?" I'd never given their goddess much thought. All I knew was that being an agathos sounded terrible.

"I know so," Mom clipped, always offended at the idea that I'd challenge her opinion on anything. "I hope she will rise again, and wipe out all the agathos who disrespected her creation and elevated themselves to the level of gods in her absence."

"That sounds very genocide-y," I replied drily. The reminder that my mom was in fact like most daimons of her generation always took me off guard. So bloodthirsty. Who had the time for it?

"Indeed," she said with a savage grin. "Though I hope when that day comes, Riot's lover will be spared. If all agathos were like her, maybe the world wouldn't be such a terrible place for us daimons."

I hadn't met the woman who was turning the agathos and daimon worlds upside down, but I somehow had to agree. The world needed more of her.

GRACE

CHAPTER 14

Today marked a week since Riot had left. A week of learning everything I could about Gaia, the war she waged on the Olympians, the Goddess of Night, and all but memorizing every prophecy that had ever been made.

A week of coming to terms with my new life. Or the loss of my old life, at least.

A week of chaste nighttime snuggles with Bullet, and secretly taking the edge off my raging desires alone in the shower.

I felt like I was constantly about three seconds away from crawling out of my own skin.

Between the agony of missing Riot and the growing urges to cement the bond between Bullet and I, I was a wreck. A restless, itchy, frustrated *wreck*. My appetite was almost completely gone. I was convinced I only slept because Bullet kept me captive in my dreams. My attention span was roughly two minutes before I started contemplating yet another shower.

It was unbearable.

I sat on the couch, theoretically reading the ancient tome Bullet had dug out on the different kinds of daimons while he poked around in the kitchen, but I hadn't seen a single word on the page.

What I needed was a book on seducing overly polite men.

Maybe I could convince Bullet to pop downstairs so I could shower again. Would that be suspicious? I'd been in there at least twice a day to take the edge off—whenever Bullet went downstairs for anything—instead of just having a rational conversation with him about my needs and finding out where his head was at.

I felt so guilty.

I couldn't stop doing it.

The agony of having *two* unfulfilled soul bonds was making me crazy.

Bullet hadn't initiated anything physical with me, and I wasn't sure I had the confidence to do that myself, even though Riot had reluctantly encouraged it. *Could* I initiate, even if I wanted to? I was always told that good agathos girls were chaste and demure, and the idea of being anything other than that still made my stomach churn a little.

I wasn't a good little agathos girl though. I never had been.

"What's going on?" Bullet laughed, leaning over the half wall that separated the kitchen from the living area on his forearms and grinning at me. He seemed to be handling the lack of bond much better than I was, which was a little bit frustrating.

"Your emotions are playing ping-pong right now," he said, raising an amused eyebrow at me.

You can do this. It's okay.

It's nothing to be ashamed of.

"What kind of emotions are you picking up?" I asked, carefully setting the priceless book on the coffee table and twisting on the couch to face him. I aimed for a casual tone of voice and failed spectacularly.

Bullet's eyes sparkled, and not for the first time I wondered what it would take to unbalance him. Maybe seeing all of the things he'd *seen* in his life made him impossible to shake.

"All sorts of things, Amazing Grace," he replied diplomatically, tipping his head to the side.

Okay. Okay, well that wasn't a *no*, but it wasn't exactly a green light either. Or was it a green light? Sugar, I was way out of my depth.

"Would you... would you come and sit with me for a while?" I asked, cringing internally at how formal I sounded. I wanted an orgasm, and yet my approach was so archaic, Jane Austen would have called me old-fashioned.

"Always," Bullet said easily, pushing back off the half wall that hid the counter and stooping slightly as he made his way out of the tiny kitchen.

Good. Good. This was good.

Bullet sat on the couch next to me—center seat, not the furthest spot away, which was good too, wasn't it?—and flopped back, his arm reaching along the back of the sofa towards me with his legs splayed in a distinctly masculine sort of way.

He didn't *dominate* the space per se. Bullet was too ethereal for that. He didn't look like he belonged in this world.

"So, what are we doing?" he asked, resting his cheek against his outstretched arm and giving me a disarmingly lazy grin. "Chess? *Les Miserables* sing along? Strip poker?"

"I'm hopeless at chess," I replied slowly, shaking my head. "And no sing along."

"Strip poker then?" Bullet's eyebrows shot up, though his face never lost that mischievous grin. There was a flash of emotion from him that I was too slow to identify, and I mourned the lack of a complete bond between us.

You can't do that, I reminded myself. We still needed to have a serious adult conversation about birth control before even entertaining that idea. Most agathos weren't blessed with children until they had met all four soul bonds, but I wasn't most agathos.

I wasn't ready for a little half agathos, half daimon baby. I wasn't sure the world was ready for that.

"Maybe, um, without the poker bit? Since I can't lie and all."

My attempt at a flirty laugh came out slightly hysterical, and I contemplated asking the Goddess of Night if she'd do me a favor and wipe this entire interaction from Bullet's memory. Mine too, for that matter.

"You wanna get naked with me, Amazing Grace?" Bullet asked, his surprise sharp against my skin.

"I did, but I'm getting the impression you don't want to get naked with me," I replied with another nervous laugh. I didn't want to compare them—I was really trying not to—but this part had been so much easier with Riot, and I had to wonder if it was because Bullet wasn't into me that way.

I'd heard what Riot had said about Bullet not dating, but Bullet had known me since I was a *child*. What if he looked at me as a sister or something? That would be horrifying, considering the less than sisterly thoughts I'd been having about him in the shower.

For the first time since I'd met him, Bullet actually looked taken off-guard. "What? I *definitely* want to get you naked. I don't want to pressure you though, that's all."

It was on the tip of my tongue to beg for a little bit more pressure, but I didn't want to make him uncomfortable either.

Bullet hesitated for a moment, and the indecision on his face was so unusual coming from him that I stayed silent and waited for him to continue.

"I always knew you'd be mine one day," Bullet said, seemingly shaking off his nerves as he spoke and plastering his usual smile back on his face. "So while I am firmly Team Virginity-Is-A-Gross-Social-Construct, one that is mostly designed to make women feel like objects that are either used or mint condition, for the purposes of this conversation, I guess I am a virgin. I should assure you though that while this whole sexy thing is new territory, I will obviously be awesome at it. Sex, I mean. I've watched, like, a billion hours of porn for research purposes."

"For research purposes," I repeated faintly, embarrassment and amusement warring in my brain. There was also a vague sense of satisfaction? Not that I liked the idea of Bullet being alone, but the darkness that lurked in my brain was a possessive beast.

"Yup," Bullet said, popping the 'p'. "I have paid particular attention to learning oral sex techniques, and I am very much looking forward to testing them out on you."

"That sounds... lovely, but don't you think we should maybe kiss first?" I suggested, scarcely believing I was having this conversation.

"That does seem a logical progression," Bullet agreed, nodding his head seriously.

I sort of regretted letting him talk so much now that we'd managed to talk ourselves into a pit of awkwardness. I should have launched myself at him the moment he sat down.

It's okay. It's fine. You can do this.

There was a strange feeling in my stomach that may have been butterflies or possibly nausea as I tucked my legs underneath me and rose up on my knees on the couch. Bullet was as still as a statue as I awkwardly shuffled towards him, my face feeling about three times warmer than usual.

"I'm going to kiss you now," I murmured.

"Okay." He didn't sound as confident as usual. If anything, he looked a little intimidated.

Please let those be butterflies in my stomach. Please don't throw up.

I focused on Bullet's lips—because *sugar*, wouldn't it be embarrassing if I missed?—and managed to suppress a nervous giggle as I closed the gap between us. The moment my lips brushed his, a thousand pound weight lifted off my shoulders. Taking the first step had been scary, but the feeling of Bullet's mouth on mine was the most natural thing in the world.

Tentatively, I moved one hand up to cup Bullet's jaw, the other gripping his shoulder for balance. His hands were equally as uncertain as they settled on my waist, his fingers flexing against me like he wasn't sure if he should pull me closer or not.

I usually tried to shove my inner monster down deep, but in moments like this, I couldn't bring myself to do it. The darkness insisted on coming out to play, and I wasn't strong enough to resist it.

My tongue swept over the seam of his mouth, encouraging him to relax, and suddenly I was the experienced one in the room, which was a little unsettling. Bullet's lips parted, his fingers digging a little harder into my sides, and I tightened my grip on him as our tongues brushed tentatively together, exploring one another. The small space between us felt like entirely too much, and I wriggled forward on my knees until my front pressed against his side, my breasts brushing his chest in a way that I should've been self-conscious about, but I couldn't find it in me to care.

Bullet groaned, his hips shifting restlessly in his seat, and the sudden rush of power I got was heady. I may not have any idea what I was doing, but this man was entirely at my mercy.

He wouldn't deny me anything, I knew that deep in my bones. It was flattering, and a tremendous responsibility all at once. I couldn't let him down.

My hand moved slowly down from Bullet's jaw, stroking gently down the column of his throat in a movement that elicited another deep, unselfconscious groan. There was something so incredibly satisfying about *hearing* how good this was making him feel. I explored the hard contours of his chest through the crisp luxurious fabric of his dark shirt, experimenting to see how I could get him to make that desperate sound again. I gently scraped over his nipples with my nails and *bingo*, another rewarding moan that seemed to reverberate between my own legs.

The logical part of my brain told me to take things slow, reminding me that I wasn't ready to go *all* the way, but that part of my brain wasn't in charge at that moment.

My fingers continued lower, exploring Bullet's stomach, the ridges and lean muscles that were evident even through his shirt, before hesitating at the waistband of his slacks. His hips were still grinding faintly against nothing, but he didn't push me to move my exploratory touch any lower even as his own desire built to inferno levels, I could feel it on my skin.

And in other places.

You should stop, the agathos part of my brain scolded.

Go a little lower, the malfunctioning side encouraged.

Maybe... a teeny bit lower. I had been so curious about a man's anatomy since I'd rubbed myself all over Riot's lap to find my release. I just wanted to feel it with my hands a little. The fact he wasn't pushing me only made me want to explore more, feeling entirely safe that either of us could say it was too much and the other would stop.

I moved my hands over Bullet's waistband, stroking down his hip to lightly massage his thigh, letting him know my intentions and giving him the chance to push my hand away. He did not. The noise he made in the back of his throat was almost pained, his teeth scraping almost desperately at my lower lip before his tongue soothed the sting.

He'd been holding himself back, I realized with sudden clarity. *All* the way back. He was suffering too, but he'd never let me see it.

I knew how it felt to be desperate for release, and Riot had taken great care to get me there, more focused on my needs than his. That was what Bullet needed right now, and I could be there for him. I wanted to be.

You can do this, I told myself as I settled my hand over the bulge in Bullet's pants, sucking in a breath against his mouth at how *firm* it was. I logically knew that, er, desire made it firmer, but I hadn't been prepared for how solid it would feel under my palm. I could have sworn it *moved.*

With more confidence than I felt, I began rubbing Bullet through the soft fabric of his dress trousers, experimenting with the pressure and the angle until Bullet was panting underneath me. His gentle, explorative kisses grew messy and uncontrolled, our tongues wrestling for dominance as his hands slid up over my ribs, thumbs brushing the underside of my breasts.

"Fuck!" Bullet gasped, his hips pumping against my hand for a few moments as warmth blossomed under my palm. His movements stuttered to a stop, and his breathing was so labored it sounded like he'd just run a marathon.

Bullet's head dropped back against the back of the couch and he wrapped an arm around my waist, tugging me down with him with a squeak of surprise so that we were snuggled up next to each other.

Satisfying him had been unexpectedly satisfying for me, and although I wanted more, the horrible itching achy sensation had abated. Or maybe I was picking up more of Bullet's emotions and his contentment was affecting me as well. Riot's emotions had felt stronger the more time we'd spent together and physical closeness we'd shared, so it made sense that I'd feel Bullet more strongly now too.

"I'll be honest, Amazing Grace, I've had a lot of fantasies about us, and that didn't happen in any of them. Next time though, I'm going to last like two hours and make you orgasm a hundred times, then trace the shape of your pussy with my tongue until I've got it memorized. Deal?"

"Um, deal?" I squeaked, still not really believing that anyone would want to put their face there, even though Riot had hinted as much already.

"Awesome," Bullet sighed. "Just give me like, three minutes to recover and clean up first."

The moment Bullet disappeared downstairs for clean clothes and I was alone, my itchy, aching desire morphed back into the steady buzz of anxiety I'd become accustomed to at Riot's absence, followed by guilt that I'd indulged in some afternoon petting with Bullet while Riot was away doing goddess knows what, followed by more guilt that Bullet was getting the short end of the stick in my attention.

I was carrying enough guilt to make any agathos proud.

Bullet walked into the bedroom where I was pacing a little manically in front of the bed, and I felt a brief moment of happiness that he felt more comfortable with me. He'd dressed in another outfit that looked straight out of a fashion magazine and oddly impractical to wear around the house—complete with tan suspenders—but I couldn't deny there was something quite debonair about his style.

He sat cross-legged on the bed and pulled out his deck of cards, shuffling them absently in his hands as he watched me pace in silence for a few minutes.

"I'm sorry, I don't mean to be so... this," I said, vaguely gesturing at myself. "It's just that Riot is stuck in Milton because of me, forced to work for some guy he doesn't like because of me, and I feel so helpless. I've caused Riot nothing but trouble, and I can't even do anything to help him."

"I can assure you Riot doesn't see it that way. However, we're kind of stuck in a holding pattern until we get Riot out from under Viper's thumb."

I made a noise of frustration in the back of my throat, continuing my pacing.

"I have a wild theory, and I think it's time to explore it," Bullet announced. I stopped my pacing to look at him, never as confident with reading him as I was with Riot. Riot tended to wear his emotions on his sleeve, where Bullet was less forthcoming with how he was really feeling.

"A *wild* theory?" I repeated dubiously. "That will help Riot?"

"Oh yes," Bullet said solemnly, nodding his head. "Very wild." He paused for a moment before breaking into the chorus from Will Smith's *Wild Wild West*.

"Bullet," I sang, giving him an exasperated look. Part of me was still reticent about speaking up—I always felt like I was making a scene—but I knew I'd need to be more assertive. If not for the trials that Bullet hinted were ahead, then just to keep him focused.

He grinned unapologetically. "Wild."

"Your theory. So you've said," I replied, forcing myself to be patient. Maybe I should have given myself an orgasm while Bullet was cleaning up to reset my bad mood.

"As I mentioned earlier, before I came in my pants like a teenage boy, I'm a virgin," Bullet continued, not a trace of self-doubt in his tone. "It's always been you, you know? I always knew it would be you."

Guilt that I hadn't also waited for him settled in my stomach, piling on to the existing list of things I was guilty about, which was ridiculous because Riot was as much my soul bond as Bullet was. While I got some bizarre satisfaction out of knowing I was Bullet's one and only, at the same time it was almost easier to just not think about it.

I assumed Riot had been with people before me, but if I reflected too hard on *that*, my inner monster would be out with a vengeance over something totally irrelevant that I couldn't change anyway.

"Oh, don't feel bad," Bullet said, flicking his hand absently. "I always knew I'd have to share, though I didn't know the order we'd meet you until recently."

"We never, er, in my dreams..." I trailed off, struggling to voice the question I'd had since the moment we met.

"No," Bullet said instantly, looking mildly offended at the very concept. "I wanted all those experiences in person, and you're hardly the type to get frisky with a stranger anyway, even in your dreams."

"I'm sorry," I said weakly. "I don't know why— I mean I should have known—"

"Don't apologize, you don't remember," Bullet interjected, his smile a little strained. I caught a brief flash of the frustration he was feeling before he tamped it down. "You have nothing to feel bad about."

He held the cards in one hand, shoving the other back through his blonde hair, and it was such an uncharacteristically stressed move from him that I immediately climbed on the bed facing him, crossing my legs to mirror his position.

"What does this have to do with your theory?" I asked in what I hoped was a soothing voice.

He wasn't quick enough to suppress his guilt, and I wondered what could possibly be causing it, because it seemed like such an un-Bullet-like emotion to have.

"Two years ago, a new club opened in downtown Milton. *Asphodel.* It was the talk of the town."

I nodded, recognizing the name. I had never been—to that or any other club—but plenty of the humans who came through the shelter were familiar with the place.

"It's owned by a daimon who moved here from London under mysterious circumstances," Bullet continued, looking down at the cream comforter like he'd never seen something so interesting. "I was curious about anyone who'd name their club after a field in the Underworld, but I had no intention of visiting the place. I didn't want to start having visions about every daimon or human I spoke to in passing, you know?"

"That makes sense," I said slowly. His guilt was rising again, and I couldn't understand why. I wanted to comfort him, but everything about his body language was closed off, rejecting my touch.

"La Nuit came to me that night and gave me a vision of going to the club. It was weird, but who am I to question a goddess?"

Bullet fidgeted uncomfortably, chancing a glance at me before returning his gaze to the bedding. It was that gesture that made the monster in me snap. I'd barely been holding it at bay anyway, and apparently that was my tipping point.

How dare he deny me his eyes? How *dare* he hide?

I hadn't done a good enough job showing it, but didn't Bullet know that he was everything to me? Didn't he understand that I craved every part of him? His wisdom, his humor, the bravado he used to mask his vulnerability. His *pain*. I wanted every drop of his agony for myself so he'd never have to feel it again.

He and Riot had each snagged a piece of my heart, and I was going to make sure they both knew it.

I closed the distance between us and grabbed Bullet's chin, tugging his head up with a little less gentleness than I'd intended.

"What. Is. Bothering. You?"

"Did you just growl at me?" Bullet asked after a moment of silence, blinking at me.

"My inner monster doesn't like you holding back from me. It doesn't like seeing you suffer," I replied, trying and failing to sound less growly. *What was happening to me?*

Bullet's eyes softened and he reached out, his fingers toying lightly with the ends of my hair.

"That's your mother talking," he scolded gently. "You told me when you were ten that she started calling all the parts of you she didn't like your "monster." There's no monster in you, Amazing Grace. Just a fierce, brave woman who questions everything and challenges and demands better when better is due. Don't hide the best parts of yourself because they make other people uncomfortable."

Well, that certainly took the wind out of my rage sails. Tears welled up in my eyes and I leaned forward, grabbing Bullet's face and smashing my mouth almost desperately against his. Bullet only froze for a second before his arms wrapped around me, pulling me up on my knees and tilting his head to deepen the kiss.

My ridiculous tears leaked out despite my attempts to hold them back, running down my cheeks and probably wetting his. I'd let out the worst part of me and Bullet had embraced it with open arms. More than that, he'd encouraged me to embrace it. To not cower in shame from myself.

It was time for me to return the favor. Even if it meant stopping this increasingly heated kiss, which I was loath to do.

Concentrate! Important discussion in progress!

"Mm, we need to finish talking," I mumbled against his lips, my tight grip on his face contradicting my words.

"But you might not want to kiss me after we do that," Bullet whined, his arms giving me a quick squeeze before releasing me.

"Rip the bandaid off?" I suggested, grabbing his hands before he could completely withdraw from me again, linking them together and resting them on his lap, forcing myself to sit back.

"I kissed him," Bullet blurted, his cheeks going pink. "The mysterious club owner from England. There's an exclusive club on the top floor, *Elysium*, that's daimons-only. I met him there. We were dancing—we didn't even speak—and I found him attractive, which was weird because my sexuality has always been Grace, you know? It was just you, forever. Anyway, he kissed me and I'd never been kissed before and I enjoyed it for like two seconds before realizing that I was kissing someone that *wasn't you* and bolted."

There was so much to unpack there, I thought I might have gone into shock figuring out where to begin.

"His name is Wild," Bullet added hesitantly. "He's pretty well known in Milton. I never saw him after that night, but he bought up a bunch of clubs around Milton under his brand, Underworld."

"Wild," I repeated numbly. "Your *wild* theory..."

"I think he's your third soul bond, and that's why I felt a connection to him like I felt a friendship with Riot. Except not the same at all, because Riot's whole emo scene kid vibe does *nothing* for me."

"Hey now," I teased, giving him what I hoped was a reassuring smile, though it probably looked a little watery. "Don't knock the scene kid look. I am very much into it."

"I can tell," Bullet replied wryly, eyes sparkling.

The jealousy at the idea of Bullet with someone else morphed into something more like curiosity, if that someone else was also mine. Maybe it was normal within soul bonds? My fathers had only ever treated each other like brothers, but they weren't affectionate with my mother in front of me either. For all I knew, they could have all been together and—

Nope. Cutting that thought off right there.

"Please tell me what you're thinking," Bullet demanded hoarsely, gripping my fingers tightly.

"A lot of things," I confessed. "Many of which are hypothetical and can be discussed later. I guess the biggest question I have is why are you so uncertain? I know you don't know everything, but haven't you *seen* all this?"

Bullet's posture relaxed, his grip on my fingers becoming comforting rather than desperate.

"My visions of your soul bonds are represented by certain tarot cards," he explained, flipping his hand over so I could see the tattoo on his inner arm. "When you met Riot, the depiction of him in my visions changed from The Devil to a devil-y looking Riot."

I traced the tattoo with my fingers, admiring the intricacy of it. Five cards were fanned out, slightly overlapping one another. The first one, closest to Bullet's wrist was one I recognized—The Fool. A skull in a jester's hat.

"That's you," Bullet said, noticing where my eyes had paused. Well, that was both accurate and maybe a little insulting? "Followed by my card, then Riot's. I got the order wrong there."

"No you didn't," I replied softly. "We did meet first. I just don't remember it."

I felt rather than saw Bullet's gratitude as he inclined his head, glancing up at me before returning his gaze to the tattoo. I wanted to explore the cards depicting him and Riot in more detail, but I decided to come back to them later in favor of looking at the ones representing the bonds I hadn't met yet.

"The next is The Chariot," Bullet said, gesturing at the fourth card which showed the striking profile of a leaping horse. On one side was a moon-like circle, which morphed into sun-like rays on the other, surrounding the whole animal. "Control, willpower, determination," Bullet continued, listing what I presumed were the traits associated with the card.

They weren't *bad* traits, but they sounded... challenging.

"And this?" I asked, tracing the shape of the final card. It looked like a globe, but it was filled with a checkered pattern, and surrounded by two thin circles that were intersected by a sun at the top and a moon at the bottom.

"The World," Bullet grinned. "Completion, integration, accomplishment. The final piece of the puzzle."

"And do you have a theory on who that is?" I asked, raising an eyebrow at him.

"I daresay I do," Bullet replied with an unrepentant grin. "But there's an order that needs to be followed here. All good things to those who wait, et cetera, et cetera."

I disagreed strongly with that sentiment, but Bullet had proven plenty of times that if he didn't want to reveal something yet, he wouldn't.

"So, why the hesitancy?" I asked, still puzzled over that. "Surely, if you felt some kind of *kinship* with Wild, and the only other comparative experience is with Riot, then the answer seems obvious."

My fingers had moved back to the depiction of The Chariot as I spoke, idly tracing the beautiful ink with my fingers.

Bullet gave me a wry smile. "Despite the snippy attitude, Riot actually likes me deep down. We spent a lot of time together growing up, and he was always the first to step in when daimons gave me shit for being the weird psychic kid."

My first instinct was to be enraged that Bullet had ever been treated that way, followed by an overwhelming rush of sympathy because I knew better than most how it felt to be the weird kid. My heart expanded with appreciation for Riot that he had stepped in and defended his friend, despite whatever hangups he had about the concept.

"*That* is why I'm not sure," Bullet continued. "Riot likes me. Wild seemed to like me." His cheeks flushed pink and I bit my lip to stop myself from laughing. "But, while I've never seen them interact, I know for a fact that Riot and Wild *despise* each other. Riot is banned from all Underworld clubs, it's a whole thing."

Oh. That was definitely a point against Bullet's theory.

"Riot makes it *seem* like he doesn't like you though," I hedged, and Bullet grinned smugly, like he was immensely proud of that fact. "Maybe it's the same with Wild. Maybe it's less that he despises him and more, you know, male posturing."

"Riot needs a little practice with sharing," Bullet chuckled. "I don't take it personally because I know deep down—like really, really deep down—he's got my back and I've got his."

Sugar, that made me feel all kinds of warm and fuzzy inside. I hadn't realized how much the relationship between Riot and Bullet was worrying me until Bullet had given me that reassurance. Some of the weight on my shoulders eased slightly, knowing that underneath all the bickering, they really did care about each other.

"With Riot and Wild, I'm less certain," Bullet continued. "It *could* be male posturing, but Riot did sell drugs in Wild's club, which Wild frowns upon, and Wild did beat the crap out of him for it, which doesn't seem like a very soul-bond-in-law thing to do. But there's no way to know for sure if Wild is or isn't yours until you see him, right? So I vote that we go see him."

I blanched. "In Milton?"

"I'm thinking... not," Bullet said with a slight frown, reaching for his cards again, shuffling them until one with three cups appeared on the top. "I had a vague vision last night that I *think* is pushing us to explore this theory, but I didn't recognize the location. I'm hoping the Fates will be generous and shed more light on it for us."

That eased my panic a little. I definitely wasn't in a rush to try sneaking into Milton while it was occupied by agathos, if I even could. The idea that I'd see people I knew, standing on the opposite side of the line they'd drawn for me... it stung.

"Do you think that this *Wild* will even want to meet me? The daimons—"

"*Adore you,*" Bullet interrupted emphatically. "Seriously, my visions are super clear on that. Daimons think you're cool as hell. Even Riot, who had the mopiest, most boring reputation you can imagine—which is honestly impressive for someone who spent his nights coked up in various clubs and seedy alleyways around town—is cool by association. With *you.*"

"Sometimes I don't know how to respond to you," I admitted, a little bemused.

Bullet grinned, pulling his hand out of my grip to shuffle his cards. "Follow my lead, Amazing Grace. What I lack in social skills, I make up for in insider information, direct from La Nuit and the Fates. I'll steer you right."

BULLET

CHAPTER 15

I was slumped on the armchair, wondering if maybe it was time to add caffeine to my diet. Surely my body would still be temple-like with just a little boost? Exhaustion was not a feeling I was accustomed to, and I didn't like it.

I'd stayed up most of the night asking the Fates questions, sitting up in bed with Grace pressed to my side as she slept, giving her the physical contact she was craving to ease the ache of the incomplete bonds. I'd had such grand plans to pleasure her all afternoon after my embarrassing performance on the couch, but she'd obviously run out of patience on the Riot situation, and that had to take priority.

It had been an unproductive night for answers, no matter what questions I asked.

Was Wild Grace's third soul bond? Where was he? Was it time to seek him out? Was Wild the third cup the card referenced? Would he and Riot be able to put their past behind them?

I imagined the three Fates, sitting there with their arms stubbornly crossed, refusing to answer. They must have gotten fed up with my line of questioning too, since they stopped giving even vague answers and abruptly pulled their presence away in a manner that felt distinctly impatient.

It was almost like they wanted me to figure out answers the old-fashioned way, without all the psychic helpful hints.

Rude.

I was missing Riot a little today. His opinion would be really helpful right now, even though he basically knew nothing about anything. Even if I was wrong about Wild being Grace's soul bond, maybe we could still convince him to buy out Riot's deal with Viper, if Riot begged hard enough. Wild would be a good ally to have, but it would be even better if Grace's soul bond spidey senses tingled for him too.

Grace was poring over a book about the war between Gaia's giants and the Olympians, brow furrowed in concern. I doubted this was a version of "Anesidora" that the agathos were ever taught about—the power-hungry, vengeful goddess who'd sought to overthrow her own grandchildren.

I thought I'd be so great at being Grace's soul bond. I'd had my whole life to prepare for it! Looking at her now, I could see I was failing in my duties. She was restless, with dark shadows under her eyes and a grayness to her pallor she hadn't had when she first arrived here.

It wasn't great to think that Grace had looked in better condition when she'd shown up here covered in blood and soaking wet than she looked now. I needed to do better.

"I'm going to make a call," I told her, standing and moving towards the outside door. I'd excused myself before to take calls from clients so Grace didn't question it, but it made me feel kind of shitty that I was being one percent sneaky. I didn't want to get her hopes up though.

By the Fates, this relationship business was hard. Communicating in person had been a lot trickier than I had anticipated, and the whole *sex* thing was a minefield I had no idea how to navigate.

In my mind, I was sure I'd perform like a pornstar, with heaps of great moves and hours of stamina. In reality, I'd come in my pants after Grace touched my dick *over fabric* for a couple of minutes.

I was going to blame my close to thirty years of celibacy for that misstep. *Next time*, I'd be awesome.

I jogged down the stairs and took shelter under the deck in front of the entrance to the shop. There was a faint mist of rain falling that would have probably felt refreshing if I was wearing a jacket over my shirt. The air was cold, winter was rapidly approaching.

In all the visions I had left for my future, I never saw another summer.

No time for bitterness, I reminded myself as I held the phone to my ear.

"*Hello*," Riot said gruffly, sounding half asleep, his voice rough.

"It's me," I replied quickly, in case he got any ideas about phone sex with our lady love.

He grunted. *"What is it? Where's Grace?"*

"She's fine. Inside, reading a book. I need some info from inside Milton."

"About what?" he asked suspiciously.

"Wild."

Silence. Total and utter silence. Why'd Riot have to sell coke in Wild's club that time? That was basically Wild's golden rule. Riot was such a self-sabotaging idiot sometimes. Or he was, pre-Grace at least.

"Why?" Riot asked flatly.

"You know why."

"No."

It wasn't a 'no, I don't understand'. It was definitely a 'no, I reject that notion'.

"Is he in Milton right now or not?" I pressed.

Riot made a noise of frustration. *"No. His second-in-command, Onyx, has been handling the clean up at Asphodel and keeping their employees from going completely savage. Wild was out of town the night everything went down. He didn't make it back before the troops showed up."*

I hummed to myself, contemplating our next steps.

The instant connection I'd felt with Wild had scared the shit out of me at the time, so I'd done my best to pretend it had never happened. Maybe it was time for me to pay Wild's dreams a visit, though there was no way I'd be going without Grace. I didn't know how I felt about interacting with him after I let him kiss me that one time. I'd beat myself up about it ever since for being such a shitty, disloyal soul bond to the love of my life.

"What are you planning?" Riot asked.

My natural impulse was to give him an evasive non-answer, since I usually went through life doing whatever the hell I wanted and relying on my connection with La Nuit and the Fates to steer me right. However that probably wasn't the way to establish a healthy trusting relationship with my soul bond-in-law, so I was going to have to give him a little something to work with.

"I suspect he's the third. And the third is required not only for Grace's benefit, but for yours."

"Mine?" Riot scoffed. *"If Wild's the third, I'd rather Grace never find him."*

"Did you want to make out with him too?"

"What?" Riot choked. *"No, the guy looked about two seconds away from hanging me from the fucking rafters by my intestines the one time I met him."*

"You do have that effect on people," I agreed.

"Why? Did you want to make out with him?"

"Kind of." I mean I had, but that was a conversation for another day.

"Do you want to make out with me?" Riot asked, sounding slightly appalled at the concept. Rude.

"My, my, are you propositioning me, Mr. Garner? I'm afraid I'll have to turn you down. 'Bad boy' is not my vibe," I teased.

"Thank fuck for that," Riot muttered. *"Could have been awkward. Also bullshit, because that's exactly what Wild is and you know it. You better have talked to Grace about this."*

"Of course," I assured him, not even caring that he was implying I wouldn't have. I found I liked that he was so protective of Grace, even if his ire was directed at me. "Anyway, it might all mean nothing. Or maybe it means something. I won't know until I track him down."

"I have reservations," Riot grumbled. *"But I trust you'll keep Grace safe."*

"Always," I promised.

"Did you check on Dare?"

My chest ached at the question, and not for the first time, I resented my gift. I had yet to *see* what Dare's troubles would be, but the Fates had implied they would be great.

"Nothing to worry about in the immediate future. I'll keep you posted."

I hung up quickly, feeling like a bit of a coward, but also knowing I'd done the right thing. If Riot was worried about Dare, he'd insist Dare figure out a way back to Milton, or send him here. Dare was right where he needed to be for now.

"Everything okay?" Grace asked as I let myself back in, heading straight for the fireplace to chuck another log on. She was right where I left her, curled up in the corner of the couch with a blanket over her legs, the crumbling old book perched carefully on her knees.

"Fine," I replied vaguely, shooting her my most charming smile.

It was mid-afternoon, and my call had woken Riot up, which was pretty normal for a daimon. If I wanted to get inside Wild's head, I was going to have to do it now.

"Wanna take a nap, Amazing Grace?" I asked, closing the fireplace door.

"A nap?" Grace replied, eyebrows shooting up. "I'm not sure I could sleep right now. I feel…" she trailed off, blushing, not that I needed her to explain how she was feeling. The need to bond had moved between lethargy, pain, and an incessant itch that I couldn't scratch. I assumed it was twice as bad for Grace who was experiencing those same feelings times two with Riot.

I mean, she hadn't brought it up, but I could *feel* her orgasms with each of the many showers she had each day, so I knew she was struggling with the urges. I was quietly proud of her—I knew enough about the agathos to know that masturbating was almost number one on the Never Ever Allowed list.

"We could just lie down and see what happens?" I suggested cheerfully, striding towards the bedroom. *Damn it, Bullet, say something seductive.* I would totally be great in bed if I could figure out how to get us to that point.

I felt Grace's excitement spark sharply at my skin, followed by a warm brush of embarrassment. Freaking adorable.

We did actually have to sleep though. At some point. And I definitely wasn't going to come in my pants this time.

Maybe.

I ditched my shirt and trousers, climbing under the blankets in my boxers while Grace stood in the doorway, hovering while she made up her mind. I draped an arm over my eyes, the blanket slipping down to my waist, giving her a moment to decide without me staring at her.

After a minute, I heard the rustle of clothes before she climbed into bed next to me, shuffling close to my side until the bare skin of her arm brushed mine. I lifted my arm enough to peek out at her, catching a glimpse of the oversized t-shirt she'd stripped down to that came partway down her thighs before she pulled the blankets over her body.

She'd been wearing it with yoga pants underneath before.

Was that a sign? Removing pants seemed like a sign. Maybe I should stretch my arm out over the pillow so she'd curl into my side? This lying on our backs side-by-side position was not optimal for seduction, that much I definitely knew.

Or maybe I should make a joke about being the little spoon and she'd argue that she wanted to be the little spoon, and then I'd be all 'yes, please!' and then we'd be snuggling. Except I'd have to do some strategic angling to keep my boner away from her ass.

"Bullet," Grace whispered, staring up at the ceiling. I could *feel* her desire. Surely, I couldn't screw this up.

"Yeah, Amazing Grace?"

"Close your eyes."

Oh. Maybe it wasn't a sign. Maybe we were just going to skip straight to naptime.

Swallowing down the disappointed sigh—directed entirely at myself because I had definitely fumbled the seduction opportunity—I closed my eyes and moved the hand over my eyes behind my head.

Maybe I couldn't make Grace see stars this afternoon, but I could get her some answers that she wouldn't remember which was... not the awesome redeeming factor I hoped it would be.

Maybe I should consider asking Riot for sexual tips after all.

Before I could give much thought to that depressing idea, Grace shifted on the bed, the blankets rustling as she moved around. I contemplated sneaking a peek at her again, but then I felt the soft brush of her lips against mine, and every thought went out of my head.

I opened one eye, semi wondering if this was a fever dream I was making up, but nope. There was my real life soul mate, carefully holding herself up on one arm and leaning over me, her long dark hair spilling over one shoulder and tickling the top of my arm.

Do not jizz your pants again, I instructed myself firmly, sending extra strict thoughts to my dick. The dick that had so thoroughly betrayed me yesterday. Not again. This time I was going to be *awesome*.

I could feel Grace's desire, but also an undercurrent of nerves that made sense, but that I also kind of hated. I never wanted her to feel nervous around me. Was she worried about making the first move? I could definitely prove she had nothing to worry about there.

I cupped the back of Grace's head with one hand, drawing her closer and coaxing her lips apart. Nothing on this Earth tasted more tempting than my Grace did—she was like the richest, headiest dessert. Rich and sultry and delicious.

"Bullet," she breathed against my lips, one hand tentatively resting on my bare chest, her fingers brushing the The Lovers card tattooed over my heart.

I fisted the back of her shirt, tugging her down on top of me and smiling against her lips as her surprised squeak turned into a giggle.

Nailed it. A+ skills with my lady love.

"Can I touch you?" I murmured, my hand resting a gentlemanly distance above her ass even as my dick pressed in an ungentlemanly way against her thigh. Shit, I probably should have paid more attention to dick placement before I pulled her on top of me.

"Yes," Grace replied hoarsely. "*Please* touch me."

Was she begging for *my* touch? The idea was ludicrous. Grace should never have to ask for anything, and I was letting her down if she was.

I released my grip on her hair and slid both hands down her body, stroking the silky soft skin of her upper thighs as her long t-shirt rode up.

My dick twitched against her thigh and Grace rolled her hips slightly at the movement, which was *really* not helping my resolve to not come in my pants again.

Her skin was *so soft* though. Like petals and silk and other soft poetic shit I couldn't think of when Grace's hips were being all writhy on my abs.

She wanted more, and I didn't want her to have to ask again.

My fingers inched up slowly, giving her time to stop me as I brushed the edge of her panties. Panties *I'd* bought her. These plain cotton bad boys were courtesy of me, and I got a weird sense of pride out of that.

Grace's hands explored my chest while I fulfilled years' worth of fantasies about memorizing the shape of her body, smoothing over her hips, kneading her full perfect ass cheeks, tentatively slipping a hand between us to brush over damp panties.

"Bullet," Grace whined, moving more insistently. It wasn't a sound she usually made, but I could feel her instinct to bond riding her hard, itching at her skin as much as it was mine.

I tugged at the waistband of her underwear and Grace happily shifted off me, pushing them down clumsily as she attempted to keep our lips sealed together. Maybe she'd feel embarrassed at being so forward when the urges died down, but I was going to do my best not to give her a chance to. I'd hold her and kiss her and praise her and do everything in my power to make her feel okay.

The moment Grace was bare from the waist down, I rolled her onto her back and propped myself on my side next to her, reversing the positions we'd started in. I kissed a soft line of kisses from her collarbone up to behind her ear, cursing the t-shirt she was wearing the entire time as my hand landed on her inner thigh, tugging her legs further apart.

Don't come.

Fuck.

She was so wet and soft and warm and *don't come, Bullet. You are not allowed to come right now.*

227

I was holding my breath as my fingers explored her folds, memorizing every inch of her, forcing myself to focus on what made Grace gasp and twitch instead of how my dick was about to explode in my boxers. Not the good kind of explosion either. Explode like a bomb, leaving nothing in its place. It fucking *hurt*.

Note to self: probably not a masochist?

"Clit," Grace gasped. "Circle it with your finger."

Ooh, all those masturbatory shower sessions were obviously paying off.

I gathered wetness from her entrance, barely resisting the urge to explore that more, before sliding up to Grace's clit and circling it as instructed.

Thank the Fates for all the instructional porn tutorials because I'd probably die of shame on the spot if I hadn't been able to find it.

"Just... a little harder," Grace moaned, tipping her head back, her hands slipping up her body to massage her breasts, pushing the stupid t-shirt up with it. I added a little more pressure, my eyes running up and down the length of her body, not sure which perfect part of her to focus on.

By the gods, Grace was so pretty. I felt kind of bad she'd been lumped with rough-around-the-edges daimon soul bonds, but also not that bad because I was a selfish son of a bitch and she was *mine*.

Before I could articulate all those thoughts out loud, Grace's soft fingers brushed at the waistband of my boxers and my brain short circuited.

"You don't have to—"

"You don't want to know how much I've thought about this," Grace breathed, cutting off my objections.

"My dick?" I asked, embarrassingly hopeful as she wriggled her hand under the fabric.

Grace made a throaty noise of assent. "I don't know if other agathos think like this but... I can't stop imagining it."

I shucked my boxers one-handed, already mentally preparing to set fire to every pair I had so my girl had easy access whenever she was feeling curious.

Her hand wrapped tentatively around my shaft and I sucked in a breath, my movements stuttering until Grace made another impatient noise in the back of her throat, reminding me I had a job to do.

Her hand felt so much better than my hand though.

Like a million, billion times better.

"It's so hard but the skin's so soft," Grace giggled, looking appropriately mesmerized.

Make her come! So long as Grace came first, it wouldn't be too embarrassing that I blew my load after two minutes tops of her hands on me. Probably.

"I'm so close," Grace whispered, bucking her hips against me. "Tell me what to do, I want to make you feel good."

"You make me feel good just by existing," I gritted out. "But, um, tighten your hand a little, that's it..."

With my free hand, I covered hers, guiding her movements the way I liked them, except it was a million times better because Grace's hand was soft and angelic. Once she'd settled into a rhythm, I gave all of my focus to the circular motions I was making with my finger, concentrating on what made Grace gasp and twitch, on the way her abs sporadically contracted as she got closer to her peak.

"Bullet," she breathed, that faint whiny tone in her voice that I found so sexy pushing me over the edge about a second after Grace.

Still counts. I still made her come first.

I half expected Grace to pull her hand away or at least be a little grossed out, but she kept pumping my shaft slowly, breathing heavily as she stared at the fucking *puddle* that had formed on my stomach, totally entranced.

I awkwardly grabbed a handful of tissues from the nightstand, keeping one hand on Grace's thigh while cleaning myself up as she gave me a soft, dreamy smile that I wasn't sure I deserved.

"We're definitely doing that again," she commanded softly. "After we nap."

Fortunately, after staying up most of the night, an orgasm was enough to tip me into the dreamscape pretty easily. I was pulled into a few visions I didn't care about at first, but that was fine since Grace seemed to be taking longer to fall asleep.

Hopefully because she was so mind blown by our afternoon activities and eager for a repeat. That would be nice.

Eventually, I was able to tug on the thread that connected us, feeling it wrap around us both as I pulled her through the dreamscape, seeking out Wild's head.

The more I visited someone, the more instinctive it was to jump into their head. After my first meeting with Wild and the kiss that I tried to pretend never happened, I had deliberately steered clear of his mind. I'd never been shown any visions of his future either, which I thought was a mercy from the goddesses, but I now realized it was probably because Grace's soul bonds were hidden from me. There had been blanks in what I'd seen of Riot's future too, before he met Grace.

We landed in Wild's dream—which was always risky business because people had weird thoughts in general—but this was the opposite of weird. It was boring. Grim, even.

"Where are we?" Grace whispered, as if worried we'd disturb the lone figure in the center of the room. We were in some kind of drab, industrial gym. Wild was facing away from us, the dark skin of his muscular back soaked with sweat, muscles rippling as he whaled on a punching bag.

Grace sucked in a breath and I grinned at her, not that she noticed. Wild was a big guy and stacked with muscle, like most Keres were. He'd been a semi famous boxer in London before he'd mysteriously quit and moved to Milton.

She was staring at him like she was memorizing him—his dark brown skin, buzzed black hair, red athletic shorts, muscular legs. Wild was a specimen of masculinity, that was for sure. That kiss years ago had been a mistake, but I wasn't blind.

"Wild?" Grace breathed, unable to take her eyes off him. I nodded, eyeing his movements. He made each hit look so fluid and easy, but I had no doubt that even at half strength he could knock me clean across the room with one hit.

"Wild," I confirmed. "He can't see us yet. I can't believe he dreams about training. This might be the most depressing dreamscape I've ever visited."

And I had seen some shit in my life.

"It's very lonely," Grace agreed softly, her gentle voice the only noise in the place except for the rhythmic thwack of Wild's wrapped fists against the bag. "He has no tattoos," she added suddenly, cocking her head to the side.

"Are you stereotyping us daimons?" I teased, bumping her with my shoulder. "Wild is a notorious loner, getting a tattoo might require too much social interaction for him. He's amassed this small empire in Milton, and his influence seems to extend beyond that, but I don't really understand how. I've never even heard him speak."

Grace frowned, leaning in close to my side.

"Does he feel like yours?" I asked, watching her reaction.

"Oh yes," Grace breathed, staring at him like she was in a trance. "He definitely feels like mine. Are we going to meet him? It feels kind of like I'm taking a shortcut. I know we met in the dreamscape, but dreams are your gift."

I grinned at her, entirely unrepentant. "First of all, I'm a daimon. I have no qualms about taking shortcuts. Second, neither of you are going to remember this anyway, but if we're going to visit him in person, we need to find out where he is at the moment. So, if you could steer the conversation in that direction, that would be helpful."

Hopefully Grace could do that without triggering her agathos instincts to be super honest about everything.

"Aren't you going to join me?" Grace asked, alarmed.

"Not for this conversation," I replied, pulling her close and pressing a kiss on her forehead. Every daimon in Milton knew I was an Oneiroi, if Wild saw me, he'd know this was all due to my influence. If Grace showed up alone, hopefully he'd think she was some manifestation of his subconscious and spill all his secrets while I merrily eavesdropped.

"Ready?" I asked, extricating myself from her so I could let her out of the invisible bubble we were in.

"Are you? You're the one that has to remember all of this," Grace replied with a sad smile, catching my arm before I could step fully away and kissing my jaw.

My thoughtful little soulmate.

"Such is the life of an Oneiroi. I'm ready if you are, Amazing Grace."

"Let's do it then," Grace said, steeling her spine and taking a few steps backwards. "If this first meeting is horribly awkward, please never bring it up."

I snorted, tugging the bubble in tightly around me so Grace became visible to Wild. He spun immediately to face her, fists raised in front of his chin, everything about his stance defensive.

Crap, in no universe did I expect him to try to fight her. Maybe this was a bad idea.

Though after one look, his expression was softening from a fierce rage to a sort of melancholy suspiciousness. I wondered what was going through Grace's head as she took in Wild's face—he had a short black beard, neatly trimmed, and a definite crick in his nose from an old injury. His bare chest was littered in long-healed scars, and his eyes had the least amount of purple in them I'd ever seen on a daimon. The almost pure crimson irises didn't help with the intimidating picture he was painting.

Intimidating, but attractive, if that's what you were into.

I contemplated pulling Grace back, but her steps hadn't faltered as she moved closer, and I shadowed her movements from a few steps back. Either she was confident that Wild wouldn't hurt her, or she trusted me to get her out if things turned sour.

"Grace," he rumbled thoughtfully in a low voice. "I'm going insane. I guess I see you everywhere now that you've disappeared."

One—he knew who she was. How did he already know who she was?!

Two—English accent. Such a shame he wasn't a chattier guy in person because that voice was an audio-gasmic experience.

Grace's steps faltered, just a foot away from him. "You know who I am?"

He tilted his head to the side, frown deepening before running an assessing gaze down Grace's body, taking in the black jeans and gray off-the-shoulder top she was wearing.

"Not your usual agathos attire," he remarked, voice filled with suspicion as his eyes darted around the room, skipping right over me. "Thought you preferred dresses with flowers on them."

This plan had really hinged on him assuming Grace was a beautiful figment of his imagination, and it seemed like that wasn't the case. He knew her name. That she'd disappeared. What kind of clothes she wore.

Well, good thing neither of them were going to remember this total screw up.

"Not preferred," Grace replied cautiously. "I have more freedom to wear what I want these days."

"Since Riot stole you away."

"He didn't steal me," Grace countered immediately, a hard edge in her voice. "He didn't have to."

Wild nodded, his jaw tight. "Where's the Oneiroi?"

Grace opened her mouth before slamming it shut again. I wasn't sure if she couldn't tell a lie or she just didn't want to.

"Tell me where you are," she commanded softly. "Let me visit you in person. You can explain to me how you seem to know so much about me."

A muscle in Wild's cheek ticked. "I can't explain anything in person."

"Why not?"

Wild shook his head. "I can't. You need to stay away, for your own safety."

Goddess, save us all from posturing alpha male bullshit.

He gave Grace another long look. "You're so beautiful," he added in a low, almost sad voice. "It's inconvenient."

I snorted, dropping the bubble as frustration welled up inside me. "Grace is sweet and kind, curious and brave. She's got a spine of steel all wrapped up in the softest, warmest package. She is beautiful, but her beauty is the least interesting thing about her."

Grace blinked up at me as I took my place at her side, draping an arm around her shoulders. Why did she look so surprised? Maybe I wasn't complimenting her enough in real life.

"I don't doubt any of that," Wild replied, his eyes flicking to me, not looking surprised in the slightest that I was there, though they narrowed at my arm around Grace. "My reasons for avoiding this have nothing to do with you. Don't take it personally."

"Our souls are intertwined. It's impossible not to take it personally," Grace shot back, surprising all three of us.

Wild's eyebrows raised slowly, the corner of his mouth twitching. I thought Riot was reserved with his facial expressions, but Wild made him seem positively animated.

"Enlighten us," I suggested, rubbing soothing circles into Grace's shoulders. He was stubbornly silent, but that was okay. I stepped all over social cues at the best of times, and neither of them were going to remember this anyway, so screw it. "Daddy issues? Mommy issues? Abandonment issues? Had your heart broken by a woman in the past and decided the whole gender is a write-off?"

"Bullet!" Grace gasped, agathos manners back in place after her slip.

"Come on," I pressed. "At least tell us if you're hung up on a life ruining ex. Grace is obsessing over it now, even if she pretends she's not."

"You're lucky I'm not going to remember this," she muttered, giving me a pointed look. She was totally thinking about it though.

"No life ruining ex," Wild said eventually, his eyes boring into Grace's like he was willing her to understand something, but she couldn't. Not unless he explained it to her.

"This," Wild began, gesturing at himself. "This is not who I am in real life."

"I don't care about that," Grace replied instantly, though I could hear the confusion in her voice. Grace and I appeared pretty much as we were in the dreamscape, though she'd always been fond of manifesting slightly more glamorous clothes for herself than what she wore in real life.

For others though... Impediments that our physical bodies had in real life didn't exist here if we didn't want them to. Someone who was wheelchair-bound could walk in their own dreams. We could fly, if we wanted to, though most people didn't dream big enough.

Surely I'd have heard or noticed something like that with Wild though.

"You will care," Wild replied with grim certainty. "Forget about me."

I felt a tug in my gut, the summons of another vision, one imparted by La Nuit herself.

"We'll see you again soon," I told Wild calmly. "You can't avoid Fate."

Wild's answering smile was predatory. "But I can fight it, and nothing excites a Keres more than the thrill of battle."

Grace struggled as the dream began to disintegrate around us, obviously unwilling to leave Wild behind. But she couldn't stay here without me, and I was being called elsewhere.

"We'll be back, Amazing Grace," I whispered in her ear, wrapping my arms around her and guiding her back to the safety of her own dreams before the Goddess captured all of my attention.

I landed outside the wrought iron gates of an impressive mansion, surrounded by mature trees and a high stone fence. We'd passed whatever test the Goddess had set for us. She was giving us some answers.

WILD

CHAPTER 16

I stood at the edge of the ring while Ash and Raven beat the bloodlust out of each other, crossing my arms but keeping myself alert and ready to move in case one of them got carried away. I'd brought Ash here a little over a week ago when she'd nearly beat the shit out of a human she'd been riling up. It was meant to be a quick trip—a day at most to get her settled with the other Keres who were recuperating here—but the agathos intrusion into Milton had hampered my plans to get back.

It was fucking outrageous, being kept out of my own town, but I didn't want to draw any agathos attention to myself, and frankly I didn't trust my judgment around them. They'd come for Grace. They wanted to snatch her away again. It was unforgivable.

I'd spent more time than usual hitting the bags myself to work out the rage I was struggling to keep under control. I wasn't much better than the other Keres who were staying out here, at this temporary retreat we used to regain control of our bloodlust.

This home needed my financial support, but I rarely spent time here. Rider, the Keres I'd put in charge of it, had the day-to-day running under control. I wasn't *needed* here. I was needed at Asphodel, where I ran all the Underworld clubs out of. Onyx was a good second-in-command, but she'd never been in charge on her own for this long.

If nothing else, I wanted to get back to my office where I had access to everything, including my network of security cameras. I could see a few from my laptop, but for security purposes, access was mostly restricted to my office.

How was I supposed to keep an eye on the girl if I didn't have my fucking *cameras*? I had assumed she'd left Milton, which would be the sensible thing to do, but Onyx had bumped into a drunken Creep and he'd confessed that Riot had been at his casino earlier in the week.

He was a little fucking weasel, but surely Riot wouldn't have abandoned her somewhere? He'd marginally moved up in my esteem, since the agathos hadn't actually managed to find her yet, but he may move down again if he hadn't actually got her out of Milton. For now, I was inclined to think he wasn't as useless and self-destructive as all previous evidence suggested.

"It was a good thing you brought her here," Rider said quietly, sidling up a few feet to my left and watching the two women in the ring whale on each other. He was a grizzly old man, almost entirely bald except for the few stubborn gray hairs he was determined to hold onto, and it was harder to find an inch of skin on him that wasn't scarred than an inch of skin that was. Most Keres didn't live as long as Rider had. "Usually they come out of the haze faster than this."

I nodded, watching Ash's rage-fueled movements carefully. Her usual red eyes were glassy and the veins in her arms and forehead were protruding, a good indication that it hadn't cleared yet.

The extended haze was an unwelcome variable when I had enough change going on to be dealing with. A few good hits should have cleared it by now, but it had been over a week.

Rider hesitated next to me and I glanced at him out of the corner of my eye, tipping my chin up to invite him to speak.

"It might be nothing," he hedged, shifting his weight uncomfortably in the way he did when his back pain flared up. "But I've seen war in my time, and this kind of flare up, where the need for destruction is like an itch that never quite goes away, is often found near battlefields. This is what we're designed for. We're drawn to bloodshed. We live to fuel it."

War?

This was fucking bullshit. I needed to get back to Milton. I'd been planning on waiting out the troops who were patrolling the roads in and out of Milton, but now I was contemplating letting the bloodlust take hold and tearing through them by force.

I tilted my head at the ring and Rider nodded in confirmation that he had it under control, so I left him to supervise. At least I could monitor a little of my town from the office I'd taken over, but the urge to check on things was incessant. Rider was too old to physically intervene if the fighters got carried away, but he'd been known to douse them with a hose if they didn't respond to his verbal commands.

I jogged up the creaking basement stairs to the first floor, where most of the temporary residents were starting to wake up and get food in the kitchen. This place comfortably housed fifteen, and there were twelve here at the moment. I'd purchased the property a year and a half ago and converted it into a halfway house of sorts for Keres. The kind of place that I'd needed when I was younger, but hadn't existed.

Not all of us wanted to be a slave to our bloodlust. Even the older daimons like Rider understood the need to quench those uncontrollable rages so we could exist in society.

It wasn't a permanent residence—just somewhere to go when they needed to reset their rage. Only Rider lived here full time. He'd worked for me in Milton, and I trusted him as much as I trusted Onyx.

Not all the way, but a decent amount.

He'd given up his office space for me to use while I was here, and I made my way straight there. Someone was cooking facon in the kitchen, and as tempting as the smell was, the sudden lack of conversation whenever I entered a room wasn't worth it.

Social interaction was an inconvenience I had neither the time nor the patience for.

The office was a small windowless room that doubled as a panic room of sorts. Why Rider had painted such a confined space navy, I had no idea. It was a suffocating sensation being in here—a built-in desk dominated by three monitors took up almost all the room, only leaving enough floor space for an office chair and a filing cabinet.

I switched Rider's laptop connection to my own, pulling up my emails on the screen and answering a few questions from Onyx and the suppliers who'd been caught up in this state of emergency bullshit in Milton. The business would be fine, but it wasn't the most lucrative week to be a club owner.

Fucking agathos.

Usually, I could disappear into the zone when I was working and focus for hours, but tonight my mind refused to switch off. I'd woken earlier than usual, when the sun was still bright outside, and felt off. More than off, I felt *sad*. Not unlike how I'd felt when the auntie who raised me had died a few years ago. It was a profound sense of grief, that someone who'd been so important to me was gone, and I wouldn't see them until the Fates cut my mortal thread and sent me to the Underworld.

I must have been dreaming of Auntie Samira.

Or maybe I was just hungry. Hunger was as good an explanation for a weird mood as anything else.

I switched to the security cameras to do a sweep of the grounds before I headed back to the kitchen to make a facon butty and bring a general air of discomfort to everyone with my presence.

The driveway that led to the country house was long and windy, with a gate partway up where the forested area had been cleared and fences added. There was a camera directed at the road and my eyes narrowed as a shiny Ford hybrid approached, headlights shining bright before the vehicle turned onto the driveway.

That wasn't going to work for me.

This place was invitation-only, and no one had contacted either Rider or I to request an invitation.

Fortunately, the access pad to unlock the gate was in this office for that reason, and I triple checked the gates to make sure they were shut before locking all the internal doors and scanning the cameras that monitored the grounds to make sure none of the residents were outside.

It wasn't like daimons had *friends* who would come and visit them. Our relationships were transactional and reliant on proximity, for the most part. The group here would fight, fuck, and keep each other entertained while they were in the same place, then part ways and probably never see each other again. That was our way.

Perhaps they were in the area and happened to be lost, but I didn't much believe in coincidences these days. The gods worked in mysterious ways, and those ways usually caused the maximum amount of carnage for mortals.

I checked the camera part way up the driveway as the car continued to make its way slowly up the winding gravel. Hmm. The hybrid SUV wasn't an unusual choice for a daimon, but one *particular* daimon did own one in that shade of electric blue. One who would be able to find this place no problem, with just a quick trip into my head.

Maybe that was why I had woken up feeling odd.

The car stopped outside the gate, and the driver cut the engine while leaving the headlights on, illuminating the dark forest and grounds.

Bullet climbed out of the driver's side, shooting an arrogant grin at the camera as he made his way around the vehicle to the passenger door. I'd only met him once, but it wasn't an experience I was liable to forget.

Before I was cursed, I enjoyed intimacy of every kind with both men and women, whoever caught my attention. Sometimes a good fuck was better than a good fight to take the edge off the bloodlust, if it was just starting up. After I was cursed, any interaction that wasn't strictly professional lost its appeal.

That was why it had been so striking when the beautiful Oneiroi had made an appearance in Asphodel two years ago, drawing every daimon in the room to him with his preternatural appeal. He was marked by the Goddess, her magic clung to him, giving him an aura that regular daimons didn't possess.

So, in spite of my natural aversion to everyone, I'd danced with him. Despite the fact that I didn't let anyone touch me anymore, I'd grinded against him and felt lust for the first time in years. I'd *kissed* him, like I was a normal daimon who could indulge in normal things, like snogging someone I found attractive on a night out when I absolutely couldn't do things like that. Not anymore.

But he'd panicked before I had. Frozen up like a statue before bolting from the club and never looking back. At the time, I thought his Oneiroi gifts had tipped him off to the reek of the gods' magic on me. To the curse I'd never told anyone about.

As he opened the passenger door, and the woman I'd greedily obsessed over, watched, and dreamed about for months climbed out, I realized that wasn't the case.

Of course, Riot wasn't the only daimon she was connected to—it was well known that agathos had multiple lovers despite their generally prudish ways. Bullet had prophetic gifts, he must have known about her all along. Grace looked at him with a shy kind of adoration as she slipped her hand into his and let him guide her back around the car to stand in front of the intercom.

Every time I saw her, even through the camera lens, I felt like my heart was going to beat out of my chest. Oxygen was suddenly hard to come by, and my fingers itched with the urge to touch her, no matter how far away she was. It was even worse than usual, having been denied her beautiful face for so long.

She was safe. The agathos hadn't found her.

The relief was short-lived, though. Why had he brought her here? I trusted daimons more than I trusted agathos, but only just.

"Hellllooooooooo," Bullet said through the intercom, unnaturally cheerful considering everything about the situation. "Where's the lord of the manor?"

Fuck, it was inconvenient being unable to speak.

I grabbed my phone on the desk, scrolling absently through my long list of contacts until I got to Bullet's name. I hadn't asked him for his number, but I made a point to obtain it. Information was currency, after all.

Me: *Get her out of here.*

Not the most eloquent of messages, but that was the key information I wanted to get across. Grace had no business being here, and it was reckless of Bullet to bring her to a house full of violent daimons even if he'd *seen* a positive outcome.

This is why I didn't trust other people. They made idiotic decisions.

Bullet: *Now why on earth would I do something like that?*

"Bullet," Grace chastised softly, her voice drifting through the intercom that I'd deliberately kept connected so I could listen in. "Don't antagonize him."

245

Him. Me. She was talking about me. For months I'd watched over her from a distance, made sure no daimons had given her a hard time while she lived in Milton, and stayed in the shadows.

And now she was talking about me like she knew who I was.

"Antagonizing daimons is my specialty," Bullet replied with an unrepentant grin. "I can't help myself."

By the moon, he was trouble. Had the Fates really paired them? Had they really landed her with that idiot, Riot?

Was Grace mine too?

The pull I felt to her would indicate yes. But I couldn't believe the Fates would lumber Grace with a man already marked out by the gods as cursed. Nobody deserved that.

Me: *Grace doesn't belong here. Why would you bring her here?*

"It really sounds like he knows who I am," Grace murmured, leaning in close to Bullet to read the message. He looked at the top of her head with a mixture of devotion and a little disbelief, like he couldn't quite believe she was real. I was sure I'd do the same if Grace was hanging all over me like that.

"I guess I have a reputation after all the stuff in Milton," she added, sounding embarrassed.

Oh, darling. I knew about you long before that.

Bullet: *We have important matters to discuss with you.*

The formal language of his message was somewhat undercut by the wink he shot at the camera. He was an arrogant little shit. Beautiful too. I supposed getting an exclusive look at the future would make any person arrogant. I'd been arrogant for far less impressive reasons.

Grace chewed her lower lip nervously, staring at the phone as she waited for my response, and the idea of denying her anything felt like I was ripping my own chest open.

Me: *Whatever your request is, send it to Onyx.*

I blocked his number, intending to unblock it later once he'd got the message that I wasn't going to discuss this any further, and shut down the intercom link. Tipping my head back against the chair, I closed my eyes and waited for the feeling of unmitigated regret to dissipate.

Whatever they needed, whatever they asked Onyx for, I would make it happen. But I couldn't see her. Couldn't get close to her.

Physically couldn't speak to her.

There was nothing for Grace here except disappointment.

GRACE

CHAPTER 17

Well, that hadn't gone the way I expected. Frustration rolled off Bullet as he tapped out messages on his phone with his thumbs, but his face was as mildly amused as usual. It was an impressive mask.

"My messages are bouncing back," Bullet sighed, raising an eyebrow imperiously at the security camera, though I had a feeling Wild was already gone.

Maybe it was a little untoward for us to show up this way—it sounded like Wild was a fairly important person among daimons, and possibly us showing up on his doorstep—or whatever this place was—had insulted him.

I got the sense it was more than that though. He sounded like he *knew* me, he knew my name. Then again, I was a little bit famous among daimons now, wasn't I? Even before all this happened, I was the only agathos living in Milton, and I would have been pretty recognizable. I couldn't blame any of them for not wanting me around when I'd brought the daimons nothing but bad luck—Wild couldn't even get home because of what the agathos were doing in Milton.

It was still frustrating though. I hadn't even got a glimpse of him, hadn't heard his voice. There was nothing to indicate whether he was really mine or not. If only I could *see* him.

"We should probably go," I murmured, giving Bullet's arm a squeeze. "He obviously doesn't want to see us."

"But why?" Bullet asked, looking thoughtful. "What am I missing here?"

I tugged slightly at Bullet's blazer and he reluctantly allowed me to lead him back to the car, sighing dramatically as he got in the driver's side. I quickly got myself settled in my seat, clipping my seatbelt in and giving the imposing house in the distance one last look. It was barely visible in the darkness, a shadowy outline beyond the gate, and I wished I could see it better.

Why was Wild here, at this grand stately home? Apparently La Nuit had shown Bullet the location during our afternoon nap, but she hadn't given him any details on why Wild was here rather than in Milton. I'd driven past Wild's biggest club, Asphodel, plenty of times, and it looked nothing like this place. Asphodel was a huge converted factory with a red brick exterior and a very industrial feel, about as opposite from this elegant property as possible.

"Put the glasses on," Bullet reminded me. I nodded, grabbing the square white glasses with clear lenses that Bullet had insisted I wear, sliding them on.

"You know, I think fake glasses have already been proven to be the most ineffective disguise out there. I should at least add a stick-on mustache," I teased, trying to lift his spirits.

His lips twitched as he focused on backing out of the winding driveway in the dark. "Those particular glasses bounce back infrared light, scrambling facial recognition software. Your face will look like an indecipherable glowing blob on any CCTV footage."

"Nothing suspicious about that," I pointed out, raising an eyebrow at him.

"Privacy is a growing concern. The glasses are weird, but not *that* weird," he replied absently, mind clearly elsewhere.

Bullet was quietly contemplative as we drove home, blasting the soundtrack to *Wicked* at an almost deafening volume. Every time I felt even the faintest brush of his negativity or frustration, it was quickly followed by rapid humming or full on singing, depending on how down he'd been. It was obviously a coping mechanism, but I had a lot of questions about why he needed to employ it so frequently.

A little anger and frustration wasn't necessarily a bad thing. It was healthy, even. Had Bullet not basically said the same to me when I'd complained about my inner 'monster'?

I turned down the music, and Bullet shot me a questioning look as I figured out how best to broach the subject. Where were all my years of training and expertise from working at the shelter when I needed them? Being in Bullet's presence left me so tongue tied.

"Do you want to talk about Wild?" he asked, fingers still drumming incessantly.

"No," I said slowly. "I want to talk about you."

"That is a grim topic," Bullet chuckled. "Why Wild refused to see us, or even use the intercom to speak to us, is a far more exciting mystery."

"You're plenty of mystery all by yourself, you know," I commented wryly. "Sometimes I feel like... like you're almost a god in your own right." I stared out the window, finding it easier to have this conversation when we weren't making eye contact.

"Me?" Bullet asked in surprise. "Why?"

"There's magic *on* you," I explained clumsily, scrambling for the words. "*In* you. I can feel the Goddess' presence all around you."

I chanced a look at him out of the corner of my eye, surprised to find an almost grim look on his face. It was a definite departure from the forced cheeriness he usually favored whenever something was bothering him.

"You can feel it because it's there," Bullet said eventually. "The connection the Oneiroi have with the divine doesn't have an on/off switch. It's like a frequency that we're constantly tuned in to."

I frowned to myself, trying to imagine what that would be like. Did he feel like he was constantly sharing his mind with someone else? I supposed he had lived with it his whole life and wouldn't know any differently, but the idea of it was... well, a little appalling, honestly.

"Do you, er, enjoy having that connection?" I asked lightly, not wanting to push my own thoughts on the matter to him.

Bullet scoffed, and I noticed his eyes darted to the volume control on the dashboard like he wanted to drown out his own thoughts with music.

"I promise, you can belt out *Defying Gravity* at the top of your lungs to your heart's content when this conversation is done," I said primly, giving him a pointed look that made him chuckle. "You can talk to me about anything, you do know that, right? With everything going on, I'm not sure I've done the best job at making you feel important—"

251

"You don't have anything to worry about, Amazing Grace, I promise," Bullet replied with a gentle smile, though I felt a small brush of sadness against my skin. "As for the connection with the Goddess and the Fates? It's a lot for any one person to bear. Let's just say I'm glad it's my burden and not yours."

I wanted to press him for more information, but I could also *feel* how much that admission had cost him.

Why was Bullet the only Oneiroi left at the house? He'd made it sound like there had been others—

"How willing are you to hide under a blanket in the backseat for your own safety so we can go through a drive-thru?" Bullet asked suddenly. "Tonight was a bust, and I'm willing to pollute my temple-like body with fries just this one time to make me feel better. And I bet you're missing meat."

So. Much.

"I'm convinced," I replied. "So long as you order me a hamburger. Then we're going to talk about why you are so determined to hide your emotions, even though you couldn't hide them from me if you tried."

Bullet grinned, pulling over as we approached the restaurant so I could move into the back. "I'll get you two burgers and all of the fries, then you'll be too busy to talk."

I had been too busy eating my burger and fries to interrogate Bullet again, and he looked altogether too smug about that. I'd planned to try again when we were back home, but the moment we pulled up in front of the barn, all thoughts of interrogations went out of my head.

I felt Riot's presence before I saw him. Bullet chuckled as I threw open the door and ran clumsily over the gravel driveway to the base of the stairs where Riot was waiting, leaning against the railing looking all devil-may-care and delicious.

Suddenly, I didn't care even a little that I'd been taught my entire life to be modest and respectable. That I'd always been taught that public displays of affection were wrong.

I couldn't think past the fact that Riot was back and I'd missed him more than anything. I threw myself into his arms and he caught me with a surprised *oomph* while I grabbed clumsily at his hair, pulling his mouth down to meet mine.

The connection between us, the not-quite bond, sparked to life the moment we touched and we both groaned at the sensation. The ache both receded and fired up all at once. Or perhaps it moved—the ache in my chest morphing to an ache between my thighs.

Riot lowered himself to the steps, guiding me down with him until I straddled his legs, silently cursing the tight denim that was keeping my legs imprisoned. If my grip on Riot's hair was painful, he didn't mention it as his own hands roughly tugged at my back pockets like he could rip my jeans off if he tried hard enough, his tongue hot and demanding as our kiss became increasingly inappropriate for our surroundings.

That ship had probably sailed when I'd straddled him.

"Fuck, Gracie," Riot groaned, his hips shifting slightly beneath me, and I was right there with him, desperate for the skin-on-skin friction my jeans were denying me.

"I missed you," I chanted against his lips. "I missed you, I missed you, I missed you."

"Are you dry humping on the stairs?" Bullet asked from behind me, voice filled with amusement. "I mean, do what you gotta do, but you'd probably be more comfortable inside," he chuckled, climbing over a grumbling Riot and still singing *Defying Gravity* under his breath as he made his way up the stairs and unlocked the front door.

Riot sighed, pressing his forehead against mine, breathing heavily. His hands ran over my waist and hips in a less fervent manner, more like he was verifying I was still there. I found myself doing the same, burrowing my hands under Riot's sweater, feeling the ridges of his stomach through the cotton of his t-shirt.

"Is he driving you crazy?" Riot asked seriously, dark red and purple eyes staring deeply into mine.

"What?" I laughed quietly. "He's my soul bond, he's a part of me. Of course he doesn't drive me crazy."

"Not even with all the singing?" Riot asked dubiously.

"I love the singing," I assured him. "And I can feel your emotions, so I know it doesn't bother you that much either. You were a little happy to see him."

Riot mumbled something unintelligible against my skin, his lips pressed against my shoulder. He could complain all he liked, but deep down, Riot cared for Bullet. More than the average daimon cared for another daimon, at least.

"Where did you go?" Riot asked, pulling back with a frown. "I wasn't expecting you guys to be out. Were you safe? The state of emergency has been lifted, but you know the agathos are still looking for you, right?"

I opened my mouth to answer before closing it again. Bullet had been absolutely confident that there was nothing to be afraid of, but I doubted that was going to reassure Riot.

"Maybe that's something we should all discuss together?" I hedged, glancing up at the apartment. Smoke was already unfurling from the chimney, and I imagined Bullet crouching in front of the fireplace, singing to himself as he built the fire.

It made me feel all gooey inside.

Riot sighed. "I'm not going to like this conversation, am I? Come on then, Gracie. As soon as this chat is done, I'm stealing you for some intense... cuddling."

I laughed as I climbed off him, snagging his fingers the moment he stood and tugging him up the stairs behind me. There wasn't any point in acting coy—I knew as soon as I had Riot alone, I was going to be all over him.

Maybe not even alone.

Bullet had turned the lamps on and got the fire going by the time we joined him. He was sitting in the corner of the couch, arms crossed behind his head, legs extended, humming idly to himself.

Riot moved to the armchair closest to the fire, pulling off his damp sweater before tugging me down into his lap and wrapping his arms around my waist. Bullet's amused expression faltered for a moment, showing a glimpse of the man underneath he was always trying to hide, before his mask slipped back in place.

Perhaps it was jealousy? I never sat on his lap with this kind of ease. The timing had never seemed right, but I hadn't really *tried* either. Maybe I'd assumed that because Bullet wasn't snuggly at nighttime that he wasn't snuggly in general, which wasn't really fair. He didn't sleep quite like everybody else.

"So, where did you go tonight?" Riot asked, sounding suspicious.

"We went out to Easton to track down Wild," Bullet replied matter-of-factly.

Riot groaned, tipping his head back against the armchair. "You do know Grace is a wanted woman, right?"

"You do know I'm a psychic, right?" Bullet countered, grinning.

"Nothing happened." I stroked circles into Riot's arm with my thumb, marveling at how good it felt to touch him again. "We didn't even see him. He messaged Bullet's phone while we were outside the gates of the property and told us to leave."

"Do you think he's your, you know, soul bond?" Riot asked, looking a little disgruntled at the idea.

"I won't know until I see him," I replied apologetically, grabbing his hand and giving it a squeeze. "Bullet seems to think so, and maybe that's how you get out of your deal with Viper. Though you're here now, so does that mean you're free?" I asked hopefully.

Riot gave a sad half smile, shaking his head. "The state of emergency has been lifted, so I was able to get out of Milton. I'm sure Viper will call me back when he wants me."

That was disappointing, but not particularly surprising. Based on Bullet's visions, it seemed like we'd have to do more than just *try* to visit Wild to get Riot out of his deal.

"Not that Wild would be willing to do me a solid even if he were your soul bond. Besides, couldn't you see that nothing would come of your trip, oh psychic one?" Riot asked Bullet, and I hated to admit that I'd been wondering the same thing.

Bullet's brow furrowed for a moment before he smoothed the distressed expression away. "Maybe it wasn't nothing. Maybe tonight's trip wasn't important. They want us to discover some things on our own, I guess."

"Convenient," Riot muttered. "So now what? The troops are gone. There are still some agathos hanging around—not in uniform—mostly picking fights and being assholes, but we can get in and out easily enough now. I'd be shocked if Wild wasn't back in Milton by dawn."

"He directed us to ask Onyx, so I guess we can do that. But as you said, you'll be summoned back to Milton by Viper," Bullet pointed out. "So you could go have a chat with Wild at Asphodel."

Riot chuckled humorlessly. "I *know* you haven't seen *that* conversation in your visions. Me walking right up to Wild on his turf is basically a death sentence—"

"What? No, we don't need to do anything that puts Riot in danger," I said quickly. I'd protect the soul bonds I had over ones I hadn't even met, even if it hurt to do so.

Perhaps I was the tiniest bit bitter that Wild had sent me away without even speaking to me. I was frustrated that he knew who I was, and I didn't know who he was. And maybe feeling a teeny bit insecure about the whole interaction.

Riot didn't even attempt to hide his smug expression that I'd gotten all protective over him, and I lightly smacked his arm without thinking about it.

"Cute, Gracie," Riot murmured. "Has Bullet been bringing out your playful side in my absence?"

Huh. I hadn't thought about it, but maybe? Bullet was playful, even in the heaviest of times. Perhaps he was rubbing off on me.

"I do tend to bring out the best in people," Bullet said solemnly, saving me from answering. "You should spend some time with me, Riot. I'm sure we can dig up one or two decent qualities if we work hard at it."

Riot scoffed, but I felt his amusement brushing against my skin. "The only thing you'll dig up if I'm forced to spend time with you is my last nerve."

257

Sugar, these two secretly adored each other under all the sniping, I could feel it. It made my heart feel funny—too light and too full at once.

That wasn't the only thing I was feeling.

I was acutely aware of how handsome Bullet looked tonight in his dark blazer and crisp white shirt, unbuttoned low enough to see the gold of the bullet he wore around his neck glinting in the light. I'd already been feeling on edge, and that was before I saw Riot, smelled his familiar scent, felt the warmth of his body under mine. In just a week, I'd forgotten how he had a tendency to entirely engulf me in his hugs, the way he had no shame about curling around me like he'd never let me go.

Between the physical overload of being back in Riot's presence after so long, the incomplete bond hanging between us, and the constant simmering want for Bullet was overwhelming, I was about three seconds away from orgasming if one of them looked at me the wrong way. Or the right way, perhaps.

"I need a shower," I blurted, trying to climb off Riot without actually touching him, in case I spontaneously combusted. I wanted some intimacy with Riot, but I didn't know how to initiate it with Bullet here, and I definitely didn't want to ask Bullet to leave.

If I could take the edge off, I'd be fine. I could handle this.

"Um, okay then," Riot replied, sounding confused. "I'll be here."

Sugar, Grace. You have got to get yourself together.

Or complete the bonds. You've got to do something.

BULLET

CHAPTER 18

I scrolled through news articles on my phone, idly checking to see if Gaia had destroyed any lives today with natural disasters. Riot relaxed in the armchair with his eyes shut, the firelight casting moving shadows over his face. The only sounds in the room were the noise of the running shower from the bathroom and the occasional crackle of the fireplace. As tempting as it was to start singing *The Music of the Night* to fill the silence, I got the impression that Riot wouldn't appreciate it. He'd always had terrible taste in music.

Grace would never say anything because she was so happy to see him she probably hadn't even noticed, but Riot looked *terrible*. There were dark shadows under his eyes and his skin was sort of pallid and gray, which I was pretty sure wasn't a good sign.

He was valiantly trying to hide his suffering, not wanting Grace to know how much the lack of bond was getting to him, but it was riding him even harder than it was riding me. Too bad I hadn't been sent any signs on when *that* would happen.

Riot made a strangled noise as we got a full on jolt of Grace's lust like an injection straight into our veins. I had no idea if my not-a-bond had caught up to where his was or not, but we'd definitely just felt the same thing. Riot jackknifed upright in the chair, eyes instantly alert.

"She masturbates a lot in the shower," I told him absently, still scrolling through my phone.

Riot choked on his saliva. "Excuse me?"

"Like a teenage boy level of self-love," I continued. "It's great, right? After a lifetime of repression—beyond repression, really, since the agathos aren't even able to *feel* lust—she's finally getting to explore what makes her body feel good."

"That's... good," Riot said slowly, giving me a strange look. Probably wondering why I wasn't taking care of all of Grace's needs, which was a fair question. Maybe because I was one percent more intimidated by this whole girlfriend thing than I thought I would be, though we'd been making progress over the past couple of days.

"But now you're here, so the violent cravings will probably go down and you can always take the edge off anyway until Grace is ready for the bond," I finished, locking my phone and tipping my head back against the couch.

And I wasn't jealous about the easy affection between them. Nope, not even a little. I didn't care that Grace had basically humped Riot on the stairs on sight. That was cool.

"How are you so fine *sharing*?" Riot asked, sounding disgruntled. Spooky, it was like he was reading my mind. *Soul-bonds-in-law, unite!* "I don't want to murder you as much as I thought I would, but every instinct I have tells me to keep Grace to myself."

260

"I've always known this was how it would be." I shrugged, deciding if I was energetic enough to walk to the kitchen and make some camomile tea. We'd stopped at the drive-thru mostly for Grace's benefit, and I was feeling gross from the fries that did not belong in my temple body. "Besides, I'm an Oneiroi. You know what that means. I want to know that Grace is in good hands."

Riot gave me a sharp look. "You're obviously not like other Oneiroi."

"Yes and no," I replied, absently humming *Who Lives, Who Dies, Who Tells Your Story* under my breath. If Riot would just agree to watch Hamilton with me, he'd get the reference.

"Bullet," Riot snapped, looking disturbed. Maybe the big guy cared about me more than he let on? That was cute. "Be serious. That isn't happening to you."

"What's not happening?" Grace asked quietly, looking between Riot and I from the doorway. She was wearing some low slung flannel pajama pants and a matching navy henley that exposed a sliver of smooth brown skin at her waist, her black hair pulled up in a haphazard bun.

I'd been putting off this conversation, but it had to happen eventually, and Riot rightfully wouldn't let me avoid it. Grace deserved to know what she was getting into.

"The Oneiroi curse," I said, doing my best spooky boogeyman voice.

"Stop it! You are *not* cursed," Riot hissed. Aww, I knew he loved me. Underneath that brooding bad boy exterior was a big ol' teddy bear. "You are such a pain in the ass," he added under his breath.

"What curse?" Grace pressed as she moved closer to us, ignoring her other boyfriend's mutterings.

"Well, I'm 29. Oneiroi don't live past 30," I told her, pushing my emotions down deep. I'd had my whole life to come to terms with it, but the idea of leaving Grace behind never hurt any less.

"What? Why?" Grace breathed. She closed the distance between us and dropped to her knees at my feet like it was too painful to maneuver her body to the couch.

This wasn't a conversation I'd wanted to have for this exact reason. Grace's fear was like cold blades against my skin.

"It's a lot for a mortal's mind to handle. The bombardment of visions, the connection to the divine. Eventually our brains sort of combust. We basically go into a coma from the brain overload, then just fade away."

I shrugged like it wasn't a big deal. *No time for bitterness.*

No time to make Grace feel anything other than happiness. That's what I should have been doing, not making her feel this abject misery.

"No. That's not going to happen to you," Grace said, shaking her head vehemently. "It's not. You're not like the other Oneiroi, anyway. Like you said, older daimons are different..."

Unable to handle her pain for a second longer without touching her, I leaned forwards and pulled her up, encouraging her to straddle my lap, wrapping my arms around her back. It was a selfish thought, but I was glad I got to hold her the way Riot had outside. Grace laid her head on my shoulder, burying her face against my neck, her tears splashing against my skin. I tightened my grip, wishing I could take away the pain that I'd caused.

Occasionally, in the dreamscape, I'd talk about my short life expectancy. Mostly when I was younger and struggling to come to terms with all the things I was going to miss out on. Grace had always been empathetic, but she'd never taken it this badly. She hadn't known me then though. Not for the first time, I was frustrated that she had no memory of me from before.

"I can't say for certain, Amazing Grace. I'm the last Oneiroi left. After we meet your fourth soul bond, my future is less certain. I still see visions of yours, though," I told her in an upbeat tone, hoping to cheer her up. "It's a good one."

A future full of traveling the world, of fame, of sad tears and happy laughter. There were hurdles too, paths that were more difficult to travel than others, but I refused to accept those were even options. Until my mind gave up on me, I'd do everything I could to make sure Grace's future was *perfect*.

"That's not going to reassure us if you're not there too," Riot groused.

You love me, I mouthed over Grace's head, stroking her back. He rolled his eyes, but there wasn't much heat in it.

"That's not a great incentive to find all four soul bonds," Grace mumbled into my neck, still sniffling.

"You wouldn't have a choice even if you wanted to," I chuckled. "It's going to happen. Sooner rather than later."

"You should have told me all this before we sought out Wild," she chided.

"If anything, that's an example of why we won't be able to put it off. I'm confident Wild is the missing piece to sever the deal with Viper. If you want Riot free from Viper's clutches, then you have to do this. Ergo, you have to meet your third soul bond, if my hunch is correct."

"Okay, so then we just don't find the fourth one," Grace grumbled. I smiled as I rubbed her back, knowing she wouldn't be able to resist when the time came. The call was too strong, and I wouldn't want her to resist anyway, not on my account.

Riot's head was tilted to the side as he narrowed his eyes at me, a silent question in them. He definitely suspected who his future soul-bond-in-law was, and I shot him a reassuring grin to let him know he wouldn't have to choose between his bestie and me. I wouldn't let Grace hold herself back for my benefit.

"I'm not going to let anything happen to you," Grace said fiercely, clinging on to me like I was about to disappear at any moment. "I'll find a way. I refuse to believe that the Goddess would give me you, only to take you away from me."

And she couldn't lie. When Grace said she refused to believe my days were numbered, she really meant it.

"If anyone could find a way, it's you," I agreed easily, not wanting to argue with her. Not wanting to point out that what she wanted was impossible, and that she shouldn't get her hopes up because my days were numbered, like it or not.

I moved my hands up to toy with Grace's hair that had escaped from its tie. It was straight most of the way down, but curled into thick corkscrews at the end, and I'd always wanted to see if they were as springy as they looked. Now that Grace was on my lap, hugging me, touching me like it was the most natural thing in the world, I wasn't going to throw the opportunity away.

She smelled so pretty. And looked so pretty. And felt so...

Sexy.

And maybe it was me searching for a distraction, or a connection after a conversation that reminded me my days were numbered, or maybe it was just Grace, because all of a sudden her sexiness was almost overwhelming to think about.

Her pajama top had ridden up further, exposing most of her lower back, and my thumb hesitated above the exposed patch, so tempted to see if the skin on her back was as silky as the rest of her. Riot smirked at me, folding his hands behind his head and leaning back.

"Feeling shy, oh wise one?" he asked, raising one judgmental eyebrow at me, like he hadn't been all *wah, wah don't you get jealous* ten minutes ago.

Grace raised her head to look at me, glancing back at Riot over her shoulder before giving me her full attention. "You can touch me," she said softly. "I know I haven't been good about encouraging you—encouraging affection between *us*—and we're both shy and kind of new to this."

The fear hadn't gone away, but the simmering arousal that she hadn't quite managed to rid herself of in the shower had bubbled up to the surface. It felt a lot more pleasant on my skin than her panic, that was for sure.

Even before Riot had shown up, Grace had been checking me out all night—probably because I was looking exceptionally suave in my new suit. When Riot had shown up, I had assumed the two of them would disappear into the bedroom, and he would take care of the arousal that was riding her from the incomplete bonds and general sexiness of her boyfriends. The way she was feeling though, the way she was looking at me... Maybe I'd be a bigger part of tonight than I realized.

It'd be a little embarrassing if we had a repeat of my performance from the other day in front of Riot though. He'd give me shit for the rest of my short life if I came in my pants, and I didn't need to be a psychic to know that.

With encouragement in Grace's eyes, I let my thumb slip under her top, brushing against soft, warm skin. How had I kept my hands *off* her in the dreamscape? Kudos to me. Ten points to Bullet for being the perfect gentleman.

265

Grace sat back on her heels, fingers toying shyly with the lapel of my jacket. There was a lot going on in her head—her emotions were like butterflies dancing just out of my reach. Riot, with his stronger bond, was observing Grace's back clearly, a pensive look on his face.

"You know, Gracie," he said suddenly, startling us both. "When you're ready, I think Bullet should be your first. Your first time. Your first *bond*."

Grace's tentative movements froze, her shock mingling with mine. Mr. How-Do-You-Share was suggesting this? I mean, I wasn't going to argue with him, but it was an unexpected development, and I wasn't someone who dealt with a lot of unexpected things in my life.

Like, the total opposite, basically.

"Why do you say that?" Grace asked, her hands resting against my chest. She wasn't ruling anything out, which was awesome for my ego. She just sounded curious.

"Because he's been waiting for you. Because he's been a constant presence in your life since the beginning," Riot said thoughtfully. In all honesty, I'd probably scored some pity points with the reminder I was going to die soon, but I was selfish enough to take them.

"I'm not saying you have to," Riot added hastily, always putting Grace at ease. "Just letting you know that I'd be okay with it. That because you met me first in real life doesn't mean you need to bond with me first."

"Excellent logic," I supplied. "If not a little unexpected from Mr. Possessive."

Grace turned to look at me, the corners of her mouth lifting. I brushed my thumb over her back again, memorizing the bumps and ridges of her spine, wondering if I'd ever get used to touching her. In real life! A real life girl.

It was more surreal being awake than dreaming these days.

266

"I'm still possessive," Riot grumbled. "Honestly, I think I should be in the room to give you pointers so Grace's first time isn't, you know, awful."

Grace's eyebrows shot up while mine slammed down, seriously contemplating that idea. In my head, I liked to think our first time wouldn't be two minutes of awkward fumbling, but was I willing to test that theory on the woman I loved? Maybe I should consult the cards.

"You okay, Amazing Grace?" I asked, forcing myself to be present in the moment and not run off and immediately ask the Fates.

"Hm? Oh yes, I'm fine." Was her voice a little breathy, or was I imagining things? Surely the idea of being watched was pretty normal for agathos? For all their emphasis on purity, they had *multiple lovers*. There had to be multiple lover stuff going on.

"I think you like that idea, Gracie," Riot added, sounding smug as he stared at the back of her head with hooded eyes. "I can feel how much you like that idea."

If I was a nicer person, I'd give Grace an out of this conversation because her cheeks were growing increasingly flushed, but I was still a daimon at the end of the day.

"I want the bond," Grace whispered, so quietly I tilted my head forward to try to catch it.

"What was that?" I asked in disbelief. Riot sat forward on his chair, elbows resting on his knees as he tried to listen in.

"I want the bond," Grace reiterated, not much louder, but Riot definitely caught it this time if his wide eyes were anything to go by. "I do. I've been thinking about it a lot, and I feel ready to take that next step. But I, um, don't want to get pregnant."

Riot made a strangled noise in the corner. "Yeah. Let's, uh, not do that. One thing at a time and all."

I smiled softly at Grace, stroking my thumb along her jaw. For all the many visions I'd been given of Grace's future, I'd never seen her pregnant. There had been plenty with a child in the background though, so I guess it happened for her somehow, after I was gone.

"So, we'll use condoms then," Riot suggested, breaking the lovey dovey staring contest Grace and I were having.

Grace's lips pursed slightly. "I have been thinking about the, er, logistics a little." Her cheeks flushed at that admission and I couldn't stop myself from grinning. "I don't know if the bonding would work with a barrier. You know?"

"You mean we solidify the bond through the magic of our jizz?" Riot deadpanned, making Grace's face burn an impressive shade of crimson.

"You jest, but the gods take jizz seriously," I told Riot, saving Grace from answering. "When Kronos sliced off Ouranos' balls, Aphrodite emerged in all her glory from his foaming sea jizz."

Grace clapped both hands over her face, groaning in embarrassment.

"Alright then," Riot replied with a shrug. "I don't have a good argument against the magic sperm theory. How do you feel about going on birth control, Grace?"

Grace dropped her hands, returning them to balance on my chest and taking a deep breath like she could exhale out the awkwardness. "I'm not exactly sure if human birth control would work on me—it wasn't encouraged among bonded agathos. We were always taught to accept children in Anesi—*Gaia's* own timing."

I snorted. "You all give Gaia too much credit. Timing, destiny, the general outline of one's life, that's all the work of the Fates. They're the busiest goddesses in existence."

"Can't you ask them if Grace is going to get pregnant then?" Riot suggested, not entirely off-base with his assumption for a change.

"I could," I replied slowly. "But when it comes to love, death, and children, they're notoriously vague with their answers. I think it's an entertainment thing for them."

"They get their kicks out of being evasive?" Riot asked drily.

"They're immortal beings in charge of every single thread of life on Earth. Of course that's how they get their kicks."

I mean, obviously. Eternity was a long fucking time, and they had a relentless job.

"Well, daimon women use human birth control all the time, if that helps," Riot suggested. "I'll go, uh, get tested and everything too. Not that I've ever not used protection, but just in case."

"Well, aren't you quite the Chatty Cathy tonight?" I teased, taking great pleasure in his uncomfortable ramblings. I wasn't even sure we could get those kinds of human diseases, but it was a good idea to be safe anyway. Except we'd have to wait until we could see one of our doctors. Riot shot me a death glare over Grace's shoulder, but it seemed less death-y than usual, because he had definitely missed me while he'd been stuck in Milton.

"Shut up," Riot muttered, slumping back in his chair. Grace shot him a reassuring smile over her shoulder before returning her attention to me—aka The Dying One—and I got the feeling she secretly liked the way her two soul bonds needled each other. As a kid she'd complained a lot about the silence in her household, and there wasn't any of that with us around.

"Okay. As soon as the birth control thing is all sorted, then bonding," Grace said assertively, tipping her chin up stubbornly. Either she was determined to beat her agathos self-consciousness, or the orgasm she'd given herself in the shower had emboldened her.

"We could still practice other things until then though... Take the edge off, as it were," Grace continued, as though she hadn't just had a solo session of taking the edge off. Though I supposed her edge was rougher than mine was—the incomplete bond was *bothering* me, so two incomplete bonds were probably driving her steadily insane.

"What'd you have in mind?" I teased, running my hands over her shoulders and down to her waist, settling at a polite distance above her hips. It never ceased to amaze me that I got to touch her this way. Touch her *at all*, even to hold her hand without the thin veil of the dreamscape dulling the sensation. She was here and warm and real, straddling my lap.

Maybe I was dead already and this was all an extended vision, a final gift from La Nuit. This seemed too good to be true.

Grace leaned forward, her lips brushing mine. "I can feel your gratitude."

"Because I am very, *very* grateful," I replied, chasing her mouth. "I would very much like to demonstrate my gratitude for your existence with oral sex."

Grace squeaked—*squeaked* like a mouse—her eyes flying open as she sat back on her heels to look at me. "Really?"

"Yeah, really?" Riot drawled, raising an eyebrow at me. "That was the least sexy proposition I have ever heard."

"*Proposition* makes it sound so seedy," I shot back, shaking my head in disappointment. "However, I can admit that I'm not experienced in this area, so perhaps it'd be wiser for me to watch and learn this time around."

270

"I thought I was in control of this conversation, but it rapidly slipped away from me," Grace said faintly. "Are you, um, suggesting..."

"He's suggesting that I taste that pretty pussy I've been dreaming about while he watches and learns the best way to satisfy you," Riot replied, sounding very pleased with the idea. "Are you on board with that plan, Gracie? You can always say no, we won't get upset."

I was so confident she'd agree, I'd have eaten my tarot cards if she said no. She may have been chewing nervously on that lower lip, but the lust that was pouring off her was so strong, it felt like grasping fingers and raking nails over my skin.

Grace *wanted.*

"Okay," she whispered. "That sounds, um, we could do that."

"On the bed then, Amazing Grace," I instructed with a grin, tapping her butt gently. "Let's make sure you have plenty of room to relax."

Grace wasted no time scrambling off me, and I grabbed her hand as she led the way to the bedroom, squeezing her fingers to let her know that she was still in charge here, despite Riot's dirty talk. She squeezed mine back, shooting me a soft smile over her shoulder before stopping at the end of the bed.

Reluctantly, I let her go, clearing some space on the dresser and hopping up, getting myself settled in. I watched as Riot prowled towards Grace like a predator with prey in his sights, and she all but melted at the sight of him.

There was no nervousness or hesitation when Riot wrapped a hand around the back of Grace's head and yanked her towards him. He didn't look like he was second guessing every move when his mouth slanted over hers, his hand fisting the side of her top, tugging her forward until their hips were flush.

I made myself comfortable while they lost themselves in their kiss, in each other, forgetting I was there in the best kind of way. I waited for the raging jealousy to hit, but it never came.

Riot had been away against his will for a while, and he and Grace had missed each other. What could be more natural than this? More right? They needed this moment.

I wasn't quite unselfish enough to walk away and leave them to it, but I didn't resent them for it either. That was a nice realization to have.

Riot growled in frustration as he pulled away just long enough to yank Grace's top off, leaving her in her pajama pants and a silky white bra that I'd definitely made the right call in buying. Both Riot and I seemed to be holding our breaths for a few seconds, waiting to see if this was going to be the moment that Grace pulled back, her shyness getting the better of her, but instead she tugged at the hem of Riot's t-shirt, encouraging him to strip too.

Huh. Maybe I should find ways to get rid of Riot more often, because the homecoming was proving to be worth it.

Riot's mouth moved to Grace's neck and I watched somewhat clinically as he paused at each sensitive spot he found, laving attention on that area while his hands slowly smoothed over her hips, giving her time to say no before his hands found the waistband of her pants, tugging them gently to let her know his intentions.

She made that breathy whiny sound that felt like a shot of lust directly to my already hard dick, and Riot pushed her pants down, her panties going with them.

Oh dear.

I was definitely going to come in my pants again.

GRACE

CHAPTER 19

Oh, how I had missed Riot.

I was feeling a little foolish now for taking care of things myself in the shower. Not that my hand had felt *bad*, but Riot's hands on me felt so much better.

In the back of my mind, I still hadn't quite banished the irritating feeling that I wasn't doing this right. That I should be in a room with Riot alone, under the blankets with the lights off, completing the bond and praying to Gaia the entire time that it resulted in pregnancy.

Nothing about that appealed to me though. I wanted the feel of Riot's mouth and hands on my body, of Bullet's eyes on my skin, of dim lamplight and exposed flesh and violent hedonism.

How could anything that felt this good be wrong?

I fell back on the mattress with a little nudge from Riot, feeling very much like caught prey as he crawled over my body, capturing my lips as I squirmed underneath him, needing friction he wasn't providing me. My painfully hard nipples rubbed uncomfortably against my silky bra, but somehow that was the line I had drawn in the sand.

The bra stayed on. For modesty purposes. Even though my lower half was entirely uncovered underneath Riot's enormous frame.

"Can't wait to see if you taste this sweet everywhere," Riot murmured against my mouth, making me blush from the roots of my hair to the tips of my toes.

What if I didn't? What if he didn't like it?

"Get outta your head, Amazing Grace," Bullet chided softly from the other side of the room. "Just *feel*."

I closed my eyes and let the thoughts swirling around my head go, concentrating on the softness of Riot's lips contrasting with the scrape of his stubbled jaw as he worked his way down my body, pausing to tease one nipple then the other through my silky bra, but keeping it in place until I was ready to remove it. He bit me gently through the fabric and my back arched involuntarily at the sudden difference between soft and hard.

The further he moved down my stomach, the less self-conscious I became. Riot's movements were deliberate, and the lust that both he and Bullet were feeling was unmistakable. Riot took his time sucking dark marks over my hip bones and inner thighs until my legs trembled, my lower body clenching around nothing.

Why didn't I want to go ahead with the bonding again? I probably wouldn't get pregnant. Surely no one got pregnant from their first time?

"I can feel your resolve slipping," Riot murmured before scraping his teeth over my skin. "No matter how much you beg, Gracie, no one is fucking you tonight. When the lust clears, you'll realize it was the right call."

Bullet hummed in agreement from somewhere entirely too far away.

But then Riot's wicked tongue ran teasingly over my slit and rational thought exited my brain entirely. I made an embarrassing noise I was sure I'd never made before as Riot settled his broad shoulders between my thighs, lifting my legs out of the way. I draped them over his upper arms in an absolutely obscene way, my hips moving of their own accord, trying to get closer to the source of bliss that was Riot's mouth.

His thumbs parted me, opening me up to him, and he slanted his entire mouth over me, french kissing me as thoroughly down there as he'd kissed my mouth.

"Delicious," he rumbled, looking up the line of my body at my flushed face. I didn't even remember opening my eyes, but I was staring down at him, contemplating grabbing his messy black hair and shoving him back where I wanted him.

"Frustrated?" he teased, his breath ghosting over my hypersensitive nerves.

"You know I am," I snapped, surprising both of us with the vehemence in my voice as I briefly contemplated using my heels to kick him into action like a horse.

"Mm, this is a fun new side of you," Riot chuckled, dipping his head before I could put my kicking plan into action. His tongue circled my clit and it was warmer and silkier and all around infinitely better than how my finger felt when I did this in the shower.

"What's he doing?" Bullet asked curiously, moving closer.

"You can't seriously expect me to talk right now," I panted.

"Try," Bullet replied cheerfully, and I vaguely felt the mattress dip as he sat near my head.

"Mm," Riot agreed, voice muffled. "Try."

His stubble scraped some particularly sensitive areas and for a moment I wondered if my soul had departed my body entirely.

"His, um, his tongue..." I began, everything coiling tight as my release built.

"Yes?" Bullet prompted. I opened one eye and found him lying next to me on his side, head propped up on his hand. His amethyst eyes sparkled with amusement, though he couldn't quite hide the heat in his gaze either, and any minor irritation I might have felt died at seeing the look on his face.

If he wanted to tease me, then two could play at that game.

I reached for Bullet's shirt tugging him closer and he caught himself with a grunt right before our heads crashed. Before he had a moment to recover, my hand was tangled in his hair, tugging his mouth down to meet mine.

Bullet wasn't confident with intimacy, but he was determined to get confident, I could feel it. I could feel it in the steely resolve pouring off of him, the way he altered his posture, settling more dominantly over me as his tongue swiped my lower lip, commanding entry in a way he'd never *commanded* me before.

I was lost to sensation. Two mouths on me, four hands exploring my body. Riot's fingers oh so slowly filled me up, first one, then a second as my body adjusted to the intrusion. He pumped slower than I wanted, as if to prolong the edge that I was hovering on.

It was too much and not enough because no matter how good it felt, it wasn't the completion of the bond. It wasn't the final tying of our souls together that I needed.

"Soon," Bullet murmured against my lips, one hand cupping my jaw. "Not today, Amazing Grace, but soon."

Riot hummed in agreement, and I was about to question when the two daimons became the responsible ones, but then Riot *sucked* on my clit, and my soul really did leave my body. Maybe it left this world entirely.

I had no idea if I screamed or if I was silent, if my eyes were closed or open, nothing. It was just pleasure upon pleasure, in waves that dragged me under and buoyed me up all at once.

My shower escapades were never going to cut it again. Not after the sucking thing. And as mortifying as it was to talk about these things, I was going to find the words to give Bullet explicit instructions on how to replicate that. It'd be worth the embarrassment.

Bullet laid down next to me, soothingly playing with my hair as Riot lowered my jelly-like legs onto the bed before propping himself up on his elbows, staring me dead in the eye as his tongue swiped his upper lip. He looked *immensely* pleased with himself, and I wanted nothing more than to replace that cocky look on his face with a half-dazed one like I was sure I had.

I wasn't sure how to go about returning the favor with my mouth, but I'd successfully made Bullet feel good with my *hand* earlier, and had thoroughly enjoyed the experience...

"Come here," I told Riot, patting the bed next to me.

Riot grinned, moving up next to me and playfully swatting my hands away. "What am I, a piece of meat to you?" he teased. "No returning the favor required, Gracie. Let me hold you for now. I don't think you're ready to meet Prince Albert yet."

"What?" I asked as Bullet laughed. "Who's Prince Albert?"

I woke up feeling *incredible*. Sated after last night and sleeping draped over Riot like a blanket. Emotionally satisfied after whatever dream Bullet had shown me.

Both guys were still asleep on either side of me—Riot snoring gently underneath me and Bullet as still as a statue, lying on his back near the edge of the bed. I'd noticed that he wasn't as cuddly in sleep as Riot was, but having them both here, the difference was stark. It was like Bullet was so absorbed in his visions, his body was completely paralysed.

Did he even like sharing a bed? I had just assumed that would be what he wanted without really discussing it with him first...

Gosh, I really needed to do better at managing multiple relationships. With Riot gone, my focus had been on his absence and the physical ache of the bond, but I shouldn't have let that detract from getting to know Bullet.

Surprisingly, I was able to climb out of bed without waking either of them, though perhaps Bullet was still lost in visions and Riot looked like he could use another couple of days' rest after his time away. I wondered if I could convince him not to shave the short beard that had grown in the week he'd been gone—it really added to his ruggedness, and I found the slight stubble burn on my inner thighs surprisingly sexy. Like a secret reminder I got to carry around with me all day of what we'd gotten up to last night.

I quietly grabbed some clothes and slipped out of the room to shower and get ready for the day. After I was done, I poked my head back in the bedroom door and found them both still asleep with a Grace-sized gap between them that made me smile. Riot had snuggled up to my pillow, and it made my heart somersault clumsily in my chest. I'd missed him so much, and now they were both here and we were all together.

It was tempting to reflect on how perfect it felt, lack of complete bonds aside, but that seemed like asking for something terrible to happen, considering I already had a prophecy hanging over my head.

Quietly, I shut the door behind me and crossed the silent living room to the kitchen, the low dawn light barely illuminating the space. I hadn't made a meal once since I'd been here, and at this rate I was going to forget *how* to cook. I'd mostly done bland, nutritious meal prep style cooking when I lived alone, and I was wasting the opportunity to be cooking for other people, which was much more satisfying.

I opted for pancakes since all the ingredients were there, putting on some coffee while I worked and eventually turning on the television for some low background noise. The footage of an earthquake on the other side of the world made my hands shake as I flipped the pancakes, stacking them haphazardly on a plate by the stove.

Was that another expression of Gaia's grief? Of rage or resentment or despair? Did she know that the Fates were calling for change? Was it a coincidence, or did every slight movement of the earth have meaning?

I thought I was scared of Gaia before, when I called her Anesidora and tried to live every facet of my life in a way that would please her. Now, I was *terrified*. The Gaia that Bullet had told me about—the one that lived in the pages of the ancient books I'd been reading—that Gaia was vengeful and power hungry, and yes she gave life, but she was also pretty happy to take it away.

The morning news show changed to a story about increased violence across multiple cities, spreading like a disease after a night of such vicious fighting in Milton that a state of emergency had been declared. For lack of any other explanation, gang violence was given as the reason, but I knew better.

How quickly this had escalated from a secret relationship between Riot and I that I'd been trying to keep from my parents to this level of unrest across multiple cities... It was unsettling.

The prophecy had made it clear that this was bigger than me, than *us*, but it still felt like a tiny catalyst for such a big response.

The pancake I was cooking was charred by the time I flipped it and I sighed, hoping the stack I'd made was enough. I turned the television off as some fluff segment came on, not in the mood to hear about magical diet pills made from never-before-discovered Himalayan plants or whatever it was they were talking about.

There was movement from the bedroom as I finished gathering toppings for the pancakes, setting them up on the dining table while the pancakes sat warming in the oven. There was a restless energy that I hadn't felt when I woke up this morning. I knew I was following some kind of order, a path that was laid out for me, and Bullet had been shown certain steps happening, but it felt like it was all going too slowly. Like all I was doing was creating more problems for people then leaving carnage in my wake.

Riot and Bullet emerged—Riot muttering irritably, Bullet grinning broadly—and I did my best to shake off my bad mood even though I knew they'd both sensed it.

"I made pancakes," I announced with a too-bright smile.

"You're too good to us," Riot murmured, kissing my forehead before shuffling towards the coffee machine.

"Thanks, Amazing Grace," Bullet added, kissing my cheek on the other side before following Riot into the kitchen to make tea.

How could I have it so good while people's homes vanished into the earth and daimon homes were attacked by agathos who didn't know the first thing about the goddess they claimed to be fighting for?

"You're frustrated," Bullet noted, steeping his tea. "Big things are coming. It was a busy night in my head."

"Are you going to elaborate on that?" Riot asked, frowning at Bullet.

"Yes and no." Bullet gave him a tight smile. "But first, breakfast. Let's not spoil the lovely meal our girl made for us."

They both worked hard to keep the conversation going as we ate. Riot filled us in on some of what had been happening in Milton, though he'd been keeping to the shadows as best he could to not draw too much attention to himself. By all accounts, the older daimons had enjoyed themselves immensely over the past week, antagonizing the agathos at every turn and using their gifts to rile up the human residents. Chaos was very much their domain, and the more Riot described, the more ridiculous it seemed that the agathos had invaded their territory in the first place. What had they expected to happen?

We cleaned up together, and I moved to the kitchen to put on another pot of coffee when Riot's phone rang. My heart sunk, assuming it was Viper, but Bullet slung an arm over Riot's shoulder like it was something he did all the time and peered at the phone screen.

"Rogue. You're going to want to get that," Bullet said lightly, not looking bothered at all when Riot absently shouldered his arm off, frowning at the screen.

Rogue. I vaguely remembered the beautiful daimon woman from the store, the one who'd distracted the human robber for me while I used my gifts to take his pain. She and Riot had clearly known each other, though I hadn't realized they were close enough to call each other.

I didn't know how I felt about that.

Jealous, perhaps.

"Hello Rogue," Riot drawled as he picked up the call, the boredom in his voice at odds with the curiosity he was feeling.

Why was he curious? What was this call about?

I could hear a feminine voice on the other end of the phone, but I couldn't make out what she was saying. She could have been talking about the weather or offering herself up on a platter for a sexual feast.

Either of those options seemed equally credible at that moment.

Bullet's arms wrapped around mine from behind, pulling them behind my back like he was restraining me. We seemed to have broken through some invisible touch barrier last night, and I was thrilled about it.

"Green is so your color," he teased in my ear while Riot watched me curiously, both eyebrows raised.

"This is not a rational response," I breathed, embarrassed they could sense my jealousy. I was in a relationship with both of them, what right did I have to feel jealous? They weren't agathos, they hadn't grown up expecting this kind of relationship.

"Feelings aren't always rational," Bullet replied cheerfully, moving his arms to rest over my collarbone instead and tugging me back against him. He wasn't usually so easily affectionate, but maybe he knew I needed it.

"No, they're not," I practically squeaked, feeling his hardness brush against my backside as he awkwardly angled his hips away from me.

"What can I say?" Bullet said without a trace of embarrassment. "I like this side of you."

"Wait, what?" Riot barked suddenly into the phone, his eyebrows slamming down. "What did you say her name was?"

He switched the phone to speaker mode, and held it out in front of him.

"*Mercy,*" the bored feminine voice responded. "*Her name is Mercy.*"

No.

No, no, no.

Daimons couldn't be talking about Mercy. My baby cousin wasn't meant to be dragged into whatever this was. This world of prophecies and shadowy goddesses and whatever else.

"Mercy?" I repeated, dragging Bullet with me as I lurched forwards. "What about Mercy?"

"*Nice of you to let me know I'm on speakerphone,*" Rogue groused, and I remembered her unimpressed expression clearly from that night at the convenience store.

"*Mercy is also* involved *with one of us,*" she drawled, sounding bored by the whole thing. "*My half-brother, Dice.*"

How could that be?

"Since when?" I asked, more to myself than anything.

"*Ages,*" Rogue replied. "*Since that little agathos crew showed up to paint the Milton community center.*"

Sugar, was that why Mercy had been so strange when I'd seen her before Joy's memorial? There had been something she hadn't wanted to tell me, and now I was kicking myself for not just telling her about Riot at the time. If I'd been honest with her, she could have been honest with me, and we'd have helped each other through all this.

I felt a strange mixture of dread and relief at the idea she might also have daimonic soul bonds. Dread at the trials she might be facing, selfish relief that I wasn't the only one.

"Guess there's something in the water at your family's place, huh?" Rogue asked drily, and I swallowed the very impolite urge to snarl at the phone. *"Anyway, I've been trying to get her to call you for ages, but she's super weird about it. She's at the house now, I'm going to put her on the phone. Talk to her about girl shit or whatever."*

Mercy was there? At a daimon's house? Why hadn't she wanted to call me earlier? Surely she knew about me and Riot by now, she should have known I'd be the one person she *could* talk to.

Rogue yelled *"Mercy!"* loud enough for us to all wince, so I guessed she hadn't been privy to that part of the conversation.

"Did you see this coming?" I asked Bullet quietly, holding his forearms and twisting my head back to look at him. His expression was thoughtful, head tilted to the side like he was examining his visions in his head on replay.

"When The Devil carried The Fool over the river, there were others on the shore opposite where I stood. Maybe they were waiting to cross too."

"What are you talking about?" Riot asked, summing up my thoughts.

"La Nuit did say there were others," Bullet added.

"Grace?"

Mercy's hesitant voice coming through Riot's phone made me freeze.

"Mercy?" I breathed.

"*Um, hello. I didn't expect to talk to you today,*" she replied. Her voice sounded so different. So much less youthful than the last time I'd spoken to her, like she'd grown up overnight.

"Why not? Rogue mentioned you weren't sure about calling me. I hope you know you can, I thought maybe you knew how to contact me..."

I'd sent her that message from Bullet's phone, but maybe she hadn't realized it was from me. Or maybe she hadn't cared? I'd left, after all. Would she be having this conversation if Rogue hadn't forced her into it?

I could hear Mercy's hesitation as she struggled to come up with an answer and my gut roiled. I guess my best friend hated me now? That was a comforting thought.

"*You're a wanted woman, you know?*" Mercy laughed nervously. "*I don't want to put you at risk. Besides, it's been kind of hectic. I met Dice and well, you know how it goes.*"

I laughed, eyes welling up with emotion. "Yes, I do know. Are you okay? Is he treating you well?"

"*Dice is great,*" Mercy said a little defensively.

"I'm sure he is," I assured her. The daimons I'd met had all been nicer than the agathos I knew.

"*Right. Sorry. I'm a little on edge, that's all,*" Mercy said apologetically.

"How are you in Milton?" I asked.

"*It's easier now that the troops have gone, but it's still kind of hard to get out of the house. Your parents just got back from Orlando, they were looking for you there.*"

They were?

"Maybe we could meet up?" I suggested. "Now that Milton is safer?"

"Sure. Maybe for an hour or something?"

It wasn't the enthusiastic response I was hoping for, but she had agreed, so that was something. The suspicion Riot was feeling scraped over my skin like nails, but Bullet continued to look thoughtful.

She's my cousin, I mouthed at Riot, frowning at his reaction. For most of my life, I thought Mercy was the only friend I had, the only one I hadn't felt the need to hide myself around until I met Riot, because I couldn't remember my interactions with Bullet.

Now that Mercy and I were in the same situation, there was no reason to hide from her. It was a *gift*. We could move forward together! She was turning 18 this week, she wouldn't even have to live with my parents anymore.

"Of course," I replied, barely keeping the excited grin off my face. "Where? When?"

"Bullet," Riot hissed, giving him an expectant look that I interpreted to mean *predict the future right now.*

"Saturday?" Mercy asked. *"Maybe by the community center? It's the only area I really know."*

Bullet kissed the top of my head before disappearing down the stairs, pulling out his cards as he went while Riot scowled fiercely at the phone. Neutral-ish ground seemed like a sensible idea, and we could hardly visit my Milton apartment without attracting attention.

"Your birthday," I said softly. "That sounds perfect."

"Um, yeah. Midday?" Mercy added. *"It's easier for me to, er, get away during the day, you know what I mean?"*

"Of course," I assured her. I couldn't imagine how stressful it would be for her if she was still living with my parents. However sorry I was feeling for myself, Mercy had it much worse.

"Your family can't know," Riot growled, making me jump at the barely disguised fury in his tone. "You need to swear that no one but Dice is coming with you. That you won't tell anyone else where or when we're meeting. Swear it, or no deal."

"Riot," I gasped, outraged that he'd speak to Mercy that way.

"Until Saturday," I promised Mercy, narrowing my eyes on Riot. I could hardly believe I was going to see my favorite cousin again. I'd been beginning to accept that I'd *never* see her again. Maybe I should go say some thank you prayers to whichever Goddess made this possible.

"I'm not sorry, Gracie," he told me, refusing to back down. "You trusted your family once before."

"Mercy isn't like that," I argued. "She's—"

"It's fine," Mercy interjected. *"I'm glad he's got your back. I swear that I won't bring anyone but Dice with me, and I won't tell anyone where or when we're meeting,"* she added flatly.

"See?" I asked Riot, with a pointed look. *Agathos can't lie.* "Nothing to worry about."

"I guess we will see," Riot replied, still looking unrepentantly suspicious. Part of me was offended, but the other part of me loved his fierce protective streak.

"See you then, Grace."

There was no enthusiasm in her tone, and I wouldn't blame her in the slightest for being offended at how rude Riot had been. He hung up the phone, shoving it in his pocket and crossing his arms defensively.

His biceps looked very nice when he crossed his arms, and I was annoyed at myself for noticing.

"That was rude."

"Okay," Riot said.

"Mercy was my only real friend before I met you."

"Okay." He tilted his head to the side, infuriatingly calm.

"I trust her with my *life*," I told him emphatically.

"Okay."

"Stop saying 'okay'!"

Riot's mouth curved, eyes sparkling. "Okay."

"I'm going to find Bullet," I announced in frustration, spinning away from him. Riot moved before I had the chance, closing the distance between us and wrapping an arm around my waist. He pulled me back against him, and as irritated as I was, there was no denying the amount of genuine worry pouring off Riot.

He'd appeased me once before and I'd ended up being snatched from work a few hours later. He wasn't about to make that same mistake twice, and I was mostly grateful for that. Mostly.

I sagged against him, resting my hands over his arm and tipping my head back on his shoulder. "Mercy is the only friend I have who doesn't have some kind of supernatural connection to me, Riot. I've known her my whole life. I trust her."

"Your heart's too big for your body, Gracie," Riot murmured in my ear. "I don't know shit about gods and goddesses, but I am pretty sure that's why they gave you me. To be the asshole who destroys those illusions you have of the world and the goodness you think resides in it."

I was shaking my head before he even finished talking. "You make me ask the questions that are hard to ask, but I still think there's nothing to be worried about."

"And I want more than anything for you to be right. I want you to be able to walk safely into Milton and have a lovely family reunion with your best friend and bond over how weird it is to have daimon soul bonds."

"But you don't think that will be the case?" I asked, feeling suddenly tired despite it only being mid morning. "Do you know Dice?"

"Not really. I know Rogue, and I knew she had a brother around ten years younger than her. It's not Dice I'm worried about."

"Mercy isn't like other agathos. She's like me. More like me than I even realized."

"And you found it hard to walk away. To leave that all behind, to shrug off the guilt you thought you should be bearing. You *still* struggle with that, even after what they put you through. How old is Mercy?"

"Eighteen on Saturday," I said quietly.

Riot grimaced, and I hated to admit he had a point. Mercy was young and maybe more easily influenced than I was, but she'd also sworn not to tell anyone. It wasn't like it'd be me and my soul bonds she'd be putting at risk if she did—it would be her and hers too.

"I want you to be right, Gracie, but we need to be smart. Come on," Riot said, patting my hip gently. The familiarity of the gesture made me melt a little more. "Let's go see what your other boyfriend has to say. If anyone can give us peace of mind, it's Bullet."

BULLET

CHAPTER 20

I spent the entire day holed up in the card reading parlor, asking the Fates questions and occasionally napping to receive visions from the Goddess of Night. Grace delivered me food and tea a few times, but otherwise left me to it after I'd ushered her and Riot out the first time they tried to interrupt my process with their questions.

The night before Rogue's phone call had been a constant bombardment of confusing, mostly terrible visions, all featuring a faceless representation of The Sun card. After the call, it became obvious that Mercy was The Sun. That *should* be a good thing—that card was generally a sign of good fortune—but everything I'd been shown over the past 24 hours had been freaking bleak. It was weird that I was seeing Mercy at all—before last night, the only agathos who'd ever featured prominently in my visions was Grace.

Maybe it was just *regular* agathos I couldn't see. Special edition agathos like Grace and Mercy were different cases.

I let myself into the bathroom and freshened up before bed, stripping down to my boxers. Grace and Riot were already sleeping, and despite my anxiety about tomorrow, something settled in me upon seeing the two of them in the bed. The moonlight spilled through the window, outlining their bodies—Grace facing my side of the bed, her hand outstretched like she'd sought me out in sleep with Riot at her back, his arm draped over her waist. He was so close that her hair fluttered every time he breathed.

I'd only ever vaguely imagined *this* aspect of my relationship with Grace—the element where she had *other* elements—it was more awesome than I expected. At least I knew Grace would never be alone, even after I was gone.

Riot had always been a friend, even when he'd forgotten about me out here, but now he was my responsibility too. It was my job to keep them both safe, and it was fucking terrifying. Especially after what I'd *seen* today.

I lifted up the blanket carefully and slid into the bed. Grace immediately shuffled slightly in her sleep, her hand grabbing my arm as her brow furrowed unhappily. That wouldn't do. Grace had never had a bad dream on my watch, and I wasn't about to let them start now.

Hold on, Amazing Grace. I'm on my way.

We were lying in the sun in a meadow of my design—heavily influenced by the Twilight movies because she'd gone through a phase where that really did it for her—staring up at the cloudless sky side-by-side.

"Doesn't this make you sad?" Grace asked, turning her head to look at me. She'd chosen a white sundress today—one that could have been agathos-friendly, were it not for the deeper cleavage than usual and the almost non-existent straps holding it up. "That you create these beautiful dreams for me and I never remember them?"

I kept my gaze trained on the sky, pasting a smile on my face. My mental shields weren't as strong as I liked them to be, and even in my dreams, I wasn't sure I could keep my anxiety about tomorrow hidden.

"I like creating beautiful dreams for you," I replied honestly.

No time for sadness. No time to reflect on the things I wish I could change.

I heard her hesitation as Grace struggled for a response, obviously reading between the lines. In the past, I'd never had to worry about that, but she knew me now. Knew when I was speaking in half-truths and giving her pretty words to make her feel better.

"Are you nervous about tomorrow? You've been so busy all day, I've barely seen you," Grace said gently, giving me a probing look.

I knew it was the coward's way out, to have a conversation with her that she'd never remember. Maybe I was a coward in real life, and I'd spent so much time living in my head that I hadn't realized it until now.

"Tomorrow isn't going to be a good day," I sighed, hating the way Grace's brow furrowed in concern. "Your mother found out about Mercy and Dice a few days ago. She's been manipulating the relationship between Mercy and Dice to lure you out."

"No," Grace breathed. "She gave her word. She'd have to tell me if she broke it—"

"Mercy isn't a regular agathos," I interjected softly. "She doesn't have the same limitations as you do. Another one of the Fates' experiments."

"What are they going to do?" Grace asked, sitting up and reaching for my hand. "Take me away again?"

"They'll never take you away from us again," I swore, grabbing Grace's hand and giving it a squeeze.

"Then what is going to happen?" Grace pressed, her grip on my hand a little frantic. "Bullet, you're going to tell me all this again when I wake up right?"

Crack went my chest. Just a giant fissure, right down the middle.

"Will you forgive me if I don't?"

"I won't know that I have to," Grace shot back, looking at me with so much devastation that I wished I could take it all back. Find a different future, forge a different path, anything but this.

There was a tug in my gut that made me jolt, and I closed my eyes for a moment, trying to arrange my face into something resembling calm before I opened them again. "I'm being summoned, Amazing Grace. I'll leave you to your dreams for now."

"No. No, we're not done talking about this," Grace replied instantly. She grabbed my arm but it was already dissolving out of this dreamscape. "Take me with you!"

"I can't. Not here."

Perhaps one day Grace would meet La Nuit for herself, but it had to be on the Goddess' terms, when she was in a form that was appropriate for mortal eyes. I could handle seeing La Nuit in this form, but most couldn't.

I appeared in front of the goddess and immediately dropped to one knee, bowing my head respectfully, partly to hide the agony on my face. La Nuit formed the throne and low bench for me, and I took my seat when she gestured towards it, waiting until the goddess was ready to address me even though it took every ounce of self control I had not to bombard her with all my unanswered questions.

"*The Spirit of Dreams,*" *the Goddess said, sounding mildly amused.* "*You are troubled this night.*"

I nodded. I was definitely troubled. Disturbed, even.

"*You have trials ahead, but you will persevere. I believe you will succeed, and spend eternity in the Elysian Fields with your beloved. You want more answers and an easier road, but part of your test of worthiness is discovering them for yourself.*"

I knew I'd have to do something I hated tomorrow. I knew that the alternatives were worse, but whenever I asked why this was the only way, why we had to go through this suffering, the answers were withheld from me.

Was reaching the Elysian Fields really worth not having all the answers?

La Nuit laughed like she could read my mind—probable—and the ethereal sound was so unexpected that it cut off my musing. The landscape around us changed, to a beautiful field filled with flowers in every color imaginable that sat on the edge of an enormous crystal blue lake. Across the water, I could make out a traditional marble temple, the interior hidden by a colonnade, with lush trees visible in every direction. A peacock strutted past my feet, the color of his feathers even more vibrant than the peacocks in the upper world.

"*Life is short, the Spirit of Dreams,*" *the Goddess' voice echoed, though I couldn't see her.* "*The afterlife is long. Choose wisely.*"

This wasn't the real Elysian Fields, of course. Just a dreamscape illusion of the real thing, but even that was enough to convince me. I couldn't jeopardize Grace's shot at the highest level of the Underworld because I wanted a way out of whatever terrible things I had to do tomorrow. Or at the very least, an explanation for why they were necessary.

Other people went through life without insight into the future all the time. It sounded terrible, but surely I could manage.

"I don't have any more questions," I breathed, unconsciously keeping my voice as quiet as possible to not disturb the perfect stillness and beauty of the illusion around me.

"You are wise, the Spirit of Dreams, and you have my favor," the Goddess' disembodied voice replied, sounding pleased with my response. "I will show you what I can. Have faith, embrace your fears, and all will be well."

The Elysian Fields vanished around me, leaving me standing in a dreary parking lot outside the Milton community center, a growing knot of dread in my gut.

I woke up, staring unseeing at the ceiling while Grace and Riot stretched and yawned next to me.

Not much surprised me or saddened me after a lifetime of visions. I'd seen more death than I could remember—both in the dreamscape and among my Oneiroi peers. I'd seen tragedy and heartbreak of every kind, and I'd found ways to cope with the ensuing misery. Mostly through music, and always through my connection with Grace.

My visions for Mercy's future had made me shed a rare tear. Maybe because she was Grace's cousin and closest friend. Or maybe it was because she was so young and had so much heartbreak ahead of her. I wasn't sure what had upset me most. One thing I was sure of was that Mercy had choices to make, and they were all pretty unpleasant.

One was definitively worse.

For all our own sakes, including hers, I needed to make sure Mercy didn't choose that option. She was too young and naive for prison. Too young and naive to take on her ruthless aunt.

"Are you okay?" Grace asked drowsily, rolling onto her side to face me and squinting through tired eyes. Her dark hair had mostly escaped its tie, creating a dark fuzzy halo around her face, and I didn't think she'd ever looked more beautiful.

I half expected to see that devastated look on her face that she'd been wearing when I'd left her in the dreamscape, but all was forgotten. I hated myself for the relief I felt.

"I'm fine, Amazing Grace," I lied, giving her my most beaming smile. "Waffles?"

I smiled and joked my way through breakfast, drumming my fingers on my thigh under the table, trying to think about positive things so Grace wouldn't pick up on my bad mood.

For the most part, it seemed to have worked. Grace was so excited to see Mercy, she was lost in her own world, more stressed about not having a birthday present to give her cousin than anything else.

I guessed the upside about already having one foot in the afterlife, ready for the Fates to cut loose my mortal thread, was that my actions had consequences, but only very briefly. I would be the one to be given the hard tasks when it came to Grace's future because I was the one that had to live with them for the least amount of time.

If I had to see betrayal in Grace's eyes like I had last night in her dreams, at least it wouldn't be for long.

"I'm going to check on something downstairs," I muttered vaguely in Grace and Riot's direction. They were in the kitchen, washing dishes as Grace recounted her favorite memories with Mercy, which didn't make me feel worse at all. In an hour or so we'd leave for Milton, and events would be set into motion that couldn't be undone.

I jogged down the steps, through my old makeshift bedroom, through the parlor, and quietly out the front door. Despite the rain, I strode down the gravel driveway and over the field to the pond where I'd taken Grace not so long ago. I wanted to be out in the open so I could see them approach if either Grace or Riot came looking for me.

Selfishly, I hoped Grace *would* come find me. I hoped she'd picked up on my emotional turmoil and cared enough to investigate. Logically, there was a very good chance she hadn't noticed my struggle. Not when she was so excited.

Keeping close to the oak tree for shelter, I unlocked my phone and scrolled to the messages from a few days ago. There was an unsaved contact there, and a lame joke sent from my phone with one sent back in reply. I wondered if Grace would have deleted the evidence, but her agathos instincts had prevented her from doing something that seemed like lying.

I hit 'call', not giving myself a chance to second guess the decision. There was only a short window where Mercy was available to talk and I couldn't miss it.

"*Hello?*" Mercy said breathlessly. Goddess, she sounded so young. Too young for this path.

"You need to do what your aunt told you to do, but you need evidence. Follow the Basilinna's plan and record everything—phone, dash cam, whatever you've got."

I heard her sharp intake of breath, followed by more rustling like she was moving around.

"*I can't,*" Mercy hissed.

"He'll find his way back to you."

"*He'll despise me forever, and I wouldn't blame him,*" Mercy replied flatly. Some of her affectations were so like Grace's, yet they were completely different at the same time. Clearly, Mercy was more abrupt.

"He'll understand when you make him understand," I assured her. Eventually.

"*Grace—*"

"—has an enormous capacity for forgiveness. Dissent is a seed that has to be sowed. Don't underestimate your importance—the Fates have big plans for you."

"*I tried,*" Mercy said softly. "*I tried so hard to keep everything hidden. To stay under the radar so they wouldn't find out about Dice, so they wouldn't use me as Grace's weakness.*"

"I know," I told her seriously. "I know that's why you kept putting it off when Rogue suggested you contact Grace."

"*If I do what they want me to do, someone might get hurt.*" She sounded resigned, and I could relate to that.

"Not fatally." I sighed, not looking forward to that part and wondering how much to tell her. I'd seen enough of Mercy's future to think she might need this act of kindness.

This act of *mercy*.

Damn it, I was in too poor of a mood to even enjoy my excellent pun.

"No one can outrun Fate. Sometimes there are different paths to take—sometimes they extend the journey, sometimes they shorten it—but if the Fates have chosen a destination for you, you best believe you're going to end up there.

"I've seen your options, Mercy. I'm telling you as a kindness to follow the Basilinna's plan. That backup option you're entertaining will only make you and Dice more miserable, and it'll fail to stop what is already in motion."

"But at least I could say I tried," Mercy whispered.

"The price to pay is too steep to gamble on a clear conscience," I warned. The Nine of Wands card appeared in my mind like the Fates themselves had put it there. "Grace had to do what scared her to set the wheels in motion, now it's your turn. Choose wisely."

With a shaky exhale, I hung up and shoved the phone back in my pocket.

Done. It was done.

I walked back to the barn as quickly as I could, too filled with nervous energy to even hum to make myself feel better. There weren't enough Broadway songs in the world to save my mood today.

I could hear Grace laughing upstairs, and I forced myself to breathe evenly and not let Grace feel my panic as I pulled a duffel bag out from under the foldout bed.

As quietly and efficiently as I could, I packed some stuff for the three of us out of the selection of spare clothes I had in storage. It wasn't ideal, but they'd have questions I couldn't answer if I started packing clothes from the upstairs bedroom.

Once I was satisfied we had enough, I snuck the bag out to the trunk of the SUV, and speed rapped *Guns and Ships* from *Hamilton* under my breath before I had a full on panic attack.

This was the way it had to be.

It would be fine. Mercy would be fine. *I* would be fine.

Grace would forgive me.

Grace was so excited, her knee had been bouncing impatiently in the front seat the entire car ride to Milton.

"I told Viper we'd be in town today," I vaguely heard Riot saying. "Our *arrangement* is ongoing until you no longer need to hide or for a year, whichever comes first," he explained to Grace. Good. She'd been struggling with the secrecy, and at least he was telling her what he could without triggering her honesty impulses.

"Did that bother him?" Grace asked. "That I was visiting Milton?"

"Yes," Riot snorted. "But he's confident all the agathos who were in Milton have left town. We always had the home team advantage there anyway. The agathos do have a camera watching your apartment though. Viper decided to leave it there so as not to raise any suspicions."

All going well, Riot wouldn't be stuck with Viper for much longer, but he'd still come in handy in the interim. Viper had a long and winding path of his own to travel.

That reminded me... I pulled out my phone, quickly firing off a couple of messages before silencing it and shoving it into my pocket. I'd already *seen* that we could safely get to Milton and relayed that to Riot, but both he and I were still looking out the window constantly like an agathos army was going to materialize out of midair.

"Did you *see* anything last night? About how today would go?" Grace asked, twisting in her seat to look at me.

She'd dressed in jeans and tan boots, with a tan wool coat over a cream blouse. Her hair was half up, secured with a cream and burgundy silk scarf, makeup applied perfectly after spending about forty minutes locked in the bathroom doing it. It was definitely a *more* agathos look than she'd been wearing lately, with the exception of the jeans, but I guessed she wanted Mercy to feel comfortable.

Should I mention the Elysian Fields? Would Grace know the significance? Would she care? Grace struck me as the type to care more about her life here rather than an abstract afterlife. Maybe I would be like that too, if I had longer on the mortal plane to enjoy it.

Riot shot me an exasperated look from the driver's seat as I connected my phone bluetooth and started blasting the *In The Heights* soundtrack to keep myself peppy.

"Bullet," Grace said softly, turning the music down and twisting further to look at me. "Your emotions are all over the place."

What would happen when Grace and I bonded and she could get an in-depth read on my emotions? Oneiroi weren't designed to share their souls with others. There was too much at stake.

No time for bitterness. No time, no time, no time.

301

"You must have seen something, you're a fucking wreck," Riot noted, a nervous edge to his voice. He absolutely did not want to be heading to Milton today, and I was right there with him.

"I see lots of things," I replied, not quite able to keep the frustration out of my voice.

"Did you ask about today?" Riot pressed.

"Obviously," I drawled. Dick. As if I *wouldn't* ask when it came to Grace's safety. *I take back all the nice thoughts I had about him.*

Riot opened his mouth like he was going to argue, but closed it again when Grace raised an eyebrow at him before returning her attention to me. How did she manage to silence him with just an eyebrow? That was *skill.*

I tapped my fingers along to *96000,* drumming my thigh a little more aggressively than usual. All these serious conversations were not good for my sunny disposition.

"I saw a lot of different options for today," I said evasively, realizing they were expecting some kind of answer from me. "It's a very important day."

"What does that mean?" Riot asked.

"I guess you can't really see Mercy, since she's an agathos," Grace sighed. If I were a better man, I would have corrected her assumption, but that would only lead to questions I couldn't answer yet.

"But why is it an important day?" Riot pressed, looking at me suspiciously through the rearview mirror.

I was going to have to give them something. Something that would ease their minds and explain my weirdness. Something that would allow the day to unfold the way it had to to minimize the amount of damage.

"You're going to meet Wild today."

"What?!" Grace shrieked, turning more fully to face me. "Really?!"

Huh. That worked better than expected.

Riot groaned. "I'm even more tempted to turn the car around now."

"Will he hurt Wild?" Grace asked, looking at me with wide trusting eyes I didn't deserve. I shook my head silently and she rewarded me with a beaming smile.

"See, Riot? It'll be fine," she said. "I mean, maybe he's not my third soul bond. We don't know for sure."

"He probably is," Riot sighed. "That time we met..."

"Yes?" Grace prompted, and I leaned forward a little, curious to hear about their infamous meeting.

"It felt personal," Riot admitted. "Like Wild was *personally* upset that I broke his rules. It wasn't like it was the first time I'd pissed off a club owner, but when he beat the shit out of me, *I* felt weirdly upset about it. It was like a personal betrayal."

That made sense to me. It felt like a personal betrayal when Riot and Dare continued being besties and forgot all about me when I moved away, but I didn't have time to be bitter about that. Or anything else.

"That does sound like it means something," Grace said gently. "It's looking more and more like your wild theory is correct, Bullet."

I gave Grace a weak smile as Riot snorted, pulling the SUV into the community center parking lot. I'd like to think we'd talk more about it later, but I doubted Grace was going to want to talk about anything else after today's events unfolded.

303

The community center in Milton was a tragic looking box of a building on the outskirts of town. Grace had mentioned a recent agathos clean up project, but a fresh lick of white paint over the miserable brown color and some vibrant potted plants outside couldn't disguise how dilapidated the structure was underneath. It was barely even used—only the humans in Milton had any use for a 'community' anything.

The parking lot was deserted except for a sleek silver SUV parked next to the covered entryway, with a nervous looking daimon and a determined agathos leaning against the side of the vehicle.

Riot parked opposite them, putting some space between the vehicles. The parking lot was enclosed by a chain link fence, and Riot scanned the quiet intersection and the overpass above before climbing out of the vehicle. He looked about a second away from tackling Grace and wrestling her back into the car, but instead he managed to grab her hand before she bounded across the empty parking spaces to Mercy, forcing her to slow down.

Mercy had the same brown skin, opal eyes and dainty nose as her older cousin, but that was where the similarities ended. Her long hair fell in tight curls around her more rounded face, and she was shorter than Grace, but it was the expressions they wore and the way they held themselves that stood in stark contrast.

Since she was a child, Grace had always had a very serene, calming presence, one that I knew would serve her well in the trials to come. Mercy definitely hadn't inherited that gene. Mercy looked like she was waiting for an attack, and she'd be ready for it when it came. If Grace's excited reaction was any indication, that look on her face wasn't entirely unusual.

"Mercy!" Grace squealed, yanking her hand free of Riot as we reached them and throwing her arms around the girl. Mercy didn't hesitate to return the gesture, despite her defensive expression, and I wasn't imagining the way she clung onto Grace a little more desperately than most people did for a friendly hug.

I glanced at the waiting daimon out of the corner of my eye, trying to figure out what he made of all this. Dice was at least a decade younger than me, with pale skin pulled taut over a square jawline and high cheekbones and no dark shadows that came with age under his red and purple eyes. His pale blonde hair was longer on the top, and artfully styled like young people who had time and no prophecy over the neck like a guillotine blade could do. He was boy band handsome, movie star handsome, and I imagined Mercy would have been thanking her lucky stars every day if prettyboy Dice had been an agathos.

I'd never met Dice before, though I had gone to school with his older sister, Rogue. It wasn't common for our kind to have daimonic siblings unless they were multiples. Usually our daimon parents only felt called to parenthood once.

Dice seemed to be a daimon made more in the me-and-Riot mold rather than like our parents' generation, judging by his nerves and the borderline adoring way he was staring at Mercy, despite the two feet gap she was maintaining between them.

If anyone noticed how uncomfortable she looked, they didn't say anything. Maybe they didn't. Grace was too excited, Dice too enamored, Riot too worried.

"I missed you so much," Grace sniffed, definitely crying a little. "Are you okay? I abandoned you, I feel terrible."

"You had to leave," Mercy murmured, rubbing Grace's back. "You did the right thing. I'm not mad at you."

Grace pulled back, gripping Mercy's shoulders as she examined her cousin's face like she was memorizing it. "Are you okay? How did you guys meet? Did you have your emergence?"

"I'm okay," Mercy replied slowly. "Dice and I met here. He came past as I was painting the building with the other agathos. I didn't know what was happening, my heart was beating so fast... Anyway, I saw him and he hid so no one else noticed. I kept coming back. It took a week for me to work up the courage to speak to him."

Dice gave her a sappy smile. He'd be embarrassed if he could see his moony face right now, I was sure of it.

"And I did have my emergence," Mercy said with a tight smile. She was *so* young, and trying so hard to be brave. When I was her age, I'd been newly holed up at the Oneiroi mansion, resenting the entire universe.

"And?" Grace pressed. Mercy's stoic facade crumbled for half a second, a flash of terror in her pale eyes.

"Hygeia," she whispered, gaze dropping to the ground.

"No," Grace breathed, shaking her head instantly, her fear feeling icy and sharp against my skin. Riot winced, and I knew he was experiencing the same thing.

Well, shit. That was some *terrible* luck. Hygeia could give the gift of good health. If Mercy was a daimon, that wouldn't matter. We could use our abilities pretty freely without physical consequences—with the exception of my melty brain—but Mercy was an agathos. Each time she gave good health to a human, she'd lose some of her own in return.

As far as I knew they recovered a lot faster than humans did, but I doubted they had a great life span if they regularly used their gifts. They were a rare type of agathos these days—humans could rely on their own medical care, the need for hygeia had decreased over the centuries.

"I wish you'd tell me what that means," Dice said roughly, a pained look in his eyes as he stared at his soul bond. Mercy barely acknowledged him, her gaze still fixed on Grace, but I could see her tense when he spoke.

Self-preservation, I supposed.

"Sorry, I'm Grace," my girl said, politely introducing herself to Dice, who nodded a little uncomfortably in return. "And these are my soul bonds, Riot and Bullet."

I wiggled my fingers cheerily, just to throw him off balance, because Riot was for sure shooting daggers with his eyeballs.

"So how are you able to be here without my mother knowing? Where does she think you are?" Grace asked, not a trace of suspicion in her voice.

Mercy opened her mouth, a flare of panic in her eyes, but Dice beat her to the answer.

"Your mom does know she's here," he said, sounding confused. "I thought it was kind of weird for an agathos, especially considering all the shit that happened with you, but she encourages us to hang out."

Good thing he's pretty, I thought with an internal facepalm. I saw a little of Dice's future last night. He'd outgrow this naivete, starting today. Poor guy.

"My mom knows about the two of you? She encourages you to come here? I mean, I know you didn't tell her you were meeting us, but Mercy... I don't know if I would have come if I'd realized that. It feels... like my mom is springing a trap."

307

I could have sworn I felt Grace's blood run cold as she took a step back, her hands falling away from Mercy's arms.

Mercy opened her mouth. Closed it again. Looking everywhere but at Grace's face. Her eyes darted between Riot and I, and I gave her a sympathetic smile to let her know I was the one that had called her. And that I understood how awful this was for her, but it was too late to turn back.

What a gift. What a curse. The first agathos able to lie.

"Aunt Faith has been gone a lot, looking for you. I haven't had very close supervision recently," Mercy said evasively.

"And my dads?"

"Valor is leading the search party. He and Earnest went to Florida, looking for you. Aunt Faith has been searching closer to home. Creed and Chance are holding down the fort at home, looking after Leon and Tobin. And me, I guess."

I felt Grace's sharp stab of sadness at the mention of her brothers. Maybe they hadn't been repeatedly told that Grace was a daimon-loving harlot or whatever the party line was if the other three parents were gone a lot.

Grace still looked disturbed. *Felt* disturbed, and I knew she was floundering at how to handle this conversation now that Mercy wasn't the secret rebel Grace had assumed she was.

"So, what now, birthday girl?" Grace asked, valiantly trying to inject some normality into this awkward, abnormal conversation. "You're eighteen. You can leave, if you want to."

That was my girl, always trying to make the best of things. Always trying to make other people feel comfortable when she was clearly uncomfortable.

Always assuming the best in others.

"My things are in the trunk," Mercy said quietly. "I'm not going back."

"You're not?" Dice asked, eyebrows shooting up in surprise. "Are you, um, moving in with me? I mean, it's cool if you are, but I'll need to run it by Rogue first."

"Mercy, what is going on?" Grace asked softly, reaching for her hand and giving it a squeeze. "Is my mom tormenting you somehow? Why is she encouraging you to see Dice? None of that makes sense. We can help you, talk to us. Do you want to talk with me alone for a minute maybe—"

"No," Mercy cut in, shaking her head, eyes darting around nervously again. "No, you can't help me."

CHAPTER 21

This is stupid. You are stupid. The words repeated in my head on a loop as I drove towards the outskirts of Milton.

I'd received a message from Bullet an hour ago that said *'Milton Community Center, 12pm. Come armed.'*

If Bullet was there, Grace would be too, and although I was determined to stay away from her, it seemed foolish to ignore a message from someone who could see the future. Especially when he requested backup.

Like he knew I'd hesitate—which was likely—he'd sent a very similar message to Onyx, but very much directed at me. Onyx was a Keres as well, and a formidable foe who brought grown men to their knees with a deceptive smile and a flick of her butterfly knife.

Usually, there'd be no question of who I'd have fighting at my side if there was a whiff of violence in the air, but the idea of showing up where Grace was with another woman at my side felt disrespectful somehow, even if Grace could never be mine. If she was ever meant to be mine to begin with.

I'd never entertained having that kind of relationship with Onyx, but I knew better than most how important first perceptions could be. I didn't want to cause Grace... undue stress. That was why I'd roped Memphis into coming with me. He was a Keres with consistently good self-control, uncreatively nicknamed after the city he'd moved to Milton from. He'd worked at Underworld for a year now, and I had been meaning to assess his suitability for a more intensive role.

Today was a very high stakes job interview. If he failed, if Grace was hurt in any way, I might have to kill him.

He sat next to me while I drove, idly scrolling through his phone and occasionally glancing out the window. We stopped at the traffic lights and I discreetly observed Memphis, narrowing my eyes slightly. He was very popular with women at the club, with his dark bronze skin, muscles that constantly seemed to be on display, curly dark hair, and his charming smile.

Maybe I shouldn't have brought him with me.

Worse, what if he only saw an agathos and attacked Grace? I should have made it clear she was off-limits. But that would raise questions.

Fuck. There was no good answer for any of this.

I'd heard whispers among the Underworld staff about Riot and Grace—Bullet was still a secret by the sound of things—and the tone of the conversations had been *excited*, for the most part. The idea of an agathos *choosing* a daimon was a novelty to them. *Good girl,* they all called her. That the agathos had come after her and tried to drag her back was an affront to daimons everywhere who prized personal choice above all else.

They liked her. Admired her, even. Saw Grace as a different kind of agathos and hoped there were more like her who'd feel emboldened by her actions and copy them.

Most daimons were idiots in that regard.

I'd seen the divine. Wrestled a god with my bare hands. Learned a humiliating lesson in return.

Grace wasn't with Riot, or Bullet, because she'd simply *chosen* to be. It wasn't their sparkling personalities or pretty faces that had drawn her to them. The Fates' needle was hard at work, weaving webs between souls of their choosing.

If their threads had stitched Grace to four agathos men as expected, she wouldn't have given Riot or Bullet a second look.

We were all playthings for the gods.

The light went green and I hit the gas, drumming my fingers irritably on the steering wheel as the clock ticked past midday. I strongly disliked lateness, and it frustrated me that Bullet hadn't given me more notice.

If I were psychic, I would never be late a day in my life, nor would I let anyone else be. It was inexcusable.

There was plenty of parking near the community center, but I had no idea if they were expecting me or what Bullet thought was going to happen—*would it have been too much to ask for something more detailed than 'come armed'?*—so I parked a block away, shrugged on my black backpack and motioned to Memphis to follow me as we approached the front of the building, sticking to the shadows as much as possible.

The car park was too exposed for us to move any closer without being seen, but I knew I had to get closer. I couldn't use my abilities on agathos, I couldn't incite them into violence—that trick only worked on humans—but to be a Keres was to be baptized in bloodshed. The promise of violence on the verge of being unleashed smelled like iron, and the air here was thick with it. It made my blood sing in my veins, my muscles flexing in readiness, my palms itching for my weapons.

That unmistakable iron tang was mystifying, since the group in front of the building appeared to be speaking calmly. I could *feel* my proximity to Grace, knew without even looking which one she was, the connection so much more potent in person than it was through a screen. Riot and Bullet I recognized, flanking her, but the other two I was less sure of.

"Is that Dice?" Memphis murmured, squinting at the man leaning against the vehicle. Memphis looked back at me and I gave him a curt nod, encouraging him to continue talking. I knew of a daimon called Dice, but since he was basically a child and not a Keres, my interest level was almost non-existent.

"He's an *Ate*. He works at Creep's casino."

I snorted, shaking my head. The Ate were daimons of rashness who encouraged humans to follow their most reckless impulses to their ruin. They thrived in casinos.

I could make out Bullet by his blonde hair shining in the sunlight and watched as he scanned the area while the others talked. Was he looking for me? I'd like to think that if I was somehow essential to what was happening here, that he'd have given me slightly more of a heads up about it.

That delicious, tempting violent promise on the air grew stronger, luring me closer to the community center. Memphis' muscles were locked tight, his hands curled into fists with white knuckles, forcing himself to stay in place.

I'd made a good call in bringing him along. Not all Keres would have the self-control to resist the lure.

There were three throwing knives strapped to the sheath around my forearm underneath my loose jumper, but I'd need the six in my leg holster, currently hidden in my backpack if this turned into a real fight. I drummed my fingers silently on my thigh where the holster would sit, assessing the situation. I couldn't do anything from here anyway. No, I had to get closer.

And I had to have somewhere safe for Grace to go if a fight broke out. Grace *and* Bullet.

Riot, I didn't give a shit about.

I pulled out my phone and tapped instructions for Memphis, telling him to bring the van closer, but to stay out of sight and grab Bullet and the girl if things went south, to take them somewhere safe. His jaw was tight as I showed him the message and passed him the keys, but he gave me a stiff nod, rolling his neck before turning and walking back the way we came, forcing himself away from the fight.

I made a mental note to put him in a supervisor role. Memphis was a daimon worth keeping around.

Go time.

As stealthily as I could, I left the cover of the shadows and jogged further down the street, away from the community center. If I could double back around without being seen, hopefully there was a dumpster behind the building which would give me enough height to climb on the roof.

If Riot, Bullet and Grace had chosen this as a tactical location, they couldn't have picked worse. While I knew I couldn't give in to the draw I felt to Grace, it concerned me that her safety was in such inexperienced hands. Oneiroi may be experts in the future, but they existed more in their own heads than in the real world.

And Riot was a fucking idiot. As evidenced by him selling drugs in *my* club.

The smell of iron was so strong in the air, I could taste it. Instead of exciting me, it made something churn in my gut. An instinct I'd felt and ignored once before because I was too cocky. I was never going to make that mistake again.

I picked up my pace, practically sprinting through the streets, weaving around the humans who were out during the daytime and ignoring their confused looks. As I passed a small side window, I saw the unmistakable signs of movement from within, the flash of pale agathos eyes before I ducked out of sight, too quick for them to notice.

This was an ambush.

GRACE

CHAPTER 22

This conversation was not going the way I had expected it to go. *Nothing* about this encounter was going the way I had expected it to go. Mercy and I had always been close, she'd never judged me for being different, and while I knew it would be weird for her to meet Riot and Bullet and for me to meet Dice, I hadn't expected it to be *this* weird. She was uncomfortable around me in a way she'd never been uncomfortable around me before, and I wasn't sure how to put her at ease.

Maybe I'd been naive thinking Mercy would be as excited to see me as I was to see her. She'd been living with the rumors of what happened at the temple and whatever poisonous whispers my parents had been feeding her. Of course she didn't look at me the same way as she used to.

Judging by the look on his face, Dice hadn't expected things to go like this either. There was definitely an early days nervousness between them that I had experienced with Riot and was still kind of experiencing with Bullet, but it was more than that. Dice was frowning at Mercy like she'd let him down somehow, and Mercy was looking at me like...

Like she was sorry.

It was a strange, suspended moment. I felt myself frowning, trying to interpret the look on her face. Bullet's hand came up to squeeze my shoulder, sighing heavily, a strangely resigned sound. Like he knew something I didn't.

Then a spike of pure unadulterated fear from Riot as the doors to the community center flew open with a bang that made us all jump.

A group of armed agathos men streamed out, seven or eight at least, dressed all in black, shouting orders at us not to move, and my heart stopped in my chest as I looked from them to Mercy.

She hadn't been looking at me like she was sorry, she'd been looking at me like she was *guilty*.

How was this possible? She'd said she wouldn't tell anyone. She said she'd only come with Dice. Her instincts—

"You lied," I breathed in stunned realization, dropping her hand like it had burned me. *Lied. She lied.*

All three daimons were already moving, ready to face the agathos head on. Riot and Bullet's fear and adrenaline combined with my own until I wasn't sure whose emotions were whose.

"I'm so sorry," Mercy whispered, reaching for me again as I took a step back. "Grace, I'm sorry!"

I scoffed, already turning away, wanting to be close to my soul bonds. "I don't believe you."

I'd never believe a single word out of her mouth ever again.

Riot was already brawling with two men and I fought the urge to scream his name, not wanting to distract him. A third agathos moved to grab him and Riot swung wildly, my heart leaping into my throat and only dropping somewhat into normal position when his blow struck, making the agathos stagger backwards.

Dice had moved away from Mercy and was easily dodging a swing from an agathos aiming for his face.

There was so much *violence*. There were no restrictions on the agathos when it came to violence against daimons, but we'd been raised to believe we were better than that. Above such barbaric practices as brawling daimons in the street. These agathos hadn't gotten the same message.

Mercy was shouting something behind me, but my eyes were seeking out Bullet, heart thundering in my chest that he wasn't in the fray with Riot and Dice. It took me a moment to realize that he'd moved a few feet away and was standing perfectly still, like... like he was waiting for something? I took a step towards him, but he shook his head subtly before mouthing at me to *stay back*.

What? Why? He wasn't hiding his emotions as thoroughly as usual, and the dread that poured off him was so thick I felt like I could taste it in the air.

"Bullet—"

Again, he shook his head, a resigned smile on his face. *Stay back, Amazing Grace.*

Before I could react, Riot's pained wheeze grabbed my attention as three agathos tackled him to the ground, the thud of his body hitting the concrete making my stomach churn.

"Riot!"

I felt like I was being ripped in two, my heart beating wildly in my chest, pulling me in both directions. Riot was in pain and outnumbered though, and I launched myself at him, not caring that the agathos were armed. In theory, we couldn't physically hurt one another, though I was second guessing that fact a little after Mercy had *lied* to me.

318

Before I could move, there were arms around me, yanking me backwards with just enough care not to hurt me.

"Get off!" I snarled, struggling to shake off the enormous man behind me. I didn't let the darkness slowly leak out, I leaned into it. Encouraged it. Reveled in it.

Unfortunately, it still didn't bring with it the ability to physically hurt my fellow agathos.

"Enough, daimon lover," the man behind me snapped. "You think I enjoy this? I don't want to touch you. You might infect me with your miasma."

If the situation wasn't so dire, I'd have rolled my eyes.

"I'm more concerned you'll infect me with your idiocy. Get *off*," I hissed, yanking my arms fruitlessly. No matter how angry I was, I couldn't physically escape someone so much bigger than me. Especially when they had my arms pinned behind my back—careful not to actually hurt me— and I couldn't so much as stomp on his instep.

Riot was still struggling fiercely, now with three agathos pinning him to the ground and only barely, while Bullet stayed perfectly silent. Another agathos approached him warily, grabbing him suddenly by the back of his jacket and roughly manhandling him as though Bullet was fighting back.

I twisted and struggled in the guy's hold, noticing that Mercy was screaming as two men closed in on Dice, who was fighting back with the kind of desperate fury that made it clear he hadn't seen this coming. He looked so *young*, 18 or 19 maybe. He shouldn't be subject to this. Mercy had lied to all of us, even her soul bond, a teenager who was now trying to fight off two grown men.

No one was holding Mercy back despite her desperate pleas for them not to hurt anyone. Why would they restrain her? She'd invited them.

"Just take us!" she was shouting. "Leave them alone, you don't need to do all this! We'll go with you if you leave them alone!"

I hated that she was right. I would go willingly if they'd leave Riot and Bullet in peace.

Mercy ran towards Dice right as he managed to flip open his switchblade and took a swing at the agathos next to him, slicing a bloody gash into the guy's bicep.

Pandemonium.

The word jumped into my mind unbidden as chaos exploded around me. The agathos howled in pain at the injury, and the guys around him panicked at the sound, not able to see what I could see.

It was basically a scratch.

But they didn't know that.

From where they were standing, the glint of the switchblade in the sunshine, it really looked like Dice had stabbed the guy. For all the aggression of the agathos, I felt like they had been waiting for that moment. They'd hoped the daimons would draw first blood. They wanted to be able to walk away from this and say *'but it was self-defense! If only that daimon hadn't stabbed us!'*

'If only that daimon hadn't stabbed us, we wouldn't have shot at him!'

That's what they'd say. That's how they'd justify it.

Bang.

Bang.

There was nothing slow motion about the gun going off. Two shots in quick succession, faster than I could blink. I didn't even realize right away who'd fired it, and I didn't care.

Time seemed to stop as everyone fell silent, looking around in slow motion to see where the bullets had gone, to see who was injured and which side of the battle they were on.

Mercy screamed, clutching at her face.

Bullet fell to his knees with a thud, the agathos next to him leaping away like gunshots were infectious.

An agathos standing close to the door of the community center held the gun in shaking hands, eyes wide as he stared at Dice's unharmed back like he was looking for the holes that should have been there, if he'd had any kind of aim.

Blood trickled down Mercy's cheek, but the bullet had only grazed her. Dice roared in anger, but I only barely registered that as my horrified gaze tracked from the man holding the gun, to Mercy, to Bullet, kneeling on the ground, hunched forward, hand clutching his bleeding upper arm, teeth gritted against a scream.

They'd shot him.

They'd actually shot him.

There was no emotion from him. Not a cold stab of fear, or horror, or surprise, or *anything*. He didn't scream.

Someone screamed. Someone was screaming and screaming and screaming, like they could heal his wounds if they were only loud enough.

"BULLET!"

It was me. *I* was screaming, struggling harder against the agathos holding me, forcing him to readjust his position so he wasn't hurting me. He growled in frustration and I growled right back, irritated beyond belief that my body wouldn't let me injure this monster. I wasn't a violent person, but these agathos deserved violence.

"It's okay, Amazing Grace," Bullet called shakily, attempting to give me a reassuring smile even though his eyes were struggling to focus on me.

It was *not* okay. Nothing about this was okay. I knew he was forcing himself to be calm for my benefit, even as blood leaked from his wound, running through his fingers despite the hand he had clamped over it.

Riot attempted to push himself up, panic in his eyes as he took in Bullet's injury, but one of the agathos above him grabbed him by the hair and slammed his face into the concrete with a sickening crunch, his boot digging into Riot's back.

I couldn't feel Riot's fear. Or Bullet's. I couldn't feel anything.

"Stop!" Mercy screamed, clutching at her wounded face, tears streaming down her cheeks. "You have Grace. I'll come with you. Stop hurting them."

"Hurting them? We're taking them inside and *executing* them," the one holding me said with a disbelieving laugh. "You finding a daimon to follow you around was a gift from Anesidora. A gift your aunt recognized would pull your cousin out of hiding. This whole endeavor is blessed by the goddess. The Basilinna prayed and it is agreed the only way to break these cursed bonds is to execute the daimons. Frankly, your miasma is so strong, I think we'd be better off putting you both down too, for your own good."

Put you down. Like we were feral animals.

I looked to the sky, tears welling in my eyes as I prepared to pray to every god or goddess I'd read about in Bullet's books, but movement on the roof caught my eye.

The briefest flash of dark red eyes, a black hood, a small nod towards the fray, and the glint of metal in his hand.

My heart was beating so fast, my mouth already dry, there was no way of physically discerning whether it was panic or the discovery of a soul bond, but my instincts knew.

Wild. It had to be Wild. I felt it in my bones.

I knew nothing about battles and strategy, but I could see that he was outnumbered and there was too much chaos. Wild needed time, a distraction, I could see that, but I needed to get to Bullet. I *had* to get that wound bandaged, I knew that much first aid at least. Blood loss was a fast killer, and he was too weak to keep the pressure on his arm.

I twisted to look at the man behind me and with a start I realized that I *did* recognize him. Maxim. An occasional golf buddy of my father, Earnest. He wouldn't know me well, but he'd seen me plenty of times throughout my life at family parties and agathos events.

And he thought I should be put down. Charming.

"If you don't let me go tend to my soul bond's injury right this second," I said in a low flat voice. "I will show you exactly why the Basilinna is terrified of me. You think you know what happened in that basement? Ask them who came to my aid before Riot got there. You think you're the scariest person here with your numbers and your weapons, but the Goddess of Night favors *me* and mine."

There was a feral edge to my voice that I barely recognized as I continued, "You would piss your perfectly pressed trousers if she communicated with you the way she's communicated with me. Perhaps I'll suggest it to her."

Maxim's hands shook as he yanked them away from me like he'd been burned. "Tend to him, I don't care. It'll only prolong his death. You cannot change what the Goddess has deemed necessary."

I was already moving, running to Bullet's side and yanking my silk head scarf out of my hair.

"I'm here," I breathed, dropping to my knees at his side. "I'm here, I'm here."

"I know," Bullet whispered, attempting to smile as I pried his hand away from the wound on his upper left arm and pulled off his jacket as quickly and gently as I could. There was an agathos nearby, the one who'd originally grabbed Bullet, but he was eyeing me like he didn't want to get too close and catch my daimon-lover germs.

Good.

With strength I didn't know I had, I ripped Bullet's shirt sleeve off, exposing the bleeding wound. Tears leaked out of my eyes as I fumbled with the scarf, wrapping the injury as securely as I could, trying not to look too hard at the *holes* in his arm, hoping that two holes meant the bullet had gone through him.

That's what happened in movies, right?

"This isn't the end for me, Amazing Grace," Bullet rasped. "I'm going to be fine, okay?"

"Okay," I agreed shakily, cheeks wet with tears. "Okay. You'll be okay."

"I'll be okay," Bullet repeated, reassuring me despite being the one suffering as I tied the scarf as tight as I could and helped him into the recovery position, worried that he was going to pass out and hit his head on the concrete. I grabbed the white shirt sleeve I'd torn off him and wrapped that over the top of the scarf, hoping if one makeshift bandage was good, then two would be better.

There was more yelling behind me, the agathos trying to herd all of us into the building, but Riot was kicking and lashing out as best he could after being pinned to the ground, and Dice was refusing to back down, swiping anyone who got too close with his switchblade. Even Mercy was getting in the way as she attempted to defend the soul bond she'd all but offered up on a platter.

I glanced at the roof and saw Wild pacing in frustration as he glared at the gunman who was still hovering near the doorway. *Too close to the wall,* I realized. Wild needed more room to do whatever it was he was going to do.

I stood, positioning myself in front of Bullet's prone form and silently daring the agathos hovering nearby to approach me.

"When was the last time Anesidora answered your prayers? Actually *answered?*" I asked the hovering guy. Silence. He looked at me like I'd grown tentacles.

"When?" I pressed. "Not the last time you interpreted her silence to mean whatever you wanted it to mean, I mean when was the last time you sensed her presence? Heard her voice? What do you really know of *Gaia?* She gave *life,* and you stand here claiming *death* in her name."

I gestured at the general carnage around us, the agathos man with the gun pausing to listen to me as well. Riot was flagging, and Bullet was thoroughly incapacitated. Only the fact that Dice was still struggling and Mercy was being a nuisance had stopped them dragging the guys into the community center, and presumably shoving Mercy and I in a car where we'd spend the rest of our lives locked in a dungeon temple.

I couldn't even call on La Nuit for assistance this time. I knew from Bullet's lessons that she couldn't appear in the middle of the day like this, with the sunlight blaring down over head. Neither could Erebus, her consort, who thrived in darkness.

There was one goddess I could ask. If I was going to tell the agathos that they were wrong to interpret her will out of nothing, then I'd be a hypocrite to do the same. She'd never answered me before, but maybe...

The agathos' eyes were on me, directing attention away from the building where Wild was still prowling like a caged tiger, looking for an opening.

Come on, I silently willed the one with the gun who was causing Wild's delay. *Come closer.*

"You," I said to the agathos holding the gun, pinning him with my harshest glare. "Do you feel good about the choices you made today?"

"I— I didn't mean to hit *her*," he stammered, dropping the gun to his side, unable to look at Mercy's bleeding face. "I'll pray for forgiveness, I'll ask the Basilinna to cleanse me for my crime of hurting another agathos."

"But not for shooting him?" I asked, shaking my head sadly as I gestured at Bullet behind me. "More fool you. Mercy might be able to tell a lie, but I can't, so believe me when I tell you the man you shot is favored by the Goddess of Night herself. She visits him, speaks to him, looks out for him. But by all means, only ask for forgiveness for hurting Mercy."

I got a savage sense of satisfaction as the man's face paled, opal eyes flicking between Bullet and me.

"Please—" he began, his hands shaking, suddenly prepared to beg for forgiveness in the face of La Nuit's wrath.

"Perhaps, you'll be so fortunate as to meet the Goddess of Night yourself, after what you did today," I added lightly. Riot made a pained noise that might have been a snort. "You are wrong, all of you. I hope that one day you'll be introspective enough to look back and realize how appallingly wrong you were, and that you'll feel some small ounce of regret for things you've done in *Gaia's* name, but I doubt you will. Not if you're so *stupid* as to think the goddess who created the Earth, life, trees, mountains, the very essence of nature itself, cares that you have big homes and expensive cars, and oversized temples paved over the Earth she created."

Maxim shifted uncomfortably, but he was still appropriately freaked out about my Goddess of Night speech, and I was glad to see this was only putting him more on edge.

"You think she admires your destruction of everything she built? You think she appreciates the way you treat her creation?" I pressed, so nervous I felt like even my ribcage was trembling inside my body, rattling so loudly everyone would notice. "Shall we ask her? Shall we find out which side of history you're on?"

A gamble.

I wasn't a gambler by nature, but we were overpowered and outnumbered, and the only reason I wasn't being restrained was that they didn't think I was a serious threat. I couldn't physically hurt them even if I had a weapon to do it. In a way I pitied these men—they'd been manipulated into thinking this was for my own good, that their actions were justified in the name of their goddess. Only their goddess would convince them otherwise.

She'd never answered me before.

To my knowledge, she hadn't answered anyone in generations.

"Try," Bullet whispered, his voice a pained rasp that made my chest ache with worry for him. "*Pray.*"

"Gaia!" I shouted at the sky, not trying to mask the pain in my voice for the goddess who'd forsaken me at every single turn. "Goddess of Earth, Sender of Gifts, Ancestral Mother. Are the acts committed here today done in your name? Do the agathos who came here with their weapons to break soul bonds apart and shed daimon blood do your will? Is your silence their approval?"

Too prideful, a voice in my ear whispered. The same voice that had told me to call Felix. *Humble yourself.*

I dropped to one knee, pressing my hands against the asphalt of the parking lot, wishing it was dirt or sand under my fingers instead, lowering my head in supplication but keeping my voice strong and clear for everyone else in the parking lot to hear. "Mother Gaia, I beseech you. If you do not wish to have these men executed in your name, please give us a sign."

I'd take a faint breeze. Anything.

Everyone seemed to be holding their breath, and for one terrible moment I gave up. I accepted that Gaia really had abandoned us, or worse, that she tacitly approved of the agathos' actions. That the deaths of Bullet, Riot, and Dice would mean nothing to her. Why would they? When had she ever cared about daimons before?

Maxim's alarmed expression relaxed into a self-satisfied grin, confident that I'd gambled and lost, and I felt Riot's spike of fear like a knife blade against my skin, traveling directly to my heart.

No. I refused to believe this was the end. Bullet would have told us if this was the end of the road.

Right?

There was a prophecy. There were things we needed to do, the promise of a better world within reach if we could figure out how to grab it.

My eyes welled up, and I dropped my face back down to stare at the unforgiving asphalt underneath my fingers, watching as a few stray tears slipped down my face and splashed against the black, soulless surface.

And then the earth moved.

From underneath my hands, beneath my tears, the ground rippled outwards like a wave, cracking the asphalt like it was a sheet of brittle chocolate.

Where my hands were, the blacktop disintegrated completely, and before I could pull away in surprise, I found my arms buried in a patch of vibrant purple crocuses up to my elbows.

I tugged my arms back with a gasp, but I didn't have time to reflect on it because Dice was already moving, ducking away from the agathos hanging off him and diving for the gunman, already stumbling from the roiling earth and hitting the back of his slackening hand, sending the gun flying across the asphalt. The man scrambled after it, falling onto hands and knees as the earth wobbled like gelatin where he stood. He'd moved out of the shelter of the building.

Wild *flew* into action as soon as the earth fell still.

It took a minute to realize that the *whooshing* sound, followed by a thud and then a scream were due to *knives*. Tiny knives that he was hurling with terrifying accuracy to incapacitate the agathos.

"Thank you, Gaia," I breathed, hands shaking with adrenaline. She'd answered. She'd actually answered. "Thank you, thank you, thank you. *Láthe biōsas.*"

Live hidden. The agathos mantra I hadn't uttered in what felt like forever, used to honor the goddess who gave us life.

And she appeared to be on our side, whatever that meant.

The three men looming above Riot had fallen away, and Wild wasted no time incapacitating them. Riot scrambled to his feet, diving over one of the agathos on the ground as well as a significantly wide crack in the earth to get to us.

Blood poured from Riot's broken nose, the beginnings of bruising on his cheek already forming, as he glanced at his surroundings, noting Wild's presence and delivering a swift kick in the ribs to an agathos who attempted to snatch at his ankles. I'd never seen Riot like this. He looked like a warrior emerging from the depths of hell to rain fire down on his enemies.

329

The agathos closest to me let out a pained *ooph*, and I was glad I'd been watching Riot rather than Wild when the knife was thrown vaguely in my direction. Mercy threw herself back against the wall, shaking with terror as blood trickled steadily from her cheek. Not enough to be alarming, but it made my heart lurch nonetheless.

"Get out of here," I yelled at her as agathos dropped like flies around me. "You think these people are going to help you? That you're ever going to be able to live among them again? You're young, but you're not stupid. Or at least I didn't think you were before today. You better find some nice humans to live amongst, because there's no place for you here."

The terrified look on her face broke my heart, and maybe I'd regret being so harsh with her when the dust had settled, but all I could see was Bullet's bleeding gunshot wound and Riot's mangled face. She'd done this. This was the plan that she helped coordinate. The betrayal she helped engineer.

How could Mercy do that to me? Had it upset her so much that I'd left? Was it driven by her own resentment at having a daimonic soul bond of her own?

I could feel my mother's hand at work, manipulating Mercy's newfound soul bond and the fear it would have inspired. I understood that my mother had seen Mercy and Dice as an opportunity to punish me, uncaring of what the effect was on her niece.

But if it had been me, I would have found another way. No matter how angry at the world I was or how much pressure was on me, I would never have put Mercy or the people she cared about in harm's way.

"Get out of here!" Dice yelled, and his voice seemed to spur her into action as she made a mad dash for her SUV. Without him. I wasn't even sure if she'd be able to drive out of here, though Gaia's small earthquake had avoided where she'd been standing.

I heard a thud of boots as Wild swung down from the roof, moving through the remaining agathos like water, leaving them alive but incapacitated on the ground in his wake before he pulled his knives free. He looked like a god of vengeance, black hood pulled up, shadowing his dark skin and blood red eyes, knife holsters strapped to his body. As silent as a shadow, he ensured every agathos was unconscious as he retrieved his blades, not speaking or looking at anyone.

Mercy's car pulled away with a shriek of spinning tires and a thud as she drove over a dip in the earth, and despite his instruction to leave, Dice stumbled after her vehicle.

"We need to get out of here," Riot yelled, his voice thick from the obviously broken nose as he jogged over to join us. I stood and grabbed him the moment he was within reaching distance, making a distressed noise in my throat at the sight of his banged up face. "S'okay, Gracie. Just a sore face."

Tires squealed as a white van drove into the parking lot, stopping right at the entry before the cracks in the ground became too deep to navigate, and my heart stuttered in my chest at the thought of more agathos coming for us.

"It's Memphis," Riot said, squinting at the driver of the van as he pulled me tight in the side, both of us standing over Bullet. "He works for Wild."

A young daimon jumped out of the van, looking tense as he strode around and opened the back doors. "Fucking carnage. Right, let's go," he ordered Riot, nodding at Bullet. "Before he loses any more blood. Or the earth falls apart again."

Wild strode right past us without looking at me, carrying an armful of bloody blades that he deposited in the footwell of the passenger side before climbing into the driver's seat while Memphis and Riot carefully carried Bullet to the back.

I followed like a lost lamb, not entirely sure whether it was a good idea to get into the back of an unknown van or not. Logically I knew it *wasn't* safe, but Wild was my soul bond, I knew it in my bones. He wouldn't hurt us, right?

Everything had happened so quickly, and I felt incredibly adrift now that the adrenaline was wearing off.

An agathos on the ground groaned, and I decided I'd take my chances with the daimons in the unmarked van. Memphis climbed out after helping Riot get Bullet inside and held the door for me. I jumped in, unable to stay away seeing Bullet looking so vulnerable. He'd lost consciousness, and his already pale skin was taking on a grayish tinge.

The door slammed shut as I kneeled on Bullet's left side, and Riot pulled out his phone to illuminate the space, holding it with one hand while the other pinched his bleeding nose with a wince.

"Should I elevate the wound?" I asked, brain frantically searching through everything I knew about injuries. "That's what you do for a sprain, right?"

Something, something, wound above the heart for blood flow or something. Sugar, why couldn't I remember this? What were you supposed to do for gunshot wounds?

I steadied myself on the floor of the van with one hand as it rumbled to life and lurched forward, careful not to jostle Bullet.

"It's not a sprain, Gracie," Riot said in a concerned voice. "I don't know if you should move his arm in case there's something, you know, *in* it. You did a great job wrapping it. I think you've done all you can do."

"There must be something else," I argued, my voice barely above a whisper. The tears flowed and flowed, and I vaguely wondered if I'd ever *stop* crying.

"I'm so sorry, Bullet," I breathed, needing to speak to him even though he probably couldn't hear me. "You should have never been hurt. There were so many things going through my head, and I was sick with the idea that you were lying there hurting, and we'd barely even spent any time together. I haven't even really told you how much you mean to me and—"

My words faltered and I took a deep breath, steadying myself on the ground again as the van turned a corner. I didn't even know which direction we were going in.

"I think he knew what was going to happen today, Gracie," Riot said softly, his breathing loud as he struggled with his nose. "He was jittery as hell on the way over here today."

Oh my gosh, he *had* been jittery. I'd been so focused on my own excitement about seeing Mercy again that I'd written off Bullet's nervous energy as the same as Riot's anxiousness.

Why hadn't I questioned him more? Did he not feel like he could have told me?

"Go easy on yourself," Riot sighed, leaning back against the side of the van, looking exhausted. "When he's all fixed up, we can sit down and talk about what he knew and when. You're beating yourself up for not noticing, but there was no reason he couldn't have warned us that a bunch of psychos with guns were going to storm out of that building."

"He knew he was going to get shot," I said quietly, the afternoon's events replaying hazily in my mind like they were on a damaged film reel. I leaned forward, carefully smoothing Bullet's blonde hair away from his face. "He moved away and told me to stay back. He knew the bullet was coming."

Why didn't you tell me? Did you know Gaia would help us?

"Gaia..." I began before trailing off. I had no idea what to say about that. What did it mean? Would it change anything?

333

"I know," Riot replied, looking grim. "I don't even want to know what will happen when that news gets out. You're like the Goddess Whisperer or something."

"Or something," I agreed faintly. "How are you feeling? Do you think they're taking us to the hospital?"

Riot scoffed. "No. I assume we're going to *Asphodel*. There's a medical bay in the basement, by the fight ring. Hopefully they've got the good painkillers. I'm okay, but my face feels fucking terrible."

"They have their own medical bay?" I blanched. That sounded like some serious fighting.

"The fight ring mainly exists for Keres daimons to work out their angry energy. It can get pretty heated down there."

"He didn't seem very happy to see me, for a soul bond," I whispered, glancing at the solid wall that separated us from where Wild and his friend sat.

Riot's bloodstained lips twitched. "He's never happy. I doubt he was thrilled to see you in danger, and Keres go a little crazy when they're around violence, it's like a drug to them. I wonder if Bullet told him to show up here," Riot mused. "The roof of the community center is an objectively weird place for anyone to just be hanging out."

"With a bunch of knives no less," I added wryly, still stroking Bullet's hair. Talking about Wild was a nice distraction from the fact that Bullet hadn't woken up. "Still, he didn't speak to me or anything. Not even to tell me to get out of the way."

Riot gave me a strange look, tilting his head to the side.

"What?" I asked, glancing up at him. "What is it?"

The van shuddered to a stop, the engine cutting abruptly and leaving us in silence.

"Wild doesn't speak," Riot said quietly, glancing towards the van doors. "Ever. I don't think he can."

The doors opened, both the daimons who'd come to our rescue standing there.

"There's a stretcher on the way up from the med bay," Memphis said, frowning at Bullet's wound. "Smart thinking, wrapping the injury."

I nodded, giving him a weak smile before turning my attention to Wild. He didn't have a single mark on him, and the dark color of his clothes hid any blood that he might have got on him. The three of us in the van probably looked in a sorry state in comparison. He was also looking critically at Bullet's wound, avoiding my gaze entirely.

"Thank you for helping us," I said awkwardly. A curt nod from Wild, still not making eye contact. "We'd probably be in a terrible situation if you hadn't shown up."

"Bullet and I would be dead, and you'd be gone," Riot deadpanned, earning himself a scowl from Wild. Riot gave him an arrogant grin back, teeth stained with blood, and I got the impression Riot was needling him on purpose. Possibly Riot was trying to provoke a reaction out of Wild for my benefit, or maybe it was for his own enjoyment, I couldn't tell.

I wasn't an overly confrontational person by nature. Or perhaps I was, but due to my *nurture*, I'd repressed that side of myself to fit the mold that was prescribed to me. That seemed like a more likely explanation, because I was feeling more than a little confrontational right now.

Of course Wild and Riot didn't like each other. *That would be too easy.* With everything that had gone on this afternoon, it seemed *ludicrous* that Wild and Riot had this dislike of each other. I wanted to smack their heads together and *demand* they sort it out.

Bullet was off the hook for now—he'd had a bad enough day already—but if he really had known he was going to be shot today, if he'd known that Mercy was going to stab me in the back like that, then Bullet was going into my bad books too.

Not kind, I chastised weakly. *Think kind thoughts. Wild had come to our rescue, and Bullet must have had his reasons.*

I shuffled on my knees to get out of the van as a wheeled stretcher appeared, all three guys working to extract Bullet from the back of the van with the least amount of jostling.

The priority was getting Bullet taken care of, whatever disagreements Wild and Riot had in the past could be settled later.

If they couldn't sort them out, they were going to find themselves on the end of a very angry agathos. The darkness had come all the way out to play during that confrontation, and I wasn't sure I would ever get that genie back in the bottle again.

GRACE

CHAPTER 23

I hovered nearby as Memphis, Riot and Wild got a painfully still Bullet settled on the stretcher, noting that Memphis and Wild looked like they did this all the time.

Memphis pushed the stretcher through a loading dock to a large service elevator that was easily big enough to fit all of us and the stretcher. I was so busy staring at Bullet, my hand resting above his knee because I was too scared to touch his arm in case it hurt, that I didn't realize Wild wasn't in the elevator with us.

He probably had somewhere important to be. More important than getting to know the woman who surely his heart was beating out of his chest for.

We came out into a service hallway that led to an open basement area. In the center was an elevated fight ring, with plenty of space around the edge for spectators, though it was all plain concrete with no seating. Memphis guided the stretcher around the ring, through a set of double doors that led to a stark gym, and then through another door beyond that contained a surprisingly sophisticated medical bay. It was all white and reassuringly sterile, and I felt myself breathe a little easier the moment we were inside it.

A no-nonsense daimon woman walked out wearing a white coat and pulling on latex gloves that snapped against her wrists. She looked to be in her 50s at least, with dark skin and tight curls that she wore in a high bun on top of her head. Her red and purple eyes flashed impatiently as she waited for Memphis to push the stretcher all the way into the room, and I slid my hand into Riot's in surprise as I took her in.

A daimon doctor?

I didn't know such a thing existed. Wasn't *helping* people antithetical to the daimon's purpose?

"My name is Dr. Martinez," she announced, already removing the makeshift bandages I'd wrapped Bullet's wound in. "Wild already filled me in when you were en route. Get out, I don't work with an audience."

I opened my mouth to protest, but Memphis appeared in front of us, wearing a grim smile. "Trust me, you don't want to argue with her. She's a doctor, but a daimon first. Let's go back to the gym and get some ice on Riot's face."

"I'm on board with that," Riot agreed. "I don't want to lose my spot as Grace's most attractive boyfriend." He winked at me and I squeezed his hand to let him know I appreciated his futile attempt at distraction.

Memphis led us back out to the gym area, guiding us to a bench at the back that had some cleaning and first-aid supplies. They were certainly well-equipped here, for what I had assumed was a regular nightclub.

He pulled out an ice pack from the freezer and wrapped it in paper before handing it to Riot. "Keep using cold compresses on it for the next couple of days to keep the swelling down," Memphis instructed. "Dr. Martinez can realign it later if need be."

Riot gave a curt nod, pressing the ice pack to his face with a wince. "This isn't my first broken nose."

Memphis snorted. "Didn't Wild give you one the last time you were here? I'm surprised he let you get in the van." Memphis cut me an assessing glance. "Well, maybe not that surprised. You've caused quite the stir around here, good girl."

"Don't talk to her," Riot said in a cool, lethal tone that was only slightly undercut by the thick slur in his voice.

Memphis smirked, pulling a couple of bottles of water out from the fridge and handing them to us. "Oh, this is going to be fun. Wait here, Dr. Martinez will command your presence when she's ready for it."

"Thank you," I told him softly as Memphis turned to walk away. "For all your help."

His eyebrows raised slightly, like my gratitude was unexpected, before tilting his head in acknowledgement and making his way out of the gym. Riot tugged my hand, leading me over to a bench seat next to the double doors that led to Bullet, pulling me down next to him.

"Well, that was not how I expected our afternoon to go," Riot mumbled, leaning forward and keeping the ice pressed to his face while I took a big swig of water. "Wanna talk about it?"

I shook my head. "Not until Bullet..."

339

I couldn't even finish that sentence. He'd be fine, right? He'd basically told me he'd be fine.

"He'll be okay, Gracie," Riot said, wrapping an arm around my shoulders and pulling me to his side. I leaned into his embrace, resting my head against him and placing my trembling hand on his thigh. Riot felt like stability and safety, but it wasn't enough to comfort me without Bullet's bright, wise presence too.

I had no idea how much time passed while we were waiting, snuggled up together on the uncomfortable bench before Dr. Martinez' clipped voice ordered us inside. Riot ditched the ice pack as I practically sprinted through the double doors, forcing myself to speed walk to the edge of the stretcher where Bullet's eyes were still shut, his breathing even.

His shirt had been removed and the wound properly bandaged. A blood bag hung from a stand next to his head, a line connecting it to his inner arm on his good side.

He's alive, I reminded myself. *He'll be fine. He just needs a little extra blood.*

"He was very lucky," the doctor announced. "Clean entry and exit wounds, didn't hit anything vital, should make a full recovery after a few weeks. You did good to wrap the wound, though you could have done it tighter, he still lost a decent amount of blood. Conveniently, he had already written his blood type in permanent ink about an inch away from where he was shot," she added drily, pointing at the 'O+' scrawled on his arm that I'd somehow missed while I was bandaging him up.

Riot snorted. "How considerate of him."

"He's sedated right now. He'll be another hour or so with the blood bag, then I'll remove the line and you can take him upstairs to rest with some medication. Hang around, if you want to."

"Yes please," I replied instantly. All the daimons we'd encountered today had been surprisingly friendly, but I still didn't feel comfortable leaving Bullet alone here. I didn't know where we'd go anyway—the car we'd come here in was back at the community center, and Bullet was in no shape to travel.

"Don't stress," Riot murmured. "Obviously the agathos know you're in Milton until Viper redirects them, and your apartment is under watch so we can't go back there. But Dare's place is empty, and he won't mind us crashing there."

I nodded, throat too thick to reply. Whatever we had to do to keep Bullet comfortable while he healed, we'd make it happen.

"They'll be looking for me," I whispered, although the doctor looked too busy cleaning up to listen to our conversation anyway. "After today, they'll be even more motivated."

Riot hummed in agreement, pulling out his phone. "I'm updating Viper now so he can do his thing. The deal was to keep you hidden until you didn't need to be hidden anymore, so he's still on the hook. And probably regretting our arrangement."

"But won't someone have followed us here?"

"If there's anyone able to cover their tracks to this place, it's Wild," Riot replied reassuringly. "He'll have sent some of his loyal followers to make sure there was no tail. Besides, he fucked up those agathos at the community center pretty thoroughly, they'll have all needed medical attention first."

"You really don't like Wild," I surmised from his tone.

"Wild doesn't like me," Riot shot back defensively. "I'm ambivalent. Though I like him more than I did this morning, I guess."

Well, that was progress. The idea of them disliking each other felt like a lead balloon in my gut. It was *wrong*. Unnatural.

341

Careful not to jostle him, I rested my hand over Bullet's upturned one, taking comfort from the warmth of his skin. Dr. Martinez continued to potter around, apparently a one-woman medical team, before coming back over to check on Bullet.

I was struggling to reconcile the idea of a daimon doctor in my head, and I felt guilty that I was probably being horribly stereotypical. Didn't it sort of go against everything daimons were designed to do, though? Maybe she only had daimon patients.

"I can see you look confused, agathos girl," Dr. Martinez said, though she wasn't even looking at me. "Your kind visit your own doctors, don't they?"

"Yes," I replied hesitantly, before clearing my throat. "The agathos have their own clinics," I added, removing myself from that equation.

"Mm. Daimons rarely bother seeking medical care," Dr. Martinez said, sounding irritated by that. "It's difficult getting a job at a daimon-only medical facility. For most of my career, I've worked with humans, but I'm now exclusively employed here."

Riot didn't seem interested in this conversation at all, and I wanted to elbow him in the ribs and ask him how this wasn't fascinating to him.

"You used to treat humans?" I asked hesitantly.

"I am a daimon of the Geras line," Dr. Martinez stated, pausing her movements to look up at me, waiting for some spark of recognition I guessed, but we hadn't covered the Geras line in Bullet's tutoring sessions. "The Geras are the bringers of old age. It's a different kind of misery to what your Moros over there inspires, but it's a misery nonetheless. Your own body failing you, new aches and pains developing with each passing day, not to mention diseases of the mind..."

I'd never given much thought to the aging process, but now I would need Bullet to intervene to ensure I didn't have nightmares about my own body falling apart in front of my eyes.

"I am driven to guide every human I encounter to old age. It sometimes puts me in conflict with my fellow daimons, but it makes medicine a suitable field for me. For my younger patients, at least," she added, with a slightly cruel smile that better fit my assumptions about older daimons.

Riot yawned disinterestedly, wrapping his arms around my waist from behind and resting his chin on my shoulder. "Oh, maybe we should organize you some birth control, Grace. While we've got a doctor handy."

My eyes widened as I turned my head to stare at him, hopefully conveying with both my eyes and whatever emotions he could pick up how unimpressed I was with that question. I mean, it was a good idea, but it was the most inappropriate possible time to raise it.

I supposed, in Riot's defense, he looked pretty exhausted and his face was hurting.

"Of course," Dr. Martinez agreed easily. "Perhaps an IUD, if you're not planning on getting pregnant for a few years. I doubt you're welcome at your regular agathos doctor these days."

"No, I assume not." The reminder took me off-guard. The little reminders of the life I'd lost always did.

Dr. Martinez nodded curtly. "When you're ready, come back and we'll discuss it. Drag the chairs closer to the bed if you'd like to sit with Bullet until the transfusion is done. Riot, I want to check that nose then you may want to clean up your bloody face," she added, nodding at a small sink in the corner. "You look a fright."

Riot grinned like he was proud of that fact, letting Dr. Martinez examine him for a few minutes before heading over to the sink, cleaning his face and returning with two uncomfortable plastic chairs for us to sit in.

He gently led me over to the sink before I could sit, carefully cleaning Bullet's blood off my hands while I stared at the pinkish water swirling down the drain. I didn't even realize that I'd had blood on me.

I wet some paper towels and brought them over to Bullet, meticulously cleaning the blood off his hands and arm as gently as I could. Satisfied that the blood was no longer taunting me, Riot and I sat down next to the stretcher, my now clean hand stroking Bullet's still one the entire time.

There was a war of emotions taking place in my chest. Despair that he was hurt, versus anger that he'd obviously known this was going to happen. The smudged O+ scrawled on his arm was practically taunting me.

Eventually, Dr. Martinez returned with painkillers for both Riot and Bullet, antibiotics for Bullet, and a written list of instructions for when they were to take them.

She removed the line from Bullet's arm with practiced efficiency as another daimon pushed open the double doors, loudly announcing his presence even as his eyes were trained on the phone in his hand.

"Oh shit," Riot said as we both stood from our seats. "Leo? I didn't know you worked here. Er, Grace this is Leo. Leo, this is... my Grace."

I smiled to myself as he stumbled slightly over the introduction, resting my hand against his outer thigh and giving it a light squeeze to let him know I wasn't offended. Our relationship wasn't exactly normal in the daimon world either.

Leo nodded his head at me in greeting, no animosity in his gaze whatsoever. I wondered if he'd earned his 'Leo' name because of his appearance—with his tanned skin, shaggy long reddish blonde hair and matching beard, he did look a bit like a lion.

"Nice to finally meet the famous Grace. There are some rooms upstairs and a communal living area for the club staff who live here. It's nothing fancy, but you're all welcome to a room here while Bullet recovers."

"That's very kind of you," I replied immediately, confused about why Wild hadn't asked us himself, or where he'd gone. To say I was curious about him was an understatement—not only as my soul bond, but at *everything*. Why didn't he speak? How did he come to own this club while he was still so young?

That he had on-site accommodation for his employees was another piece of the incomplete puzzle.

"We'll go up the service lift with the stretcher, then transfer Bullet to the bed to sleep off the drugs," Leo continued.

He looked to Dr. Martinez, who gave us a curt nod, rattling off care instructions and telling us she'd come up to check on Bullet periodically.

Leo released the brakes on the stretcher with practiced ease, and Riot moved to help him guide the contraption out of the medical wing. I rushed ahead to open doors where Leo directed me.

"We do this a lot," Leo said drily, looking amused at the probably bewildered expression on my face. "There are fights down here each night, big money makers. There's always at least one employee who gets their ass kicked and has to be transferred upstairs from the medical wing."

"Oh. Is that a requirement to work here? The fighting?" I asked, not so subtly trying to understand more about the mysterious Wild.

"What? No, not at all. It's mostly the newbies who come here—either to work off some rage or thinking they'll be badass as fuck, enter a fight, leave with thousands of dollars and start a new life. It never happens, which is why the bossman built a living area for our broke asses," Leo chuckled. "I don't fight. Not my bloodline, ya know?"

"He means he's not a Keres," Riot explained. "Back in the day, the Keres were in the thick of every battle, fueled by bloodlust. Nowadays they have to make do with organized fights."

Leo nodded in agreement, guiding us through the elevator doors when they opened, revealing an open concept living space with an enormous kitchen along one wall, a dining table long enough to seat twenty people, and enormous sectional sofas facing a wall-mounted television. Everything was very industrial looking—polished concrete floors, exposed beams, and gray and black furnishings—but it was comfortable and obviously well lived in.

In the corner where the long kitchen island ended was a black metal spiral staircase, and I kept looking back over my shoulder as we passed through the living area, curious as to what was at the top of those stairs.

The corridor Leo led us down with doors leading off it was easily wide enough to pull the stretcher down, and he led us to the very end and through some double doors into a large, comfortable room with a queen-sized bed, a dresser, and a small bathroom off the side, all done in the same neutral colors as the communal living area.

"This is the fancy guest room," Leo chuckled. "No bunks, and you've got your own bathroom. Everyone's sleeping now, but they'll be up soon. There's a small, daimon-only club on this level, through a couple of walls, and the main club downstairs, so you're probably not going to get much sleep at night."

I hadn't even considered that, but we probably should try to nap in preparation for being up all night. Riot and Leo lifted Bullet onto the bed on the count of three and I winced as the movement jostled him. He looked so frail, lying there shirtless with his left arm tightly bandaged.

"There's food in the kitchen, help yourself," Leo said, clapping Riot on the shoulder before letting himself out. The lack of ceremony daimons had when it came to greetings and goodbyes was quite refreshing. There was none of the unspoken politics that existed in the world of the agathos.

I kicked off my shoes and dropped my jacket on a chair in the corner, vaguely registering the blood splatters on it, but not wanting to look too closely. Riot seemed to have the same idea, stripping down to his boxers and heading straight for the bathroom, where I heard the shower turn on.

"Now do you want to talk about it?" Riot called from the bathroom, making me smile the teensiest bit.

"Yes. No. I don't know," I replied, moving to stand in the bathroom door but keeping my eyes averted. Gaia had *moved the earth* at my request. It was almost too big to comprehend. "But we probably should try to get some rest anyway. Maybe I'll feel more ready to talk after I sleep on it."

I almost snorted. Was I going to feel more ready to talk about Mercy's betrayal and Bullet's injury after a *nap*? Obviously not. I probably needed years of therapy to properly address those topics.

"That's true. We'll have all night to talk, with the thudding bass of terrible house music pounding in the background," Riot agreed drily. "Go rest, I'll join you soon."

I climbed into the bed next to Bullet, tugging the sheet over both of us, my heart aching at how still he was. Could he find me in the dreamscape when he was sedated? I hoped so. It made the prospect of a nap a lot more appealing, even if I wouldn't remember it.

"Wake up soon," I whispered to Bullet, my lips pressed against his right bicep. "I miss your humming and the way you shuffle your cards when you're thinking, and drum your fingers on your leg when you're frustrated. Wake up and come back to me so I can yell at you for getting hurt and not giving us any warning."

As soon as the bass started thumping, all of us were awake. Bullet groaned, throwing his good arm over his eyes, and I immediately sat up, looming over him a little.

"You checking me out, Amazing Grace?" Bullet rasped, giving me a weak smile. I made a sound of disagreement in the back of my throat as I pulled a pillow out from under Riot's head, much to his chagrin.

"Don't even start with me, Bullet," I warned, giving him a stern look. "I have a bone to pick with you. Sit forward a bit, you need some water."

"Just don't pick my arm bone," Bullet joked weakly as he let me help him up and I pushed the pillow behind him.

The reminder of his injury did ease my ire a little. Riot blindly patted the nightstand, managing to turn the lamp on and shove a bottle of water at me, all without opening his eyes before his face relaxed like he was going back to sleep.

Maybe he was. Riot of all of us was used to the daimon sleep schedule.

I unscrewed the cap and held the bottle up to Bullet's lips, noticing the brief flash of vulnerability on his face before he tried to hide it, but his emotions weren't as easy to disguise, he was *nervous*. I helped him drink while staring at his arm, trying to discern if there was any blood seeping through the bandage and finding it clean.

"Are you mad at me, Amazing Grace?" Bullet asked softly, reaching for me. I sat crossed legged at his side and linked our fingers together on his good hand.

"That depends on how much you knew," I replied tiredly. How did people wake up and start their day at nighttime? I felt like my body was rejecting the concept of being awake. "And as mad as I am, I'm three times more *glad* that you're okay. Bullet wound aside."

"I'm collecting them," he quipped, eyes glancing down at his chest. I frowned as I leaned forward, realizing for the first time that there was a puckered scar barely visible underneath the rose tattoo on the right side of his chest.

"That's where I got the nickname from," Bullet explained.

"I'm pretty sure it's because you wore the bullet around your neck, like some kind of weird trophy," Riot said, voice muffled by the pillow. The gold of the small bullet on the chain glinted in the low lamplight, catching my eye.

"Mm, that too," Bullet agreed.

There was a knock at the door interrupting our conversation, and Riot immediately got up to investigate with a warning look at me to stay put, pausing to pull on his jeans before he disappeared around the corner into the small corridor that led to the door. I listened for voices, but all I heard was an amused snort from Riot before he returned with a duffel bag he'd already unzipped and was digging through.

"What is that?" I asked.

"We're going to be here for a few days while I recuperate," Bullet said, head tipped back against the pillows. "They're spare clothes."

"So you did see literally all of this coming?" Riot confirmed, pulling out a black tailored shirt and wrinkling his nose in distaste. Surprisingly, considering how much grief he'd given Bullet about his abilities, Riot didn't seem nearly as upset as I was.

"Most of it."

"Logically, I know you can't always tell us what's going to happen, but you couldn't have given us *some* warning? Gaia answered me! You got *shot*, Bullet!" I said exasperatedly.

"Chicks dig scars, right?"

"Please be serious, I've never been so terrified," I sighed. I knew Bullet used humor to deflect, but very occasionally, I needed him to just have an honest conversation.

Bullet gave me a sad smile while Riot sat quietly on the end of the bed, still yawning before wincing at the pain in his bruised face. "I didn't know Gaia would answer you. I knew *something* would happen, something that you did, but it wasn't clear in my visions what that was. Probably because neither the Fates nor La Nuit can predict what Gaia will do. And getting shot was an unfortunate byproduct, obviously, but sometimes getting shot in the arm is the *best* option."

There was silence for a moment while my mind ran through various worst-case scenarios at warp speed. What was the alternative? Had he seen someone die?

"You're going to have to elaborate a little more," Riot deadpanned.

"What if I just didn't? And we all moved past this?" Bullet proposed hopefully. "No use beating a dead horse and all that. Besides, we're in the belly of the Underworld club network, under the nose of your mysterious third soul bond, and isn't that something you'd like to talk about right now? No? Oh dear, I think I'm feeling faint from the pain medication," he said with a dramatic sigh, closing his eyes before peeking out under his lashes at me.

Riot snorted as I gently swatted Bullet's leg. "You haven't even had any pain medication in a while, you're due for more. And fine—you saw worse options, so you opted to let us go through this still terrible option, and now you're recovering from a gunshot wound. Did you know that Mercy... that Mercy would do what she did?"

Bullet's smile turned sympathetic, and I felt Riot's concern as he fed off the emotions I was putting out.

"Yes."

I shook my head, picking at the blanket. "I can't understand it. I did stupid things when I was a teenager too, but she put peoples *lives* at risk today. Not only my soul bonds, but hers too. What did she expect to happen?"

"Your mom and that scary priestess probably fed her some carefully worded bullshit about it being the right thing to do and how she was saving you both," Riot suggested. "I doubt they outright told her they intended to kill us. She seemed pretty upset about that."

"Mercy was hurt too," Bullet pointed out. "That bullet that scraped her face must have stung."

Guilt roiled in my gut because I'd told her to run. To go find some humans to blend in with. We weren't quite the same as humans and tried to avoid going to their doctors so as not to raise questions. Would she be able to get medical care for her wound?

Maybe I was too harsh when I'd sent her away.

"Don't feel guilty," Bullet said, a plea in his voice I wasn't used to hearing. "Mercy... She's got a lot of challenges ahead of her. You're not the only agathos to have caught the eye of the divine, but Mercy won't be alone for long, I promise you that."

"Could we check on him?" I asked quietly. "Dice? I can't even imagine how I'd feel if one of you had deceived me that way."

"I can call Rogue, but be prepared for her to completely lose her shit," Riot said, scrubbing a hand down his face.

"As she should," I murmured. I'd do the same for my brothers, and we weren't even close.

I'd have done the same for Mercy.

With a reluctant sigh, Riot fished out his phone and began scrolling through it. Bullet was unusually silent as he fished the velvet bag of tarot cards out of his pants pocket with his good hand, taking me by surprise. I hadn't even realized he was carrying them.

As soon as Riot held the phone up to his ear, I extended my hand, silently asking for it. I didn't even know the extent Riot had gone to in order to keep me safe, but I knew it was a lot. This mess I could clean up on my own.

Riot handed over the phone unhappily and Rogue's dry, unimpressed voice filtered through the moment I pressed the device to my ear.

"I hate you, your girlfriend, and her stupid cousin."

"I deserve that," I replied evenly, ignoring the pang that went through my chest at the idea of being hated by anyone.

"Ugh. Don't you dare be nice and apologetic," Rogue sighed, sounding bored. *"My brother came home with a busted jaw and fucked up ribs because of you and your bitch cousin. Mostly your bitch cousin."*

"I can't apologize for her. I wouldn't even if I could."

It wasn't really in my nature to be unforgiving—I hated the idea that anyone could be irredeemable because I'd feared that I was, and that was a terrifying thought. I wasn't sure I could ever forgive Mercy though. I could never excuse what she'd done.

"Okay, fine," Rogue said. *"I don't hate you. You seem kind of okay, actually. For an agathos. I don't know what happened. Mercy was here early in the morning, kind of jittery but mostly normal. Then she got a phone call and was straight up bizarre after that."*

I frowned. "It was probably my mom calling her."

"*No, it was a man's voice,*" Rogue replied. "*She snuck away from Dice to take the call, so I followed her and tried to eavesdrop because her jitters were weirding me out. She was very secretive, I couldn't hear much.*"

"I guess it could have been one of my dads," I hedged, frowning to myself. I glanced at Bullet, surprised to find he had a sheepish expression on his face.

"It was me. You put her number into my phone when you messaged her that time," Bullet said, wincing like he was steeling himself for my wrath.

"*Who is that?*" Rogue asked, listening in on our conversation.

"Bullet," I clipped, narrowing my eyes at him. Not only had he *known* about Mercy, he'd spoken to her! Called her on the freaking phone. I had put her number in his phone, so my ire was as much directed at myself as it was him.

"*Oh, the Oneiroi? Damn. Now I kind of feel bad that your cousin got my idiot brother. He's an Ate daimon, it's hella unimpressive.*"

A baby grizzled in the background and Rogue made a rhythmic shushing sound like she was bouncing it on her hip.

"Is Dice okay?" I asked hesitantly, feeling foolish even as I said the words. Of course he wasn't.

The idea of Riot or Bullet betraying me the way Mercy had betrayed him was... unimaginable. Wild hadn't immediately attached himself to me and even that was distressing me.

Rogue made a noise of disgust. "*No. But they barely even knew each other, and he's acting like they were married for twenty years and she stabbed him in the back. In the beginning, he was just disappearing all the time. Then a couple of weeks ago, he brought her over for the first time. She'd come here and*" *they would sit on the couch in my living room with two feet between them and make me feel like I was their babysitter or something, it was a nightmare."*

My lips twitched in spite of myself at the total revulsion in her voice. I'd never met a woman like Rogue—agathos women were always light and effusive outside of their homes, even if they weren't happy about something. My mother was the master at putting on a polite show for acquaintances.

"Anyway, he'll live," Rogue continued, impatiently shushing the baby again. *"He followed your girl as far as he could when she ran, but his ribs were broken so he couldn't keep up."*

"Oh." I didn't know what to say to that. I'd told her to leave, she'd done as I asked. And yet the idea of her out there all alone...

"She headed further into Milton, not back towards Auburn, if it helps," Rogue said offhandedly.

Despite my anger, worry churned in my gut. She didn't know anyone, she was only *just* 18, and if word had got out about what she'd done, being in daimon territory didn't seem like a good idea for her right now.

"I can hear your panic through the phone," Rogue laughed, a surprisingly rich, throaty sound compared to her monotone voice. *"Look, Dice has eyes on her, and he's not going to let anyone hurt her. He's not going to hurt her either. But he does want to talk to her, and it'll be an unpleasant conversation."*

The baby gave such an outraged cry that I startled and Rogue swore loudly. *"Gotta go. The sprog requires sustenance. Make sure you make all those boys of yours wrap it up—you do not want one of these things. Laters, good girl."*

The call cut out suddenly and I stared down at the phone in my hand, a little bewildered by, well, all of it.

"You want me to try to find out where Mercy is?" Riot asked, reaching for the phone. I nodded a little helplessly, feeling awful for accepting his offer when Mercy's actions could well have gotten Riot killed. The instinct to protect her warred with the raging hurt in my heart that she'd put there, and my own demand that she leave.

I looked at Bullet, unable to keep the hurt out of my voice. "You not only knew, you *talked* to her. Why didn't you say anything? Was this really the only option? Couldn't you see how much this would *hurt* me?"

Bullet's expression was resigned. He straightened on the bed as best he could, wincing in pain as he jostled his arm and my hands flexed, automatically wanting to reach for him, to soothe him.

"There were multiple options, but they all kind of sucked," Bullet said slowly. "I called Mercy and told her to follow the Basilinna's orders because her half-cocked plan to get out of it would have left Dice with a permanent spinal injury and put Mercy in jail. Believe it or not, most teenagers aren't master strategists."

I opened my mouth to argue before slamming it shut again. Obviously the alternative sounded horrific and I was glad that hadn't happened.

"You got injured in Dice's place?" Riot asked, frowning.

"I've been shot before, I knew I could handle it," Bullet replied, entirely too nonchalant about it.

"Bullet!"

"I knew you wouldn't get hurt," he offered, giving me what he probably thought was a comforting smile.

"Strange, how that doesn't make me feel better," I sighed, rubbing my temples. The incessant pounding of the bass was already making me irritable, and it had only just started.

"I did offer Mercy some ideas," Bullet said cryptically, staring unseeing at the wall. "We'll have to see whether she followed my suggestion or not."

"Fuck's sake," Riot muttered, aggressively typing on his phone. "Viper won't give me any information on Mercy."

"Why?" Bullet asked before I could, sounding puzzled. "Doesn't he do anything for a price?"

"Anything except double up jobs," Riot replied bitterly. "That's how Dice has eyes on her. She's on Viper's radar."

"Interesting," Bullet murmured while my heart dropped into my stomach. *Interesting?! Was this not the same guy who had been holding Riot hostage all this time?*

"I know you're worried, Amazing Grace," Bullet said softly. "I know in your head, Mercy is your baby cousin and you struggle to see her as anything different, but trust that she can handle whatever's coming her way."

I flopped onto the bed, knowing Bullet wouldn't outright lie to me—though lying by omission was apparently a gray area—but struggling with the idea of Mercy being anything other than a teenage girl with zero real world experience.

"I'm going to go find us some food," Riot announced, pulling a pair of trendy sweatpants and a matching hoodie out of the bag, giving them an exasperated look. Riot's style was much more low maintenance than Bullet's, and on any other day I'd enjoy watching Riot grumble about getting so dressed up.

"It's all going to be fine, Amazing Grace," Bullet said quietly. "You'll see. I'd take a thousand bullets to keep you safe."

After eating the microwave meals Riot had brought in for us, Bullet had taken more pain medication and conked out while I'd showered, taking advantage of the fact that Bullet had packed spare clothes for me.

These were definitely not like the clothes he'd stocked in the upstairs closet I'd been using at his place. It was like he'd purchased these and then kept them in storage because he wasn't sure if he should give them to me or not.

The underwear in this duffel bag was a *lot* skimpier than the stuff back at the barn apartment—all silk and lace and incredibly impractical. But after I'd showered and slipped on a matching emerald green bra and panty set, I had to admit I felt *sexy*, so maybe there was something to be said for tiny underwear.

I pulled out a black knit sweater dress that had long sleeves but only fell to mid-thigh, which was a lot shorter than the dresses I usually wore. By the time I'd finger combed my hair and pulled it into a ponytail, Riot had fallen asleep again too.

I took a moment to stare at both of them—safe and *not* covered in blood—and appreciated that they were mine, if not *all* the way mine yet. That was something I wanted to rectify as soon as possible, and if I wasn't terrified to go down into that fight ring at night when it was probably full, I'd have gone and asked Dr. Martinez about birth control right away.

Instead, I decided to go to the staff common area we'd walked through and assuage my need for caffeine if I was going to stay up all night. Bullet *had* said multiple times that no daimons took any issue with me, and everyone I'd met here had been really lovely.

Okay, maybe not *lovely*, but no one seemed to have a problem with me. Except maybe Wild himself, but I got the impression that I was perfectly safe in his domain. He might not want to see me, but he definitely didn't want to see me hurt, either. It was a bold assumption to make about someone who'd never said a word to me, but he'd shown up out of nowhere to show off his knife throwing skills when we were in trouble, and that had to mean *something*.

Had Bullet arranged Wild's presence there too? Almost certainly.

There were some simple black pointed flats with thin ankle straps that I slipped on, glad I didn't have to wear my boots again that definitely had blood on them.

The kitchen was empty except for one intimidatingly beautiful woman. She was standing at the counter but turned to look at me, her crimson eyes running down me from head to toe in an assessing fashion. I blushed, old insecurities at being judged and found wanting reared their ugly heads.

Sugar, she looked like a model. Her features were sharp and perfectly symmetrical, emphasized by her short black hair that was buzzed on the sides and longer on top, styled to one side. The fitted gray tank top and rips in her tight jeans revealed that her legs were probably as covered in intricate tattoos as her arms were.

"I like your tattoos," I said softly to break the awkwardness, not entirely sure *what* to say, but wanting to demonstrate that I was no threat. That I wasn't like the other agathos she'd undoubtedly heard about. Her tattoos *were* beautiful—intricate depictions of the Zodiac from what I could see. I could make out the two Pisces fish on her forearm, twisted towards each other against the background of their constellation. On her opposite upper arm was the Sagittarius archer—a centaur, it's arrow notched, pointing up towards her collarbone.

358

"Dare did them," the woman said, arching an eyebrow at me. "You've probably heard of him, he did your boyfriends' ink too. You're dressed up, planning on partying with the daimons tonight?"

"No, uh, my *boyfriend* packed some clothes. I didn't expect to be staying here."

"We're probably the same size, I'll find you a pair of sweats," she replied dismissively, as though she wasn't doing me a huge favor. "I'm Onyx Li, by the way. And you're Grace the good girl."

I blinked at her, wishing I'd leaned against the kitchen counter or made some effort to look less out of place. "Yes?"

"I've been calling you 'good girl' since you moved here," Onyx explained with a smirk. She looked *outrageously* cool. I would look ridiculous if I tried to pull off that sultry confident expression. "Can't stop now, it's a habit."

I got the feeling she'd passed that habit on—Memphis had called me 'good girl' downstairs too.

"You knew when I moved here?"

"Oh yes," Onyx replied, turning her attention back to the coffee machine. "Do you drink coffee, good girl?"

"Ah, yes. I do." The nickname made me smile, maybe because Onyx said it in such an affectionate way.

"I'm Wild's VP of sorts," Onyx said, fussing with the machine.

Jealousy rose in my throat like bile. Was it a purely professional relationship? Or something more? Is this why he was avoiding me? She was *stunning*—cooler and more self-assured than I could ever be. If it came to choosing between us, it wouldn't even be a competition.

No wonder Wild had disappeared the first chance he got.

"Anyway," Onyx continued, oblivious to my inner struggle. "Wild has been keeping an eye on you since you moved here." She tilted her chin up towards the topmost corner of the room where I spotted a security camera. "He's got eyes over most of Milton."

He'd been watching me? I guess that explained why he sounded like he knew who I was when we'd gone to that country house to meet him.

Why had he never approached me if he'd seen me before though? Maybe that was why he'd never approached me. He'd seen me on camera and found me lacking.

Onyx fiddled with something at her hip while I contemplated what this all meant. There was no dismissing Wild's avoidance of me as a simple coincidence if he'd been aware of me for months.

Bullet had seemed so certain that I'd have four bonded someday. Maybe that meant the onus was on me to pursue Wild? It wasn't really done in agathos circles. The woman tracked down her soul bonds, but any *wooing* was meant to come from the man's side.

"Did you really summon *Gaia*?" Onyx asked. "Anesidora, whatever."

Well, word had spread about that incident quickly. "I wouldn't say summoned. I guess I asked for her opinion."

"Obviously," Onyx replied wryly. "Clearly, that is much less impressive. Nothing incredible about that at all. Just a regular Saturday, right?"

"I wouldn't go that far," I said weakly.

She hummed thoughtfully. "Don't worry, I'm not going to go around announcing that. You probably should try to direct the conversation away from that too, if it ever comes up. People will either love you, loathe you, or want to keep you as a pet if they find out what you can do."

It shouldn't have surprised me, not even a little, that word had gotten out about the whole small earthquake incident, but the idea of people looking at me like some kind of 'Goddess Whisperer' like Riot had called me was unsettling to say the least.

The agathos loathed me already. My mother wouldn't be proud that Gaia herself had answered my call. She'd be furious that I made her look bad.

I was startled when Onyx pushed the cup of coffee into my hands, so lost in my own thoughts I hadn't realized she'd finished making it. The sharp edge of something pushed into my palm and I tried to shift my hand to see what it was, but Onyx's grip was firm. She shot a pointed look towards the camera before pulling her hands away.

"In case of emergency," she said with a playful wink. "Good luck, good girl."

Too curious about what was in my hand to care that there was no creamer in my coffee, I hurried back to the bedroom, slipping through the door as quietly as possible so as not to wake the guys.

After scanning the mostly bare room for cameras and thankfully finding none, I leaned back against the door and opened my palm. The unassuming object stared back at me, and I glared at it like the reason for it would magically manifest in my mind if I stared hard enough.

Why had Onyx given me a key, and what did it unlock?

CHAPTER 24

"You sure you're going to be alright?" I asked Mom, leaning against the wall with my hands jammed in my pockets as she fussed with her blood red lipstick in front of the hallway mirror.

She turned and gave me a scathing look, flipping her straight black hair over her shoulder as she moved. "I am perfectly capable of looking after myself. Who do you think raised you? How do you think I managed before I had a big strong son to occasionally show up in town and fuss over me?"

My lips twitched. "It's a mystery to me."

"Ach, when are you going back home?"

"Sick of me already, Ma?" I teased, grinning at her.

I *could* go home. The state of emergency in Milton had been lifted, and Riot had boarded up the studio, ready for me to sort it out, plus I was more than a little homesick. It didn't feel right leaving my mom here on her own with all the attacks on daimons by fired up agathos though. I thought it would peter out over time, but if anything it was getting worse. I lowkey wondered if the agathos higher ups were stoking the flames deliberately, though I had no idea what they could be telling their people. As far as I knew, Riot was stuck in Milton working for Viper, but keeping himself hidden while his girl was.... somewhere. I didn't know where, and he hadn't shared that with me, but hopefully she was safe.

They'd basically gone underground. Daimons didn't bother with people who minded their own business, and in my head, their disappearance should have been the end of it. Apparently that wasn't how agathos worked, though.

"You're letting those assholes keep you out of your home, it's an embarrassment," Mom clipped, turning her attention back to her reflection. "I raised you better than that."

"You barely raised me at all," I pointed out, earning me an eye roll. Daimons weren't exactly hands-on parents. They weren't wired that way.

Mom shot me a withering look. "I'll be back tomorrow. I'm going to stay the night at—"

"Please don't tell me," I begged, contemplating covering my ears like a kid.

"I *would* be proud if you came home and told me about your many lovers," Mom sniffed. "You are a terrible Philotes, you know. Perhaps you wouldn't mother hen me so much if you fucked someone from time to time."

"Noted," I replied, laughing before I could stop myself. I pushed off the wall and gave her a kiss on the cheek. "Be careful."

"You're doing it again. Go find some willing lover tonight to take the edge off before you drive me completely insane," Mom instructed haughtily as she walked out the door, her impractical silk black trench coat swishing behind her.

I wouldn't do that. An orgasm might take the edge off my mood, but I could easily do that myself with just my hand for company. I occasionally tried to have meaningless sex with strangers, but my dick rejected the idea completely. I had to at least feel *interested* in them as a person, ideally intrigued by them, to get it up. Why the Goddess of Night gave a Philotes daimon such a choosy cock was beyond me. Maybe Bullet could ask her for me? From memory, he chatted to the goddess from time-to-time.

I pulled on my black bomber jacket and sneakers, locking up behind me and heading towards the daimon block of businesses within walking distance, keeping alert as I moved down the dark streets. The streetlights weren't illuminating the area nearly well enough to give me any peace of mind, especially since there had been some far more subtle agathos attacks recently. A couple of days ago, a daimon walking past a dark alleyway had caught a knife between the ribs—he was still holed up in a makeshift basement clinic a daimon doctor had set up nearby.

As much as it stressed me out to risk the same, I'd started coming here each night to help out. Daimons weren't community-oriented by nature, but all the local adults had naturally started coming together in the past few weeks to protect each other's turf. Safety in numbers and all that.

It was kind of nice, in a kumbaya, beers-around-the-bonfire kind of way. I was probably the only one who thought that way, but whatever.

"Dare," Axe grunted in acknowledgement as I approached his bar. He was leaning against the wall, smoking a cigarette and probably glaring away all of his potential customers. He was a grizzly old Keres daimon with skin tanned from years of working outside, exorcising his bloodlust by working on an oil rig, and feathered greenish tattoos that made me want to cry whenever I saw them. I could do a great cover up if he'd give me the chance.

"You look particularly feral tonight," I noted, sidling up next to him.

He rolled his eyes. "Haven't you heard? They found the agathos princess they're all looking for earlier today."

My heart stopped beating. Completely stopped in my chest.

"What happened?" I snapped, taking Axe off-guard.

"Uh, I guess the daimons fought back. With knives by the sound of it. And maybe there was an earthquake? I dunno. Anyway, she got away and the agathos are even more worked up now. Should be a rough night."

"I need to make a call," I muttered, already pulling my phone out of my pocket as I slipped down the alleyway where I'd confronted those agathos teenagers what seemed like years ago.

I pulled up Riot's contact details and paced the narrow space as I waited for him to answer.

"Hey."

"Hey?!" I exploded. "I just found out from some random dude that the agathos came for your girl again and got knifed for their efforts, and you answer with 'hey'?! You're an asshole."

"I deserve that," Riot chuckled, though it sounded weird and thicker than usual. *"It's been a shitty day, and now it's going to be a shitty night because I'm on my way to Viper's to basically be his stand-in while he fixes this mess, bitching about how I brought all this on myself for bringing Grace to Milton in the first place."*

I didn't want to be a dick, but I kind of agreed with Viper on that front. What had he been thinking?

365

"Don't judge," Riot muttered tiredly. *"I tried to talk her out of it, but her cousin swore she wouldn't tell anyone that she was meeting us. Turns out some agathos can lie, so watch out for that."*

"Some agathos have daimon boyfriends," I pointed out. "I don't think we can assume anything anymore. I take it by your grumbling that you're all physically okay? You sound weird."

"Broken nose," he replied. *"They smashed my face into the ground. I'm not complaining though, Bullet got shot."*

"What?!"

"In the arm," Riot added hurriedly. *"He got lucky. Or maybe it wasn't so much luck as he saw it coming and minimized the damage as much as possible. He's sleeping off the painkillers at Asphodel."*

That was nice of Bullet to help them out. He'd been a good friend to Riot and me when we were younger, and I felt like a bit of an asshole that I basically only saw him now whenever he wanted a new tattoo.

"Asphodel?" I asked, halting in my pacing. "How did that happen?"

"Wild came to our rescue," he replied, sounding amused. *"There was a, uh, small earthquake—I don't even know how to explain that—and then boom. Wild appeared throwing knives off the roof like a fucking ninja, taking down agathos left and right. You know I've never been a fan of the guy, but I'd probably be dead if he'd shown up later, so kudos to him, I guess."*

I snorted at the begrudging respect in his voice. Riot had taken plenty of beatings over the years, but the asskicking Wild had given him had been one of the worst. He'd basically spent a week on my couch sleeping it off and avoiding his dad's wrath.

I never envisioned Wild and Riot being anything less than sworn enemies after that.

"Why did he help you?" I pressed, confused. "There's no love lost between you guys."

"It wasn't for me," Riot said, sounding like he was trying to laugh but his broken nose was irritating him. *"Wild intervened for Grace."*

"I feel like I'm missing something here," I admitted, frowning at the red brick wall. "Why would he help out *your* girlfriend? How would he even meet your girlfriend?"

There was an awkward silence on the other end of the line, which was weird because there were never awkward silences between me and Riot. We'd known each other since pre-K.

"Agathos women have multiple boyfriends, remember? Multiple soul bonds. Four of them, chosen by the Fates or something," Riot said awkwardly.

Oh.

Ohhhhhhhhh.

"So, uh, he's one of her *soul bonds?*" I confirmed, stuttering over the weird term. Daimons didn't have anything like that.

Well, they didn't before. Why did it hurt to ask that question?

Maybe because I was a jealous son of a bitch. Of all the daimons I'd ever met, I was the one who wanted a relationship most. A meaningful, intimate relationship where I could fulfill my sexual needs without feeling like I was sacrificing pieces of my soul to do so.

"Yeah. Sorry I didn't say anything earlier, we were trying to reduce the number of backs with targets on them. Me, Bullet, and Wild."

"And one other."

"And one more," he agreed cautiously after a painfully long pause, a whole bunch of words left unsaid between us.

Why not me? It could be me. There was no reason for it not to be me. How did two people go about finding out if they were soul bonds or not?

There were shouts from the street and I growled in frustration. "I need to go. Another fight. This conversation isn't over."

"Be safe," Riot instructed as I hung up.

Usually, I was the most reserved of the daimons who showed up here at night. I didn't look for fights, for the most part. I joined in because it felt like the right thing to do. Not tonight. Tonight I wanted blood. I wanted to feel bones crunching under my fists, hear the thud of unconscious bodies hitting the ground, and then I wanted to get in my truck and drive straight to Asphodel with my foot pressed to the gas the whole way, for reasons I couldn't even fully explain to myself.

I collapsed on the fold out bed as the sun was rising, after a five minute shower to wash the blood and dirt off. I'd almost drifted off when my phone started buzzing next to my head and I groaned as I felt around for it, cracking my eyes as little as possible to see whose name was on the screen.

Bullet.

Shit, I was probably going to have to take this one.

"Hello," I mumbled, mouth half pressed into the mattress.

"You can't come back yet."

That woke me up.

"Fuck that. The only reason I'm not driving back right now is because I can barely keep my eyes open. I'll be home by tonight," I snapped.

I had a vague theory to explore, and I was going to explore it, *god damn it.*

"You can't," Bullet sighed, and I felt a little bit bad for snapping at him because he sounded like absolute shit.

"You're going to have to do better than that, Bullet. Why can't I come home? The state of emergency is over. I should have come back anyway."

"But you haven't for a reason," Bullet replied softly. *"And you can't. Something is going to happen, and you'll never forgive yourself if you aren't there."*

"What's going to happen?" I asked hoarsely, my mind immediately going to my mom.

"Just stay in Jersey, okay? It's important. Please. I'm not in the habit of begging, Dare."

"I know you're not," I murmured, feeling resigned. "Can't you tell me if she's you know..." *Mine.*

"I don't have the answers you're looking for right now," Bullet said sympathetically. That sounded like psychic speak for 'I'm not going to tell you', but whatever. I knew Bullet well enough to know he wouldn't tell me something if he didn't want to.

"Thanks for the heads up, I guess," I sighed.

The phone cut out before I could ask any follow up questions. Like "are the agathos going to fuck up my mom's life?" or "is your girlfriend also my girlfriend?"

I had no reason to think that, not really. I'd never seen her, never met her. Riot had been so cagey about everything that all I knew was her name and the fact that she was agathos from Auburn who used to work at the shelter in Milton. I still couldn't shake the *hope* that the Fates or the

Goddess or whatever divine power was up there had gifted me a connection as precious as a soul bond seemed to be too.

As much as I wanted to check in with Riot and Bullet again, the failed attempt at either getting Grace back or just killing Riot and Bullet—people here seemed to be undecided on that front—had sent the agathos into a frenzy. There had even been talks that a *second* agathos woman had been taken, and I wondered if that was the cousin Riot had referred to. Maybe it was only Grace's family that had whatever gene it was that drew them to daimons, because nothing like that was happening here.

The only agathos-daimon interactions happening around here bordered on homicide. There weren't any deaths yet that I knew of, but it was only a matter of time.

I'd woken up earlier than usual because Axe was blowing up my phone, insisting they already needed extra muscle. Car full after car full of mostly older, infuriated agathos men had come in waves, either getting out of the vehicles to pick fights or hurling bottles out their windows as they went past.

It was all well and good to come here and pick fights with us, theoretically, but it wasn't like it was only adult daimons around here. Many of the daimons in this neighborhood had children who'd been impacted by the violence, and there were a lot of humans who were just trying to go about their lives, baffled as to why their town seemed to be silently at war around them.

The agathos never injured humans directly, but they didn't have to in order to ruin their lives.

I stumbled in after another relentless night of violence, ditching my dirtiest clothes at the door so I didn't trek any through my mother's tomb-like model home, and quickly checked by her room to make sure she was safe and sound in her bed. Satisfied she was fine, I went to grab some clean clothes from my bag to take to the shower, but a text message distracted me.

Onyx: *Good girl, holding court.*

I frowned at the screen, wondering if she'd messaged me by mistake. I'd spent a lot of time inking Onyx, but I wouldn't call us *friends*. Casual acquaintances at best.

Before I could respond, a video attachment came through and my curiosity got the better of me.

I didn't recognize the weird cafeteria vibe setting, but I assumed it was at Asphodel. There was a group of people, all daimons, standing around one beautiful woman, chatting with her like they'd known each other their entire lives.

And Goddess, she was beautiful.

Smooth brown skin, thick black hair, sparkling agathos eyes that weren't even that creepy on her. She was smiling at something someone said—a genuine smile, one that made the edges of her eyes crinkle, which surprised me. In my mind, all agathos smiled like politicians on the campaign trail, all pearly teeth and cold eyes, but Grace wasn't like that.

She was wearing an unexpectedly sexy outfit—a short black skirt paired with a man's shirt she'd tucked into it, the sleeves rolled up to her elbows, showcasing slim elegant forearms and smooth, glowing skin I was dying to ink. By the way she kept tugging at the skirt like she could make it longer if she fidgeted with it enough, I guessed she wasn't used to showing off so much leg.

371

Pity, because her legs were *glorious*. Grace had crossed them at the ankles, and I wanted nothing more than to kneel at her feet, pry her legs apart, throw one of them over my shoulder and bury my face under her tiny skirt.

It was more than that. More than *desire*. It was like a yank in my gut that felt like it was going to drag me towards her through the screen. My heart was pounding in my chest, blood rushing in my ears as I stared at this enchanting woman. A beacon of light in a sea of shadowy daimons.

I was so caught up in my perverse staring that it took me a minute to recognize Riot's hands on her waist, the dark purple moon phases I tattooed on his knuckles staring at me accusingly.

What the fuck was I doing? This was Riot's girl and I was ogling her like a fucking creep, feeling jealous that he got to touch her. It wasn't like Riot and I hadn't shared before, but those were one-night only events. Quests to show a girl the best time of her life while we joked about which one of us was better in bed.

It was obviously me.

But this wasn't the same thing. Was it? I should feel wrong about lusting after my best friend's girl, but there was a part of me that felt like she should be mine.

Riot and Bullet and Wild's girl, I reminded myself. Whatever. Semantics. She wasn't *my* girl. Or maybe she was, and that was why I was so attracted to her?

There was a weird, uncomfortable feeling in my gut that may have been hope or possibly indigestion. It seemed like a weak argument when she had a whole circle of daimon admirers standing around her in the video. Who's to say I was any different from one of them?

You are being stupid. Philotes daimons don't have relationships.

My mother would keel over dead if someone told her she had to be monogamous.

Then again... Keres daimons didn't have relationships. Moros daimons didn't have relationships. Oneiroi daimons definitely didn't have relationships. They died in their late 20s.

Shit. Was Bullet okay? He was nearly 30.

Surely, if he was tied to Grace, that meant he wasn't about to kick the bucket any day now.

I forced myself to lock the screen and threw the phone aside before I could replay the video and stare at her all over again. Maybe this was why Bullet warned me away? Had he seen some future where I interfered in their relationship somehow? Tried to impose myself on Grace's life when I didn't belong there?

That would be such a piece of shit move. I wouldn't do something like that, surely.

My phone buzzed again and my resolve crumbled instantly as I dived on the foldout couch and grabbed it.

Onyx: *Everyone here is half in love with her already. It's impressive.*

Why was Onyx sending me this? I couldn't tell if it was some weird attempt at keeping me updated on Riot or if she was trying to antagonize me. We weren't close enough to be gossiping about the new girl in town via text.

Me: *Why are you telling me this?*

Okay, not my most subtle work, but whatever. Three little dots appeared instantly, like Onyx had been staring at her phone, waiting for me to reply.

Onyx: *Because I am a moderately intelligent person.*

You + Riot + Bullet = weird childhood buddies

Bullet + Wild = instant sexy connection

Riot + Wild = instant angry connection

Riot + Bullet + Wild = obsessed with Grace

Grace = agathos

Agathos = four-man harem

Ergo, you = probably the fourth man

Huh. No wonder Onyx was Wild's second-in-command, she really didn't miss anything.

I felt like I was the fourth man, but she was basing her assumption purely on the fact that I was close with Riot, and I used to be close with Bullet too. It was unusual for daimons to have the kind of friendships we had, but it wasn't the strongest argument.

Also, Bullet and Wild had an "instant sexy connection"? What the fuck did that mean? Bullet had been a sexless robot all through high school. In hindsight, I realized he'd probably already seen Grace in his visions and was staying loyal to her in advance. That was kind of cute.

Me: *It's a nice theory, but I've never even met her.*

Onyx: *I've seen firsthand that a daimon can get hooked on this girl through a video on a screen. If you're behind Grace's door number 4, you owe me a giant leo tattoo on my back, free of charge.*

Me: *If I'm not, I'll charge you double.*

I snorted, chucking my phone aside. I'd never wanted to lose a bet so much. Shit, if I was lucky enough to be able to claim just a small piece of that beautiful woman to myself, I'd happily give Onyx free tattoos for the rest of my life.

I contemplated contacting Bullet again and demanding answers, but I remembered enough of his abilities from a decade ago to know that wasn't a good idea. Sometimes he just didn't know the answer, and often when he did know, he had good reasons for not sharing them.

He'd told me I'd regret it if I left right now, and I forced myself to trust him. If Grace wasn't meant to be mine, it was probably better that I keep my distance anyway. I didn't want to lead the agathos in Jersey right to her doorstep.

Another message came through from Onyx, and I groaned as the picture loaded. It was a selfie she'd taken with a bemused looking Grace. Onyx's arm was slung around her shoulder and she was smirking at the camera, while Grace's face was turned to face her, eyebrows lifted slightly and a smile playing around her mouth.

She was so beautiful. So fucking beautiful.

You are not allowed to jack off to pictures of your best friend's girl.

Not until you know for sure that she's your girl too.

Onyx: *Remember your gratitude for me sending you these updates when you're tattooing a giant lion on my back, free of charge.*

GRACE

CHAPTER 25

I stretched in the bed as best I could with half of Riot's not insignificant body weight covering me, pointing and flexing my toes and forcing myself to wake up as night fell. I'd slept fitfully again, hating this sudden adjustment to my sleeping pattern, but after a few days, I was slowly getting the hang of it. Or I was tired enough to collapse after being up all night, but at least I got some rest.

For five days, we'd killed time at Wild's complex while Bullet's arm and Riot's face recovered. It had been unexpectedly nice. They were resting a lot with the painkillers, and I'd had horrible period cramps, so we spent the time enjoying the extra snuggles, and pretended that anything supernatural didn't exist.

The Underworld club network was like a huge family—even some of the employees who worked at other establishments lived in this building. While I wasn't an agathos in many ways, one of the most agathos things about me was that I liked being around people. I needed time to decompress afterwards, but I got genuine joy from interacting with people and hearing their stories—a feeling Riot and Bullet absolutely did not share. Every chance I'd gotten, I'd been out in the communal employee area, meeting the daimons that worked here.

They'd been *extremely* interested in me, especially in what had happened at the community center, but their questions seemed to dance around what they really wanted to know, and I'd spotted Onyx giving out warning looks whenever they got too close to the topic of the earthquake.

Either she'd picked up on my discomfort when we talked about it, or Wild didn't want it discussed. For all his absence, I got the impression that nothing happened here if he didn't want it to happen.

Riot had been glued to my side the entire time we talked to anyone, giving them all distrusting looks that the daimons seemed to find hilarious. Mostly because the altercation between Wild and Riot was apparently a thing of legend, and they were baffled that Riot was even allowed on the premises.

Unfortunately, at some point during the night, Viper would summon Riot to do whatever jobs he wanted him to do. Riot never talked about where he went or what Viper asked him to do, but there was no mistaking the toll it was taking on him. He'd redirected the agathos again after we'd shown up in Milton and undone all his hard work, and I got the impression he was punishing Riot for it in the jobs he was giving him.

I needed to find Wild. He was doing an *excellent* job at avoiding me, and maybe he didn't want me which was... well, not fine, but something I would have to come to terms with. Regardless of that, I was still hopeful that he could get Riot out of this arrangement. Bullet insisted that's what the Fates were telling him, constantly referencing the Three of Cups card.

I couldn't see it. His description made it sound like that card was a celebration of friendship, like... like the three of *them* had to bond, their relationships separate from their ones with me.

377

Which was fine in theory, but Wild wouldn't so much as look at any of us. Maybe I'd gotten too used to Riot and Bullet's rapt attention, and the way they'd given it to me right from the beginning. This was probably the reminder I needed that for all the specialness of the soul bond connection, however incredible it felt, most daimons wouldn't want to be supernaturally tied to an agathos.

I couldn't blame Wild for that. I wouldn't want to be tied to an agathos either.

What would they think of me now? Surely the agathos at the community center had told them about the encounter with Gaia. Would they fear me more? Hate me more? Reassess their position on things and have a change of heart?

It was a nice dream, but I couldn't imagine how they'd feel if they knew there was a prophecy.

"Good evening," Riot yawned, the arm that was draped over my waist pulling me even tighter against him. "You're thinking very hard."

"Are you running out of patience, Amazing Grace?" Bullet teased from my other side, having silently woken up at some point. Bullet was so still when he slept that sometimes I worried he wasn't even breathing. Then, suddenly his eyes would open and he would be completely awake, just like that.

He was still a little bit in my bad books after not telling me about Mercy, but he'd also been miserable with his injured arm and the heavy painkillers Dr. Martinez had prescribed him, which had cooled my ire somewhat.

"I am running out of patience," I agreed, my mind shifting back to my elusive third soul bond.

"What does that mean?" Riot asked, peeking at me through one eye, black hair sticking out in every direction.

"It means I want to find Wild tonight. And if he's not going to come to me in the common area where I've basically been loudly announcing my presence each night, then I'm going to go to him."

"Yeah?" Riot asked, looking more alert.

Bullet hummed knowingly. "Big night tonight."

"Thanks for that, Mr. Cryptic," Riot muttered. "Is it safe?"

Bullet laughed. "Bit late if it wasn't. We're already in the belly of the daimon club beast, we have been all week. Go out and explore. You're safe here."

"You won't join us?" I asked, wriggling out of Riot's grip to sit up and look at Bullet.

He gave me a sad smile and shook his head slightly, not reaching for me. I *hated* that we'd taken two steps back over the past week, and that I needed to be the one to move forward. Bullet was waiting for me to bridge the gap, to come to him and let him know that all was forgiven.

Was it?

"I don't want to start getting visions about everyone I come across," Bullet explained. "Besides, I'm overdue for some quality meditation."

"If you're sure," I said slowly, knowing the lack of alone time had been difficult for him recently. "We won't be long, and—"

"Seriously, no excuses necessary," Bullet laughed. "Go. Have fun. See if you can track down Wild. Dance a little. Viper's distracted tonight, so Riot is a free daimon. See where the night takes you."

He sounded like he very much knew where the night was taking me and I shook my head, trying not to smile.

My period was finished and I'd had the IUD inserted by Dr. Martinez the day after we arrived, when we'd gone downstairs to realign

Riot's nose. Between my time of the month and their injuries, it had been an incredibly *chaste* week, though the almost constant snuggling had abated the worst of the bond pressure, and I was ready for more.

Maybe ready for everything? The last obstacle was out of the way, the only thing stopping me from bonding with them fully now were my own hangups about intimacy. The irritating shame that I was determined not to let win.

I climbed out of the bed and made my way to the bags of clothes I had to choose from. Not only did I have the duffel bag of stuff Bullet had packed, but Riot had shown up yesterday with the suitcase of random things Viper had grabbed from my apartment to make it look like I'd packed and fled.

There was a lot more *club wear* in Bullet's collection, but I wasn't sure how comfortable I'd be in it. One of the dresses was so skimpy, I'd originally assumed it was meant to be a slip.

"Oh," I gasped, pulling out a rust-colored cotton dress from the suitcase. It was one of my summer ones, a pinafore-style top that crisscrossed in wide straps over the back, and it had a full skirt. I usually wore it with a t-shirt underneath, but it could work...

"Ooh, I am *excited*," Bullet said gleefully, not actually able to see what I'd found from where he was sitting, but reading my emotions instead. Or perhaps referencing the future.

"I'm going to shower," I announced, smiling to myself as I gathered up my makeup and supplies. I wouldn't look like a daimon, or even a particularly sexy human, but I'd feel a little bit rebellious while still being comfortable, and hopefully my dance partner for the evening would appreciate the more revealing outfit.

But would it be enough to tempt Wild?

I emerged an hour later, incredibly conscious of my exposed back and shoulders, not to mention the lack of bra under my thin cotton dress. I'd pulled my hair back to a low bun and gone extra dramatic with my dark eye makeup, hoping it would make the garment look less like the sundress it was, then picked out my dressiest gold hoop earrings that I hadn't realized I'd been missing.

The entire time I'd been staying at the barn, I'd tried to dress less agathos-y, to wear less makeup and fuss with my hair less. They were all things that would have bothered my mother, and I got a petty kind of satisfaction out of knowing my casual appearance would have bothered her.

But these past five days, being surrounded by glamorous people, I'd started making more effort with my hair and makeup before I left the room. With my limited options, I'd had fun putting cute outfits together, even if they were a little more scandalous than what I'd usually wear.

I'd realized I enjoyed those things, and I didn't have to not enjoy them just because my mother valued them. I could like putting on makeup and trying on outfits because I liked them, not because appearances were important to the agathos.

It's not like my mother would approve of this outfit anyway. She'd probably call me a harlot, or worse.

"You look like a sexy terracotta pot," Bullet sighed dreamily as I reentered the bedroom.

"That was not what I was going for."

I blinked at him, wondering if I should have picked the skimpy slip dress instead.

"What is wrong with you?" Riot asked exasperatedly, cutting Bullet a side eye with no real heat in it. He was already dressed in clothes that I knew were more formal than his usual tastes—dark dress trousers and a black shirt that stretched deliciously over his chest. "Your compliment game needs serious work. Gracie, you look fucking edible."

"I'm not sure that's what I was going for either, but thank you," I laughed, my face heating instantly. "You look really nice too."

I discreetly slid the key Onyx had given me into the pocket of the dress, just in case, and pulled a pair of tan block heels out of the case and slipped them on, surprised at how quickly I'd adjusted to wearing more comfortable shoes after spending all of my teen and adult years in heels. I still didn't know exactly what the key opened, but that mysterious spiral staircase in the corner of the common area seemed like a pretty safe bet.

I really hoped I would see Wild somewhere public tonight, that I'd put myself out there and he'd come to me, but I'd carried the key on me at all times since Onyx had given it to me. She didn't seem like the type of person to do things lightly.

Bullet made his way around the bed and waited as I finished doing up the ankle straps, shirtless and in sweatpants as he had been all week so he could dress without disturbing his injury. I could tell he hated it—Bullet was not accustomed to being anything less than perfectly put together.

I stood and gave him a tentative smile, my eyes shooting down to his bandaged arm before moving back to his face. The two feet between us felt like a gulf.

"I'll wait outside," Riot announced, slipping out of the room.

"How's your arm feeling today?" I asked, eyeballing the bandage like I could see through it to the wound beneath.

"Better."

His expression was as unreadably cheerful as usual, and I wondered not for the first time why Bullet was so difficult for me to understand.

No, that wasn't entirely right. One thing I did understand was that I could never comprehend the amount of information in Bullet's brain. He'd *seen* so much, learned so much, and had so much responsibility about what he did with that knowledge.

That wasn't even considering all the things he knew about me. The one-sided relationship we'd had for my entire life.

"Give me something," I whispered, resisting the urge to reach up and smooth over his brow the moment it furrowed. "I know it's a burden to know the things that you know. Logically, I understand you tell us what you can when you can, and that sometimes I'll question if you made the right call, even though I can't possibly comprehend what it's like for you to make those decisions."

Bullet sucked in a breath and I felt his surprise brushing against my skin. Surprise and *relief.*

"We won't always agree, but I don't want this tension between us either," I finished, shrugging a little lamely. I thought I'd know exactly what to say, but when I was standing right in front of him, the words seemed to fly out of my head.

"I was prepared for you to never forgive me," Bullet admitted, and I felt myself frowning. "I've loved you my whole life, Amazing Grace—"

I sucked in a surprised breath at the frank, honest admission.

"—and I guess I thought that the only obstacle standing in our way was the fact we hadn't met, and once we had overcome that hurdle everything would fall into place and be easy."

I gave him a wry smile. "As far as hurdles go, it was a pretty big one."

"Neither of us are destined for an easy life," Bullet agreed, his answering smile a lot less easy than usual. "What I'm awkwardly trying to say is that I wasn't prepared for the real-life relationship aspect of us, and that was without the goddesses all throwing more obstacles in our path. I'm sorry that I let you down."

I shook my head. "You didn't, and I'm sorry that I made you feel that way. I can't comprehend the pressure you're under, and I have no idea how you navigate it. Relationships are hard even without all the extra considerations we have to deal with, but we have to talk to each other, okay? Be as open as we can be, within the limitations imposed on us. I'm not going to give up on you, and I hope you're not going to give up on me."

Bullet swallowed, and my always smiling, cheerful, mischievous soul bond suddenly looked vulnerable. "I'd never give up on you, Amazing Grace."

"Good." I grabbed his face and pulled him towards me, liking that we were the same height now that I was wearing heels, and pressed our lips together. "Talk to me next time, please," I whispered against his mouth before gently coaxing his lips apart with my tongue, a week of pent up lust ready to explode out of me.

Bullet groaned what may have been a sound of agreement, his good hand resting on my waist, fingers brushing the bare skin of my back as he tilted his head to the side, tongue tangling with mine.

I really couldn't let myself get worked up right now. I was wearing a thin dress with no bra, and I'd be broadcasting to the entire club with my chest at this rate.

"*Mmph*, later," I mumbled, forcing myself to pull back. "I have a plan to execute, remember?"

Bullet's lips twitched, mask of amused calm back in place, but I could feel that he was more settled. If only there was a complete bond between us.

If only there were some way I could make that happen tonight.

I took a step back before my feet froze, my brain catching up to the most important thing Bullet had said. *I've loved you my whole life.*

I couldn't just walk away from that admission. There were rules, a certain way those words had to be handled—

"Go," Bullet said softly, gently spinning me towards the door. "I'll still be here when you get back, and I'm ready to hear those words whenever you're ready to say them. Good luck on your mission, Amazing Grace."

In the back of my mind, I realized I should have been grateful for the escape he'd given me so I didn't feel pressured to say something I wasn't sure I was ready to say. But as I walked away, I knew in my soul that wasn't the case.

I loved Bullet, and I couldn't tell a lie.

"Ready to go?" Riot asked, leaning against the wall in the corridor, locking his phone and sliding it into his pocket the moment he saw me, giving me every ounce of his attention.

Oh dear. I loved him too.

The realization made me want to cancel this whole ridiculous plan I had to track down Wild, drag Riot back into the bedroom and...

And?

Seal the bonds?

Yes. Seal the bonds.

"We should go before we miss out," Riot added, reaching for me the moment I was within his grasp.

"Miss out on what?"

"Tacos, obviously," Riot replied, shooting me one of those delicious half smiles that made butterflies erupt in my stomach.

Maybe I could put off the bonding plan a little longer. Long enough to get tacos.

"You didn't think I'd let you drink on an empty stomach? What kind of soul bond do you think I am?" Riot teased.

"A really thoughtful one," I replied, melting a little inside. Not that I was planning on getting drunk anyway, but food did sound like a great idea.

Riot looked back over his shoulder, eyebrows raising slightly like he was saying *really? Me, thoughtful?* He didn't give himself nearly enough credit.

In the distance, I heard the steady thud of the music mixed with the sound of laughter and voices as we made our way through the back employee-only corridors. Logically, I knew the people in the club were probably just drinking and dancing like people did in movies, but I couldn't help the little hint of the agathos paranoia in my head that told me they were doing drugs off each other's bodies in the middle of a mass orgy.

"Isn't it kind of early for there to be people here?" I asked. "Not that I know a lot about clubbing, but it feels early."

"It is," Riot chuckled. "But it's Friday night and plenty of people come in after work for drinks. It's best to get in early, Asphodel on a Friday night is packed. The line outside is ridiculous."

In the deserted corridor, I finally asked Riot the question I'd been dying to ask him all week. "Why was Wild so mad when you, um, you know?"

"Sold coke on the dance floor?" Riot suggested, smirking at me.

"Yes, that." I could understand why an agathos would get upset about it, but all the daimons I'd spoken to this week had been very relaxed about that sort of thing. They were all staunchly behind Wild, but they didn't *hate* Riot for what he'd done. Mostly, they just seemed amused by it.

"The fight ring in the basement is illegal," Riot explained. "Wild is super strict on everything else being above board. I assume because he doesn't want to draw any unwanted attention to his other activities. It's not a den of iniquity just because it's a daimon club, Gracie," Riot teased.

My face flushed because that had basically been where my mind had taken me.

"No, of course not," I agreed. "It sounds like the fight ring serves a function as well as entertaining people."

Riot nodded, giving my hand a reassuring squeeze. "You would not like a Milton where the Keres didn't have a safe space to work out their aggression. I mean, that's what it was like for years, but it wasn't fun. A lot of brawling in the streets."

Huh. The way Riot described it, the organized fighting in the basement sounded almost philanthropic. My brain wanted to immediately reject that as undaimonic, but I forced myself to check my assumptions. Almost everything else I knew about daimons had been wrong, why not this as well?

"Um, where are we going?" I asked, realizing that Riot was leading me down some metal stairs that led to the back parking lot we'd arrived at when Wild and Memphis had driven us here last week.

"There's a food truck out back," Riot said. "They always park up here on a Friday night, and they have the best tacos in Milton."

"Is it safe for us to leave the building?"

Please say 'yes'. I wanted tacos. Meat ones, preferably. Everyone who lived here was vegetarian, and they seemed to survive solely on convenience food like frozen mac n' cheese that was stored in industrial sized freezers in the common area.

I didn't want to admit I'd been too scared to leave the property, but it had been convenient that I hadn't needed to go anywhere for the past few days.

"I checked with Bullet," Riot said quickly. "He didn't foresee any trouble, and most of the Underworld staff who aren't working will be outside getting food too. They're not going to let anything happen to you, and neither am I."

"Everyone has been so kind. I guess I assumed they wouldn't like me because of all the trouble I've brought with me," I admitted, smoothing out the nonexistent creases in my dress.

Riot scoffed. "They think you're the coolest agathos bad girl that ever existed, and now I have to share your attention. It's even worse now that they know you have two daimon boyfriends. A lot of daimons don't really understand the whole soul bond thing, they think you're just, you know, freaky in bed or whatever."

"That's supposed to make me feel better?!" I squeaked. While everyone had been remarkably relaxed about my relationships with both Riot and Bullet, I'd never assumed that was the reason why.

They'd laugh their heads off if they knew you were the virginest virgin to ever exist, I thought wryly. I was rectifying that tonight, no doubt about it.

"Sure," Riot said easily, giving me an amused look as he pushed the fire door open and led me outside. "Though I'll be keeping an eye out to make sure no one else thinks they have a chance with you."

I could practically feel the possessiveness pouring off him, and it warmed me from the inside out despite the chill in the air and the entirely unsuitable outfit I was wearing.

"What if my fourth soul bond is here?" I challenged, keeping my voice low as we made our way into the crowd of daimons. It wasn't a total impossibility—there were two different clubs and the fight ring in this

388

building, all filled with daimons. Maybe I wouldn't meet Wild tonight, but someone else.

Riot muttered something that sounded like "*I doubt it*" as he guided me to the front of the line and we ordered our food.

We carried our food over to some barrels that had been set up as standing tables, joining a few of the other daimons I'd met over the course of the week, who all whistled and hooted over my dress until Riot was looking a little purple in the face, even underneath the lingering bruises.

"Hey! It's my twin!" a woman I didn't recognize yelled, joining the small circle we'd made around the barrel and giving me a slightly drunken smile.

"Me?" I asked, confused. We didn't really look alike except for the similar build, black hair and brown skin, though hers was lighter than mine. Our features were completely different, and frankly if anyone else would have called us twins, I'd have bitten back a snarky retort about all brown people looking the same.

"Yeah, twinnie," she said, snagging a bite of taco from an affronted looking daimon next to her. "Gross," she said, wrinkling her nose. "Once you've had my abuela's tacos, nothing else compares."

"Stellar," Riot said, leaning forward across the table. "What the fuck are you talking about?"

"Yeah, what are we talking about?" Onyx asked, sidling up next to me. I'd watched her work the crowd on her way here, deftly finding the balance between giving people attention but not getting drawn into conversations with them.

She was wearing a dress a lot like the one I thought was a slip, paired with combat boots and layered silver necklaces.

She really was one of the most attractive women I'd ever seen. Self-consciously, I peeked up at Riot, reassured to find his eyes still on me.

"Shoo," Onyx added, getting rid of the other daimons around the barrel until it was only the four of us. "Where were we?"

"I was telling good girl here about how we're twins," Stellar said, slurring her words slightly.

"Mm I guess so," Onyx said, narrowing her eyes on Stellar. "If your eyes are malfunctioning."

Stellar giggled, and I could have sworn Onyx shied away like the joyful sound repulsed her. "Well, Viper's options were limited on such short notice."

Riot stiffened next to me and Onyx raised an eyebrow, clearly intrigued as she leaned forward.

"I see. And what did you have to do?"

"Sit in a car," Stellar laughed. "Easiest two hundred bucks I ever made. I was trying not to laugh the whole time because Viper was wearing a black wig and made me draw these terrible moon tattoos on his knuckles, he looked ridiculous."

"I'm sure," Riot replied drolly, his own moon phase tattoos shifting as he flexed his fingers, and I fought a smile. "Where did you go?"

"Boston. Can you believe I've never been?"

"No. It's unbelievable," Onyx deadpanned. "Why Boston?"

I was wondering the same thing. Boston was only two and a half hours from Milton, and it wasn't exactly light on agathos.

"Oh, so the other girl could take the Greyhound to Maine," Stellar said absently. "The one with curly hair and the fucked up face. What was her name... Purity or Chastity or something?"

"Mercy?" I rasped.

"That's it! Not very chatty is she? And Viper is the worst company, so that part wasn't ideal. He was way more interested in her than me, and I've been fucking him for years, I'm so embarrassed about it. Anyway, Riot, are you still dealing? I've got a craving for some—"

"Riot's a changed man," Onyx interjected smoothly. "And I know you don't think you're going to get anything on Underworld property."

"Ugh, yeah. You and your *rules*," Stellar groaned. "Maybe I'll hit up the casino instead. Nice to meet you, twin!"

She stumbled off, but not before planting a messy kiss on a laughing daimon woman as she went past.

"Stellar is the hottest mess you'll ever meet," Onyx said drily, staring after her with one imperious eyebrow arched. "She doesn't actually work here. She doesn't really work anywhere, she just does odd jobs for people like Viper."

"So, the agathos probably think you're in Boston?" Riot mused.

"That'd explain the violence," Onyx said. "There's been fighting in the streets there these past couple of days. Didn't Viper update you? Aren't you the client?"

Riot snorted. "Theoretically."

Onyx hummed thoughtfully and I wondered if maybe she could convince Wild to take on Riot's debt. Wild had told us to take whatever our request was to Onyx...

"If, theoretically, we weren't satisfied with Viper's methods and were looking for an alternative, um, provider," I began, not entirely sure how to ask for what I was asking for.

"I would definitely recommend you take a walk on the *wild* side," Onyx said with a wink. "I'll pitch it to him, but he's far more likely to take up the idea if you suggest it."

"What makes you think that?" Riot asked, leaning around me to observe Onyx. That Wild was my soul bond wasn't common knowledge, though I supposed the daimons must have come up with their own theories for why we were staying here.

Onyx gave him an expression that so clearly said *you can't be serious*, no words necessary. Maybe she'd figured it out?

"Picture time, good girl," Onyx announced, pressing her face next to mine and bringing her phone up for a selfie.

"You really like photos," I said, grimacing at the slightly shell shocked look on my face in the photo. At least there wasn't sauce on my chin.

"What are you doing with all these images?" Riot growled, wrapping an arm around my waist and gently pulling me to the side so he could loom over Onyx, staring at her phone. I couldn't see the screen, but she didn't try to hide it from him as she did whatever she was doing, and I trusted Riot would intervene if she was messaging an agathos.

Onyx had taken selfies with me almost every day we'd been here. I had mostly assumed she was sending them to Wild as a way of keeping tabs on me while I was on his property. That theory seemed even more likely if she'd guessed at the supernatural connection between me and Wild.

I caught a flash of confusion from Riot, noticed the slight frown on his face, but as quick as I'd spotted it, it was gone.

Okay? I mouthed.

He nodded, giving Onyx a strange look. *Later*, he mouthed back.

Oh yes, we were definitely bonding tonight. I wanted the in-depth insight into Riot's psyche that the bond would bring. I wanted him to be irrevocably mine. I wanted to walk into a crowd with Riot at my side with absolute certainty that there was no power on this Earth who could tear us apart.

Not just Riot. Definitely not just Riot.

I imagined Bullet sitting upstairs alone, clumsily shuffling his cards with his injured arm, his confession of love hanging in the air between us, and my plan for tonight seemed even more ridiculous. Why go find my third soul bond when I hadn't even cemented things with my first two?

Riot pressed a kiss against my temple, taking the empty plate from my hands and dropping it into the garbage can behind us. "Well, as much as I'm not excited to see the guy, I'm willing to swallow my pride if it gets me out of this fucking deal with Viper. Ready to get a drink, Gracie?"

I nodded, despite my craving to get back upstairs to Bullet. I'd done proper makeup tonight, broken out the highlighter and everything, the least I could do was go inside the club.

"Elysium," Onyx called as we headed back to the building. "Go straight up to Elysium."

I waved at her in thanks as we squeezed through the crowd. "As if we were going to go anywhere else," Riot scoffed. "Asphodel is packed with humans, and I'm not sure we can afford for you to play Lady Luck tonight."

Instantly, my instincts pressed on me to go to Asphodel instead, unhappy that I was deliberately depriving humans of the chance to bestow my gifts on them.

"Quick," I urged Riot. "Give me another reason why we have to go to Elysium."

Riot looked back at me over his shoulder and I saw the understanding dawn on his face. "Er, there might be humans at Elysium who desperately need a serving of luck?"

A blatant lie and we both knew it, but even that was enough to stop the itch under my skin that wanted me to immediately go and use my magic touch on humans. That '*might*', that word of possibility gave me an out, even in my own head.

"Thank you," I murmured on an exhale. "I'm surprised the Stellar thing didn't set me off, honestly."

Riot snorted. "I mean, probably because she looks nothing like you and Viper looks nothing like me. It's such a bad lie, it doesn't even count."

He shook his head silently, probably cursing Gaia a million different ways in his mind for the limitations she put on the agathos.

"He didn't have a stand in for Bullet," I pointed out, choosing to focus on that instead of on the fact that Mercy had been in the car. *Maine*. Was it a coincidence that Felix's brother, who'd been banished on an outreach trip had also ended up in Maine? Was there something for agathos there?

"The agathos might have assumed Bullet's wounds were fatal," Riot said quietly, linking our fingers together tightly. That thought immediately made me want to turn back and go find him.

While I refused—outright refused—to believe there was some kind of curse that would take Bullet from me, I couldn't deny that any mention of his mortality made me anxious. Even though it was totally fine and nothing was going to happen to him.

He wasn't like other Oneiroi. Our connection was proof of that.

Bullet would live as long as the rest of us, and I refused to entertain the idea that he wouldn't.

"Here we go," Riot said. "Welcome to Elysium."

GRACE

CHAPTER 26

Goosebumps appeared on my arms as we approached the shiny black double doors with a neon sign reading *Elysium* emitting a low pink glow from above. Surprisingly, the darkness of the space made me feel more comfortable rather than less. I was always a bad agathos though.

A bored looking bouncer waved us through with barely a second glance, and Riot looked back over his shoulder as we entered the club like he expected the bouncer to change his mind and punch him.

"That will never stop being weird," Riot muttered. "At any club, but an Underworld one in particular."

I was too engrossed in taking in the club, the first one I'd ever been in, to respond. A long bar dominated one side of the room, with bottles of alcohol lining the wall behind it, glowing ethereally under the pink and purple lights that made up the whole space. It was both more and less than I expected—definitely less seedy and sinful, but also less glamorous at the same time, more *mundane* even. Colored lights and pounding beat aside, it was just a square room with a bar and dance floor surrounded by black leather couches and oversized ottomans.

That wasn't so intimidating.

The glamorous, scantily dressed daimons lounging on the furniture like nymphs sunning themselves on a rocky coastline were slightly more intimidating.

My stomach roiled, and my pulse picked up in a distinctly nervous way, rather than a soul-bond-nearby way. Why did I think this was a smart plan? I wasn't a good agathos, but that definitely didn't mean I was cut out to run with daimons. I didn't fit anywhere.

"I am so overdressed," I told Riot, leaning in close and raising my voice above the music so he could hear me. He wrapped an arm around my waist, pulling me tight against his side as we observed the room from a deserted end of the bar.

"How did you feel when you looked in the mirror tonight? Before we came down here?" Riot asked, scanning the room. His head was on a swivel, looking for threats, but his thumb moved reassuringly over the bare skin of my back, his attention never far from me.

I thought about the question, trying to remember how I felt before I saw all of the beautiful women in slinky microdresses and sparkly rompers that I desperately wanted to wear, but would probably have a modesty-induced panic attack if I ever tried.

"I felt good," I said slowly, leaning a little further into his side. "I felt pretty."

"That's all that matters then," Riot replied, giving my waist a squeeze and shooting me a deliciously tempting smirk. "So long as you *feel* good, who gives a fuck about what everyone else is wearing? For what it's worth, I think you're the sexiest woman on the planet no matter what you're wearing."

A bartender appeared at that moment, and Riot was busy ordering us drinks before I had a chance to come up with a sappy yet awkward reply.

"Here," Riot said, handing me a bright pinkish red drink in a tall glass filled with fruit and leaves, and grabbing a beer for himself. "It's a raspberry mojito. Want to go sit and people watch? Wild is usually all over this place, keeping an eye on things. I'm sure he'll be down before long."

Most of the seats were already taken, the dance floor still fairly empty, but we managed to find an oversized armchair that we both squeezed into, my legs angled over Riot's and his arm wrapped around my waist as I sat sideways to fit. Maybe it wasn't such a bad thing to be wearing a knee-length dress. At least I didn't have to worry about anything being on display that shouldn't be.

I sipped the cocktail through the patterned paper straw and almost moaned at how delicious it was. Agathos were usually beer-and-wine only, mostly for special occasions. I wasn't even entirely sure what kind of alcohol was in this, but it was my new favorite thing.

We people watched for a few minutes as I memorized the faces of each person behind the bar, not really needing to because I already knew Wild wasn't here. I'd feel it if he was, but the pull towards him remained as faint as it had been since we arrived here five days ago and he'd promptly disappeared.

"Why do you think he hasn't come to see me?" I asked Riot quietly, voicing the insecurity out loud.

Riot hummed, drumming his fingers lightly on my hip in time to the beat and taking a long swig of his beer as he contemplated his answer. "I thought I was a loner, but Wild is a whole different level of hermit. Everyone around here idolizes him, but they're not his friends. Not even Onyx, I don't think. So maybe you scare him a little."

"I definitely scared you a little in the beginning," I teased.

"You're very intimidating," Riot agreed with a smirk. "Then again, maybe Wild just hates me too much to be around you."

Riot shrugged like it wasn't a big deal, but I could feel the shame he was trying to suppress. He struggled more with the idea of the person he'd been than I did.

I leaned in to kiss his cheek, garnering some amused glances from the nearby daimons who'd been watching us curiously since we walked in. The ones who weren't employed here and hadn't been watching us all week.

"Did you see your dad at all that week you were here?" I asked quietly. A daimon woman stood up from the couch opposite, pulling insistently on her friend's arm and looking longingly at the dance floor. Her friend—if that was even the right term for two daimons, Riot always insisted they didn't have friends—groaned but eventually capitulated, balancing on impressively high heels and tugging her dress down before following the other woman onto the dance floor.

"I *saw* him," Riot said, rolling his eyes. "Shaking some human down for cash outside the casino. According to Viper, who took great pleasure in relaying this to me, my dad then picked a fight with two agathos troops a couple of days later."

"Oh my goodness—"

"He's fine," Riot said, waving a hand absently. "Well, broken collarbone, but mostly suffering from a heavy dose of embarrassment."

I knew he hadn't been a good dad to Riot, but I still felt a little sorry for him. The past week here with so many young daimons had only solidified Bullet's theory that the younger generation were made a little differently from their parents, and I pitied the older daimons who seemed to be built without empathy. The only daimon I'd met who actually scared me a little was Dr. Martinez, who was probably in her early fifties.

We finished our drinks while Riot discreetly pointed out some of the people in the room, and it really seemed like he knew *everyone*. Considering how much people had crowded around us during the week, it was strange how much space we were being given. Like all the daimons here had been instructed to leave us alone.

"Let's dance," Riot suggested with a mischievous smile, setting our empty drinks on a side table.

"I can't dance like that!" I squeaked, glancing at a couple near us. The two women seemed to have started a trend—more and more daimons were making their way onto the dancefloor. "I don't know how."

Riot chuckled. "It's not exactly choreographed, Gracie. All you have to do is hold on to me and make yourself feel good. We've had a little practice with that, remember?"

He winked at me and my mouth dropped open at the sheer audacity of him bringing the time I gyrated all over him up, my entire body heating at the memory.

Why were we here again? I was giving Wild five minutes to show up before I dragged Riot away. I had bonding to do.

"Come on," Riot said, pouncing on the lust he'd obviously picked up from me. He stood, lifting me with him and grasping my hips until I was steady on my feet. I wasn't a big drinker anyway, and since Bullet didn't drink at all, it had been a while since I'd had alcohol. My face was pleasantly warm, and everything felt a good sort of tingly, but I was pretty sure I was done. One fruity drink was enough.

Riot led me out onto the dancefloor and I let him pull me into his arms, his hands resting on my waist, just high enough that his thumbs could brush the exposed skin of my lower back. I rested my hands on his chest, trying to ignore all the people around us who were probably staring at the awkward agathos girl.

399

"Make yourself feel good," Riot murmured, his lips brushing the shell of my ear. He angled his hips slightly, his thigh in between my legs, not quite high enough for where I wanted him. *Needed* him.

I closed my eyes, not recognizing the song but letting the beat move my body, focusing on the feel of Riot's warm, solid chest beneath my palms, the way his hair occasionally tickled my shoulder when he bent his head close, the rough pads of his fingers moving against the soft skin of my lower back.

Suddenly, it didn't matter at all that we were in a room full of daimons. I didn't care that I was the odd one out, I didn't even care that I still hadn't felt the slightest inkling of Wild's presence nearby.

Screw him, a quiet voice in my head muttered. The dark, bitter part of me that I was used to squashing. *You shouldn't have to dangle yourself out here like bait to make a man whose soul is tied to yours give you a sliver of his attention.*

I'd let my insecurities overwhelm me when it came to Wild, to the detriment of the relationships I *could* have been focused on. Should have been focused on.

"Gracie?" Riot asked, lifting his head and looking at me with concern in his eyes. "Where did you go?"

"Nowhere," I said, shaking my head to clear it.

"What's wrong?" His grip on my hips tightened like he was worried I'd slip right between his fingers. He always held me like that.

Like I was on the cusp of disappearing.

"I love you," I blurted out, my own hands tightening on his shirt in case he tried to bolt after that less than romantic declaration, made while surrounded by sweaty grinding bodies.

Riot blinked at me. "Me?"

"What? Yes, obviously you."

"Thank fuck for that," Riot sighed. "I'm so in love with you. It makes my chest hurt." He grabbed my wrist and gently moved my hand so it was resting over his heart. "Right here. It feels all tight and weird."

"Well, hopefully you love me. Either that, or you're having a heart attack," I laughed.

"You've gotten cheeky this week, staying around all these daimons. But yes, it's definitely love," Riot agreed with a sultry half smile, lifting my hand off his chest and kissing the inside of my wrist. The small gesture seemed to travel from the surprisingly sensitive spot, all the way up my arm before dispersing into my body, making me aware of how *needy* I felt.

"I'd like to go back to our room now," I whispered, fisting Riot's shirt.

"What about your very important mission?" Riot teased, his thumb rubbing circles over my inner wrist.

I made a show of looking around the room, squinting at the daimons behind the bar. "Nope, he's not here. Let's go."

Riot laughed, a proper rich and delicious sound I wasn't sure I'd *ever* heard him make before, so I wrapped my arm around his waist, tucking myself into his side as he led us out of the club. We got a few knowing smirks from some of the daimons behind the bar who I'd already met, but I couldn't find it in me to be embarrassed.

There was nothing shameful about this. We loved each other! We were written in the stars by the Fates. It was beyond time that we made it permanent.

The journey back to our room was a blur. I was glad Riot was taking the lead because my brain was a hazy mess and despite my resolve, I was still the tiniest bit nervous about the actual physical act itself.

I wanted to seal the bond with Bullet too, maybe Bullet first, but what would they both think about that?

Would the act itself hurt?

Would I *bleed*? Goddess, please don't let me bleed on the sheets. They weren't even my sheets.

"You sneaky little Oneiroi," Riot laughed quietly as we walked into the dim bedroom. It took me a moment to realize that all the lights were off and the room was illuminated by *candles*.

"Where did you even get these?" I asked in amazement.

"Onyx," Bullet replied cheerfully, sitting in the armchair in the corner. "She was very obliging."

Riot hummed thoughtfully, and I made a note to ask about that message she sent earlier and why she was so invested in my relationships. *Later*, I'd ask later. I wasn't in the mood to talk about Onyx right now.

The candlelight made Bullet's blonde hair look like spun gold, and when he looked up at me, tarot cards shuffling idly in one hand, his amethyst eyes seemed to almost glow. He was incredibly beautiful in an almost otherworldly way.

Next to me, Riot's muscular arm was draped over my shoulders, his closeness easing the forceful ache of the unfulfilled bond, but not enough. The darkness, the hunger within me, gnawed almost painfully at my insides, following my train of thought. It was like a dam breaking inside of me, weeks of pent up lust almost bringing me to my knees.

Riot groaned next to me as Bullet smiled.

"My, my, what sort of depraved thoughts are you having, Amazing Grace?" Bullet teased, his usually playful tone back after five days of strained happiness. "Your arousal feels exquisite, you know. Like you're licking my skin."

402

That should have put a dampener on my desire, but if anything, it had the opposite effect.

"Gracie," Riot said slowly, gently clasping my chin between his fingers and guiding my face towards him, holding me in place as he looked for something in my expression.

"There's no going back after this," he warned, even as his grip on my chin tightened and he pulled me nearer, his pupils dilating.

"I love you. I don't want to go back."

I could have sworn Riot melted a little. Those three words might be a secret weapon when it came to him.

"And I love you, and *fuck* I want you. But I meant what I said the other day about you and Bullet. I know you two have had a rocky few days, and if anything, that confirms why you two need this so much. With his abilities, the burdens he carries... You legit *need* to be able to read Bullet's state of mind when he can't tell you what he's wrestling with."

"You're my favorite soul-bond-in-law," Bullet said dreamily while I stared adoringly at Riot, touched at how much he'd thought about this.

"I'm your only soul-bond-in-law," Riot replied with a smirk.

"For now," Bullet said lightly as I stepped out of Riot's grip and encouraged Bullet to stand by grabbing his good arm. I'd felt the brush of disappointment Bullet tried to hide as I'd given Riot those three words, and it was unacceptable to me.

Bullet stood in front of me, shuffling almost restlessly like he didn't know what to do with his limbs. Even with all the inches of tattooed skin on display, the planes and ridges of chest and abs stealing my attention, he looked almost adorable.

"Can't you see how I feel about you in the cards?" I teased gently, giving his arm a reassuring squeeze.

He gave me a small smile and shook his head. "There are some things they like us to discover in our own time."

"I'm kind of glad, is that terrible?" I asked. "I'm glad that we have at least this one thing I can tell you for the first time, that I can see the look on your face when I say it, and I'll actually *remember* it."

Bullet smiled a little sadly and I pushed myself to keep going, even though this heartfelt talk didn't come naturally to me and I sort of wanted to melt into the ground.

"Maybe it's fast between us, but it doesn't feel fast. It feels like I've known you my whole life."

"You have, Amazing Grace," Bullet said gently, squeezing my hand. "I know you don't remember it, but I like to think in the back of your mind somewhere that I still exist in a locked vault of memories."

"I like to think that too," I agreed, because the idea that every interaction we'd ever shared had slipped through my brain like sand through my fingers was too sad to contemplate. "That's why even though we haven't known each other in person very long, I know how I feel about you. I know I have this sense of rightness and completion when you're near. I know I love you. I *love* you."

Bullet's smile was *radiant*. It wasn't like his usual Cheshire Cat grin meant to hide and deflect, it was an expression of pure joy.

"I've loved you all your life," he said easily. "I thought I was in love with you, but that feeling of meeting you in your dreams was nothing compared to meeting you in real life and getting to know you all over again. I love you, my Amazing Grace."

Desire was coiling low in my core, every inch of my skin feeling too sensitive, too understimulated, too everything. At the same time, Bullet's words sort of made me want to cry, which probably would have ruined the mood.

"Bond with me," I commanded gently, glancing over my shoulder to see if Riot was still okay with this. It had been his idea, and it felt right that Bullet and I were each other's firsts after a lifetime of hidden memories.

Riot waggled his eyebrows playfully at me. "Should I stay or go?"

"Stay," I said immediately, glancing up at Bullet who nodded in agreement, his soft smile turning into something a little less warm and fuzzy and a little more predatory.

I blew out a long breath before leaning forward to brush a light kiss over Bullet's lips, making him chase me as I pulled away. "Make me yours," I whispered.

"I've always been yours, but I'll gladly make it official."

BULLET

CHAPTER 27

Grace unbuckled her heels, kicking them off clumsily before pulling me towards the bed, the blush darkening her cheeks visible even in the low candlelight.

"I'm nervous that I won't be any good at it—" she began.

"Sex?" I blurted out. Admittedly not my most seductive moment. Damn it, I'd been doing so well with the smooth romantic talk, but then all the blood in my body had rushed to my dick and my brain wasn't functioning.

Grace coughed slightly. "Er, yes. That. I don't really know what I'm doing."

"I'll do all the work," I volunteered immediately. Riot chuckled quietly, flopping into the armchair in the corner. It was a laugh of absolute disbelief probably, but I didn't have a chance to accuse him of being an overconfident manwhore before Grace's lips were brushing against mine, stealing all of my attention.

"You two can bicker later," she murmured against my lips, her restless hands moving against my chest giving away the nerves she was trying to hide.

"There's no pressure," I told her in between light kisses, forcing myself to think with the head at the top of my body. The words were a reminder to myself as much as to Grace. "Maybe it won't be earth shattering this time around, but we'll figure it out."

"I know. I'm nervous, and need to get out of my own head a little."

"That I can definitely do," I promised, not entirely sure I was able to deliver, but if Riot was going to stand by and give me instructions, we might be okay. Maybe this double virgin whammy hadn't been a good idea. Riot would know what he was doing at least.

Grace pulled impatiently at her dress like the thin fabric between us was too much, and any doubts I had about doing this crumbled. She leaned forward and pressed her lips to The Lovers tattoo on my chest while I slowly undid the buttons and belt tie of her dress with my good hand, quietly grateful she wasn't wearing a bra so I didn't entirely humiliate myself.

"You're so beautiful," I said quietly as she shimmied out of the fabric, leaving her standing there in a pair of white lace panties that had Riot quietly groaning.

"So are you," she whispered, quickly pulling her hair free of its tie and tugging it forward so it covered her breasts. "Maybe I should have had more alcohol."

"Hm, I don't think so," I disagreed, guiding her onto the bed. "The shyness will pass and, hopefully, you'll want to remember this."

"I will," Grace said with certainty. "I don't want to have any more forgotten memories with you."

She laid back and I propped myself over her on my good arm, cursing the stupid bullet wound as I bent down to capture her lips in a kiss. Ever since I'd watched Riot go down on Grace the other night, I'd thought about almost nothing else—getting shot aside—and I was determined to make her see stars with my tongue.

Grace relaxed into the kiss, her lips parting readily for me, tongue brushing eagerly against mine. Already I felt her self-consciousness slipping away, and I scraped my teeth lightly over her lower lip, wanting her to focus on the sensations rather than the thoughts in her head.

I moved slowly down her body, kissing her neck and collarbone, the swell of her breasts that were rising and falling heavily with her short breaths before pausing to swirl my tongue around each pointed nipple. I catalogued each reaction as I licked, sucked and bit lightly, glancing up each time to catch the way Grace's lips would part or her head would tip back.

"Bullet," Grace breathed, her hand tentatively reaching for my head, giving me the *lightest* nudge downwards.

Damn it. If she started giving me instructions, I was going to come in my pants again.

She lifted her hips as I tugged at the waistband of the skimpy lace panties I was very glad I'd bought her, and I yanked them roughly down past her knees until she could kick them off.

Before the shyness could return, I was in between her legs, memorizing the scent of her desire and slowly licking over her slit.

Grace sighed, her thighs falling open further, and I smiled against her skin as I arranged her legs either side of me.

Heaven. This was heaven. I didn't need the Elysian Fields when I had Grace wet and wanting beneath me. I didn't even need oxygen.

Okay, maybe oxygen. Everything else was superfluous though.

"Don't tease," Grace said breathily, tugging lightly at my hair. I vaguely heard Riot's quiet laugh in the background and Grace's corresponding *humph* of annoyance. "I can't take it, not tonight."

"Then move me where you want me," I challenged, looking up the line of her body with a grin.

Grace's eyes narrowed and I expected some hesitation, but apparently she was wound too tight for that. Her grip on my hair became a little more demanding as she all but *shoved* my face down. I internally reminded my dick to *wait* as my tongue swiped over Grace's folds, and she tugged me up slightly to her clit.

Apparently satisfied with my position, she held my head in place while I explored that sensitive bundle of nerves she'd spent so long getting acquainted with in the shower. I circled it lightly, flicking it experimentally with my tongue before lightly sucking like she'd told me Riot had when she was half delirious with pleasure.

I was nothing if not a fast learner.

"Bullet!" Grace gasped, her upper body curling up and her grip on my hair bordering on painful as her release hit. There was something deeply erotic about the way her abdomen contracted as she came, and I desperately wanted to pull back and stare at her pussy as she orgasmed, but that might make the shyness return.

"Keep going," Riot instructed lazily from the corner. "Lick her through it. Make her come again."

Alright, I could do that.

Grace squeaked as I resumed my ministrations, her legs kicking a little like she wanted to push me off, but her hand still keeping my head in place. Contradictory little wildcat.

"Oh my stars," Grace whimpered, body still writhing underneath me despite my efforts to clamp down on her hip with my good arm. "It's never going to end. It feels *too* good."

With a pained noise like it was costing her a lot to do it, Grace pulled my head away and I licked my lips while giving her my biggest, most grateful smile. She tasted like sunshine. Or peaches. Maybe apricot. Whatever it was, it was my new favorite flavor.

Grace smiled back at me, her eyes a little more hooded than usual. "Lie back," she instructed. "You're hurt, you need to keep the weight off your arm."

I didn't even question it. Just moved up to lie against the pillows on my back while my very naked girlfriend watched me with a coy smile on her face. I'd happily take orders from her all day long. Her shyness was gone for now, hidden in the recesses of what she'd always referred to as her "darkness" or her "monster". The part of her brain that was a little more daimon than agathos.

"Pants off," she announced, and I lifted my hips obediently while she tugged my sweatpants down. She didn't even seem to care that I had to wear ugly, easy access clothes right now because of my injury. Grace looked at me like I was just as sexy in sweats as I was in a well-tailored pair of trousers.

I wasn't wearing boxers because the less clothes I had to pull on one-handed the better, and Grace bit her lip as she yanked my pants down all the way, my dick curving all the way upwards and already leaking precum.

After she'd shoved my head against her pussy, it was a small miracle that it wasn't more than just precum.

"My eyes are up here," I teased, not at all offended that she was staring at my cock like it held the answers to all her problems.

"So they are," Grace murmured, her eyes sparkling. These few days had been good for her—seeing that she wasn't reviled in the daimon community had lifted a weight from her shoulders. Her gaze dropped back to my dick which twitched eagerly under her attention. "It looks a lot bigger now that I'm contemplating putting it in my body."

"We can stop right here," I assured her, gripping my shaft and stroking it slowly because it was starting to *ache*, but I didn't want to pressure Grace if she was changing her mind. "We could try again another day."

"No, I don't want to stop," Grace said, shaking her head as she shuffled up the bed on her knees towards me. I heard Riot moving closer, and I almost exhaled in relief.

"Let me help you relax, Gracie," he announced, dropping onto the bed next to me, eyes on Grace. "You're doing so good, beautiful. You're being so brave."

Riot's low assurances coupled with the porny voice actor tone he was using were like Grace kryptonite. There was no sign of hesitation in her eyes as he guided her over my lap until she was straddling me.

Completely naked. Straddling me.

Don't come. Don't come. Don't come.

Riot pulled her head down towards him, gripping the back of her neck in a dominant hold that I suddenly realized I had no interest in replicating while Grace steadied herself with her palms on my chest, her wet heat hovering an inch above where I wanted her and her breasts temptingly close to my face.

The moment their lips met, Grace's body went completely pliant. Her hips lowered, her pussy rubbing ever so slightly over my dick, making us both gasp at the contact.

"Make yourself feel good, remember?" Riot instructed against her lips before yanking her in again, his tongue sweeping her mouth as one hand slid up to toy with her nipples.

I rested my good hand on Grace's hip, encouraging her downwards and I could have sworn her nails dug into my chest in reprimand. Fuck, why was that so hot?

I wasn't sure I wanted her to go full whips-and-chains on me, but if she wanted to tie me to the bed and sit on my face, I wasn't going to say no. I'd probably beg.

Slowly, Grace's hips rolled, her body tilting to rub her clit on my shaft, and I loved that she was using me to take her own pleasure.

She broke her kiss with Riot, switching her attention to me, and I guess I was discovering all my unknown kinks because that was fucking hot too. As her tongue swept against mine, there was no part of me that gave a fuck she'd just been kissing him.

If anything, I was glad. Grace was a goddess and she deserved to be worshipped like one.

"More," she gasped against my mouth, reaching between us. "I need more. Are you ready?"

Was that a rhetorical question?

"I'm ready," I almost laughed. I mean, I was 29. I had been waiting a very long time for this.

Don't come! I ordered my body as Grace's hand wrapped tightly around my shaft and her hips lifted, lining me up with her entrance. *Seriously. Don't come. This will be so fucking embarrassing if I come before I'm even all the way in.*

Riot will never let me forget it.

I bit my lip so hard I was surprised it didn't bleed as Grace sunk down, her nails digging into my chest even harder in a way that I guessed was more from discomfort now.

"Are you okay?" I asked, my voice guttural.

"Try to relax," Riot instructed gently, his hands constantly moving over her body, petting and soothing at the same time.

"It feels like pressure. Mostly pressure," Grace said eventually. "And it kind of stings."

"Go slow," Riot advised. "Kiss your man, and relax."

I was about to ask him to clarify which man, but Grace leaned forward and pressed her lips against mine, answering the question I hadn't asked. With each stroke of her tongue, each nip of my teeth, Grace sunk further down, her tight, wet heat feeling about a billion times better than I'd even imagined it.

"Fuck," I rasped against Grace's mouth, my abs contracting wildly. "Fuck. This is like... I can't even explain how good you feel."

"You don't need to explain it," Grace breathed, head tipped back and eyes drifting shut. "I can feel how good you feel. Concentrate, focus on the bond between us. Can't you feel it changing?"

Honestly, I'd been pretty focused on the sensation in my dick, but when I pushed that aside, I realized Grace was right. There was a warmth in my chest that was growing and expanding, like a ball of sunlight, warming me from the inside out. The connection between us that had felt like a tenuous thread now felt like it was made of titanium.

Grace's emotions didn't merely flutter over my skin, they echoed in my heart. I could always draw from that place inside me and find her there, understand what she was feeling, check that she was okay, fill her with all the love I had for her that threatened to overwhelm my own senses sometimes.

Grace was a permanent part of me.

She was also very, very close to orgasm.

Riot blew out a long breath next to me, and I didn't need any kind of bond to know he was insanely jealous right now, but his time would come. To his credit, he kept his attention completely on Grace, still stroking her and teasing her breasts as her movements picked up. Her hands slid up to grip my shoulders and she lifted herself all the way up on her knees before slamming back down, her ass hitting my thighs in a way that I was pretty confident I'd masturbate over for the rest of my short life.

I licked my thumb and brought it to the juncture of Grace's thighs, needing her to peak in the next three seconds before I did, and she moaned softly as I brushed her clit, her walls fluttering around me.

How the fuck was she getting tighter? Logically, I had known this would happen, but I hadn't been prepared for the way her pussy gripped me like a vice as she peaked.

My movements picked up speed and I thanked all the goddesses in the universe when we both crested at the same time. The feeling wasn't entirely dissimilar to how it felt to travel through the dreamscape—like I was being dispersed into a billion little pieces and reassembled again, except it was infinitely better. I felt like I was being remade as a different man.

A better man. One who walked at Grace's side for as long as I had left on this Earth instead of waiting, forgotten in the shadows of her mind.

Grace slumped against me, her breath hot against my neck, and I felt her hand reaching across my body to rest on Riot's arm.

"I don't think I've ever heard Bullet so quiet," Riot remarked, shaking with silent laughter.

"I just had an out of body experience," I replied drowsily, my forehead resting on Grace's shoulder. "I'll be back to my usual obnoxious self shortly."

The bond between us felt like it was humming, bright and strong. I could feel Grace's contentment, her *relief*, her bone deep satisfaction. There was the slightest prickle of shame, a hangover from a lifetime of judgment, and I focused on that little dark spot in an otherwise glowing ball of sunshine, pouring my own love and happiness into it, polishing until it shone as brightly as the rest of her.

Grace sighed again and I felt her smile against my skin. "I have no idea why I put this off. This is... everything."

If Riot was upset, he did a great job concealing it, but I got the feeling he wouldn't have to wait long.

My visions had told me it was a big night for all of us, and it was only just beginning.

GRACE

CHAPTER 28

I don't know how long I dozed against Bullet's chest, lulled to almost sleep by the current that ran between us, soothing away my insecurities, flooding me with love, surrounding me with comfort and safety. The bass pounding from the clubs felt more soothing than irritating because I was too freaking happy to care about anything other than what had just happened, the sensations coursing through my body.

The bond was everything I thought it would be and more. More all encompassing, more fulfilling, more *intense*. There was no off-switch that I knew of, and it would definitely take a while to get used to having someone else's feelings so present in my mind and body. I didn't know how Bullet was going to keep things from me now with this tether between us, though if anyone could find a way to keep a secret, it would probably be Bullet. A battle for another day.

Despite the overwhelmingness of it all, how *big* it all felt, I didn't want to slow down. I couldn't. Not when I felt so off-balance. It was like one of my soul bonds was securely moored to me and the other one was flailing in the wind, and that wasn't acceptable.

I wanted more.

I wanted Riot.

He'd valiantly attempted to tamp down his jealousy and longing while Bullet and I were intimate, but it was hovering close to the surface as he laid awake next to us, his eyes on me the entire time.

Bullet snored gently underneath me and I smiled against his skin, turning to place a light kiss on his chest before carefully disentangling myself.

Riot was alert the moment I shifted, reaching out to help me off Bullet without waking him. I didn't know if my being awake would bother Bullet through the bond or not, or if I'd feel the things he felt in his visions throughout the night. It was going to be a learning curve for both of us.

"You wore him out," Riot teased quietly, pulling me into his arms.

I kissed Riot's cheek before climbing off the bed, glad most of the candles had burned all the way down while I was this naked. "I'm wide awake. Shower with me?" I suggested, aiming for casual. Riot's surprise brushed against my skin, but he didn't hesitate to follow me into the small bathroom.

The moment we were inside with the door shut behind us, I was second guessing myself. The light was jarringly bright, not like the low candle mood lighting in the bedroom, and I was self-conscious about my body and the fact that I'd just been with Bullet and would Riot even be interested in me after that—

Riot leaned around me to turn on the water, stripping out of his clothes with an absolute confidence that silenced my internal stream of self doubt.

"Stopped overthinking things yet?" Riot asked with a raised eyebrow, his naked body pressed against mine as he leaned in to check the water temperature.

"No. A little. I don't know," I admitted, letting him guide me under the warm spray.

"There's nothing to overthink," Riot replied easily, wrapping himself around me. "We're going to wash, and you're going to relax, and we'll maybe make out a little, then we'll dry off, get dressed, and find some microwave popcorn in the kitchen while loverboy snoozes."

It took a moment for his words to register while I let the warm water run over my body, Riot's solid heat at my back.

"What?" I asked. "No, we're not doing that. We're bonding."

Riot made a strangled noise. "You just lost your virginity, Gracie. Aren't you sore—"

"Virginity is a social construct," I interjected, parroting Bullet's words. It was basically the opposite of what I'd been told my whole life, but I'd given the idea some thought over the past week and decided I quite liked it. While there'd been some discomfort, I hadn't felt like a tamper evident seal was being ripped open like I'd been conditioned to think. I hadn't seen any blood either.

What if I was exclusively interested in women? Would I be a "virgin" forever, no matter how many partners I had? The more I thought about the whole virginity concept, the more I questioned everything I'd ever learned.

"I'm a little sore, but not nearly enough to stop me," I told Riot firmly. "I mean, unless you don't want to, of course. I don't want to pressure you."

Riot grabbed my shoulders, spinning me to face him. Naked. So very naked. "Don't want to?" Riot repeated incredulously.

"I know the whole idea of sharing me was something you were struggling with, and you watched me and Bullet together—"

"That was my idea, remember?" Riot said with a dry chuckle. "And, I don't know. I guess it wasn't as weird as I thought it would be. I was jealous that I didn't have that kind of bond with you even though I know we'll find our way there eventually, but actually *seeing* you together was fine. Kind of hot, actually." He shrugged like that wasn't a huge deal. "I get the feeling you're bossier with Bullet than you would be with me, it was fun to see that side of you."

I had no idea how to respond to that.

I'd been vaguely aware that I was getting quite demanding with Bullet, but he had looked at me with so much lust in his eyes that I didn't question it. I was a little embarrassed afterwards when I saw the crescent shaped marks I'd left on his chest and shoulders with my nails. The man had been shot a few days ago, yet I was clawing at him like a feral cat.

Riot reached past me to the bottle of liquid soap, pumping some into his hands and rubbing them together before massaging it into my shoulders. I tipped my hair back into the water, forgetting that I hadn't intended on washing it, but Riot's soothing touches were making me boneless. Also, if I opened them, I wouldn't be directing my eyeballs in a very ladylike direction.

His movements weren't designed to stir me up, not really, but I was already so close to being stirred up that it didn't matter. The lightest brush of his fingertips over my breasts and my knees were wobbling.

Maybe one peek. Surely he wouldn't have gotten in the shower naked with me if he minded me looking?

"Gracie," Riot warned. "You're hurting. You said so yourself."

I gave him a pointed look as I discreetly washed away the evidence of Bullet and my lovemaking between my legs.

"Actually, I said I'm 'a little sore', which is a lot less dramatic than 'hurting', and anyway, it's a good kind of ache," I told him primly. I meant to pull my hand away, but I was struck by a sudden rush of inspiration. I left my fingers where they were, slowly drawing upwards to circle my clit. *That* wasn't sore.

"You are trouble," Riot mumbled, watching with entranced eyes. "And I'm trying so hard to be good."

"Maybe I like you better when you're bad," I teased breathily, my entire body sparking to life again at the very first sensual touch. Maybe I was being mean, teasing Riot this way, but I didn't think I'd be able to rest until I made him mine.

Aside from the fact that I *loved* him, and I was ready for this step, the lopsided bond felt like it was yanking me down, and I worried it was dragging him down with me.

"I'm barely keeping it together," Riot murmured, his hands flexing at his sides.

The movement of his hands subconsciously drew my gaze downwards and I tried to cover up my surprised reaction. He had a piercing! On his... member! Sugar. There was a small metal ball at the tip that I assumed connected by a thin bar to one on the underside of his... penis.

Oh my gosh.

Didn't that *hurt*?

Maybe it felt good.

Would it feel good for me?

"I meant it when I said it was sexy watching you, and my instincts are roaring at me to claim you, and *fuck*, Grace," Riot continued, oblivious to my stream of silent questions. "I'm not going to be able to keep it together if you keep fucking *touching yourself*."

"Is that supposed to put me off?" I challenged lightly. "The idea of you out of control doesn't scare me in the slightest, Riot. You should know by now that I want every part of you."

"Fuck! Fucking temptress," Riot growled, wrapping an arm around my waist and hauling me against him, trapping my hand between us. I could feel the love and affection pouring off him, and I leaned into that warm fuzziness to reassure me when the slightly feral look on Riot's face gave me pause.

His mouth crashed against mine, and I'd barely caught up to the fact that we were kissing, that his tongue was battling mine for dominance before he pulled away, leaving me leaning after him. Then suddenly his finger was there, pressed against my lower lip, a question but not quite a command.

He was definitely too worked up to be my gentle, always-checking-in-on-me Riot, but he was still careful and reassuring, even if it wasn't with his words.

That was more than okay. I wanted Riot's rough edges as well as the refined ones.

I parted my lips, maintaining eye contact with him as he pushed his middle finger into my mouth, using the heel of his palm to push my jaw gently back up. Following my instincts, I slowly teased his finger with my tongue, relishing the way Riot's eyes darkened and the little tic in his jaw that gave away how affected he was.

He pulled the digit free with a pop and brought it between my legs with zero preamble, roughly shoving my own hand out of the way before skimming my clit just lightly enough to send a bolt of electricity through my entire body. His hand lingered there, wet finger toying with my sensitive nerves, pressing harder before suddenly backing off, featherlight followed by glorious pressure.

421

My hands found his biceps, suddenly not confident in the stability of my legs.

Riot's finger moved slowly to my faintly sore entrance, tracing teasing circles that had me rocking into his hand, seeking more. He made a low noise in the back of his throat as he slid one finger into my channel, the heel of his hand roughly rubbing my sensitive nerves.

"You're sore," Riot rasped again, massaging my inner walls oh so gently.

"I like it," I countered breathily, tipping my head back. "I can't lie. Believe me when I tell you that it feels *good*."

Riot added a second finger, and the sting increased but so did the pleasure. He angled me so my back hit the cool tile walls and braced himself over me with a hand next to my head, his upper body curled over me as I writhed on his palm.

"Please, Riot. I need you," I gasped.

"First of all, you never need to beg me for anything, Gracie. I'll always give you anything you want, *everything*. But this is our first time, and I am not fucking you against a shower wall," Riot rasped.

"Okay," I agreed breathily as my inner walls fluttered around his fingers and words became hard. "Maybe next time."

"Mm, maybe next time. That's it, Gracie, come on my fingers. Then I'll dry you off, spread you out on the bed, and Bullet can cover his eyes if he doesn't want to watch us."

All of that sounded wonderful. Maybe. I didn't really understand what he was saying while my brain was short circuiting. As the waves of bliss faded, Riot flipped the shower off and guided me out of the stall, drying me with gentle care despite the tight set of his jaw.

He wrapped my towel around me, clumsily tucking it in above my breast before taking a step back to dry himself off. I gave him about five seconds to do it before I launched myself at him, crashing into his chest and flinging my arms around his neck, my tongue demanding entry against his lips.

More, more, more.

I wanted him to the point I felt crazed with it. Like my need for Riot was an illness I'd left unchecked too long instead of seeking medical attention like a reasonable person with a healthy sense of self-preservation.

We stumbled out of the bathroom still intertwined, the door banging behind us as we crashed into every possible obstacle on the way to the bed.

Bullet was sitting up, the blanket over his lap to cover his nakedness, watching us with a serene smile like he knew all along that this was going to happen.

"Want me to leave?" he asked genially, though it sounded like he already knew the answer. I really hoped he hadn't been bombarded with visions of Riot and I making love right in front of him.

"Don't care," Riot grunted, spinning me at the foot of the bed to face Bullet and pulling me back against him. "Gracie?"

"Stay," I panted as the towel fell away and Riot's hands moved to my breasts, fingers rolling my nipples expertly as my head fell back against his shoulder. Vaguely, I remembered that I was very naked and maybe I should try to cover myself up, but I couldn't find it in me to care.

"One day—" Riot murmured in my ear, voice full of filthy promise.

"—I'm going to bend you over the bed—"

He took a step back, thumbs running down my back and settling on the dimples at the base of my spine.

"—And spread these pretty legs—"

His hands drifted further down, sliding out over my hips and down the outside of my thighs.

"—And I'm going to kneel at your feet and eat your pussy from behind while you're bent over and begging for more—"

"Holy fuck, Riot," Bullet muttered, looking as pink in the cheeks as I felt.

"—And only when you've come on my tongue and you're crying out for more will I stand up, grab your hips, and finally, *finally*, give you my cock," he finished in a low voice, suddenly gripping my hips exactly where he said he would and tugging me back against his prominent erection, sans towel, the cool metal of his piercing kissing my skin.

Then the gentle hands were back as Riot encouraged me to face him, his wry smile a little more intense than usual as he encouraged me back onto the bed and laid over me.

"You said I never had to beg you for anything," I rasped, wondering when it had gotten so hot in this room.

Riot's answering grin was criminal, his bulging arms braced either side of my head, solid body hovering an inch above mine and still too far away. "But sometimes you'll want to."

I kind of wanted to now.

"But not today. Today, I'm being a *gentleman*," Riot said drily, eyes flashing with amusement even as he dropped his hips, rubbing his hardness through my folds. The smooth metal of his piercing against my sensitive nerves made me suck in a surprised breath, eyes widening at the sensation of different textures rubbing against me.

"You're always a gentleman to me," I managed to gasp out, wrapping a leg around his hip and encouraging him closer. "Even with your filthy mouth."

For a few moments he rocked against me, that piercing I was becoming very fond of as it stoked the embers of my arousal into an inferno.

Riot's lips tilted upwards as he *finally* reached between us, lining himself up with my entrance and pushing forward with a slow, smooth thrust. For all his dirty talk and demanding hands, the motion was careful, giving me time to adjust to him, to tell him to stop. And I knew with absolutely certainty that if I told him to stop, he would with no questions asked.

That faith in him made it easy to relax. For both legs to wrap around Riot's hips. For my head to tilt back in ecstasy as the metal of his piercing moved against my inner walls and Riot seated himself fully inside me, our hips flush, his hard chest brushing over my painfully sensitive nipples.

The bond seemed to expand and unravel in my chest, growing from a small knot of thread to a strong solid rope that ran between us. It started a base in my heart, an endless pool of connection and feeling that was all Riot. Like with Bullet, that pool felt like a cool, glowing sea of silver moonlight made up of every memory I'd ever had with Riot, and every memory there was to come. Every emotion he had now, and every emotion that he was yet to experience.

It was all encompassing, yet somehow only scratched the surface of the potential between us, and I knew I'd spend a lifetime exploring this connection if the gods were kind enough to give us that time.

The constant achiness, the ever present itch of the unfulfilled bond, it all disappeared in a snap. For the first time since I met Riot, I felt *truly* relaxed.

Riot's movements had stopped while the bond changed and formed, and I felt his mixture of shock, awe, and gratitude as he took in what was happening. He rumbled a noise of satisfaction, burying his head against my neck, his breath fanning out over my collarbone.

"Gracie," he murmured reverently.

"I know," I whispered, running my fingers through his dark hair. "But I'd really like you to move now please."

Riot chuckled and I felt the bed shake with Bullet's silent laughter.

"Say 'fuck,'" Riot teased, propping himself up to look down at me. "Just one time."

My face heated at the very idea, but I knew my reaction was ridiculous. He was literally inside me! Surely, if I could have *sex*, I could say a curse word.

"Riot," I said slowly, exhaling. The crimson in his pupils glowed extra bright in the dim lamplight, his slow smile predatory.

"Yes, Grace?"

I could have sworn Bullet was holding his breath in anticipation.

"Could you please... *fuck* me now?"

"With pleasure, pass me a pillow," he ordered Bullet, who immediately chucked one at him, groaning with pleasure at the sound of me saying a naughty word. I could feel Bullet's desire ratcheting up through the bond, and sugar, there was something to be said for this multiple lovers thing.

Riot moved up onto his knees, encouraging my hips up to tuck a pillow underneath me before hooking his elbows under my knees and sliding back into me, and then he wasn't gently making love to me anymore.

He was definitely *fucking* me, his thrusts deeper and harder, reaching that spot in me that made everything clench and tingle in anticipation with unerring accuracy every time.

My mouth opened on a silent scream as heat coiled in my belly, unprepared for how *good* the new position and his increased intensity felt.

Both Riot and Bullet were exuding lust through their bonds and I idly wondered if I could get high off this level of desire before I clenched around him, shattering into a million pieces.

Riot's movements didn't falter throughout, though he was clenching his jaw so tightly it looked painful. As I slowly came back to reality, Riot found his release, bracing himself over me as warmth flooded my channel. My head fell to the side and I watched the veins in his biceps bulge, smiling to myself at the *feel* of his satisfaction.

I wanted Riot to feel like this always. Like he'd just fitted a missing piece of his soul into place. That was how *I* felt.

"You good?" Riot mumbled dazedly, pulling out with an embarrassingly wet noise and collapsing next to me. He half landed on Bullet's leg and Bullet kicked him lightly in the back as he pulled his legs away, laughing quietly.

"S'all good," I managed to get out, my voice a little slurry. The bass was still pounding from every direction of the building, but it didn't bother me at all. I wanted to tuck myself between my two bonded and take a nap.

My two *bonded*. Not soul bonds, not just *potential* but honest-to-Goddess bonded.

Well, maybe I wanted to clean up first. Reading my mind, or maybe reading the bond, Bullet climbed out of bed and I heard him wetting a washcloth in the bathroom. They were mine. Riot and Bullet were both irrevocably *mine*. Tomorrow and the day after and the day after that, I would have to think about prophecies and goddesses and why Wild didn't want me, but for a few hours in the dark with the incessant beat of house music filtering through the walls, none of that mattered. All that mattered were the two men I loved, whose souls were now completely intertwined with my own, and I was never letting them go.

CHAPTER 29

I climbed the spiral steps to my apartment in the early hours of the morning, boots clanging on the metal staircase as I dragged my exhausted body up. *Sleep. I needed sleep.* I'd been starting each night with a brutal workout before showering and then spending the night running the fights downstairs, or working behind the bars upstairs. I had to keep busy. I had to avoid temptation.

I had to know her location at all times.

Just *where* she was though, not *who* she was or *what* she was doing. I couldn't let myself think about the fact that Grace Bellamy, the beautiful agathos woman I'd been keeping watch over for the past six months, the one who I felt an undeniable connection to that could only be ordained by the divine, was on my property. Sleeping a few feet away from me, under my roof.

Probably fucking one or both of her lovers.

I couldn't decide if the visual made me aroused or angry.

Don't think about that.

Bullet was on the mend, according to Dr. Martinez and Onyx, who were both keeping tabs on them. Riot's face was mostly back to its usual state—a mixture of morose and arrogant. Grace was uninjured and, if anything, had been thriving while she was here, enchanting every daimon she came across with her open mindedness and genuine interest in their lives.

That she was so at home amongst *my* daimons, the ones who I'd deemed worthy of protection, gave me a swell of pride I had no business feeling. Not when their little group would be ready to return to the Oneiroi property in the country any day now, where apparently they'd been hiding out. I didn't have eyes on Grace out there, wouldn't have even known that's where they'd been if she hadn't mentioned it to Onyx.

The time Grace had spent there had been hell for me. Away from my watchful eyes, ensuring that no daimon fucked with her. But it was for the best that she left.

The sooner she was away from me, the better.

The curse the gods had placed on me clung to my skin like a thin layer of oil I could never wash off. It was slimy and suffocating, and no matter how hard I worked out, how much I sweat and fought, no matter how much I tried to exorcise this stain off my soul, I couldn't get rid of it.

It couldn't be removed. It was adamantine law that the word of the divine was final—no god or goddess could undo what another had done. It could be *changed*, but it could never be reversed.

No woman deserved that kind of baggage. Especially not one like Grace. She was blessed by the gods. I'd stood on the roof of the shitty community center building and watched her drag a response out of a goddess I'd long since assumed was dead. She'd fallen to her knees, humbled herself, and demanded a response, and Gaia had granted her one.

429

I'd tried my best to keep that information quiet, swearing Memphis to secrecy and only informing Onyx who was my eyes and ears on the ground. It was spreading anyway. Viper had found out, either from the screechy cousin or from Dice, and Viper didn't respond to my requests for silence. He'd have probably listened to Grace, but him meeting her wasn't a risk I was willing to take.

Grace had effortlessly charmed everyone she'd come into contact with—every daimon with a chip the size of Texas on their shoulder that worked here, and even the daimons who were visiting Elysium two nights ago when she'd shown up had watched her like she was a miracle. Not in a sexual way, or I'd have stormed out of my office and blinded them all for their insolence. They'd watched Grace like she wasn't quite real.

I was no better. Every time I looked at her, even through the filtered lens of a security camera, I wanted to *possess* her. It was beyond just wanting to fuck her—which I did—it was something darker, more permanent than that. She already had two lovers, and I knew agathos women had four. I knew those relationships were predestined.

I knew I was one of them. I'd known from the first moment I'd seen her, all those months ago.

It had taken every ounce of my not insignificant self control not to drag Grace out of the back of that van at the community center and sit her on my lap in the front seat where she belonged.

I knew it would all be over if I had. If I had touched her, made eye contact with her, the *connection* between us would strengthen. For both of our sakes, I needed to put some distance between us. Forever.

I could take care of one thing for Grace before she left though. It wasn't particularly in my nature to forgive people who'd pissed me off, but I'd make one single exception for Riot. Onyx had been borderline hostile in her attempts to convince me. Besides, it was clear Grace wasn't going to give him up, and he seemed like marginally less of a fuckup in her company. Not so much less of a fuckup that he hadn't got himself involved with Viper, but that was an easy fix. There wasn't much Viper wouldn't do if the price was right.

If Riot pissed me off again, he would have bigger problems than being banned from my establishments. The day I'd busted him on the cameras selling coke in Asphodel, my reaction had been unexpected even to myself, and it had gone a long way in deterring any copycats.

I'd taken it so *personally*. I'd never even met Riot before that day, and yet somehow his actions had felt like a deep betrayal. I wouldn't be surprised if he had permanent injuries after the beating I'd given him.

That idea didn't sit well with me, and I wasn't naive enough to think it was a coincidence. Grace was the link that tied us together.

I shoved my key into the lock for my apartment at the top of the stairs, pausing when I realized it was already unlocked. Odd. Onyx had an emergency key, but she never used it, and it was very unlike me to forget to lock it. My heart beat harder in my chest and I briefly wondered if I was losing the plot. It wasn't like anyone would be idiotic enough to fuck with me here. My daimons knew better.

Shaking my head, I let myself into the apartment, taking a few steps inside to see if Onyx was here, but the door clicked shut behind me instantly. I whirled around, only to find the angel that haunted my every living moment with her back pressed against the door, a fiery challenge in her multicolored eyes I'd never seen before.

That Keres hunger that I tried so hard to control rose up inside me, and it took all the willpower I had not to cross the small distance between us and hoist her up against the wall, pull her legs around my waist and see what kind of knickers she was wearing under that pretty little agathos dress.

Lust was a welcome reprieve from *bloodlust*, but I'd terrify her either way.

"Why are you avoiding me?" Grace demanded, hands balled into fists at her side. It looked more like a nervous reaction than an angry one, like she was steeling herself for this confrontation. "Why go to the effort of helping us and bringing us back here if you want nothing to do with me?"

Silence. That's what I responded with because that was all I could ever respond with. My arrogance had made sure of that. Even the idea of trying to speak made my throat ache.

"Why won't you tell me?" Grace asked, her voice cracking, the feeling echoed right down my chest.

If it was anyone else, I'd walk away. Ignore them and go about my lonely life in peace. I'd followed this woman from a distance for *months* though, she'd owned my soul long before she knew I existed.

I couldn't keep her, but I could give her an explanation. I could *show* her what I couldn't tell her, and then I would send her away.

I tilted my head, indicating for her to follow me as I wound around the furniture in the tight space, stopping in front of the bookshelf. I opened the hard copy of *The Iliad* that was sitting face out on the shelf, revealing the doorknob behind the fake cover, allowing myself a small smile as Grace made a noise of surprise behind me.

Only I had this key. I quickly unlocked the hidden door and pushed the shelf inward, heading inside my minuscule private office and leaving the door open for Grace to follow, letting her stay near the exit where I hoped she'd be more comfortable.

I was so much bigger than her. Even with this connection between us, I was surprised she was willing to be alone with me.

I felt Grace's presence behind me as I sat down at my desk, the bank of monitors coming to life as I tapped away on the keys, going through the authentication process.

From this workstation, I could access all the cameras across all my properties, as well as some across town that weren't attached to my properties. I was not a man who liked to be unprepared.

Blowing out a breath that I refused to admit was due to nerves, I pulled up the feed I wanted to show Grace, bracing myself for her reaction.

"Sugar," she breathed, moving closer to my chair. "Is that my apartment?"

THANK YOU

You made it to the end! Yay! This book was a lot longer than Run Riot, so I'm glad you're still hanging in there.

Silver Bullet has been an absolute joy to write, despite all the angsty stuff. I adore these characters, and I particularly loved spending time in Bullet's head. It's an interesting place! Book three, Wild Game, won't be too far away—I won't be able to stay away from the mysterious Wild for long. The State of Grace series will have five books in total.

I've noticed a few people wondering about agathos and daimons and how much of this mythology I made up. To make for easy reading, I've simplified the mythology a lot, but an agathodaímōn was a "noble spirit" in ancient Greek religion, and a kakodaimōn was an "evil spirit". The Oneiroi, Moros, Keres, Philotes etc. are daimonic children of Nyx (though I've called her La Nuit or the Goddess of Night), as were the Fates, and Gaia is Nyx's sister and a primordial goddess. Those spirits, both good and bad, were all immortal gods in their own right. The existence of mortal descendents with abilities is my own invention, as is the specific worship of Gaia by the agathos.

I have a few thank you's to make, starting with YOU, dear reader. It means the world to me that you took the time to pick up my book, and I'm grateful for each and every one of you that makes this dream possible.

This book was written during another round of lockdowns here in New Zealand, so I definitely have to thank my husband and daughter for their patience while I was chained to my laptop, trying to balance real life and the fictional worlds in my head.

To all my beta readers, you are incredible. Special shout out to my girl, Lucy, for always being there for me, as well as TS, Rory, Steph, and Ashley. You are all incredible. To my ARC team—I love all you wonderful humans! Red Line Editing, you always knock it out of the park.

I also feel like I should thank Stephen Fry for writing three excellent concise books—Mythos, Heroes, and Troy—which were all immensely helpful while writing this book and planning the overall series. If you have even a passing interest in Greek mythology, these books are a great starting point.

For the latest news and teasers, join the Colette Rhodes Facebook Group or subscribe to my newsletter.

Colette x

GLOSSARY

TYPES OF AGATHOS MENTIONED:

Arete = Virtue
Eusebia = Piety
Eutychia = Good Luck
Hygeia = Good Health
Sophia = Wisdom
Sophrosyne = Self-Control
Soteria = Safety

TYPES OF DAIMONS MENTIONED:

Apate = Deceit
Ate = Delusion
Dolos = Trickery
Geras = Old Age
Keres = Violent Death
Moros = Doom
Oizys = Misery
Oneiroi = Dreams
Philotes = Sex, Affection

BULLET'S SOUNDTRACK TO LIFE

What'd I Miss - Hamilton

Seasons of Love - Rent

La Vie Boheme - Rent

The Bare Necessities - The Jungle Book

Don't Rain On My Parade - Funny Girl

Put On A Happy Face - Bye Bye Birdie

My Shot - Hamilton

I Have A Dream - Mamma Mia

Take A Chance On Me - Mamma Mia

Waterloo - Mamma Mia

In The Heights - In The Heights

Singing In The Rain -

Listen - Dreamgirls

You Can't Stop The Beat - Hairspray

Defying Gravity - Wicked

The Music of the Night - Phantom of the Opera

Who Lives Who Dies Who Tells Your Story - Hamilton

Guns and Ships - Hamilton

96000 - In The Heights

ALSO BY COLETTE RHODES

STATE OF GRACE:

Run Riot

Silver Bullet

Wild Game

Dare Not

Saving Grace

SHADES OF SIN:

(MF monster romance)

Luxuria

Superbia

Gula

THREE BEARS DUET:

Gilded Mess

Golden Chaos

LITTLE RED DUET:

Scarlet Disaster

Seeing Red

KNOTTY BY NATURE:

(RH omegaverse with T.S. Snow)

Allure Part 1

Allure Part 2

EMPATH FOUND:

The Terrible Gift

The Unwanted Challenge

The Reluctant Keeper

DEADLY DRAGONS:

The (Not) Cursed Dragon

The (Not) Satisfied Dragon

STANDALONE:

Dead of Spring (MF - Hades & Persephone retelling)

Blood Nor Money (RH - vampires)

Fire & Gasoline (MF - wolf shifter fated mates)

Printed in Great Britain
by Amazon